Sit! Stay! Speak!

Sit! Stay! Speak!

ANNIE ENGLAND NOBLIN

wm
WILLIAM MORROW
An Imprint of HarperCollins*Publishers*

This book is a work of fiction. References to real people, events, establishments, organizations, or locales are intended only to provide a sense of authenticity, and are used fictitiously. All other characters, and all incidents and dialogue, are drawn from the author's imagination and are not to be construed as real.

P.S.™ is a trademark of HarperCollins Publishers.

HarperCollins books may be purchased for educational, business, or sales promotional use. For information please e-mail the Special Markets Department at SPsales@harpercollins.com.

FIRST EDITION

Designed by Diahann Sturge

Chapter opener photo © GlobalP via iStockPhoto

Library of Congress Cataloging-in-Publication Data has been applied for.

ISBN 978-0-06-237926-9

18 19 OV/RRD 10 9 8

For all of my dear friends working in animal rescue,
tirelessly devoting their lives to those without a voice.
You are making a difference.
You are making this world a better place.

Sit! Stay! Speak!

CHAPTER 1

Adelaide Andrews stared out the living room window and into the yard across the street where an elderly man, who she could only assume was her new neighbor, was frolicking through the sprinkler in his underwear. He was at least eighty years old and was very spry for his age. Every time the water shot up into the air, so did the man's legs. It was as if he were involved in some kind of synchronized sprinkler event in the Olympics.

Nobody came to ask the man to go back inside. Nobody asked him to stop. Nobody offered him a towel or chased after him with a fistful of medications, which he'd clearly forgotten to take. When the sprinkler stopped several minutes later, so did the man. He didn't even bother to shake himself off as he bounded up the steps and disappeared back inside the house.

This wasn't what Adelaide had in mind when she moved from Chicago to the Arkansas Delta. She'd left the midwestern city to *escape* insanity, not to move in next door to it.

She turned back to the sea of boxes that covered her living room. She'd spent all day sorting and hadn't even made a dent. She halfheartedly opened the box nearest her. Inside she found a hodgepodge of items, an indication that this had probably been one of the last boxes she'd packed up.

Looking up from the box, Adelaide scanned the room. Her aunt Tilda had died and left the house to her almost six months ago, and it was obvious that it had been empty for entirely too long. Well, not empty, exactly. Aunt Tilda died in the middle of the night—a stroke, the coroner said. Clearly, from the look of the place, her aunt hadn't planned on dying. When she said in her will that she wanted everything to go to Addie, she'd meant it. Not even the toilet paper had been disturbed since the day of the funeral. She'd had several calls from the only real estate agent in town to see what had been left to her, but Addie couldn't bring herself to do it. Yes, the hardwood floors needed to be refinished. The walls needed to be repainted. The ceiling fans needed to be replaced, and all of this was just in the living room. She heard her aunt's voice in her head. *Someday this house will be yours, Addie. I hope you'll take care of it like I have.*

Addie hadn't really believed her. What twelve-year-old pays attention to those kinds of things, anyway? Fifteen years later, the words hovered above her like the dust collecting in the corners of the walls. She'd let her aunt down over these last few months. She'd let everyone down, it seemed.

She sighed and pushed her blond hair off her neck, piling it high on top of her head. Her thoughts went back to Chicago. To Jonah. To what life had been like before she'd inherited a house that needed more work than she had money. *Jonah would have liked this house,* she thought. Addie knew that if he were here, they would have stayed in town after the funeral. Jonah would have picked through each piece of furniture, each knickknack. He would have asked for stories about each one, stories Addie had long forgotten.

She rested her head against the coffee table. It had a glass top, something her aunt had brought all the way down here from Chicago. It wasn't worth much, as far as Addie could tell, but her aunt loved it and stuck cards from relatives underneath the glass. Each time Aunt Tilda had a visitor, she'd tell them about whichever relative happened to be resting underneath that visitor's coffee mug. Today there was no coffee, and there were no visitors. There was no Jonah. Addie let her hair fall back down onto her sticky neck and said out loud to no one, "I've got to get out of here for a while."

The Mississippi River in Eunice, Arkansas, looked nothing like it had when she'd crossed the bridge in Memphis. It was smaller, tranquil almost. Addie stood with her toes touching the water. She hadn't been down to the levee since the last time she'd visited Eunice. Even this close to the water, it was hot outside. She found herself wishing she'd just stayed inside with all the unopened boxes and dusty furniture—at least there was air-conditioning.

Gazing around, Addie realized that this was no longer the nice, clean picnic area that her aunt had taken her to during her childhood visits. The tables were overgrown with weeds, and there was an obvious odor of trash in the air. This place hadn't been taken care of in a long time.

Addie bent down to wash out her flip-flops when she heard a noise coming from behind her. She turned around to face a small wooded area. The noise grew louder. It sounded like a whimpering, but all she saw were bushes. She shoved her feet into her shoes and walked in the direction of the noise. She pushed her way into the first set of bushes, where a thin layer of trash covered the ground. Off to one side there was a large, black trash bag.

The trash bag was moving.

Addie crept closer to the bag. She bent down and touched the plastic. It had been tied in a tight knot. Digging her fingers into the plastic, Addie ripped the bag wide open. The object in the bag stirred, whimpering slightly. It lifted its head and tried to move, but failed. It was covered in blood and blood-soaked newspaper and dozens of crumpled packages of Marlboro Reds.

Addie was looking at a dog.

Shaken, she quickly ran back to her car and popped open the trunk, grabbing the blanket she kept for emergencies. Kneeling back in front of the trash bag, she gingerly moved the dog from the sweltering ground to the blanket. It made little effort to escape even though it was terrified.

With the dog laid carefully in the front seat, Addie threw her car into reverse and pulled out of the parking lot, trying desperately to remember where she'd seen the sign for the town's veterinary clinic. She knew it was on the main road, so she drove until she saw the redbrick Dixon Veterinary building on the horizon, praying that the dog would still be breathing by the time she got there.

CHAPTER 2

Addie burst through the doors of the Dixon Veterinary Clinic, her arms wrapped around a blood-soaked blanket. "I need help, please!"

The leggy woman at the front desk looked up from her cell phone and replied, "I'm sorry, but we're closed."

"Please!" Addie nodded to the mass she was carrying. "This dog. It needs help."

"Ma'am, I . . ."

"This dog is dying," Addie hissed. "You show me where the vet is."

"Back this way. He's back this way," the woman replied, opening the doors to the back of the clinic.

Addie followed her, trying not to clench the dog too tightly in her arms. She could still feel it breathing, but its breath was ragged. "I don't know if he's going to make it," Addie continued. "I just found him like this. Who . . . who does this?"

"Dr. Dixon!" The woman rapped heavily on a closed door. "Dr. Dixon, open up! It's an emergency!"

A small, wiry man with salt-and-pepper hair opened the door. "Wanda? What is it?"

Addie didn't wait for Wanda to answer. "I found this dog. He's been . . . I don't know . . . I think he's dying." She pushed past the man and laid the dog down on the table inside the room. "Please help him."

Dr. Dixon stepped over to the table and unwrapped the blanket. "Sweet Jesus. What happened here?"

Addie stepped back from the table, taking a breath for what felt to her like the first time in minutes. "I don't know. I don't know. I was taking a walk. I heard a noise. I found him like this."

The vet's hands hovered above the bloody mass in front of him. "He seems to be alive. I'll take a look. Why don't you have a seat in the waiting room, okay?"

Addie opened her mouth to protest, but Wanda caught her elbow and whispered, "It'll be okay, honey. Come on out here with me."

Addie nodded and followed the receptionist through the doors. As she left, she noticed another man standing at the back of the room, his eyes fixed on her. She hadn't seen anyone else in the room until now. It occurred to her how she must look. What it all must look like.

"I'm so sorry," Addie apologized. "I didn't mean to yell at you earlier."

Wanda smiled and sat down next to her. "It's okay, honey. I know you were scared. I didn't see what you had in your hands until it was too late. Otherwise I never would've tried to send you away." She had a thick, southern drawl that put Addie at ease. She sounded like Aunt Tilda, even though she couldn't have been much older than Addie. There were lines that formed around the corners of her eyes that contradicted the sprinkling of freckles across the bridge of her nose. "Where did you find that poor thing?"

Addie swallowed. Her mouth felt very dry all of a sudden. "I was taking a walk over by the bridge . . . just outside of town . . . right before you get to the Mississippi line . . . you know, over by the casino?"

Wanda raised a perfectly plucked eyebrow and replied, "What were you doing on that side of town? That's no place to be alone, especially at night."

"I . . . I didn't know," Addie admitted. "I just moved here."

"How did you even know to get over there?"

Addie looked up from her hands and at the woman sitting next to her. "My great-aunt was Tilda Andrews. I used to visit her in the summer. When I was a kid, that was where she took me to have picnics . . . of course, that was fifteen years ago . . ."

"Oh, Miss Tilda!" Wanda exclaimed. "Of course! I should have known. I heard you moved into her old house. You must be Adelaide. I used to come out and take care of her cats once she got too old to come to the clinic."

"You're that Wanda? Wanda Carter? Aunt Tilda used to talk about you all the time. She loved you."

Wanda clasped Addie's hands in hers. "What a small world. I'm so glad to meet you, even if it is under these circumstances. We'll have to be friends now, you know."

"I'm just here for a few months—long enough to get the house sold," Addie replied.

Wanda frowned for a second and then flashed Addie another smile. "Well, we can be friends until then!"

The doors swung open and the man from the back of the examination room strode out. He looked in the women's direction and said, "Miss Wanda, Doc says you can go on home. He says to tell you"—he nodded in Addie's direction—"he'll be out in just a few minutes."

"Is the dog okay?" Addie asked. She released Wanda's hands. "Is he going to live?"

"I think he's going to make it." The man gave her a lopsided smile. "But I'm not the doc, so don't hold me to it."

Wanda stood up and brushed off her pale pink scrub pants. "I've got to get going, Addie." She walked over to the reception desk and scribbled something down on a Post-it note. "Here's my number. We'll get together soon."

She hurried out the door, leaving Addie alone with the stranger who stood there silently, his hands shoved into his jeans pockets. Addie watched him, unsure of what to say. He was tall, very tall, at least six foot four. He was what her mother would have called strapping. He had wheat-colored hair that fell just above his brow line, and a wide mouth that Addie assumed held perfectly straight teeth to match his perfectly straight posture. Even though he was looking at the floor, she could tell his eyes were blue. He was young, but older than she. Maybe thirty? She couldn't tell just by looking at him.

He reminded her of a farmer, like most of the men in Eunice. He was wearing work boots that were caked in mud, and his jeans and white T-shirt were also slightly dingy. He looked like he'd just come in from off a tractor somewhere, and Addie didn't know why, but the image made her want to giggle.

After what felt like hours, Addie mustered up enough courage to break the silence. "I didn't see you standing in the room with Dr. Dixon. I'm sorry I interrupted you all. I was a bit frantic."

The man shrugged and replied, "It's no big deal. We were just talking cattle."

"I'm glad he was still here," Addie said. "I didn't know where to take him. I just remembered seeing this place the day I got into town. I'm the only person on the planet without a GPS."

When he didn't respond, Addie continued. "I've just been here a few days. My aunt died. She left me her house. I don't even know what I'm doing here. I haven't been here since I was a kid. I just wanted to go for a walk. I didn't know the camping grounds had turned into a trash dump."

His eyes snapped up to her and he replied, "You were down by the old campgrounds? What were you doing down there so late?"

"It's not safe at night," Addie cut him off. "I know. I know."

"So you're the one who moved into Miss Tilda's place?" He stuck out his hand. "I'm Jasper. Jasper Floyd."

Addie stood up and moved toward him. His hand practically swallowed hers. "I'm Adelaide Andrews. I didn't move here, exactly. I'm just sort of . . . passing through."

"I'll have to tell my mother that I met you."

"Do I know your mother?"

"No, I'm sure you don't," Jasper replied. "But she and her friends have been dying to know what's been going on over at Tilda's. The place had been sitting empty for so long people were beginning to talk."

"Talk about what?"

Jasper adjusted the green Floyd Farms hat on his head and said, "You're really not from here, huh?"

There was an awkward pause and Addie breathed a sigh of relief when Dr. Dixon walked into the room.

"I think your dog is going to live," the veterinarian stated. "No broken bones, just a lot of blood. There were some cuts that required stitches, and some bite wounds. And I think he might have been shot."

"Shot?" Addie sputtered. "You think he was shot?"

Dr. Dixon adjusted his wire-framed glasses and replied, "I don't know. It was a clean exit. He's going to lose an ear. But I don't think there is any internal bleeding."

"But he'll be okay?" Addie could barely speak. Her anger was bubbling.

"In a couple of days you can take him home."

"He's not my dog," she admitted. "I found him. Down by the river."

"I figured as much," Dr. Dixon replied. "He's not the first I've seen. I can call animal control in the morning. But I should tell you—they'll probably have me put him down. His care will be expensive. And he's a pit bull on top of that."

"I don't live here," Addie continued. "I mean, I do. But not indefinitely."

Jasper and the veterinarian shared a look.

Addie choked back a sob. "Please don't call animal control. I'll pay his bill. I'll keep him."

"We can work that out when you come to pick him up." Dr. Dixon smiled at her warmly. "It's late, and there's nothing more you can do for him tonight. Why don't you go on home?"

"Okay." Addie felt her jeans pocket for her car keys. "Thank you so much."

The veterinarian waved her off. “It’s fine. Everything will be fine.”

“I’ll check on him tomorrow, if that’s okay,” Addie replied.

“Better give him a couple of days before he’s ready.”

Addie nodded and turned toward Jasper. “It was nice to meet you, Jasper.”

Before he could respond, Addie was out the door and into the muggy May night, leaving two bewildered men staring after her.

CHAPTER 3

EUNICE WAS A LITTLE TOWN OF TEN THOUSAND PEOPLE NESTLED deep within the heart of the Arkansas Delta. It was the kind of place where people worked, lived, and died generation after generation. It was the kind of place oblivious to the outside world. It was the kind of place Addie had come to in an attempt to escape, but she couldn't shake the events of the previous evening.

Groggy, she sat up in bed and rubbed her eyes. If she was going to be bringing a dog here, she'd have to get the house in order. There was a shed out back that she planned on cleaning out as well. Once she mustered up the energy. "At least I've got some motivation," she said out loud to her empty house.

The house was rather adorable. It sat on a large lot on a dead-end street. The neighbors had kept the yard work up after Aunt Tilda died last autumn. Addie guessed that was what Jasper had meant when he mentioned the house sitting empty, although she didn't know why people would care. Her aunt had kept the house, a nineteenth-century bungalow, nice and neat. It was small, as bungalows usually are, but there was plenty of space for one person. The house had a steeply pitched roof covering a wide porch that Addie was in love with. As a child, she'd spent many summer nights playing on that porch. She pictured herself lounging there at night, maybe with a good book and a glass of wine. The living room was nice and large, and there were two bedrooms for Addie to choose from. Unlike the carpet that Addie was used to in the houses in Chicago, her aunt's house had hardwood floors throughout, and she was still getting used to the creaking noise they made every time she walked. The kitchen overlooked the backyard, which had once held a beautiful garden.

The outside of the house could use a fresh coat of paint, Addie mused, but she had no idea where she was going to find the odd shade of yellow it had been painted. *Yes, there is some work to do,* Addie thought, *but it's nothing I can't handle.*

It wasn't the kind of house in which Addie had ever envisioned herself living. Of course, this wasn't the town in which she'd ever envisioned herself living. The only place she'd ever called home was Chicago, and there, she'd only ever lived in an apartment.

The phone rang, and Addie shook herself out of her daydream.

"Hi, Mom."

"Adelaide, honey." Her mother's voice was smooth and calm. "How are you? You were supposed to call last night."

Addie swung her legs over the side of the bed. "I'm sorry, Mom. I was so tired, I must have fallen asleep."

"What have you been up to?"

"Just unpacking, mostly. How is everything?"

"Oh, we're good. You know Jerry. Retirement is boring him. I expect he'll be back at work before the summer is out."

"I still can't believe he actually retired!" Addie giggled. "Is he marching around shouting orders at the cats?"

"More like marching around shouting orders at his wife," Addie's mother grumbled. "Once a marine, always a marine."

Addie rolled her eyes, even though her mother couldn't see her. "Oh, I know."

"He said to tell you hello."

Addie grinned into the receiver, picturing the gruff hug her stepfather had given her the day she left Chicago. "Tell him I said hello, too."

"Addie, there's something else. The reason I called. Jerry finally sold his house in Wisconsin." Her mother paused, exhaling. "He wants to give you some of the money."

"No way. I don't want Jerry giving me any money. That's his money."

"I told him that's what you'd say."

"I have savings."

"But he wants to do this for you," Addie's mother replied. "I know you have some savings, but that won't last forever. It has been years since the last time I saw that house, but Addie, honey, it needed work. Even then."

"I know," Addie conceded. "But I think I can fix it up enough to sell."

"I'm sure you can."

"And I know that there are a few antiques that I can refinish and sell—some old furniture."

There was a pause and her mother said, "You sound like Jonah."

"Mom, I've got to let you go," Addie said. "I've got a lot to do around the house today."

"Oh, sweetheart," her mother began. "I didn't mean to upset you."

"I'm not upset," Addie replied. "Just busy. We'll talk tomorrow."

"So you'll take the money?"

Addie sighed. "As a *loan*. I'll pay Jerry back. With interest."

"Fine, fine."

"I love you."

"Love you, too."

Addie threw herself down onto the bed. She stared at the ceiling for a long time before sitting up, grabbing her jeans, and pulling them on. She felt bad cutting off the conversation with her mother. But it was just so hard to hear his name. So hard. She shook her head, and the shake resonated throughout the rest of her body. *I've got too much to get done today,* she thought. She rolled off the bed and headed to the hardware store determined to get started on the renovation of her new temporary home.

There was nothing that Adelaide Andrews hated more than feeling out of place. And once inside Linstrom's hardware store, that's exactly what she felt. The inside of the store looked nothing like what she was used to back home in Chicago.

"Can I help you with something?" A man in a red-and-white-striped apron appeared in front of her. "You look a tad lost."

"I know what I'm looking for," Addie replied. "But I don't know where to find it."

The man chuckled. "Is there a certain project you're working on?"

"I'll be refinishing some furniture soon." Addie glanced down at her list. "I need to repaint the outside of my house. And I need to replace the showerhead in the bathroom. And I need to plant a garden. Also, how much would it cost to have my floors refinished?"

The man held up his hands and took a step back. "Whoa, whoa there, one thing at a time. Let me see this list."

Addie handed him the list. "I'm in over my head, aren't I?"

"Well . . . like I said, let's just take it one thing at a time," the man responded. "I think you could start with replacing that showerhead. You can find those over in aisle 13."

"Okay, thanks." Addie was relieved to have some direction.

"My name is Tom. Holler at me if you need help finding anything else."

Addie waved at him and wandered off in search of aisle 13. As she stood in front of the different showerheads, she closed her eyes, trying to remember what her shower looked like. She wished she'd taken a picture of it with her phone. "Maybe I don't need to shower," Addie wondered aloud. "Maybe I can just run through the neighbor's sprinkler."

"I'm pretty sure that's illegal in all fifty states," said a voice behind her.

Addie turned around to see Jasper standing in front of her. "You might want to tell that to my eighty-year-old neighbor. That seems to be his favorite pastime."

"That doesn't make it any less illegal."

Addie raised an eyebrow. "What are you, some kind of lawyer?"

"I used to be." Jasper reached above her to pluck a showerhead from the shelf. "Here, I think this one will probably work for general purposes."

"And now you just hang out in the hardware store assisting confused young girls?"

"Something like that." Jasper's face was expressionless, but Addie could tell he was trying to stifle a smile. "You aren't so young."

There was an awkward silence, and Addie was relieved that this time she wasn't shaking Jasper's hand as it happened.

"Well"—Addie held up the box with the showerhead inside—"thanks for your help, Counselor. I've got to go and find some hundred-fifty-grit sandpaper." She brushed past him, clutching the box to her chest. She could feel his eyes on her, and she wondered what Jasper meant when he said he "used to be" a lawyer. No wonder he made her nervous.

And for Addie, that was almost as bad as feeling out of place.

CHAPTER 4

Two days later, Addie sat in the waiting room of the Dixon Veterinary Clinic. This was the day she was picking up the dog she'd found—the dog she thought would surely die.

"Addie!"

Addie looked up. Wanda waved her over to the reception desk.

"Addie, honey, how are you?" Wanda flipped her rust-colored hair behind one shoulder. "I'm sorry I had to skedaddle the other night. My four-year-old was driving the babysitter crazy."

"Oh, that's okay."

"Hey, what are you doing tonight?" Wanda leaned over the desk excitedly. "Do you want to go to the county fair with me and Bryar?"

Addie furrowed her brow and replied, "Who's Bryar?"

"Oh, Lord. I'm sorry. That's my son!"

Addie searched for an excuse not to go. It didn't seem like a good idea to make friends when she wouldn't even be in town more than a few months. Friends meant connections and connections meant growing roots, which was certainly *not* Addie's first plan. "I really have a lot of work to do at the house, and I shouldn't leave a puppy alone, should I?"

"Well, it ain't gonna take a week," Wanda replied. "Besides, it'll be fun. Old Man Alcee makes the best funnel cakes this side of the Mississippi."

A funnel cake did sound pretty good. "Sure," Addie said finally. "But just for an hour or two."

"Great!" Wanda clapped her hands together. "I'll take you on back to get your pup. He's perked up some since you last saw him."

Addie followed Wanda into a sea of barking dogs. At the end of the hallway, Wanda pushed through a set of doors, and they were surrounded by kennels.

"This is where we board dogs that are staying with us," Wanda yelled over the noise. "Your little guy is back here somewhere."

Addie was anxious. She hoped she was doing the right thing by taking this dog home. *Of course,* she thought, *what are my options? Let him die?*

Toward the back of the room, Wanda opened up a kennel and reached inside. "Come on, buddy."

Addie held out her hands. Wanda handed him to her, and in that instant, Addie was in love. He shivered underneath her arms, and Addie nuzzled him and whispered, "It's okay now. It's all okay now."

When Addie got home with the dog, she carried him inside and placed him gingerly down on the dog bed she'd bought the day before. He was still shaking, and Addie was desperate to make him comfortable.

"Please don't shake like that. I won't hurt you."

She sat back. He was just a puppy, but Addie knew that by the size of his paws, she probably shouldn't be able to see each of his ribs beneath the skin. He needed to gain weight. There were several places on his body that had been stitched up, and the damaged ear had been repaired, leaving half of it. Every inch of his body seemed to be covered with a scratch or a stitch. Despite his pitiful appearance, his black-and-white coloring was beautiful. He had a little black circle around one eye on his otherwise white face and muzzle. She wanted to pet him but was afraid she'd hurt him—so much of him was broken open and raw.

She stroked the top of his head, staring at his mangled ear. It looked like it had been torn off. Several places on his skin had bite wounds and tear marks. It didn't make any sense to her. Why had someone shot him? Why had someone dumped him? More importantly, why had Dr. Dixon not seemed surprised to see a dog in such terrible shape?

Addie realized it wasn't just the pain of the stitches that was causing him to shake. It wasn't just the new house, the new bed, the new surroundings. He was terrified of her. He was terrified of what she might do to him. She thought about everything she'd heard about pit bulls over the years—the locking jaws, their genetic predisposition to be vicious, and how many communities had banned them. After she'd left the wounded puppy at the clinic, she'd rushed home and done some research on pit bulls, and she now knew enough to know that the first two, at least, weren't true at all. Looking at him, at his sweet face, she couldn't imagine that he would hurt anyone.

It was then that she noticed he was no longer shaking. He had fallen asleep beneath her touch. "I think I'll call you Felix," she whispered. "That name means 'lucky' and that is for sure what you are." Addie was ecstatic to have found Felix. She could always take him back to Chicago with her when she was done selling her aunt's house, but she was happy that she wouldn't be totally alone while she was here. Even with the bite marks and half an ear missing, he was the cutest thing she'd ever seen.

She thought about what "back to Chicago" really meant. Most of her friends were married with children and living in the suburbs, something she and Jonah swore they'd never do after they got married—leave the city. Yet here she was, miles away from everything and everyone she loved. Jonah wasn't with her. She was alone.

Addie glanced down at Felix. Well, maybe she wasn't entirely alone. Maybe this dog was kindred. He looked an awful lot on the outside like she felt on the inside. She had a feeling that Felix wasn't the only dog to have been dumped bleeding and struggling for his life. There was something fishy going on in the town of Eunice, and Adelaide Andrews was determined to get to the bottom of it, but first she had to get ready to meet Wanda since she'd agreed to go to the fair with her and her son. There had been no use trying to get out of it—she'd figured out quickly that Wanda was not a woman to be argued with when she made her mind up about something.

She checked the time on her cell phone and stood awkwardly in front of the bathroom mirror. Just like almost everything else in the house, the mirror was a throwback to another time—another life. She remembered standing in front of this mirror every day the summer she was twelve, wishing she was back home in Chicago with her mother. But now Chicago meant old memories; it meant Jonah. She shook the memories from her head and began to focus on tonight. And tonight, she looked okay, she guessed.

Her long blond hair was pulled back into a ponytail, and her thick, blunt bangs fell across her forehead, resting just above her eyes. She liked her hair this way—it pretty much always looked the same, but that meant there was less of a chance she could mess it up. She was wearing a blue-and-white gingham sundress with her favorite pair of white Chuck Taylors. Addie loved the way the sundress pushed up her boobs, which were her favorite feature. She was five foot five and a curvy size eight, but she had the breasts of a larger woman. Most of the time she kept them at least partially hidden beneath a cardigan, but it was too hot for all of that tonight. Besides, it wasn't as if she had an actual date, so she didn't know why it mattered so much to her what she looked like, but she was satisfied with her appearance nonetheless.

Addie looked down from the mirror when she heard her phone ring. "Hello?"

"Hey, hon. It's Wanda. Bryar and I are here. Come on out."

Addie padded into the living room where Felix was asleep. She hadn't realized that a puppy could sleep so much, although a call to Dr. Dixon eased her concern. He'd told her that it was probably the first time Felix had a warm bed and food to eat. From the looks of him, he'd spent all of his short life outside, fighting for just about anything he could get to eat. He hadn't really moved since she'd brought him home. She'd taken to carrying him outside because he wouldn't walk around while she was watching him. His eyes were still so wide and frightened. Addie hoped he'd be okay for a few hours while she was gone. She put down a few old newspapers just in case he couldn't wait until she got home. She wasn't sure what to expect from him just yet. She just hoped the couch was safe. She'd heard horror stories about dogs tearing up furniture and flooring, doors, and even windows. Adding to her list of fixes around her house wasn't her idea of a good time. She slipped out the front door, locking it behind her. She waved to Wanda and hurried out to the car.

"Hey!" Wanda shifted her huge Bonneville into drive.

Addie reached for the seat belt, and replied, "Hey! Thanks for picking me up. I know this is a small town, but I probably never would have found the fairgrounds."

"Addie, this is Bryar." Wanda gestured to the freckled redhead sitting in a booster seat in the back.

The little boy waved at Addie. "Hi. I'm four."

"Hi, Bryar," Addie replied. "I'm twenty-seven."

"My mom is older than you" was his response.

"Not by much, kiddo." Wanda snorted. "I'm just thirty."

"You don't look thirty," Addie said. "Of course, I don't know what a thirty-year-old is supposed to look like."

"Me either," Wanda replied. "I don't know how they're supposed to act, either. I live with a four-year-old. Other than the clinic, this is the first adult interaction I've had in months! Oh, the joys of single parenting."

"Are you and his dad D-I-V-O-R-C-E-D?" Addie spelled out the word, not wanting to trigger a reaction from the backseat. When Wanda didn't answer right away, she added, "I'm sorry. That's totally none of my business."

"Oh, no, no." Wanda waved her off. "It's fine. We were never married. His daddy is actually in P-R-I-S-O-N."

Addie sat back in her seat. "Oh . . . I'm sorry."

"Don't be. He's an S-O-B." Wanda winked. "As long as he stays where he is, everything is gravy, baby!"

From the backseat, Bryar dissolved into a fit of giggles, repeating, "It's gravy, baby!" over and over.

Addie and Wanda both began to laugh and Addie felt herself relax for the first time in weeks. Maybe she could go out with Wanda from time to time. A little friendship wasn't going to hurt anything, was it?

CHAPTER 5

By the time Wanda pulled into the grassy lot at the fairgrounds, it was almost full. A man wearing a bright orange vest directed them to the nearest spot.

"Is this the parking lot?" Addie asked. "The grass?"

"Yep," Wanda replied. "All the spots on the dirt are already taken. I hate parking in this grass. It ain't been mowed in weeks. Watch out for chiggers."

"Chiggers?"

"Yeah, you know, chiggers."

"I don't know what a chigger is."

Wanda laughed over her shoulder at Addie. "I keep forgetting you're a Yankee."

"I'm from Chicago. That's the Midwest." Addie followed Wanda and Bryar into the throng of people, trying to forget she'd ever heard the word *chigger.* Ahead of them, the fair stretched out in a hazy display of cotton candy and dirt. Looking down at her shoes, she realized that white had not been the right choice.

"What do you want to ride first?" Wanda asked her son, looking down at him as they approached the ticket booth. "Anything but the Ferris wheel."

"Mama! That's my favorite!"

"No, sir," Wanda replied. "You puke every time."

Addie scanned the crowd looking for a food cart. The more she thought about eating a funnel cake, the more her mouth watered. There was a white cart to the right of where she was standing. "While you two duke it out, I'm going to go get a funnel cake."

As Addie walked toward the cart, she noticed two men standing off to the side. They were arguing feverishly. One of the men, tall and broad, was waving his hands in the air as he spoke. He was bald, and the russet-colored skin on the top of his head was glistening with sweat.

The other man, the smaller of the two, cowered as the bigger man loomed over him. He had skin the consistency of glue, the liquid kind school children used, and it was about the same color. The closer Addie got to the food cart, the more she noticed the pockmarks covering the second man's face.

Addie strained to hear what they were saying.

"You owe me money," the first man growled. "You need to pay me my money."

The second man rubbed his hands on his filthy jeans and replied, "C'mon, man. You know I don't have it. I need more time."

"I don't got the time you need." The first man's voice was low and controlled. "You know better than to come to me making bets your ass can't cash."

The second man dug his shoe into the dirt.

The first man watched him, wrapping his hands around a package of cigarettes and then dropping the crumpled package to the ground. He put the last cigarette to his lips and let out a long sigh, and his face relaxed. Then he put one of his massive hands onto the second man's shoulder. "How about you do me a favor instead, huh?"

The second man slumped under the weight of the hand. "What do you want me to do?"

"We'll talk about that later." The first man pushed the second man forward, and they began to walk.

They neared Addie, and they were coming at her fast. The little man knocked right into her as he tried to keep up with the bigger man. "I'm sorry, missus," the little man said. He glanced in her direction but wouldn't look her in the eye.

"Watch where yer going!" the big man boomed. He caught Addie's eye. He kept her gaze but said nothing else. His dark eyes bored into her.

They were gone before Addie could respond. She waved to Wanda in the distance and yelled, "I thought you said Bryar couldn't ride the Ferris wheel." She hurried up to her friend, eager to shake the two men and their odd conversation from her memory.

"His friend Timmy wants to ride it, too." Wanda popped a piece of funnel cake into her mouth. "Maybe this will be my lucky year. Let's walk around for a little while. Bryar's going to be with Timmy and his mom for a while."

Addie followed Wanda as she began to head toward the outline of the fairground, where all the booths were set up. "How can it be so hot at five o'clock at night?" she mused, accepting a fan from one of the political candidates that had set up shop. "It feels like my back is sliding down onto my legs."

"Oh, honey, don't use that." Wanda plucked the fan from Addie's hands. "You don't want people to think you'd vote for him."

"I'm trying not to die of heatstroke."

"Walter Lee put his mama in a home last summer and moved his twenty-year-old child bride into his mama's house," Wanda drawled. "He said it was because his mama has Alzheimer's, but everybody knows it was because she didn't like his new wife."

"Was all of that on the back of the fan or something?"

"You'll thank me later."

All around Addie the fair buzzed. Nobody seemed to be bothered by the heat or the dust or the smell of fried everything. Women pushed baby strollers through the clumpy grass and over power cords. Children with faces covered in sweat and cotton candy ran past the slow-moving adults. Somehow, despite the noise, the cicadas could still be heard chirping their early evening prelude.

Suddenly Addie noticed that Jasper Floyd was standing three booths away. His head was bent low, talking to the man sitting in front of a sign that read FLOYD FARMS.

Did he ever change clothes? Or shave? Addie was sure he was wearing the same thing he had been wearing both times she'd seen him before tonight—his uniform of mud-caked boots, jeans, and a white T-shirt. His face had not seen a razor in days. This time he was wearing a green cap as well. It also read FLOYD FARMS.

Jasper looked up and caught her staring at him. He gave her a slow smile before returning to his conversation. Although his eyes stayed on her for a bit longer before he gave his full attention back to the man in front of him.

"Well, look who's smiling at you, Adelaide." Wanda gave Addie a playful jab in the ribs.

"Why wouldn't he smile? Isn't that polite?"

"I've known him since elementary school, and he's never smiled at me," Wanda replied. "Jasper Floyd is the most serious man I've ever met."

Addie looked down at the empty paper plate she was carrying. "He caught me staring at him. I'm pretty sure he was obligated to smile at me."

"He was a lawyer, you know," Wanda continued. "Had his own practice in Memphis."

"Then what's he doing here?"

"Well"—Wanda's green eyes danced with excitement—"his daddy got real sick last year and can't run the farm all by himself anymore. And there was no way Jack Floyd was gonna sell that farm to anybody. No way. So Jasper came home to help take care of business. Been here ever since."

"No wonder he never smiles."

"Well, he's smiling at you." Wanda linked her arm through Addie's. "Let's go talk to him. Who knows? Maybe you can even make him laugh.

"Hey, Jasper," Wanda called out. "How's it going?"

"Same as always, Wanda." Jasper shifted on his feet, folding his arms across his chest. "How are you two tonight?"

"We're great," Wanda replied before Addie could open her mouth. "I haven't seen your mom too much around town lately. How's she doing?"

Jasper stiffened. "Mom doesn't get out much anymore. She spends most of her time taking care of Dad."

Addie watched him. He was curious to her—he didn't talk like any farmer she knew. Which she admitted weren't too many. He had perfect posture and perfect teeth, and Addie wondered what else was perfect and lurking underneath his purposely rumpled exterior.

"Addie?"

Jasper and Wanda were staring at her. "Huh? What?"

"Jasper asked you if you'd gotten your showerhead put in," Wanda said.

"Oh!" Addie's face flushed. "No. Not yet."

"Mommy!" Bryar ran up to Wanda and tugged at her purse strap. "Guess what?"

Wanda reached down and lifted him up onto her hip, and replied, "What, honey?"

"I rided the Ferris wheel three times and didn't get sick! Three times!"

"That's great, baby!"

"Mommy?"

Wanda placed him back on his feet. "What?"

"Uh-oh."

Addie jumped back as a tidal wave of vomit flew out of Bryar's mouth and on the ground in front of them and all over Wanda's shoes.

"Oh, Bryar! Yuck!"

"Sorry." Spit dangled from Bryar's bottom lip.

"It's okay, baby. It's okay. I think we probably better go home."

"Okay, Mommy."

Wanda turned to Addie and said, "I'm sorry. I don't think the B-Man needs to be riding anything else tonight."

"Oh, that's okay," Addie replied. "I think I've seen just about all I need to see, anyway."

"Come on, baby," Wanda whispered to Bryar. She picked him up.

"Are you sure you have time to take me home?" Addie asked, following after them.

"I can take you home, Adelaide," Jasper said. "I'm headed out anyway. I need to get home before it gets dark."

"Thanks, Jasper," Wanda called over her shoulder. "You're a lifesaver." She headed off toward the grassy parking lot, Bryar's head lolling on one of her shoulders.

"Wanda didn't even wait for you to change your mind," Addie said.

Jasper gave Addie a crooked smile. "I've found that Wanda very rarely waits for anything."

"So," Addie said. "You and Wanda went to school together?"

Jasper nodded. "We did. She was a couple of years behind me."

"So you're . . ." Addie trailed off.

"Thirty-four," Jasper finished.

"Oh," Addie replied. She was starting to feel the conversation going nowhere. "I'll be twenty-eight in July."

They continued to walk in silence until Jasper stopped in front of a hulking John Deere tractor. "Here we are. Climb on up."

Addie glanced around the parking lot. Maybe Jasper was talking to someone else. "You want me to do what?"

"The tractor. Climb on up."

"On the tractor?"

Jasper took hold of the side and pulled himself up. "Come on. There's plenty of room inside."

"You drove a tractor to the fair?"

"I did."

"Why?"

"Are you going to climb up here or not? I don't have all night."

Addie grabbed Jasper's outstretched hand. "I don't think I'm dressed for this."

"There's no law that says you have to be wearing overalls," Jasper replied. His tone was gruff, but he was smiling down at her.

"I don't think I've ever ridden in a tractor before."

"Well, then, Miss Addie, you've not lived."

Addie situated herself inside the cab of the tractor next to Jasper. The engine started with a lurch and Addie grabbed onto the bottom of the seat. "Is this the way you get around town? I can't imagine this is economical."

"Most days you'll find me driving a 1970 Ford Bronco Sport."

"Fancy."

"It's my baby," Jasper replied. "All original. My dad gave it to me when I was fifteen."

"I got a 1989 LeBaron when I got my license," Addie said.

"At least you got to drive it," Jasper continued. "I wasn't allowed to take the thing off the farm until I left for college."

"Well, then why did your dad even give it to you?"

Jasper's grip on the tractor wheel tightened. "That's just my dad."

They bounced along, quiet twilight hanging between them. Jasper didn't look over at Addie for what felt like hours. She thought that she probably could have walked home faster than the tractor was moving. Cars passed them on both sides, and occasionally Jasper pulled over to let a stream of vehicles pass.

"I picked up Felix from Dr. Dixon today." Addie broke the silence. "He's doing much better."

"You named him Felix, eh?" Jasper asked. "That's not a bad name. I'm glad he's better. He looked pretty rough the other night."

"Hey, can I ask you a question?"

"Sure."

"What kind of a person shoots a dog and throws him in the trash?"

Jasper stopped at the top of Addie's street. The tractor gave an exhausted sigh as he cut the engine. "I don't think I can get down your street. You may have to walk from here."

"That's okay," Addie replied. "But you didn't answer my question."

"The kind of person with no regard for the life of another living being."

"I can't understand it."

"I'm glad you can't understand it. *You* should be glad you can't understand it." Jasper jumped down and walked around to help Addie out of the cab. "I can walk you the rest of the way."

"That's all right. I'm not far from here."

"I've been to your house before," Jasper said. "Your aunt Tilda made the best fried pies in the state."

"I wish I'd also inherited her skills in the kitchen," Addie said. "Thanks for the ride."

"Anytime."

Addie bent down to scratch at her leg. It felt like something was biting at her ankles. "Hey, Jasper," she called after him.

"Yeah?"

"What's a chigger?"

CHAPTER 6

In the dream, Addie was helpless. She stood, hands glued to her sides, as the man in the white coat pulled back the white sheet.

"I'm so sorry, ma'am."

Addie opened her mouth to speak, but no sound came out. She was trying to scream. "Please cover him back up!"

"I'm so sorry," the man said again.

"I'm so sorry."

"I'm so sorry."

"I'm so sorry."

"I'm so sorry."

"I'm so sorry."

She reached past the man and grabbed Jonah. She shook him. She slapped him. She cursed at him, but he wouldn't wake up. "You should have listened to me," she cried into his lifeless chest. "I told you not to go."

Addie bolted straight up in bed, her hair clinging to her neck and face in sweat-soaked clumps. Her heart was racing, and it took her a few seconds to realize where she was. It was the middle of the night.

She jumped when she heard a small whimper beneath her. Peering over her bed, she breathed a sigh of relief when she saw Felix looking curiously up at her from the bedroom floor.

"Hey, buddy." Addie reached her hand down to pet him.

Felix flinched and backed away. He kept himself hunched down, just out of touching distance from her.

"I wish you'd trust me," Addie murmured disaffectedly.

Felix cocked his head right and then left. He inched closer to her, but stopped just short of brushing her fingers.

"So close," Addie said. "Let's go outside."

Felix's ears perked up when he heard the word *outside*. He followed Addie to the back door, his nails making a *clack, clack, clack* noise on the hardwood floor.

Addie opened the door, and he stopped. "Please just go outside," Addie begged. "You're getting to be too big to carry." When she reached down to pick him up, Felix shot down the porch steps and into the backyard. Addie shut the door behind them and sat down on the steps as Felix pranced around the yard looking for a perfect spot. It was progress.

The garden stretched out in front of her in a mass of overgrown weeds and flowers. The rice paper plants that her aunt Tilda had loved so much had almost completely taken over the yard, in some areas preventing any light from breaking through beneath their leaves. Luckily, the bulb over the back door was still functioning, and Addie was thankful for some light.

Addie knew she needed to do something about the unruly

thicket the plant had created, but she didn't have the first clue about where to begin. She supposed she ought to call a landscaper, just one more thing to be added to the list.

She squeezed her eyes shut, trying to wipe away entirely the fading memory of the nightmare she'd had. When she opened them, Felix was waiting expectantly at the bottom of the stairs, but Addie was looking past him to the shed at the back of the yard. She walked back into the house and rummaged in the kitchen drawer for a flashlight. And it worked! It was her lucky day.

The shed was locked with a padlock. The padlock was new—probably something a well-meaning friend of her aunt's had placed there for protection. However, the door was rotting all around the lock. Addie curled her fingers around the door and pulled. There was a cracking noise that sent Felix barking to the other end of the yard. "I've almost got it," she said.

The next time she pulled, the door came flying off its hinges, sending Addie into orbit. She landed in the grass, and the door landed on top of her. She didn't move until Felix delicately took one of her flip-flops off with his mouth and ran off. "Get back here," she called to him from underneath the door.

Felix ignored her and settled happily with her flip-flop into the grass.

Addie groaned and pushed the door off her. "Give me back my shoe!" She pushed herself up and started toward Felix, who ran off every time she got close. After a few minutes, Addie gave up and turned her attention back to the now doorless shed. "That dog," she said under her breath.

The door hadn't been the only part of the shed that was rotting, but Addie was surprised to see that it was in overall good shape on the inside. The dust, however, was another story. There were two small windows on either side, but they were so caked with dust that Addie had trouble seeing what else was inside, even with the light from the flashlight. She hobbled back inside the house and returned a few minutes later with a new pair of shoes.

The shed was packed. Addie scanned the light around the room. There were plastic tubs and boxes stacked on top of furniture stacked on top of more furniture. It was like her aunt had been stacking pieces of her life in there for years. In one corner there was a table with several chairs stacked on top of it. It looked a lot like the dining room table Aunt Tilda had kept in the kitchen when Addie was a kid. She crept closer and let the light hover over it. It had seen better days. The paint was flaking and cracked, and she could hear Jonah in her head saying, *Why would someone paint an antique? Amateurs!*

Addie turned when she heard a scuffle behind her. Felix was standing in the doorway, flip-flop in his mouth, staring curiously at her. She sat the flashlight down on a nearby box and grabbed at the stack of chairs on top of the table. One by one she carried them inside.

The table was a more difficult task, but she was able to take it apart, leaf by leaf, and carry it. Once she had everything inside, she stood back and admired the dusty mess she'd made. Both she and Felix left sooty footprints all over the linoleum floor in the kitchen, the door to the shed was propped precariously up against the shed. She knew that the table and chairs were splinters waiting to happen, but Addie felt alive for the first time since she'd seen the mighty Mississippi River.

CHAPTER 7

Dr. Dixon peered into the kennel where Felix sat hunched in the back corner. Every time the kindly veterinarian attempted to open the kennel door, Felix shrank farther inside.

"He really, really didn't want to get into his kennel this morning," Addie said. "I had to put a piece of cheese inside of it, and then once I got him in, he looked at me like I tricked him."

"I guess technically, you did," Dr. Dixon replied, a wry smile on his lips. "It's okay, Addie dear. He'll come around."

"I've been putting the medicine on him just like you told me to. He doesn't like it, but he doesn't seem to be in any real pain."

"He looks good." Dr. Dixon's eyebrows knitted together. "He's beginning to heal nicely."

"But you look concerned."

"Well . . ." Dr. Dixon trailed off, running his hands through a patchy spot of hair at the top of Felix's head. "His hair was a little thin when you brought him in, and I think it might be worse. We need to do a skin scraping to rule out mange."

"Mange?"

"Let's just be sure." Dr. Dixon produced a small, flat razor from a side drawer.

"Is that going to hurt him?" Addie asked. "I don't want that to hurt him."

"He'll feel a little pinch." He scraped a small section of Felix's head and wiped the contents onto a glass slide.

"I'll be right back." Dr. Dixon patted Addie on the shoulder.

Addie reached over to pet Felix. He inched forward and licked her hand. "I'm sorry, buddy," she said. "I promise I won't trick you anymore."

Felix allowed her to scratch him underneath his chin for a few seconds before Dr. Dixon appeared in the doorway, a small bottle in his hand.

"Felix appears to have some Demodex."

"He has what?"

"It's a form of mange. Don't worry, it's not contagious. It just means he may lose some more hair, and you're going to have to give him some medicine for a month or so." Dr. Dixon held up the bottle. "This is ivermectin. You'll need to give this to him orally once a day."

"Okay."

"Sometimes this happens, especially with bulldog breeds," Dr. Dixon said. "It's not uncommon. I've seen it before."

"That reminds me," Addie began. "The night that I brought Felix in . . . that night . . . you said that his wounds were something you'd seen before."

"Yes."

"Well, what did you mean by that?"

Dr. Dixon nudged his glasses up higher onto the bridge of his nose. "I have seen many, many dog injuries as a result of a couple of farm dogs getting into a fight."

"But Felix had been shot, too."

"Yes," Dr. Dixon said. "But it's also not uncommon for farmers to shoot an animal that they don't think will live."

"Instead of taking the dog to you?" Addie asked. "Is it also common for farmers to take their animals off of the farm while they're obviously still alive, wrap them up in plastic bags, and dump them down by the levee like garbage?"

"I'm not sure I know what you're getting at."

"I don't know what I'm getting at, either," Addie replied. She was exasperated that she couldn't explain herself. "I just don't understand why someone would do what they did to Felix. He *belonged* to somebody, and I think we both know it wasn't a farmer."

"This is a safe town," he replied. "Most people around here are good people. But you need to be careful down there by the levee. And I'd put that mange medicine in something yummy before you give it to him."

Addie closed the door to the exam room and headed up to the front desk. She wished she had a friend down here, someone she could talk to about things. Nothing she said seemed to come out right when she didn't get to talk through her thoughts first with someone else. Nothing sounded the same inside her head as it did coming out of her mouth. Her mother always told her she got it from her father. Her aunt had been the same way. She missed Jonah.

"Addie, baby, here are the pamphlets Doc was talking about," Wanda called out, nodding in the direction of the double doors leading back to the examination rooms.

Addie smiled over at Wanda. "Okay, thanks."

"You never told me about what happened after the fair," Wanda whispered.

"Nothing happened. He gave me a ride home," Addie said. "In his tractor."

Wanda began to giggle. "You're kidding!"

"It was actually kind of cute."

"I'm going to give Jasper a call," Wanda said, "and tell him if he offers you a ride in his manure spreader you just might fall in love."

"I have no idea what that is," Addie replied. "But it sounds awful."

"It is exactly what it sounds like."

"Gross!"

The women dissolved into a fit of giggles. When Wanda caught her breath she said, "You're doing a good job with Felix. Doc says so. How is everything going with the house? Have you managed to get that dang shed cleaned out yet? The last time I went in there was with your aunt, and it was bursting at the seams."

"I'm trying." Addie looked over at the kennel. "He is still pretty scared. Not that I blame him. And the house still needs a lot of work. I'm taking it one day at a time, but I'm thinking I bit off more than I can chew."

"Happens to the best of us."

"But I am excited to see what all is in that shed."

"Don't worry about the mange," Wanda said. "It's common, 'specially when people don't do nothin' that they're 'sposed to for their animals."

"Seems to be a running theme around here."

"It's a runnin' theme everywhere, darlin'."

"I guess I just never realized."

Wanda patted Addie's hand. "Your aunt Tilda was wonderful with animals. She took excellent care of her cats, and I bet you have the same touch."

"You have her cats now, don't you?" Addie asked. "Can I see them?"

"I do!" Wanda's eyes brightened. "Hey, why don't you come over one night this week? I'll cook supper, and you can see the little devils."

Addie hesitated.

"Bryar would love it."

"Okay," Addie replied. "I'd love that, too. Thank you!"

"Thanks, nothing, sugar. That's what friends are for."

CHAPTER 8

ADDIE STOOD ON THE DOORSTEP OF WANDA'S HOUSE, POISED TO ring the doorbell. Above her, menacing clouds loomed, casting shade throughout the yard. She thought about Felix alone in the house. She hoped he'd be okay if it started to storm. He wasn't at all happy with his new medicine. It made him itch worse than before, and Addie was beside herself not being able to explain to him that it was for his own good. Before her finger reached the button, the door swung open.

"You're here! Great!" Wanda exclaimed. "Come on in!"

"Thanks for inviting me to dinner." Addie grinned. "I was starting to feel very hostile toward my microwave."

The entire house smelled of suppertime, the word her aunt had always used. In Chicago, people called the last meal of the day dinner, but in the South, she learned, they called it supper. And supper was glorious. Addie's stomach growled. She followed

Wanda to the kitchen. The place was small, but it was comfortable. From her spot by the stove, Addie could see Bryar watching television in the living room. He sat in his underwear on a child-size recliner.

"Is Bryar watching the Weather Channel?"

Wanda sighed, bending down to pull the tuna casserole out of the oven. "Yes. The kid is obsessed with weather."

Bryar bounded into the kitchen, a broad smile on his freckled face. He looked up at Addie and said, "Hi! Wanna come watch TV with me?"

Bryar led Addie toward the living room. "Sure," Addie said. "But do we have to watch the Weather Channel?"

"Yes. There's a storm coming."

"Is that what the weatherman says?" Addie sat down beside the small recliner.

"Uh-uh," Bryar said, shaking his head back and forth. "She says it is going to miss us."

"Well, that's good, right?"

"There's a storm coming," Bryar repeated. "It's coming here. I know."

Wanda piped up from the kitchen, "That's what he always says. He's only right about fifty percent of the time."

"Mama!" Bryar shrieked, turning around backward in his chair. "I said! I said!"

Wanda put her hands up in the air and replied, "I know, I know. Come on now, it's time to eat."

The three of them gathered around the table in the kitchen. Addie had never seen such a spread. She didn't know the first thing about cooking, despite her various attempts to learn. If it didn't fit in the toaster or the microwave, it didn't get cooked.

"This looks amazing." Addie gawked at the food. "I haven't had a meal that looked this good since Jonah made me . . ." She trailed off, realizing that Wanda would have no idea who she was talking about.

"Who's Jonah?"

"Oh, just someone I used to know back in Chicago," Addie said, waving off Wanda's question. "He was an amazing cook."

"Don't you like to cook?"

"I think I'd like it better if I wasn't so terrible at it," Addie admitted.

"My granny taught me to cook when I was just knee-high to a grasshopper," Wanda replied.

"Since you were what?"

"Since I was a young'un."

"Aunt Tilda tried to teach me every summer," Addie said. "But it never took."

"My granny didn't think a woman could keep a man if she couldn't cook, but feedin' and keepin' ain't the same thing at all."

"I guess not."

Wanda stirred the pot. "So how is Felix doin' with that medicine?"

"Getting him to take it is an all-day event. He won't take a treat from my hands, so I have to put the medicine in the treat and leave it on the floor. Then I have to leave the room completely before he'll even think about eating it."

"You can hardly blame the poor dog. He's not had much reason to trust people."

Addie dug her fork into the casserole. "Oh, I know. He seemed terrified at your office the other day, but he's a good boy. He never growls or tries to bite."

"You'd be amazed the difference a little love can make," Wanda said, giving Addie an encouraging smile. "He's just a puppy."

Addie was about to respond when the doorbell rang. A large figure loomed on the other side of the kitchen window, hidden by the curtains.

"Who in the . . . ," Wanda mumbled, pushing her chair back.

The doorbell rang again.

"I'm coming!" Wanda yelled. "Hang on to your horses!" She opened the door and her irritation vanished. "Bobby!"

"Wandeeeeeeeeeee!" the man on the other side of the door exclaimed. "I missed you, little sister!"

"I was wonderin' when you'd finally show up at my door," Wanda gushed, dragging him inside. "I 'bout thought you was dead!"

"Uncle Bobby!" Bryar squealed, jumping out of his chair and knocking over his glass of milk. "Hi! Hi, Uncle Bobby!"

"Bryar, calm down!" Wanda scolded halfheartedly, stepping aside so that her son could jump into Bobby's arms. "Addie, this is my brother, Bobby."

"Hi." Addie smiled at the hulking figure in front of her. "It's nice to meet you."

"You too," Bobby replied. "I didn't mean to interrupt supper."

"Nonsense!" Wanda said, clucking her tongue. "Pull up a seat. Delight us with stories of the open road!"

Addie smiled to herself, listening to Wanda and Bobby's excited conversation. She wished sometimes that she had a brother or sister to share a bond with.

"Everybody sit! Sit!" Wanda commanded, placing Bryar back in his chair at the table. "This supper isn't going to eat itself!"

Bobby went about filling his plate with his sister's cooking. He was eyeing the food as hungrily as Addie had, and she was grateful she'd fixed her plate beforehand.

"So, Miss Addie," Bobby began, his mouth full of casserole, "what brings you to our fine town?"

Addie grinned. She liked him. "You might have known my aunt. Tilda Andrews. I inherited her house."

Bobby's eyes widened. "Oh, yes! She made the best fried pies around. I was sorry to hear about her passing."

"Unfortunately, I didn't inherit her talent for baked goods," Addie admitted. "And thank you. So, what is it that you do?"

"I was a long-haul trucker," Bobby replied proudly. "Been on the road for fifteen years."

"Wow, I bet that's interesting."

"It was," Bobby agreed. "Wrecked my rig about a month ago, and I ain't had the time or money to get 'er fixed."

"Oh," Addie said, "I'm so sorry. I'm glad you weren't hurt."

"Bruised a couple of ribs." Bobby leaned back in his chair and patted his hearty midsection. "Got rear-ended on the Manchac Swamp Bridge in Louisiana. Held up traffic for hours."

"How come you're not still in Mississippi with Doreen?" Wanda asked.

"Things with me and her ain't goin' so well."

"She get tired of ya?"

"More or less." Bobby let out a throaty chuckle that turned into a cough. "Hell, I've gotta stop smoking."

"It would help if you weren't spending so much time over with Redd. The man smokes like he's having his last meal."

"I've only been back in town a week," Bobby said. "How'd you know that I've been stayin' with Redd?"

"Mama told me," Wanda replied. "I figured he had you up to

no good, otherwise it wouldn'ta taken a week for you to come visit your little sister."

Bobby picked at his teeth with his pinkie finger. "So far he's the only man in town decent enough to have offered me a job."

"You know that work ain't decent, Bobby Carter. And it sure as Jesus ain't honest. That man is crookeder than a three-dollar bill."

"He's what?" Addie asked, breaking into their conversation.

"Just something our granny used to say," Bobby replied. "What Wanda's tryin' to say is that she don't like Redd much."

"Oh." Addie picked up her plate and started toward the sink. The conversation Wanda and Bobby were having felt like something that should be private—especially since Addie didn't even know who they were talking about.

"You don't have to do that!" Wanda jumped up. "You're the guest!"

"I am capable of clearing my plate," Addie said. "Besides, I've got to get going. Felix must be going crazy by now."

"Addie!" Bryar called from the table. "You stay to play!"

Addie walked over to the little boy and ruffled his hair. "I can't tonight, kiddo. I have to get home to my dog. And didn't you say there was a storm coming?"

"Yes."

"Then I have to go before it starts!"

"I'll play with you, bubba," Bobby hollered from the table. "What do you want to play?"

"No." Bryar crossed his arms firmly across his chest. "I want Addie."

"You're gonna hurt your old uncle Bobby's feelings," Bobby said. "We can play whatever you want."

"Whatever I want?"

"Sure."

"I want to play Weatherman!" Bryar squealed. "You be the storm! The mean storm!"

Addie hugged Wanda and let herself out, leaving the cozy scene going on inside. Part of her wished she could stay. She looked up at the sky as she hurried out to her little Honda, parked on the street next to Bobby's massive F-150. There was a rumble in the distance, clouds circling menacingly above her. She looked up at the sky darkening around her, thinking that maybe Bryar knew more about the weather than his mother gave him credit for.

By the time Addie made it back to her house, the power was out all over town, and the rain was pouring down in opaque sheets. She used the last minutes of daylight to rustle up a few candles.

Once she'd gotten Felix settled and given him a treat to keep him from barking at the flickering candlelight, Addie found the sandpaper on the counter and sat down on the floor—sandpaper in one hand and glass of wine in the other. Jonah had liked to use electric sanders, but Addie never got used to them. She felt like it rushed the job, made the relationship between her and the wood somehow impersonal. Jonah thought that this was a silly excuse for taking twice as long on a project.

"Well, you're not here," Addie said aloud. "It's just me now, and I'm doing it my way." It exhilarated her to say those words out loud. One of the worst arguments they'd ever had was over sanding. Addie took a sip of her wine. She'd told Jonah that in one of the books he'd given her about refinishing wood, it had said that power tools could be too harsh on delicate pieces. He'd told her that she read too much. "But you gave me the book," she'd said to him.

"I didn't expect you to read it from cover to cover," he'd replied.

"That's what books are for," she'd said, before skulking off to their bedroom. She could hear the electric sander clear into the early morning hours. She hadn't known then that the piece he was working on had really been for her, that his need to finish by the morning for her birthday was more important than anything else. How surprised she'd been when she'd walked downstairs to find breakfast sitting on that beautiful bench in the breakfast nook, and sitting next to her orange juice was a ring—a diamond ring. Before she could react, Jonah was down on one knee.

Addie wiped a stray tear sliding down her cheek. She drank more wine. *Always sand in the direction of the grain—never perpendicular to it or at an angle,* she told herself. But she couldn't see the direction of the grain; the tears were blurring her vision now, flowing freely.

Outside the thunder boomed, sending Felix into a frenzy. He bumped into her elbow, and the glass fell out of her hands and shattered.

"It's okay, it's okay," Addie said to him. He was in her lap, and she didn't quite know what to do. She leaned down and put her arms around his shivering body. "I won't let anyone hurt you," Addie said, nuzzling her wet cheeks into his fur. "Don't be afraid." It felt good to feel his little body pressed into hers, soft and warm. Maybe she hadn't been able to keep Jonah safe, but she could surely keep her dog from trembling beneath her fingertips.

After a few minutes, Addie released him and stood. Without hesitation, Felix scrambled up and followed her into the bedroom. He sat on the rug by the bed watching her as she felt around for her pajamas.

Outside, the thunder and lightning seemed to be edging closer and closer. Addie shivered and slid under the covers. She lay there, her eyes open, and listened to the storm rage. She wasn't sure why she was already in bed. Had there been power, she probably would have been sitting in front of the TV, feeling guilty about all the work that needed to be done on the house. Felix had been taking up so much of her time that she'd put off projects that should have been started already—namely, the work on the floors and the garden. She made a mental note to make a few calls in the morning.

Rolling over, Addie squinted at the floor below and whispered, "Felix? Are you down there?"

There was a sharp clap of thunder, and Addie felt Felix brush up against her extended hand. She stroked his head, and when he didn't back away, Addie ran her hand up under his chin and rubbed. Felix made a low, guttural noise at her touch, a noise that sounded almost like a cat purring.

The thunder sounded again, and Felix tore away from Addie, his paws grasping at the sheets. To Addie's astonishment, Felix leapt up onto the bed. She lifted up the covers in time for him to crawl underneath them.

"You are the weirdest dog on the planet," Addie mumbled as Felix's cold nose pushed against one of her thighs. "Get comfortable. This is going to be a long night."

Addie wasn't sure how long she slept, but she woke up to total darkness and the sound of sirens going off outside.

Addie could feel Felix panting next to her. She felt her nightstand for the flashlight. She shone it around the room, blinking her heavy eyelids. What was going on?

The wind was howling, the sirens were howling, and from where she sat in bed, Addie could see the shadows of the trees bowing over through the curtains.

"I think we need to get to the bathroom," Addie croaked, reaching underneath the covers for Felix. He let out a small noise in protest but didn't shrink away from her grip.

Addie stood up with Felix pressed against her. She knew, from her summers spent with her aunt, that the house didn't have a cellar. The best place would have to be the bathroom—more specifically, the bathroom tub. She remembered a storm similar to this the last time she'd stayed with Aunt Tilda. Addie had been in a panic to find that the house didn't have a basement. All the houses in Chicago had basements. But her aunt had calmly explained that the bathtub would keep them safe as could be, and they had spent the entire night in the tub pretending to be pirates of the high seas. Despite the storm roaring outside, Addie smiled.

Felix squirmed out of her grip and dropped to the floor, his claws clack-clacking on the wooden floor.

She managed to get him corralled into the bathroom, and lifted him up into the tub with her. "This is just great," she muttered to herself, the flashlight illuminating the porcelain white of the tub. "I'm going to die in a bathtub in Arkansas with a one-eared, mange-ridden pit bull."

Both Addie and Felix jumped when a clap of thunder shook the house. There was a burst of lightning and a piercing crash. It sounded like something had smashed right through her house. She scrambled out of the bathtub and followed the beam of her flashlight into the kitchen, from where the noise was coming.

Addie didn't need her flashlight to see the chaos unfolding in front of her. In the kitchen, jutting through the window above the sink was a giant tree limb, branches and all. It writhed in protest, trapped by the house. Shards of broken glass covered the floor, the wind shifting them at its will. From where she stood, Addie could feel the sting of rain against her face. Somewhere in the distance, Felix barked. And Addie, turning on her heel to find her phone, began to think that being found in a bathtub in Arkansas didn't sound like the worst thing that could happen to her after all.

CHAPTER 9

THE STORM HAD ALL BUT CEASED BY THE TIME THE FIRE TRUCK, paramedics, and half the town arrived at Addie's doorstep along with the first glimpse of daylight. She sat on the porch clutching her head in her hands as Felix growled from his kennel in the living room.

"I said I'm fine." Addie pulled away from a paramedic. "I wasn't anywhere near the kitchen when it happened."

"It's just my job," the man grumbled.

"Fine." Addie sighed. "But if your hand brushes my left boob again, you'll be the one asking for assistance."

"I think we're all done here."

Addie glared at him. She wished she'd taken the time to change out of her pajamas before she had called 911. All she was wearing was an old T-shirt that scarcely covered her rear end. The first responders wouldn't let her go back into her house until they deemed it secure.

As the paramedic strode off, a brown Bronco pulled up in front of Addie's house. Addie's breath caught in her throat when Jasper stepped out. He was wearing blue shorts and a white fitted T-shirt. Instead of his usual work boots, on his feet were running shoes. Morning stubble traced his jawline. He looked like he'd just woken up. Addie watched as he spoke with one of the men hovering around the fire truck. The man was pointing toward the downed limb. Jasper was rubbing his chin and nodding. Addie couldn't take her eyes off him. She felt her cheeks flush hotly, and she began to think about what it might be like to wake up next to him, to feel his unshaven face brush her skin.

"Carl Thomas says you almost clocked him for trying to examine you," Jasper said, making his way up the steps to Addie.

"He would have deserved it," Addie replied. "What are you doing here? I've never seen so many people turn out for a limb through a window." She hoped he couldn't see her daydream written all over her face.

"Not a lot to do in this town," Jasper responded, his lips twitching amusedly. "I was getting up for a morning run when this came over the radio. I recognized the address."

Addie let out an exasperated sigh and stood up. "The fun never ends at Adelaide Andrews's place."

"So you're okay?" Jasper questioned. His eyes met hers briefly, studying her intently.

"I'm fine," Addie replied, her hands moving to her burning cheeks. "I was in the bathtub with Felix when it happened."

Jasper raised an eyebrow.

"I wasn't bathing with my dog at three A.M., if that's what you're thinking," Addie continued, rolling her eyes. "The sirens were going off, and I figured it was the safest place. So I was in the bathtub with Felix, but we weren't in the bathtub together."

"Uh-huh," Jasper responded, this time breaking into a full-fledged grin. "Is that your bath buddy in there barking?"

"Yes. He doesn't like his kennel. But I was afraid with all these people crawling around that he'd go berserk and try to eat someone," Addie said.

"Did he eat your pants?"

He was trying to get a rise out of her. Addie met his gaze. "You're all just lucky I was wearing anything."

Jasper's gaze dropped from her eyes to her legs. "I don't know if I'd consider that lucky."

"Ms. Andrews?" They were interrupted by a man in a firefighter's uniform. "There's not a whole lot more we can do here, but we've done some basic cleanup. You'll need to have someone come and remove that limb as soon as possible."

Addie shifted, placing a hand on her hip. "You mean you can't remove it? I thought that's what you were here for."

"No, ma'am," the man replied. "You've got to get that done for yourself. I told Ms. Tilda years ago that tree out there was a goner."

"Great," Addie muttered. "Just great."

"Thanks, Joey." Jasper nodded. "I'll see if I can't get someone out here today."

"Do you know someone?" Addie questioned. "How much does a thing like that cost? I'm going to go broke fixing this damn house."

"Don't worry about it. I can do it myself with a little help from one of the guys on the farm."

"Really?"

"Sure."

"Wow, thanks." Addie smiled for the first time all morning.

"How about I come back here in a couple of hours, and we can go from there?" Jasper asked. "I'll need to go get a few other things back at the farm."

"Perfect." Addie was still smiling. "I need to get cleaned up, anyway. Maybe put on some pants."

"See you later," Jasper called over his shoulder as he headed back down the porch steps. He stopped when he saw Addie's neighbor standing in the yard across the street.

"My neighbor is a lunatic."

"What?" Jasper turned back around toward Addie. "You mean Augustus Smoot?"

"Is that his name?" Addie squinted past Jasper to the man across the street. He was standing in his underwear and holding a black umbrella. He was stoic, almost like a statue, watching the scene unfold in Addie's yard. "I haven't actually met him. But he stands out in his yard in his underwear at least once a week."

"That sounds like old Auggie."

"You know him?"

Jasper scratched the stubble on his chin. "I know him. He used to be a county judge. Before that he was a lawyer here in Eunice. All of that was before my time, but my father knew him well."

"What happened to him?" It was hard for Addie to believe that her neighbor had ever been a regular person.

"Nobody really knows," Jasper said. "The rumor, and mind you this is just a rumor, is that he went crazy after his wife, Eleonora, died of cancer. That's been at least fifteen years back."

Addie stood up and walked down the steps to where Jasper stood. "That's really quite sad."

"Most people don't go crazy because they're happy with life."

Just then a woman pulled up to Augustus Smoot's house in a yellow Neon. She got out of the car and left the engine running. Addie had never seen the woman before, but it wasn't the first time that she'd seen the car parked in his driveway. She was a little, round woman with toffee-colored skin and brown hair sprayed into a pristine bun. She was wearing white sneakers that looked like the kind of shoes nurses wear.

Jasper and Addie watched the woman scurry up to Augustus, grabbing him by one of his bony arms. Without a word, he dropped the umbrella and followed her inside the house.

A couple of hours later, a brown Bronco once again pulled up beside Addie's house. The running shorts and sneakers were gone and he was back to his uniform of broken-in denim, T-shirt, and work boots. Addie felt overdressed in her cutoff shorts and lime green tank top.

"I've got a couple of guys bringing a truck out to help with the tree."

"Great," Addie replied, opening the door for him to enter the house. "I would have spent all day just looking for people to come out and help me."

"I needed a break from the farm anyway," Jasper admitted. "You want to grab some lunch first?"

"Sure." Addie shrugged. "There are a few restaurants in town I've been dying to try."

"I know the perfect place," Jasper replied. He grinned down at her. It'll be an hour or two before the guys can make it over, so we have plenty of time."

"So you're taking a break from the manual labor of farm work to do . . . more manual labor?" Addie asked, as she followed him down the steps. "That makes sense."

"It's not all manual labor on the farm," Jasper replied. "There is a lot of that, yes, but I also oversee the day-to-day business. That requires quite a bit of sitting at a desk and crunching numbers."

"That sounds even worse."

"It can be."

"I thought about getting a business degree in college," Addie said. "But then I remembered that I'm terrible at math."

"So what did you opt for instead?"

"I have a liberal arts degree," Addie replied. "And I know what you're going to say."

Jasper folded his arms across his chest. "I wasn't going to say anything. Except what does one do with an arts degree?"

"Open a furniture store with her fiancé." Addie's heart jumped into her throat as soon as the words were out of her mouth. That wasn't what she had meant to say. Avoiding his gaze, she stared out the window and said, "Because, you know, who needs a business degree to open a business?"

"So you know a thing or two about furniture?"

"A little."

Jasper took a right turn and slammed on his breaks for an elderly woman and her poufy white dog. "You made furniture?"

"No," Addie replied. "It was an antique and refinished furniture shop. Jonah was the brains behind the operation."

"Jonah?"

Addie wished she hadn't opened her big, fat mouth. "He was my fiancé."

"But not anymore?"

"Not anymore."

Jasper pulled into a parking lot in front of a small white building. "Here we are."

"Do you need to get gas or something?" Addie asked.

"No. This is where we're eating."

"Jasper, this is a gas station."

"I know." Jasper threw the Bronco into neutral. "This place has the best catfish in three counties."

"But it's a gas station."

"Just get out of the car, Adelaide."

Addie stepped out onto the pavement. "Lord have mercy, is it hot out today."

Jasper laughed, stepping around the front of the car to meet her. "Now you're starting to sound like a proper southern woman."

"Do proper southern women eat at gas stations regularly?"

"They do if they like catfish."

There was a line of people winding to the back of the station when they stepped inside. They were all facing a glass case holding an array of glistening fried foods. "Why don't you go sit down and hold us a spot?" Jasper asked. "What sounds good to you?"

Addie slid into one of the orange booths at the back of the room, years of grease coating her legs. "I'll just have whatever you're having."

"That's a pretty tall order."

"I can handle it."

There were people everywhere, but most of them were taking their orders to go. Addie recognized some of them, people she'd seen at the grocery store or other places around town. It felt like they were all staring at her, as if they somehow knew she was an outsider.

She didn't belong.

At the very back of the store there was a man smoking, his head bent low, reading a newspaper. Each time Addie glanced over at him, he was grinding another cigarette into the overflowing ashtray. It was the same man Addie had seen at the fair. He caught her staring at him and gave her a long, slow smile that made Addie nervous. The smile turned to a scowl when he saw Jasper.

"Do you know that man?"

"Who?"

"The guy sitting in the back."

Jasper slid a Styrofoam plate over to Addie. "I got you fish and chicken gizzards."

"Chicken what?"

"Gizzards." Jasper licked his fingers. "I got myself gizzards and livers, but I thought I'd start you off slow."

"What in the hell is a gizzard?"

"It's part of the digestive tract. It's fried. You'll like it."

"That sounds appetizing."

"Just try it."

Addie did as she was told and popped the gizzard into her mouth.

Jasper watched her intently. "You like them?"

"Kind of chewy," Addie replied. She swallowed and took a bite of the fish on her plate. "The catfish is amazing, though. I haven't had catfish in years."

"I told you this was the best place for catfish."

Addie looked up from her plate. The man at the back of the store was walking toward them, another cigarette lit between his fingers. His heavy black boots shuffled along the linoleum floor until he stopped in front of their table.

"Afternoon, Jasper."

"Hello, Redd."

"Haven't seen you 'round here in a while."

"Been busy over at the farm."

"I reckon you've been damn busy with all that land you recently acquired."

"I reckon," Jasper replied.

"You sure showin' your lady a nice time here at the greasy spoon."

"I'm not his lady," Addie spoke up.

"You lookin'?" Redd eyeballed her.

"Not for you."

Redd chuckled, and then began to cough. After a few seconds he recovered and said to Jasper, "She sure got a mouth on her, don't she?"

"I don't know." Jasper stabbed at a piece of fish on his Styrofoam plate. "Sounds like she's got some taste to me."

Redd flicked his cigarette and the ashes drifted down onto Addie's plate. He reached across their table and ground out the cigarette in their ashtray before shuffling toward the door. "Well, you have a nice day."

Jasper was silent, his jaw set in a hard line. After a few tense seconds he grabbed their plates and threw them in the trash can. "Sorry about that. Do you want me to get you something else to eat?"

"What was that all about?" Addie asked. She slid out of the booth and stood up next to Jasper.

"It was nothing."

"How do you know him?"

"The same way I know everybody in this damn town," Jasper replied, motioning for Addie to follow him. "I went to high school with him."

"Who is he?"

"His name is Redd Jones."

"He doesn't seem to like you much."

"The feeling is mutual."

"I saw him at the fair a couple of weeks ago. He was arguing with some man. I think it was about money."

"Sounds about right," Jasper said through clenched teeth. "C'mon, let's get back to your place. We've got work to do."

Chapter 10

From one end of the yard, a black-and-white ball of fury came racing toward Jasper and the other workers in the yard at full speed. "Whoa, whoa!" Jasper shouted, holding his hands up in surrender. "Adelaide, call off your dog!"

Two of the men took off toward the back gate, allowing Felix to give chase, his good ear standing on end and his tongue hanging out the side of his mouth, strands of slobber flying in all directions.

"Felix!" Addie ordered, stepping in between Felix and Jasper. "Sit down!"

Felix screeched to a halt. He whined and stretched out in front of them on his belly.

"I thought for sure he was going to take my legs out," Jasper said.

"That dog is a menace," another man chimed in, his chest heaving up and down as he gulped in buckets of air. "He coulda taken out my legs."

"It would have been a bit higher than your legs," Addie replied. She leaned down to pet Felix. "He wouldn't have bitten you. But you call my dog a menace again, and I might."

"Remember they're here to help you," Jasper whispered. "For free." He walked toward the back of the kitchen window, his brow furrowed. "It's really not as bad as it looks. I think we can have this fixed pretty quick. But what's going on with your shed over there?"

"I broke the door."

"Looks like you did more than break it." Jasper put his hands on the splintered wood. "It is completely off its hinges."

"It's useless anyway," Addie replied.

"I think you're right," Jasper said. "But I can probably secure this one until you can get another one."

"Is there anything I can do to help?"

"I could really use a glass of sweet tea."

Addie motioned for Jasper to follow her inside. "I don't have any tea made."

Jasper stopped at the doorway. "You don't have any sweet tea?"

"No, but I guess I can make some real quick." Addie shrugged. "I don't have any sugar, but I have some artificial—"

"Just stop right there," Jasper cut her off. "Don't go saying things like *artificial sweetener* down here. Not if you want to make any friends."

"What is it with you people and sweet tea?"

"You people?" Jasper raised an eyebrow. "What is that supposed to mean?"

Addie let out an exasperated sigh. "Southern people!"

"You just keep diggin' that hole deeper and deeper."

"You want some water?"

Jasper didn't answer. He was staring at the table and chairs strewn about the kitchen. Finally, he said, "Did the storm blow in some debris?"

"That's not trash!" Addie placed both of her hands on the tabletop. "It's my aunt's old dining room set."

"How old?"

"Old," Addie replied. "But just because it's old doesn't mean it's trash."

"You're going to fix it?"

"Refinish it, yes."

Jasper peeled a piece of paint off one of the chairs. "And this is the kind of thing you did? With that other guy?"

Addie nodded. "It's going to look great when I'm done."

"I'm sure it will," Jasper replied. "Let's get some of the broken glass out of the way. Maybe let these guys work in peace."

"Okay," Addie agreed. "I got most of it up off the floor this morning so Felix wouldn't cut a paw. That's the last thing he needs."

Addie set to work finding a box in which to put the pieces of broken glass. "I tried to use a plastic bag this morning. Imagine how well that worked out."

Jasper stood over the counter by the window where the limb was nestled, and replied, "I'm going to pull some of these bigger chunks of glass out of the window. I don't want it to shatter when we pull the limb out. That will make for an even bigger mess."

"I found a box!" Addie hollered from the living room. "I'll bring it in to you!"

When Addie returned, box in tow, Jasper was leaning over the sink, one hand wrapped in a paper towel. On the counter next to him were several drops of blood and a bloody shard of glass.

"What happened?" Addie surveyed the scene in front of her. "What did you do?"

"What did I do?" Jasper quipped. "What did I do? The damned piece of glass cut the hell out of my hand."

"Let me see it," Addie demanded. "Is it bad?"

"Aside from the fact that I'm bleeding like a stuck pig, I think I'll live," he replied drily. "I'm fine."

"Let me see," Addie repeated.

Begrudgingly, he held out his hand to Addie. She unwrapped the paper towel to find a jagged two-inch gash on his palm, blood still oozing.

"I think you're right." Addie looked up at Jasper. "You'll live. But I need to clean and bandage this cut."

"Fine," Jasper replied, rolling his eyes. "It's really not that bad."

"Hush!" Addie was already in the bathroom searching for peroxide and cotton balls. "Do you want your hand to get infected and fall off?"

"I'm not nine," Jasper said, exasperated. "You can't threaten me with that and actually expect me to believe it."

"Hold your hand over the sink," Addie instructed. "Don't move it." She turned on the water and ran it over Jasper's hand. Then she poured peroxide over the cut.

"Yes ma'am."

Guiding him from the sink, Addie put his hand, palm up, on top of hers. She gently dabbed at the wound with a dish towel. As she held him, she felt a small tremor run up her spine, all the way to her head. Even her hair began to tingle. She looked up to see if

Jasper had noticed. He was staring at her, studying her. Without taking his eyes off her, he laced his fingers with hers and pulled her into him.

Addie couldn't breathe.

From outside a horn honked. Jasper let out a curse and tore himself away from Addie and strode toward the living room window. Pulling back the curtain, he said, "It's Bob and Jim." Without another word, he let himself out the front door, leaving Addie staring achingly after him.

Chapter 11

Addie sat idly on Wanda's front porch, watching cars zip past in Eunice's version of a Friday evening rush. It reminded her of living in Chicago, and for a brief moment she missed the smell of the city. She missed her mother and Jerry. She missed the smell of the Polish diner down by the Apollo Theater. Everything moved slower in Eunice. Nobody was in much of a hurry to do anything. It was as if people were stuck in a constant haze of summertime.

"Here you go," Wanda broke in, handing Addie a tall glass filled with a pinkish liquid. "I make the best peach margarita in the world."

Addie wrinkled her nose and replied, "I have to admit, I'm not a fan of any kind of margarita."

"Lord, girl. Can't you just say thank you? Drink up or it's gonna be a long night."

Addie took a sip from her glass. "Not too bad."

"Not too bad?" Wanda snorted. "Not too bad? It's the best peach margarita in the Delta."

"You forget I'm from Chicago," Addie teased. "But it's good! I wasn't trying to insult you."

"Oh, what do you know, city slicker?" Wanda laid on her thick southern accent. "Y'all don't know nothin' about drinkin'."

Addie took another sip. "I can see why my aunt liked you."

"I miss her bunches," Wanda said. "She helped me out more'n I can say when I was going through hell with Bryar's daddy. That woman could make any situation a comedy."

"She led an interesting life. I guess she had to look at things from a different perspective. Like you said, to keep from going crazy."

"She didn't like talkin' about her life, kinda like you." Wanda nodded toward Addie. "Never opened up too much about nothin'. But there was always talk around town about, you know, some kind of romance gone bad."

Addie sat her glass down on the table in between them and said, "Aunt Tilda never told me too much. I stopped coming to visit her when I was twelve. After that summer, I spent most of my summers babysitting or doing something else in the city. I thought my world was too big for Eunice. I suspect she might have told me more once I got older. As a kid, I remember thinking it was strange that she lived down here all by herself with her closest family in Chicago."

When Wanda didn't say anything, Addie continued.

"She's actually my great-aunt on my father's side. My dad left when I was little. I don't even remember him. My mom raised me by herself. Aunt Tilda and my mom were always pretty close despite my dad leaving. My mother had a lot of respect for her, doing what she did."

"What did she do?"

Addie turned to Wanda and said, "Now I don't know if any of this is true. All I know is what my mother told me. So you'll have to take it with a grain of salt, because who knows where my mother got the story."

Wanda's eyes widened. "Tell me! Tell me!"

"My aunt supposedly ran off from Chicago with a musician in the 1930s. I guess he must've been from Eunice or someplace close." There was a mischievous gleam in Addie's eyes. "My mother told me that my aunt told her once that this musician 'played me like his fiddle and never did make an honest woman out of me,' which sounds just like something Aunt Tilda would say. I guess after this guy left her, she decided to stay here and make a life for herself."

"Wow," Wanda replied after a few seconds of silence. "That sounds scandalous *now.* Can you imagine what it must have been like back then?"

Addie nodded and said, "I know. It's hard for me to picture my aunt with anyone. She never acted like she wanted a husband or kids, you know?"

"She used to say that men were only good for one or two things and neither of them was marriage!" Wanda giggled. "Hey, speaking of men . . . how come you didn't tell me that Jasper was the one who removed the tree limb from your window? I had to hear it from Mrs. Johnson when she brought her cat in to be neutered."

"Who's Mrs. Johnson?" Addie asked. "And why is she talking about Jasper and my kitchen window?"

"Oh, honey." Wanda waved a hand in the air. "You have a lot to learn about living in a small town. Everybody talks. And I mean everybody. You're new in town. You're a single woman. And suddenly Jasper Floyd starts showing up at your house in his running shorts in the wee hours of the morning? And there you are not wearing any bra and standing on the porch in front of God and everybody?"

"What?" Addie sputtered, her hands flying up to her chest. "That's what people are saying about me?"

"I can't even imagine all the questions Jasper's mother will have to answer at church on Sunday," Wanda replied. "Old widow Johnson could lick a skillet in the kitchen from the front porch."

"What?"

"It's just something my granny used to say. It means she's a gossip."

"How is it that *my* life is the most interesting topic of conversation around town?" Addie threw herself back into the chair. "My neighbor runs around in his yard half naked and nobody even seems to care."

"You mean old Mr. Smoot?"

"Yes."

"Everybody just expects that from him," Wanda said. "But you and Jasper . . . well, now that's a story!"

"It's not like anything interesting happened," Addie grumbled, settling back into her chair.

"Oh, no?"

"No." Addie's mouth was set in a hard line. "Apparently being touched freaks him out. He and Felix are a lot alike."

"Well, that's it," Wanda said, pulling Addie up out of her seat. "I'm calling my brother and we're going out tonight."

Addie shook her head. "I can't. I have too much to do at home."

"No excuses. Bobby's friend Jennifer owns a sports bar downtown. It'll be fun. Put on a bra and you can call it damage control!"

"I always wear a bra," Addie replied, "except when a huge tree branch crashes through my window at three A.M."

"Don't take it personal," Wanda said. "You were bound to be the talk of the town, but it makes it all the more delicious that the town's most eligible bachelor doesn't need directions to your house."

"Nobody needs directions to my house!" Addie threw her arms up in the air. "I live right smack-dab in the middle of this godforsaken town."

"Well, you're not staying anyway, right?" Wanda took a sip of her drink. "So what do you care what all the old biddies are saying?"

"I guess I don't."

"Exactly. So let's go get ourselves gussied up!"

Addie twisted uncomfortably from the backseat of Bobby's truck and said, "There is no way I'm wearing this out in public."

"What on earth are you talking about? You look great!" Wanda replied, turning around to face her. "Don't she look great, Bobby?"

"Mmmhmm . . . ," Bobby replied. "Good, good." He wasn't even looking in Addie's direction.

"See?" Addie said. "Bobby can't even look at me!"

"Bobby's an idiot," Wanda said, rolling her eyes.

"Then why did you ask him?" Addie yanked at the hem of her dress. She wasn't sure how she had allowed Wanda to talk her into wearing one of her dresses. Wanda was at least two sizes smaller than she was. Everything felt squished.

"Just stop worrying. I swear, for the life of me, I've never seen a girl as pretty as you worry about so much."

Despite what people in town might have been saying about her, it wasn't like Addie to wear anything that came above her knees, and she certainly didn't like to wear anything that clung to her. But somehow Wanda had talked her into a black cotton dress that came down only to midthigh. There were thick straps at each shoulder, with the sweetheart neckline resting just above her cleavage. Even though it was entirely too hot, Addie desperately wanted a cardigan. She checked herself in the rearview mirror one last time and said, "Okay. Let's do this."

"Good girl!" Wanda jumped out of the pickup.

Addie followed Wanda and Bobby across the street to a small building nestled in a row of businesses. The sign above the bar read JENNIE'S JOINT in neon orange letters. It didn't look like much on the outside, but from the inside this was the place to be on a Friday night. There were people everywhere—sitting in booths, sitting at the tables, and standing up at the bar talking and drinking—and there was a live band playing in the back. Much to Addie's relief, nobody seemed to notice when the three of them walked through the door.

Bobby raised his hand above the throng of people and shouted something unintelligible. A tall woman with dark hair down to her waist came bounding over to them.

"Bobby!" the woman exclaimed as Bobby engulfed her in a hug. "Why didn't you tell me you were back in town? I woulda saved ya a place!"

"Didn't know it until just a couple of days ago," Bobby replied, shrugging his thick shoulders. "Addie, this is Jennifer Taylor. Been buddies since we was kids."

The woman stuck out a slender hand to Addie and said, "You can call me Jennie."

"It's nice to meet you." Addie smiled at the woman. "This place is crazy! I didn't even know this many people lived in this town!"

"Oh, it's always like this on Friday nights," Jennie replied. "The Burle Brothers sure can draw a crowd." She motioned to the band. "Come on over to the bar, and I'll get y'all something to drink!"

"I'll have a mango margarita!" Wanda called out, squeezing her way up to the bar. "Addie, sugar, what do you want?"

"Not a mango margarita." Addie rolled her eyes. "I'll take a Guinness and a shot of bourbon."

"I like you," Jennie replied.

Addie took the shot. The warm liquid slid down her throat. It had been a long time since she'd had a drink like that.

"Hey, Vic!" Jennie shouted to the man behind the bar. "I need a rum and diet for the lovebirds over there."

Wanda gave Addie a sharp jab in the ribs. "Don't look now."

Jasper Floyd sat at a booth adjacent to the bar, and he wasn't alone. There was a woman next to him. They were sitting close to each other—unnervingly close—having a conversation that appeared to be very private.

Addie sucked in air. Who was this woman? She didn't look familiar. She looked like she had come straight from work with her smart blazer and matching skirt. Her jet black hair fell in a perfectly straight line at the middle of her back. Even from where Addie was standing, she could see the woman's perfect olive skin. Perfect. Perfect. Perfect.

She was perfect.

The woman stood up and started to walk toward the bar. Lord, she was tall. Addie felt like a bug waiting to be stepped on as the woman passed her in her four-inch heels. Addie turned away, her hands groping for the glass of Guinness. The glass tipped on its side, sloshing half of the contents onto the floor and onto Addie.

"Shit!"

The woman stared at Addie for a few seconds, her face emotionless, before turning her attention to Vic. "I'm sorry, but I ordered a drink a while ago and have yet to receive it."

"Where's the bathroom?" Addie asked Wanda.

"In the back," Wanda said. "Want me to go with you?"

Addie shook her head. "I'll be back. Get me another shot."

She stalked off toward the bathrooms, toward where Jasper was now sitting alone. That was just all she needed—to be covered in beer and have to talk to him, while he was here with a gorgeous woman. Addie tried to ignore Jasper as she passed him, but he cut her off at the door.

"What happened here?" Jasper's gaze wandered from Addie's face to the front of her dress, which clung damply to her skin.

"I spilled beer on myself. Move, please."

"You should be more careful." He made no attempt to move.

"You should bite me."

Jasper ran his teeth over his bottom lip and replied, "Is that an invitation?"

"Are you drunk?" Addie leaned in closer to him. He didn't look drunk.

"No. Are you?"

"No."

"Well, now that we've got that settled . . ."

"Get out of my way, Jasper."

Jasper's eyes danced over her body playfully. Finally, after what seemed like forever, Jasper stepped aside, allowing Addie passage.

"Thanks," she said, shoving past him. "You're a real gentleman."

"Are you mad at me about something?"

Addie turned back around to face him. "What are you talking about?"

"You seem angry."

"I'm not," Addie replied. "I'm just wet, cold, and smell like stale beer."

Jasper opened his mouth to respond but thought better of it. Instead, he pushed her back into the alcove between the bathrooms. He pressed her up against the wall, his eyes pleading with hers.

The heat from Jasper's body coupled with the cool wood of the wall against Addie's back was too much for her to take. She grabbed his shirt collar and pulled him down to her level, where their mouths met for the first time. He kissed her with such a hunger, such a desperate hunger, that Addie forgot about everything else except his lips on hers—everything except being the answer to whatever it was that he needed.

When Jasper finally pulled away from her, he was smiling. "You don't smell like stale beer," he said. "You smell like fresh strawberries in the summertime."

"Thanks," Addie murmured. She looked down at Jasper's hands, still intertwined with hers. The cut on his hand was still there, the flesh puckered slightly. She thought that it would probably scar, her mind wandering away from the moment just long enough for her to remember that there were people just beyond them talking, laughing, and drinking. There was another woman waiting at a table for Jasper and another shot waiting for Addie at the bar up front.

CHAPTER 12

By the time Addie made it back up to the bar, Bobby and Wanda were sitting at a table, looking over the bar's menu.

"Not a lot to choose from," Bobby said. "Wanda didn't tell me you all was wantin' to eat until we got here."

"Do they have potato wedges?" Addie was suddenly starving.

"The best in town."

"Here's your shot." Wanda narrowed her eyes at Addie. "Everything okay? You look kinda funny."

"Well, I did just spill beer all over myself," Addie replied.

"I'm sorry about you-know-who," Wanda said. "I didn't know he was going to be here . . . with someone."

"Of course you didn't know," Addie agreed. "Besides, it's not like it should matter to me."

"I've never seen her before," Wanda continued.

Addie's back was facing Jasper and the mystery woman, and she resisted the urge to turn around and stare at them. "So you don't know who she is?"

Bobby snorted into his beer. "No tellin' where he picked her up the way he throws his money around like there ain't no tomorrow."

"You don't have any cause to say that. Just because you don't like what he did." Wanda rolled her eyes.

"What did he do?" Addie was dying to know what Bobby was talking about.

"When he moved back he bought the old Jones farm, which was in foreclosure," Wanda explained. "Their land borders his parents' land. It made sense."

"He didn't have no right. He had no right buyin' that place," Bobby cut in. "That land should have stayed in the family."

"Maybe the family should have paid their mortgage," Wanda said. "You know just as well as I do where their money goes."

Bobby stood up from the table, his big hands balled into fists. "I'm going to get another beer."

"Ignore him," Wanda said over the bass of the band. "He doesn't know what he's talking about. He listens to whatever Redd says like it's the gospel."

"I take it Redd's family doesn't like Jasper too much?"

"Their families don't like each other much. The Floyds have that big, commercial farm. The Joneses had a little, ramshackle place. I think it bothered Jasper's daddy the way the Jones place looked. He used to make comments about it when we was kids."

"Why would he do that?"

"You just have to know Mr. Floyd," Wanda replied. "He's not a bad man. But he isn't one to hold on to his thoughts."

"So Jasper and his dad are a lot alike."

"The apple don't fall too far from the tree." Wanda nodded. "But what Bobby failed to mention is that Jasper paid way over what it was worth. He paid the banknote, and made sure the Jones family got some money in their pockets."

Addie bit the bottom of her lip. "That man. I just don't know what goes on in his head."

"Let's get another drink, shall we?" Wanda slid out of the booth. "Maybe then we can start to make some sense of the men around here."

Addie clinked down an empty shot glass and smiled placidly. She felt warm and happy and . . . had she mentioned warm? It felt like years since the last time she'd felt this way. And truthfully, it had been.

"We've got a real treat for y'all tonight," the lead singer of the band crowed from the makeshift stage in the back. "We're gonna play two brand-new songs. Come on out onto the floor for a listen!"

There was a cheer from the crowd. People began to take their drinks and move toward the stage. Wanda grabbed Addie by the wrist. "C'mon! You ain't gonna want to miss this!"

"I can see from here just fine," Addie said. In fact, she could see more than just fine. She could see that woman's hand on Jasper's arm. She could see her whispering something to him as he stood up to walk toward the stage. She didn't want to get any closer.

But Wanda wasn't having it. "Come *on,*" she urged. "Trust me; you don't want to miss this."

Begrudgingly, Addie followed her into the ocean of people. She followed her all the way to the back of the bar until they were standing next to Jasper.

"Hey," he yelled over the music. "I wondered where you went."

"I'm here with Bobby and Wanda."

"What?"

After several failed attempts to reply, Addie shook her head at him. She turned to Wanda, but she had disappeared into the crowd. The music finally stopped, and Addie felt relieved. She just wanted to go back to their table at the front—far away from Jasper and that woman.

"Come on over here for a minute," Jasper said. "There's someone I want you to meet."

"I better go find Wanda."

Jasper motioned for her to follow.

"I'm tired of following people tonight," Addie grumbled. "You are all so bossy."

"Hold that thought." Jasper waved at a man at another table. "Have a seat. I'll be right back."

Addie sat down next to the woman and tried to muster a smile. "Hi."

"Hello," the woman replied. "You must be Adelaide. Jasper has told me so much about you. I'm Harper."

Her lips were the kind of red that Addie had seen only on the covers of magazines. "It's nice to meet you," Addie replied.

"Jasper tells me you just moved to town?"

"A few weeks ago." Addie wondered what else Jasper had told her. "How do you know Jasper?"

"Oh, Jas and I go way back. I've known him since law school."

Great. A beautiful lawyer. "So you're a lawyer, too?"

Harper nodded. "I'm Jasper's partner in Memphis."

The way she said *partner* made Addie's stomach hurt. She looked past Harper to Jasper. He caught her eye and winked. She looked away. "What brings you down to Eunice?"

"Jasper and I had some business to take care of." Harper took a sip of her drink. "We always come to Jennie's afterward."

"That's right," Jasper chimed in, appearing in front of them. "Just crossing some t's and dotting some i's." He sat down next to Harper.

Harper reached down and placed her hand on Jasper's leg. "Adelaide and I were just getting to know each other. You know how much I enjoy meeting your friends."

"Well, it was nice meeting you." Addie stood up. "I really need to go find Wanda. I hope you two have a great night." She turned around and hurried as fast as she could to the front of the bar. Her head was swimming.

"What's wrong, Miss Addie?" Bobby asked when she reached the bar. "Your face is all flushed."

"I just need another drink is all."

"What can I get ya?" Jennie asked.

"Something strong."

"You got it."

"I seen you back there talking to Jasper," Bobby said. "Did he say somethin' he shouldna?"

Addie tipped back the shot. And then another. The warm feeling returned. "I'm fine." She smiled at Bobby. "Where did your sister get off to?"

"No tellin'."

Jasper was headed toward them. "Can I talk to you for a minute?" Jasper asked Addie.

"What?"

"Do you want to go outside?"

"No."

"How much have you had to drink?" Jasper was focused on the several overturned shot glasses.

Bobby stepped in between Addie and Jasper. "I don't think she wants to talk to you, *Mr. Floyd*."

"I don't think I was talking to you, Bobby."

"I don't think I give a shit."

Jasper sighed, putting a hand to his temple. "Look, I know Redd's got your nose out of joint . . ."

"Don't even say his name," Bobby growled, clenching his fists. "You don't even deserve to say his name."

When Bobby reared his fist back, Addie shot between them as fast as her unsteady legs could carry her. She caught Jasper at the elbow. Although not sure that she could control the octave of her voice, she said as quietly as possible, "Jasper and I are just going to step outside for a minute."

"Like hell you are," Bobby snarled, his ruddy cheeks on fire. "He's leavin', but he ain't leavin' with you."

Addie put her hands up against Bobby's chest. "It's okay, but thank you for looking out for me. You're a good friend."

"Go on then," Bobby huffed. He was scowling, but his fists had unclenched. "Don't bring him back in here, Addie. You hear me? Don't you bring him back in here."

Jasper opened his mouth to reply, but Addie gave him a look and said to Bobby, "You got it. Order us another round, okay?"

Bobby skulked off.

Once Addie was outside, the adrenaline mixed with alcohol was coursing through her veins and she was starting to feel sick.

Finally, Jasper said, "That was pretty stupid. Getting in between two grown men like that. Seriously, what were you thinking?"

"I didn't see any grown men. I saw two boys having a pissing contest."

"You don't know anything about it."

"I know enough."

"Oh?"

"Just go home," Addie replied. She felt very tired. "I've had too much to drink to be having this conversation."

"I can see that."

"But what else is there to do in this damn town," Addie continued. "Drink whiskey and listen to shitty bands play."

"If you hate it so much what are you doing here?"

"I miss Chicago."

Jasper stepped closer to her. "Then why don't you go back? Go back there to that fiancé of yours."

"I can't."

"Why not?"

Addie's hand clasped the door handle. She closed her eyes and tried to ignore the sick feeling she had in the pit of her stomach. "I can't go back there," she countered. "I can't go back there and be with him because he's dead."

"Shit, Addie. I'm sorry." Jasper raked his hand through his hair. "I didn't know."

"Of course you didn't know," Addie snapped. She faced him. "That's why I'm here, okay? My fiancé died almost two years ago. I couldn't live in that city anymore. I couldn't stand the sympathy. I couldn't stand seeing his parents. I couldn't stand seeing his friends. Most of all, I couldn't stand talking about it."

Jasper stood with his hands jammed down into the pockets of his jeans. He said nothing, but he didn't take his eyes off her the way so many people did when she told them about Jonah. Addie felt the weight of his stare, and the weight of her words, and the weight of everything she'd had to drink over the last few hours. Holding it all, her knees buckled and she sank down onto the concrete.

"Hey, now. Don't cry." Jasper knelt down beside her.

"I'm fine," Addie lied.

Using him for support, Addie steadied herself on her feet. She wanted to stay there and let him comfort her. She wanted to cry. She wanted to beat her fists angrily into his chest while he held her.

Addie pushed herself away from his grip. She smoothed her dress, straightened her shoulders, and said, "I better get back inside. They'll be wondering where I am."

"Are you sure you're okay?" Jasper's face looked worried, but he made no second attempt to touch her.

"I said I'm fine."

Just then, Harper appeared in the doorway. She clutched her purse, wide-eyed. "What on earth happened in there?"

"Nothing." Jasper stepped away from Addie. "Just small-town gossip."

"Honestly, I don't know why you insist on coming here with these roughnecks."

"I am one of these roughnecks."

"Hardly," Harper scoffed. "Well, Adelaide, it was nice to meet you, but I think I'll be calling it a night."

"It was nice to meet you, too," Addie replied.

"Are you coming, Jasper?"

Jasper nodded. "I'll be right behind you."

"You want me just to meet you back at your place?"

Jasper cleared his throat. "Uh, sure. Yeah, sure, that's fine."

Addie glared after Harper and then focused her attention back on Jasper. "Go on," she said. "Just go on with *her.* I'm fine."

"I don't want to leave you like this."

"I said I'm fine."

"I know what you said, but you don't look fine."

"Well, you don't want to keep Harper waiting," Addie said. "Besides, I don't want Bobby coming out and seeing you here."

Jasper crossed his arms over his chest and said, "I'm not afraid of Bobby Carter."

"I know you're not." Addie rolled her eyes. "Please just go. I don't need you to feel sorry for me."

"I don't feel sorry for you."

"I don't need your help, either."

"Fine." Jasper's jaw was set in a hard line. He was angry, but Addie could tell by the look in his eyes that he was hurt, too. It made her feel even worse. He strode off into the darkness, and he didn't look back at her. She waited until the taillights of his Bronco disappeared down the street before turning and stepping back inside the bar—where the buzz of fluorescent lights and several shots of whiskey awaited her.

CHAPTER 13

THERE HADN'T BEEN ANY MEN SINCE JONAH. TO BE PERFECTLY honest, there hadn't been much of anything. What she hadn't told Jasper that night, what she hadn't told anybody, was that she blamed herself for Jonah's death. It happened two months before the wedding. It had been raining all day, and Addie was late meeting him for an appointment with the caterer. Jonah hadn't even wanted to use this caterer because she was an hour outside the city, and he didn't want to do anything that took him outside the city, but Addie insisted. They'd argued about Addie being late. In fact, Addie argued herself all the way into a taxi where she promptly hung up on him. She refused to answer the next five calls from him, and when she got home, he was already gone. He left a note apologizing. He'd gone to see the caterer alone. He hadn't wanted to miss the appointment and risk messing up the menu so close to the wedding. The food had been so important to Addie.

Jonah never saw it coming, never saw the semi cross the center line. They told her he likely didn't feel anything at all; it happened so fast. Maybe if she'd answered her phone, told him to wait just a few more minutes . . . *We can call the caterer and reschedule,* she should have said. *Don't worry about it. I love you.*

Sometimes she wondered if she'd ever be able to stop thinking about the words she hadn't said.

But Addie awoke the next morning in the same clothes she had been wearing the night before; she woke up thinking about Jasper and the kiss they'd shared. There was a chemistry between them that she wanted to ignore but just couldn't. The memory of his lips on hers was both infuriating and scintillating. She rolled over to escape her thoughts and heard a muffled yelp from beneath the covers. Felix wormed his way to the pillow beside Addie. She was grateful to have him with her, in spite of all his quirks. In fact, maybe she loved him so much *because* of them.

"Good morning, buddy."

Felix rolled over on his back and licked Addie's face. Ever since the storm, it was like Felix was a different dog. He no longer backed away at her touch. He no longer hid under the couch when she came home. He no longer growled at every living thing he saw. He was still fearful, especially when it came to men, but he was altogether a much happier dog than he'd been when Addie had first found him clinging to life down by the levee. Felix was beginning to trust her, and it made Addie's heart swell every time he looked at her with his blue puppy-dog eyes.

"Let's get some breakfast." Addie slid off the bed. "Well, breakfast for you. Coffee for me." Her entire body felt stiff, and she remembered why she rarely drank.

The two padded their way into the kitchen. Addie busied herself fixing Felix's food as he waited by his bowl eagerly. He whined when she poured his kibble, his tail making a *thump, thump, thump* sound against the tile floor.

While Felix ate, Addie stood beside the coffeepot and stared out her new kitchen window into the backyard. Jasper had ordered a beautiful window, she had to admit. It was much nicer than the one that had been destroyed by the tree. The yard still looked frightful, and the door to the shed still needed to be fixed. She glanced over at the table and chairs. They were coming along nicely. It had been so long since she'd had a project—had a finished product of which she could be proud. She wished Jonah could be here to see it, if only for a second.

Addie shuddered to think about her conversation with Jasper the night before. Much of the night was muddled, but she remembered exactly what she'd said. The thought made her want to crawl back under the covers until Christmas. She hadn't wanted him to know. She hadn't wanted anyone to know. She picked up her phone and dialed her mother's number.

"Addie? Hi!" Her mother's voice came booming from the other end. "How are you, sweetie?"

"I'm okay, Mom," Addie replied. "I just called to check on you and Jerry."

"Oh, we're good . . . you know. The usual—working on the house."

Addie sighed into the phone. "Me too. I'm not getting much accomplished, though."

"What's wrong?" Concern filled her mother's voice. "You don't sound like yourself."

"It's nothing. I just miss you guys, that's all."

"We miss you, too!" her mother replied. "Are you sure you're okay down there all by yourself? In that house all alone?"

"I like alone," Addie reminded her. "That was the point of coming here. To be alone. Besides, I won't be here forever. A few months, max."

"I don't have to like it, Adelaide. I just wish you'd talk to someone about things . . . you know."

Addie rubbed her throbbing head. This was not the direction she had intended for the conversation to go. "I'm tired of talking, Mom."

"You're talking to me."

"You know what I mean."

"Yes, I know what you mean," her mother replied. "Maybe it's time for you to meet some new people."

"That's actually why I'm calling." Addie saw a chance to change the subject. "I got kind of drunk last night . . ."

"Oh, Adelaide."

"Mom, let me finish," Addie said. "I got a little drunk last night and acted like an idiot. I think I said some things that I shouldn't have."

There was silence as her mother thought about it. Finally she said, "Well, you know what your aunt Tilda always did when she stuck her foot in her mouth?"

"Ate her foot? I don't remember Aunt Tilda apologizing to anyone . . . ever."

"It was rare. But it happened. Except she was a lot like you—she had trouble saying the words. So she baked."

"You want me to bake?"

"I don't want you to do anything, kiddo," her mother replied.

"But, at least for your aunt Tilda, baking was a way to relieve stress and apologize all at the same time."

"I relieve stress with paint thinner and sandpaper," Addie replied. "But I do have all of Aunt Tilda's cookbooks upstairs in the attic. I guess it can't hurt to try something new."

Her mother's laugh jingled through the phone. "I would suggest the recipe for fried pie."

"Okay. Love you."

"Love you, too."

Addie threw her phone down on the couch and walked to the kitchen. She just needed to think for a minute. She walked over to the counter and cut off a twelve-inch piece of cheesecloth and soaked it in tung oil. Maybe if she could remove all the dust from the table she'd been sanding, she'd feel better. She strapped on a particle mask and got to work.

Addie was so engrossed in what she was doing that she didn't even hear the doorbell ring. It wasn't until Felix began to bark that she looked up. Wanda was standing in the doorway looking horrified.

"What on earth are you wearing on your face?" she exclaimed.

"It's just a mask." Addie pulled the mask off her face. "It keeps the dust particles from the table out of my lungs."

"Did you do all this?" Wanda ran her hand along the now smooth table.

"Yup," Addie replied. "I found it in my aunt's old shed out back. I think it's the same one she had sitting in here when I was a kid."

"What will it look like when you're done?"

"Similar to how it looks now. I'm just going to stain it," Addie said. "So what's up?"

"Well, you left your clothes at my house last night." Wanda handed Addie a plastic bag. "I washed them for ya."

"Thanks. Come on in."

"Hey, Felix." Wanda leaned down and scratched Felix behind his ears. "I could hear you barking all the way from the street."

"I thought you had to go in to work today."

"I do. But not for another hour or so." Wanda jammed her hands down into the pockets of her scrubs. "So, last night was kind of crazy, huh?"

"It's definitely on my top ten."

"So what happened with you and Jasper?"

"What do you mean?"

"Come on, Addie. Don't think I didn't notice your face all puffy like you'd been cryin' when you came back inside." Wanda sat down at the kitchen table. "I didn't say anything last night 'cause we were with Bobby. But I'm not blind."

Addie sat down next to her friend. "I was just trying to get him out of there before your brother changed his mind. He didn't want to leave. We argued about it. That's all."

Wanda placed both of her hands palms down on the table. She stared down at the prints left on the glass. "Look, the reason I came over here . . . well, I wanted to apologize."

"Apologize?" Addie was surprised. "What do you mean? You didn't do anything."

"I didn't mean to push you into going out. Gettin' all dressed up. I didn't think about how maybe you came here to get away from people, not see more of 'em . . . you know . . . after . . . what happened in Chicago."

"So you've heard about that."

Wanda looked over at Addie, her big green eyes full of tears.

"Your aunt told me the month before she died. I'm so sorry. I just didn't think."

"It's okay." Addie reached over to take Wanda's hand.

"Miss Tilda didn't tell me much. She was forgetting an awful lot by then."

"We were getting married," Addie said. "It was a car wreck. Jonah, that was his name, was pronounced dead at the scene . . ." Addie trailed off, not sure whether she could keep her voice steady enough to continue. "It was the worst day of my life."

"I'm so sorry, Addie." Tears streamed down Wanda's face. "I'm just so sorry."

"I don't want to talk about it. I'm tired of talking about it. I'm tired of people feeling sorry for me." Addie hesitated and then added, "Please don't feel sorry for me."

Wanda wiped at her tears with the paper towel Addie handed her. "I don't. I mean, I won't. I just don't know what to say."

"I spent the last year being sad. I don't want to be sad anymore. I came here to try out some other kind of emotion."

"And then mean old Jasper Floyd makes you cry."

"I actually owe him an apology."

"Oh, really?" Wanda raised an eyebrow.

"Yes," Addie replied. "My mother suggested I make Aunt Tilda's famous fried pies, but I can't even boil water."

"Well then, it's a good thing you've got me." Wanda jumped up from the table. "But I don't believe I have a recipe for fried pies—well, not like your aunt could make them."

"I have her recipe box around here somewhere," Addie mumbled, following Wanda halfheartedly around the kitchen.

Wanda stopped in her tracks. "You have her recipe box?"

"Yeah."

"Girl, get that thing out."

Addie did as she was told. Her aunt Tilda's recipe box didn't look like anything special. In fact, it looked just like everything in her aunt's house—old and covered in dust—when she found it tucked behind a cast-iron skillet in the kitchen cabinet. She'd considered throwing it out, not knowing what it was at first. It took her a minute to realize she'd seen it before, many times, during the summers she'd spent with her aunt. It was the little wooden box she pulled out before she began cooking every meal. Her aunt never looked at any of the recipes she pulled out. She just licked her index finger, leafing through them with surprising speed. Once she found a recipe she liked, she pulled it out and set it on top of the box. She wouldn't look at it again until she filed it away.

Many of the recipes were written on index cards or scraps of paper. Some of them had been ripped out of magazines, but those were few and far between, and most of them had been marked up one side and down the other, proof that Tilda's special touch could be tasted in everything she cooked.

"Here it is," Addie said at last, pulling a yellowed card out of the box. "I hope it's the right one. It just says 'fried pies' on it."

"Tilda Andrews didn't have but one fried pie recipe," Wanda replied. "What's it say we need?"

"Apples, brown sugar, nutmeg, cinnamon . . ." Addie tore her eyes away from the card and focused on Wanda. "Can't I just buy a pie and pretend I made it?"

"You can't feed a store-bought pie to the likes of Jasper Floyd," Wanda said. "You want him to think you're cheap and easy and lazy?"

Addie shook her head from side to side, wide-eyed. "A store-bought pie can say all that?"

"It can say that and more." Wanda stared into Addie's empty cabinets. "You think Jasper's mama feeds him store-bought pie?"

Addie didn't know how to respond to that question. She'd never met Jasper's mom. Did his mom still cook for him? Was that normal? She couldn't remember the last time her mother cooked for anyone, let alone her adult daughter.

Wanda sighed and slammed the cabinet doors shut. "Put that recipe in your pocket, honey, and grab your keys. We've got some shopping to do."

CHAPTER 14

The road to Jasper's farm was mostly unpaved. Felix stirred occasionally from his nap in the front seat to growl at the bumpy ride. It was funny to Addie that Felix liked to ride in the car. There were days when he was afraid of his own shadow, but if there was a car door open, Felix was going to jump in. It didn't matter how far they went—the second Felix was in the seat, he fell asleep.

It was the first time that Addie had seen the Delta countryside since her visits with Aunt Tilda. The land was lush and green, and miles of cotton and cattle stretched out in front of her. Here the mighty Mississippi deposited rich soils over millions of years. She remembered her aunt calling it the land of rivers.

After several miles, Addie came up on what looked like an old farm. Although the land had been tended, the buildings were in terrible disrepair. The graying boards of the barn were leaning to one side, and it looked to Addie like a strong gust of wind might bring the whole structure toppling to the ground.

The house was almost completely demolished, with only the remnants of a chimney left standing. There were pieces of the house everywhere—from what Addie could tell, a native stone house.

This must be the old Jones farm, she thought. Bobby's accusations from the night before ran through her head. If Bobby was that upset, she could only imagine how the Jones family must feel. Addie had no desire to see Redd as angry as he'd been the night of the fair, and she wondered if the rest of the family was like him.

She didn't notice the Floyd farm until she was upon it. Her breath hitched in her throat as she took in the magnitude of the property. She turned left up the driveway, the house growing larger and larger as she approached.

The house was an 1830s mansion, which from the outside gave Addie a sense of antiquity, a farm meticulously kept over time. Addie had never seen anything like it in her entire life. The vast house, dwarfed only by the vastness of the land surrounding it, stood in the shade of at least four pin oak trees.

Addie hesitated. She considered throwing the car in reverse and flying back down the driveway before anybody had the chance to notice she was there. She didn't really need to apologize, did she? After all, Jasper *had* pushed her. He'd wanted to know.

She looked over at Felix, who panted excitedly. Addie guessed she didn't have much of a choice now. She was already here. And the pies would go bad if she didn't find someone to eat them. Rolling the windows down a few notches, she said to Felix, "Sit here. I will be right back." She'd just drop off the food and leave. No big deal, right?

Addie opened the back door and pulled out the basket full of food. She took a long look at the house before trudging up the front steps and up onto the huge wraparound porch.

Addie rang the doorbell, and when a middle-aged woman answered the door, panic began to rise in her throat. She hadn't thought this through. She hadn't even called first. She didn't even have Jasper's number! What kind of a person shows up at the house of someone she doesn't even know well enough to have a number for?

"Hello. I'm . . . I'm Adelaide Andrews," Addie stammered. "I'm . . . I . . . I know Jasper. I brought him these." She shoved the basket at the woman.

The woman looked lost for a few seconds, and then much to Addie's relief, broke out into a broad grin. Jasper's grin, she realized. She was a squat, round woman with bright blue eyes hidden behind square bifocals.

"Well, hello!" The woman had a deep southern drawl, thick as honey. "Come on in, darlin'. I've heard so much about you."

"You have?" Addie was dumbfounded. "At church?"

"What?" The woman ushered Addie inside. "No, from Jasper, of course. I'm his mother, Artemis Floyd."

"I thought so. He has your smile."

"And you, my dear, look quite a lot like your aunt Tilda." Artemis turned to wink at her. "I was quite fond of your aunt. She was like a second mother to me."

She led Addie down a wide hallway of deep mahogany wood floors covered by vibrant oriental rugs. Addie had little time to take in her surroundings before she was standing inside one of the largest kitchens she'd ever seen in her life.

"What have you made us, Adelaide?" Artemis asked, peeking inside the basket.

"Call me Addie, please," Addie replied. "They're fried pies."

"Oh! I love fried pies."

"I wanted to thank your son for helping me with the tree-in-window incident," Addie said. "I hope they taste okay. I've never actually made them before."

"I'm sure they're wonderful," Artemis replied. "You must stay for Saturday supper."

"I couldn't. I didn't even tell Jasper I was coming."

Artemis waved off Addie's concerns. "Nonsense. He'll be thrilled."

"I really would love to stay," Addie continued. "But I've got my dog in the car. He'll go crazy if he's left out there for too much longer."

"I cannot send you home on an empty stomach," Artemis replied. "Besides, who can say no to grilled pork tenderloins, green beans, and cheese grits?"

"That sounds glorious," Addie admitted. "But . . . what's a . . . grit?"

Artemis looked at Addie, a bemused smile forming on her lips. "Well, bless your heart! I forgot that you aren't from here. Grits are . . . well, they're a coarsely ground corn, sort of like porridge."

"Oh," Addie said. "I think I saw a recipe for something with grits in my aunt's recipe box."

"You're in possession of Tilda's recipe box?"

Addie nodded.

"I can't believe that woman didn't take that box with her to her grave, God rest her soul," Artemis replied. "That woman was the best cook in three counties."

"I remember." Addie winced at the thought of her aunt smelling or tasting the sorry excuse for pies she'd fried up earlier. "I'm not much of a cook myself."

"You wouldn't mind to let me take a look at those recipes sometime?" Artemis asked. She was staring intently at Addie.

Something told Addie that she should say no. It didn't matter to her—she didn't figure she'd get much use out of the box's contents. She probably would have showed it to Wanda, but she hadn't asked. A little voice inside her, Aunt Tilda's voice, said that Artemis knew she shouldn't be asking, either.

"A woman's recipes are like her diary," her aunt Tilda had told her once. "They aren't meant for anyone else's eyes but hers."

Before she could answer, Addie heard footsteps hurrying toward them from the front of the house. A man wearing a green Floyd Farms T-shirt came rushing into the kitchen. He bounded toward the women, his arms flailing. "Ms. Artemis! Ms. Artemis! Come quick, there's a rabid animal in the chicken coop!" he screeched.

"Calm down, Clyde," Artemis said, barely rising from her seat. "I'm on my way. Grab the .22 from the case."

Addie followed Artemis outside and around to the right side of the house, quite a ways out. She could hear the chickens before she saw them. Once she got close enough to witness the commotion, she saw a fury of black and white racing around and around the wire fencing.

Clyde was behind them with the shotgun in hand. He was out of breath. He raised the rifle to his shoulder. "Hold yer ears, ladies. Then cover yer eyes. You ain't gonna want ter see this."

Addie squinted at the muddy mass running in circles around the coop. It looked oddly familiar. "Wait!" she yelped. "Wait, don't shoot! That's my dog! Felix! No! Felix!"

Artemis and Clyde stared open-mouthed at Addie as she ran. Neither was sure what to make of the frantic young woman in front of them.

The closer Addie got to the coop, the more she realized that Felix wasn't trying to eat the chickens. He was licking them as they squawked their protests. Each time a chicken got close enough to Felix, he stuck out his tongue and gave them a good lick. He waited in the mud, hiding, until a chicken wandered over.

He stopped when he heard Addie's voice, cocking his head to one side as she scolded him. "Felix, you crazy dog! What is wrong with you?"

Felix rolled over on his back, wiggling in the dirt and chicken poop. He licked the air, he licked the chickens, he licked the mud, and he licked himself.

"That's your mangy dog?" Clyde asked incredulously. "You're lucky I didn't shoot that thing when I first saw him molestin' them chickens."

Addie fixed her gaze on Clyde. She put her hands on her hips and replied haughtily, "He's my dog, yes. And he's not mangy. I mean, he has mange, but he isn't *mangy.*"

"I didn't know there was a difference," Clyde said. "I beg your pardon."

"You can't just go shooting first and asking questions later," Addie continued, exasperated.

Clyde gripped the shotgun so tightly that his knuckles were white. "I don't know what side of the Mississippi you think you're on, Miss, but 'round here ain't no woman tell a man what to do with his gun."

Addie ignored him and busied herself getting Felix out of the chicken coop. Once Addie entered his space, Felix gave chase, and the whole thing started up again. She was so busy pursuing her dog that she didn't notice that Jasper had come in for the evening and had been watching the scene unfold.

"I'm never taking you anywhere again," Addie said to Felix, dragging him by his collar from the chicken coop. "You're staying in the house forever. Forever!"

When Addie looked up from scolding Felix, Jasper was standing in front of her, arms crossed. He was laughing.

"I'm so sorry," Addie said to Artemis. "I guess I rolled the windows down too low and he wiggled out."

"Oh, honey," Artemis said, "that was more fun than I've had in weeks."

Clyde, who was less than amused by Felix's antics, stood rigid next to his employers. "That dog coulda killed all them chickens."

"You hate those chickens, anyway," Jasper cut in.

"I guess Clyde loves the chickens more than we realized," Artemis said. "Adelaide and her dog are staying for supper."

Addie tightened her grip on Felix's collar. "That's okay, Mrs. Floyd. We're both covered in chicken poop. I think it's time to call it a night."

Jasper cleared his throat and stepped in front of Clyde. "I'll take Felix and get him hosed off." He looked Addie up and down as she tried in vain to wipe off the thick muck. "And you can take a shower at my place if you want. I live in the carriage house behind the main house. C'mon. I'll show you."

Addie followed Jasper, silently wallowing in her humiliation.

"You can probably let go of that poor dog's collar," Jasper said finally, turning around to grin at Addie. "He obviously couldn't help himself."

Addie let go of Felix's collar, and Felix happily followed Jasper, nudging at his hand with his nose as they walked. "I made you fried pies," Addie blurted out. "I just wanted to apologize for last night. I had too much to drink, and I said some things I shouldn't have."

"Forget about it," Jasper said. "You should be apologizing to me for having to bathe your devil of a dog."

Addie grinned. She was relieved that he wasn't angry. "I am sorry about that. I don't think Felix likes Clyde very much."

"Nobody likes Clyde."

He stopped at the door of a house smaller than the mansion. "This is it. Go on in and take a shower, and I'll get Felix cleaned up. I've got sweats and T-shirts in the bottom drawer of the armoire. You can wear that until your clothes are clean."

"I don't want to put anybody out. I can just go home. I didn't mean to interrupt everybody's day like this."

"Too late for that now," Jasper said. "Besides, I'm not going to be the one to explain to my mother that you skipped out on supper." Jasper whistled to Felix. "Let's go, buddy. No more chicken love for you tonight."

CHAPTER 15

The carriage house was neat as a pin. It wasn't anything she would have expected from a man living alone. Everything seemed to have its place; even the toiletries in the bathroom were lined up according to height. Jasper was the most organized person she'd ever seen, and Addie sure hoped that he never looked inside her medicine cabinet. She blushed at the thought.

As in the main house, there were beautiful rugs laid over the hardwood floors. Artemis's touch, Addie thought. There was a television, a couch, and a couple of chairs in the living room, but nothing else of substance. Off to the right, Addie could see the kitchen. She went left down a short hallway and into the only bedroom.

The bed was made so neatly, Addie wondered if Jasper had ever even slept in it. The crisp, white comforter looked brand-new. Next to the bed was a dark wooden nightstand that held several books and a pair of glasses.

In the bottom drawer of the armoire there was a pair of gray sweatpants. Hanging above the sweatpants were several T-shirts. She took a second to riffle through them. Most of them were the plain white shirts in which she normally saw him dressed. There were a few she'd never seen before. She picked the one that had OLE MISS written on the front in faded, red-and-blue letters, resisting the urge to snoop through the rest of the house before heading to the bathroom and shutting the door.

It was no wonder Jasper offered to let me clean up, Addie thought. Her hair was caked with mud, and she was covered in feathers all the way down to her very dirty flip-flops. Her mind flipped back to the night before and Harper. She wondered if she'd stayed here, showered here, woken up here this morning. If she had, there was surely no trace of her. She bet Harper wouldn't have been caught dead in a chicken coop with a practically hairless pit bull.

She didn't want to go to dinner at Jasper's parents' house. What if they hated her? The first time she'd gone to dinner at Jonah's parents' house, she'd felt the exact same way. He'd put off introducing her to them, even though they were both professors at the college she and Jonah attended in the city. She'd never taken any of their classes, as they were both high-level history teachers, but she knew who they were. Everybody knew who they were. Their home in an affluent suburb of Chicago looked exactly like Addie had pictured it—piled high with books and art and smelling slightly of pipe tobacco. However, she hadn't been greeted with the warm reception she'd expected.

Jonah's father had been admittedly more friendly than his mother, but both had been cold. Neither one of them had spoken more than three words to Addie the entire time she was there, even though she'd attempted multiple times to make conversation. She'd reached out and taken Jonah's hand under the table, searching desperately for some comfort, but he'd jerked himself away from her, slurping his soup and avoiding eye contact with anyone. It was only later, months later, that she found out his parents blamed her for Jonah quitting graduate school just one semester from finishing. The fact that their only son was more interested in the chairs historical people sat in rather than the actual people was not acceptable to them.

She shook her head to clear her thoughts, flinging mud onto the mirror. Her denim skirt and red tank top reeked of wet dog, but she forgot about everything when she stepped inside the shower. It felt the way all showers were supposed to feel. When she emerged minutes later, she found Jasper sitting on the couch with Felix snoring at his feet. "Your water pressure is amazing. I could have stayed in there all day."

"It's not the pressure," Jasper replied, slinging one arm over the back of the couch. "It's the showerhead. I'm guessing you haven't installed yours yet?"

"The showerhead is the least of my concerns right now."

"You've had that thing for at least a month."

"I don't think I've even lived here a month."

"I'm pretty sure you have," Jasper replied. "It's been just about a month since I met you for the first time at Doc's clinic."

"You're the only person I know who can start an argument over a showerhead." Addie rolled her eyes. "I guess you were probably a pretty good lawyer, huh?"

"Technically, I'm still a lawyer," Jasper said.

"That's what Harper said."

"Oh, yeah? What else did she tell you?"

"She told me lots of things."

"Oh?"

"Yep," Addie replied. "She also told me that she was your partner in Memphis."

"She's taking over the practice."

"Why are you giving up your practice?" Addie asked. "I mean, Wanda told me a little about it, but not much."

"I'm sure she did," Jasper replied drily. "My father had a stroke last summer."

"I'm sorry, Jasper."

"I thought maybe my father's condition would improve, but the doctors say he won't walk again, and it's just too much for both of them to bear the responsibility of this farm alone, especially right now during harvest time." Jasper looked down at his fingernails. "It's likely I won't see the inside of the courtroom again for a while."

"Do you miss it?"

"Some days."

"You could always practice here in Eunice, couldn't you?"

"I could," Jasper said. "But I don't have any interest in helping Old Mrs. Johnson sue her neighbor's cat or helping my high school buddies divorce their cheating wives. Besides, I'd have to pass the bar in Arkansas. Memphis is in Tennessee, you know."

"I know." Addie rolled her eyes. "What kind of law did you practice in Memphis?"

"Criminal, mostly." Jasper stood up from the couch. "I did take on a few smaller cases for some friends, but most of the time I handled criminal defense cases."

"That sounds exciting."

"I suppose protecting my chickens from rabid Yankees is just as exciting."

"I'm from the Midwest." Addie crossed her arms over her

chest. "Not everybody north of the Mason-Dixon is a Yankee, you know."

"We better head on in to the main house." He motioned for her to follow him. "My mother will be wondering where we are."

Addie looked down at the clothes she was wearing and said, "Your mother is going to think I'm completely insane. First I show up unannounced with terrible food, then Felix terrorizes her chickens, and now I'm wearing your clothes."

"I'm sure she loves you already."

"She is going to think I'm ridiculous."

Jasper grinned. "As long as she's not having the same thoughts as I'm having right now, we'll probably be fine."

Addie felt her face grow warm. She wasn't sure how to respond to that. "What will I do with Felix?"

Jasper reached down to scratch the dog's ear. "Oh, he and I had a little talk while you were in the shower. He'll be just fine here while we eat."

"Are you sure?"

"It will be fine," Jasper reassured her. "Now come on."

"Whatever you say, Counselor. But if he eats your bed I will not be held responsible."

"It'll be my word against yours."

As they walked, Addie felt someone watching her. Clyde appeared in front of them as if he were an apparition. "I'm headed home, Mr. Jasper. Been a long day."

"Evening, Clyde," Jasper said.

Clyde grunted a response to Jasper, but his eyes were on Addie, and she felt the hair on her arms stand up. Even after they continued on their way, she couldn't shake the feeling that he didn't like her and he wanted her to know it.

Jasper stopped when they got to the front door. "My father can be . . . difficult," he said. "Just keep that in mind."

Before Addie could answer, the door swung open and Artemis stood in front of them. "Come in, come in. Why are you all standing out here?"

"Thanks again for having me." Addie stepped through the doorway.

Artemis led them down the hallway, but this time they took a right before the kitchen.

"Mom?" Jasper said. "What are we doing in here?"

"We have company. I thought it might be nice to use the formal dining room," Artemis explained, shrugging.

Jasper raised an eyebrow. "Does Dad know?"

"He's already at the table," Artemis replied, gesturing toward the room.

"We usually just eat in the kitchen," Jasper whispered to Addie. "You must be pretty special."

"I'm wearing your sweatpants," Addie whispered back. "I'm not special; I'm embarrassed."

Addie followed Jasper and his mother into the dining room. A long, wooden table lay in front of them. The food glistened under the chandelier, and Addie remembered that she hadn't eaten that day. She was famished.

At the end of the table a man sat, staring at the three of them. He said nothing, but his eyes were narrowed as if he was carefully assessing the situation.

Artemis cleared her throat and said, "Adelaide Andrews, this is my husband, Jack Floyd."

"It's nice to meet you, Mr. Floyd," Addie replied cheerfully as she took a seat. "And please, call me Addie."

"I like Adelaide better if it's all the same," Jack answered. "It's nice to meet you as well."

Jasper mouthed, "I told you so" from across the table.

"Jack?" Artemis said. "Would you like to say the blessing?"

"Fine." Jack bowed his head. "Dear heavenly father . . ."

Addie watched Jack through her eyelashes. If she hadn't known he was disabled, she never would have guessed it. Jack Floyd was every bit as strapping and broad-shouldered as his son. He had the same perfect teeth, and same booming voice. His complexion was darker than Jasper's—Jack's once dark hair was now salt and pepper. His forehead and corners of his eyes showed signs of age. When Jasper confessed that his father had been the victim of a stroke, she'd harbored a completely different vision.

". . . Amen," Jack finished. "Let's eat."

Addie watched as Artemis picked up a large white bowl, spooning some of the contents onto her plate. "These," Artemis said, passing a bowl to Addie, "are grits."

Addie spooned the grits onto her plate and brought a forkful to her mouth. "Yum. These are wonderful!"

"We usually have grits for breakfast. Without cheese," Jasper explained. "Grits are traditionally a breakfast food."

"I didn't know what they were until a couple of hours ago, but now I'm not sure how I lived my life without them."

Artemis laughed and pushed another steaming platter toward Addie. "Spoken like a true southerner. I think you're going to be just fine here."

"Where are you from, Adelaide?" Jack broke in.

"I'm from Chicago," Addie replied. "But I spent two weeks every summer until I was twelve down here with my aunt Tilda."

Jack didn't respond and continued to eat in silence. Addie followed suit and concentrated on her cheese grits. Neither Artemis nor Jasper made an attempt at conversation.

"You have a beautiful home," Addie said finally.

"Yes. It is," Jack agreed. "It was built in 1835 by my great-great-grandfather, and it's been kept in immaculate condition, as I'm sure you can see." He gestured around the dining room.

"My father's a very humble man," Jasper said.

"Nothing to be humble about," Jack sniffed. "The Floyds have owned this farm since 1830."

"That's amazing."

"Indeed," Jack agreed. "Floyd Farms' cash crops arc cotton and soybeans."

"Why those crops?" Addie asked. "I hear cotton and soybeans are used together all the time down here. Is there a reason?"

"Smart girl." Jack gave Addie a wry smile. "We alternate between the two. Simply put, cotton takes the nitrogen out of the soil, and the soybeans put it back. We're on a three-year rotation."

"Are those your only crops?"

"Those are the moneymakers," Jack said. "We have a small watermelon patch that we open up to the public over the Fourth of July."

"You have a celebration here?"

"We do," Artemis said. "We eat watermelon and then shoot off fireworks. We didn't have a crop last year, so we're making up for lost time."

"Why didn't you have a crop last year?"

From the other end of the table, Artemis quietly cleared her throat. "We had some issues pop up last year that kept us . . . busy."

"I'm sorry," Addie said.

"What for?" Jack demanded. "Did you put me in this chair?"

"No."

"Then don't be sorry."

"Give her a break, Dad," Jasper cut in. "The nurse put you in that chair an hour ago. You want to chastise someone, go chastise the person who gets paid to put up with you."

"Jasper thinks he's in charge since he came home to help his crippled old man around the farm," Jack said, turning to face Jasper. "But maybe if he'd been helping years ago, his old man wouldn't be a cripple."

"Jack," Artemis said. "That's enough."

"The jury's still out on that one." Jack was staring intently at Jasper. "What do you think, Counselor?"

"I don't know, Dad." Jasper met his father's gaze. "Maybe you should ask a better lawyer."

Jack shifted his gaze back down to his plate and not another word was spoken. Addie had never been more relieved than she was when Artemis stood up to clear the plates.

"Let me help," Addie said, jumping up.

"Nonsense," Artemis replied. "You and Jasper go on now."

Jasper was already making strides toward the door. Addie followed him out into the summer heat. The air was thick, and so was the silence hanging between them as they trudged toward the carriage house.

When they got to the front door, Jasper stopped. He put a hand to the back of his neck and let out a long sigh. Finally he said, "Don't let my father get to you."

"Are you talking to me?" Addie asked. "Or yourself?"

Jasper shrugged. "Whichever one of us will listen."

"I'm not good with parents." She winced as thoughts of Jonah and the dinner at his parents' made its way back into her head. "It's never been my strong suit."

"Oh, really?"

"Not my first awkward family dinner, I'm afraid."

"You didn't make it awkward."

"I'm sorry I upset him, anyway," Addie said.

"Breathing upsets him," Jasper replied. "He's been angry at me for the last year."

"Because he thinks it's your fault what happened to him?"

"He's never quite forgiven me for going to law school," Jasper said. "I was supposed to come home after I graduated from college. I was supposed to take over the farm. Get married. Have a family. Be just like him."

Addie could see that he was gripping the door handle so tightly that his knuckles were white. She wanted to grab his hand and tell him he wasn't alone—that he wasn't the only one who felt guilty and that maybe they were both being too hard on themselves. Instead she kept her hands planted firmly at her sides and said, "Well, you're here now. That's got to count for something."

"It doesn't matter." Jasper shook his head. "Let's get inside and see if Felix has destroyed my house."

"If he's eaten your couch, just don't forget that it was your idea to leave him alone," Addie replied.

"You better hope he held up his end of the bargain." A grin began to spill across Jasper's face. "Otherwise, you're going to owe me a lot more than a basket of fried pies."

CHAPTER 16

EUNICE HAD ONCE HAD MONEY, AS MANY RIVER TOWNS IN THE South had. The houses in the oldest part of Eunice—the downtown area—were a reminder of a long-lost splendor. Many of the houses had fallen into disrepair; their owners seemingly evaporated into thin air, vanished during a summer heat wave. Jagged windows, rotting doors, roofs that were caving in, and squatters that meandered in and out could be found on any one of the cobblestone streets. Even historic buildings where bullets from the Civil War, the only war that really mattered in the Delta, were still lodged into the walls had been forgotten. The years had changed the beauty that Addie remembered from her childhood to something ugly. Something angry.

Addie wondered if the person responsible for hurting Felix lived in one of the decrepit houses that they often passed during their daily walks. There were dogs running loose everywhere.

Some were chained to trees in unruly yards. They barked and lunged and whined. In their eyes was a longing for a life different from the one they had been allotted.

It broke Addie's heart.

She supposed she could have listened to Jasper and the others when they told her not to venture too close to these houses—not to venture too close to the levee. But her odd curiosity was something she couldn't ignore, and very often Addie's walks with Felix led them to the end of one of those cobblestone streets.

Addie tried to amble down the street, but Felix wasn't having it. The evening was surprisingly cool, and his lanky puppy legs beat against the cracked pavement. Felix gave the leash a tug, and Addie broke into a sluggish jog. Addie's mind wandered back to Jasper and the morning after the storm. He'd been wearing shorts and running shoes. Maybe she could convince him to take Felix jogging once in a while.

Addie didn't notice the two men sitting in lawn chairs in the front yard of one of the houses until she was upon them.

"That's an interesting-looking dog you've got there," said one of the men. It was the same man from the fair. Addie wouldn't soon forget his complexion.

"Thanks." Addie recognized the second man immediately. It was Redd Jones.

Redd stood up, crushing a beer can beneath his muddy boot. "He missin' an ear?"

"He is," Addie replied. Felix tucked his lips up under his gums and flashed his teeth. He let out a low, guttural growl. "You better not come any closer."

"He ain't gonna hurt me."

"I don't know about that."

Redd took a long, slow drag from the cigarette between his thick fingers. "Where'd you get him?"

"Found him."

"Oh, yeah? Where?"

Addie tightened her grip on Felix's leash. She didn't want to tell him anything. "I don't remember right off hand."

The other man opened up the cooler between the lawn chairs and pulled out a beer. "You want one?"

"No, thanks," she replied. "I need to be getting home."

Redd stepped onto the sidewalk. "I saw you out with Jasper Floyd a while back. You ain't from around here, are ya?"

Addie took a step back onto the street. The sounds coming from Felix's throat became louder. "I'm from Chicago."

"A Yankee."

"Hardly." Addie snorted.

"Leave it to Jasper to buy himself a Yankee girl," Redd said. "Guess the women here ain't good enough for such a fine gentleman." He flicked his cigarette. Ashes floated down onto Felix's nose.

"Now, come on," the other man said. "Ain't no reason to talk like that to her."

"Shut up, Frank."

Disgust welled up inside of Addie and pieces of it spilled out onto her face. "Jasper didn't buy me."

"Jasper buys whatever hard work won't get him," Redd replied. He squinted one of his eyes closed. "Which is the same thing as sayin' Jasper buys everything. And everyone."

"Come on back now, Redd," Frank said. "Sit down and have a drink. We're supposed to be celebrating tonight."

"I said, shut up."

"Does he always talk to you like that?" Addie asked Frank. She knew she shouldn't be antagonizing Redd. She knew it, and yet she couldn't help herself. She realized that he might be drunk, and the thought made her even more uncomfortable than she already was.

Frank didn't respond. He pretended to concentrate on the beer can in his hands. When he looked up, Addie smiled at him. He gave her a shy smile in return.

"Ain't nothin' for sale around these parts." Redd took a step back, blocking Addie's view of Frank. His heel caught on the curb and he stumbled. "You better get on, now."

Without another word, she started back down the street, pulling Felix along after her. He continued to growl long after they were home, standing at the front door for hours with his head cocked, his good ear listening, listening to the summertime concert of crickets and bullfrogs and—it seemed to Addie—a voice in the air that only he could hear.

CHAPTER 17

"What do you mean you don't have sweet tea in Chicago?" Bobby stared at Addie.

"Well, we have it. You can make it or buy it in a jug at the store," Addie replied. "But most of the time you can't order it in a restaurant."

"A person can't order tea in a restaurant?"

"You can order it. But it won't come sweetened." Addie sighed. "You'd have to use the sugar packets at the table."

"Well, that's just un-American," Bobby muttered.

"Oh my God. What is it with you people and sweet tea?"

"You people?"

"No, no. I'm not getting into this again." Addie held her hands up. "I'm sorry about the sweet tea, but I did make cookies."

"Really?" Wanda looked up at Addie, surprised.

"I still had a bunch of stuff left over from the pies." Addie shrugged. "There was a recipe for sugar cookies in the recipe box that I thought I could get through without screwing up."

"Well, look at you!"

"It was really easy," Addie confessed. "I'm still too scared to try anything else."

Bobby and Wanda reached for the cookies. They chewed for a few agonizing seconds before Wanda said, "These aren't bad." She reached for another. "Pretty good, actually."

"Hand me the hammer, will ya?" Bobby grinned at her, his mouth still full.

Addie pawed through Bobby's huge rolling tool case. "Hey, Wanda? Do you have the hammer?"

"Yep. Hang on." Wanda placed a final nail into a new wooden floorboard. Felix howled from inside Addie's bedroom each time he heard the hammer hit a nail. He'd been so terrified when the tools came out, he'd hidden under the bed and not come out.

"I really appreciate you all coming over to help me with this," Addie said. "All this house repair stuff is pretty overwhelming."

"Don't sweat it." Wanda handed the hammer over to Bobby. "We love it, don't we, big brother?"

"Yes ma'am," Bobby replied. "I'd work construction for a living if it paid the bills."

"Besides," Wanda continued, "Bryar's in hog heaven sitting in front of your TV. You have more weather channels than we do."

"I'll need to come back sometime soon to treat this wood," Bobby said, standing up. "That's part of the reason some of these old boards is rotten. Whoever done it didn't treat it."

"I can treat it," Addie replied. "It's putting the boards in that I can't do."

"What do you know about treatin' wood?"

"A little." Addie shrugged. "I refinished that table in there in the kitchen."

"Really?" Bobby asked.

"And the chairs."

"I'm impressed, Miss Addie."

"You should see the things Bobby's made over the years," Wanda bragged as the three of them shuffled inside. "Last summer he made Bryar a wooden pedal car."

"That's awesome!" Addie said. "So is it mostly woodworking that you do?"

"I do a little bit of everything." Bobby's ruddy cheeks flushed an even deeper red. "I don't create nothin' sittin' in a seat all day and night on the truck. When I'm home, it's how I unwind."

"That makes sense," Addie replied.

"You know the chair attached to the bathtub in the bathroom?" Bobby jerked his thumb toward the back of the house.

Addie nodded and replied, "Yeah, I had to take it down when I moved in because it took up the whole tub."

"Well, toward the end Miss Tilda couldn't get around real well. She didn't want nobody to come in and help her," Bobby said. "So I put in that chair and attached it with a pulley system so that she could sit down on the chair from outside the tub and then pull herself over the lip of the tub. That way she didn't need her legs to lift her over."

"That was nice of you."

"It was easy. I miss your aunt. She was a good woman. Always gave me work when I needed it."

"Speaking of work," Wanda said, "did you see that big HELP WANTED sign at the corner of town? Looks like the Floyds are hiring people to get them all set up for the Fourth of July celebration this year."

"I didn't even know they was havin' it," Bobby replied. "Ain't been to one of their shindigs in years."

"We must've been kids," Wanda agreed. "Back when we were all still friends."

"Couldn't pay me to go now."

"I'm sure someone could pay you."

Bobby stifled a laugh and wiped his brow with the back of his hand. "You're probably right. But it ain't my first choice."

"I think I'm going to go," Addie spoke up. "It sounds like fun."

"I'd actually been thinking about taking Bryar," Wanda replied.

"You've gotta be kidding me," Bobby grumbled.

"You should come with us." Addie nudged Bobby.

"I'd rather eat bark."

"You'd rather what?"

"I'd rather eat bark," Bobby said again. "I'd rather eat the bark off a damp, old, rotting tree than spend five minutes anywhere near the Floyd farm."

"Jasper's not the ogre you think he is."

"But his daddy is, ain't he?"

Addie felt her face flush. Bobby was right—why would anyone want to spend time with Jack Floyd, especially if they weren't being paid?

"Don't be that way, Bobby," Wanda continued. "There's no reason to hold a grudge against Jasper for something he didn't even do to you."

"What—do you have the hots for Jasper, too?" Bobby asked. "I mean, everybody knows about Adelaide, but you, too?"

"Everybody knows what?" Addie stopped what she was doing to stare at Bobby. "Everybody knows what about me?"

"I don't think it would hurt to show the Floyds some kindness," Wanda said to her brother. "Wouldn't hurt you a bit."

"Who needs kindness when ya got money?"

"Come on, Bobby."

"Jasper Floyd is a bastard," Bobby said, losing patience. "Everybody knows it . . . except you two, apparently."

"What does everybody know about me?" Addie repeated.

Wanda ignored her. "I owe him everything, Bobby. Everything."

"What are you talking about?"

"Who do you think helped me get custody of Bryar?" Wanda replied. "Who do you think helped make sure that his daddy's family only got supervised visitation? Who do you think made sure the charges against Bryar's daddy stuck? Sure wasn't you. Sure wasn't *Redd Jones*. You don't know anything about the kind of person that he is."

"Of course I didn't know," Bobby said. He rubbed his thumb and index finger across his forehead. "You never told me none of that."

"Jasper didn't want me tellin' no one," Wanda replied. "Said the last thing he wanted was for everyone to know. I'm not asking that you like him, but don't you dare talk about him like you know anything just because Redd Jones doesn't have the sense God gave him to come in out of the rain."

"Damn it, I wish you'd told me."

"It wouldn't have been hard to figure out if you'd been payin' attention."

Bobby sighed. "I know you think you got it all figured out, but I could help you sometimes," he said to Wanda. "I ain't book smart, but I got my talents."

Addie's eyes lit up. "Hey, Bobby, could you help me with something?"

"I thought that's what I was doin'."

"Well, could you help me with something else?"

"Sure." He followed Addie out the kitchen door and toward the shed. "What happened to your door?"

"It's a long story," Addie said. "But what I need help with is inside."

"Lord, it's hot in here." Bobby swatted at the dust.

Addie pointed to the back of the shed to an object covered by a sheet and propped up on several boxes. "See that back there?"

"The sheet?"

"There's a porch swing underneath it."

Bobby climbed up on a stack of boxes and pulled back the sheet. "This what you're wantin'?"

Addie nodded. "I can't carry it by myself."

"Where do you want it?" Bobby hoisted the swing off the boxes.

"The front porch, if you can." Addie grabbed one end.

"I wouldn't hang that up with those rusty chains," Bobby said once they had the swing on the porch. "Don't look safe."

"I won't," Addie replied. "I don't even know if I'm going to hang it up at all."

"Well, why not?" Wanda wanted to know. "A porch ain't a porch without a swing."

"We can hang it up, no problem," Bobby said. "They got chains down at Linstrom's. I can run down and get ya a couple."

"That would be great."

"I ain't got a lot of cash right now to buy 'em . . ." Bobby trailed off. His face was crimson.

"If you'll hang the swing for me, I'll buy the chains," Addie replied.

"I can stay here and keep workin' if y'all want to go on ahead," Wanda broke in.

Bobby slung a beefy arm around Wanda's shoulders. "Let's get this floor finished, and then we'll head on out. And you"—he pointed at Adelaide—"I hope you've got some sugar left after those cookies. We're makin' sweet tea tonight."

CHAPTER 18

ADDIE SAT IN THE CAB OF BOBBY'S TRUCK. SHE WASN'T SURE what to say to him without Wanda as a buffer. She was grateful he'd offered to hang up the swing, but now she wished that she'd put him off for a couple of days.

"Hey," Bobby said, breaking the silence. "I got some tools at my place that would make it easier to hang that swing up. Care if we run by there real quick?"

When Bobby turned onto the familiar cobblestone street, Addie realized where they were going. The truck came to a stop in front of Redd Jones's house. Addie remembered that Bobby had mentioned living with him the first night they met. She shifted uncomfortably. "I'll just sit here if that's all right."

"Come on in," Bobby urged. "You ain't got to sit outside in this heat."

Addie followed him up the crumbling steps. The grass was as high as her knees, and it beat against her bare skin as she walked. When she leaned down to scratch at her legs, she could see through the missing slats in the backyard fence. She veered away from Bobby to get a better look.

"You coming?"

"Yeah, sorry." Addie could see nothing but dirt.

The inside of the house was sparse. There wasn't even a couch in the living room—just the two lawn chairs that had been in the front yard the day Addie had run into Redd and Frank. There was a huge television hanging on the wall, and a mattress and several ashtrays full of cigarette butts on the floor. Addie and Bobby were alone in the house.

"Make yourself at home," Bobby said. "I'll be right back."

Addie wandered through the massive expanse of the downstairs. Almost every room looked the same—a mattress on the floor surrounded by ashtrays. Window units sagged in every room, dripping water onto the wooden floors. Dirty dishes overflowed in the kitchen. And there was a smell, a distinct smell that Addie couldn't quite put her finger on. The house, at one time, must have been beautiful. She wondered what the original owners would think if they could see it now.

The last room that Addie entered was different from all the rest. It was fully furnished and clean. There was a four-poster bed and another huge television set on the wall. The room didn't match the rest, and Addie knew instantly that this room belonged to Redd. She looked around the hallway to make sure that she was still alone before she moved farther into the room. The first drawer on the nightstand was halfway open, and Addie couldn't resist going over to peek inside. There was a gun sitting atop a stack of papers, a .38-caliber handgun, but it was different from any that she had seen before. An intricate design had been carved into the barrel and stock—roses, it looked like to Addie. It was beautiful. She didn't know much about weaponry, but she knew enough to know that this gun was special. It wasn't the kind of gun that a person used every day.

She set the gun gingerly on the top of the nightstand and picked up the papers that had been lying beneath it. Each page held a few numbers, a name, and a bunch of other words that Addie didn't understand. The first page read:

PROSPECT #56807/Black Betty
Sire: Grand Champion Whiplash
Dam: Roho
Champion bloodline (yes)
Gameness (yes)

Each page went on and on like this. She was still trying to make sense of it when she heard someone coming down the hallway. In a panic, she shoved the paper and the gun back into the nightstand.

"Addie?" Bobby stuck his head inside the room. "Girl, what are you doing in here?"

"I was just . . . I was looking for the bathroom," Addie managed to squeak out. "This house is so damn big, I guess I got lost."

"Well, this ain't it." Bobby motioned her out of the room. "The one downstairs ain't workin', so you'll have to go upstairs."

"That's okay," Addie replied. "I can hold it."

Bobby shrugged. "If you say so. I got the tools we need. Let's git."

Addie didn't protest. She followed him out into the Delta sunshine, past the tall grass and crumbling steps, and into the safety of Bobby's truck. She didn't look back as they drove away.

CHAPTER 19

THE ROAD TO THE FLOYD FARM SEEMED PARTICULARLY BUMPY as Addie sat in the passenger seat of Wanda's car. She was nervous, and it was a feeling she couldn't shake. She couldn't figure out why. The last time she'd seen Jasper had been at the farm, and they had left everything just fine.

"What's wrong with you today?" Wanda asked. "You've been quiet since I picked you up."

"I'm fine."

"Okay, whatever."

"I swear, I'm fine!"

"I still can't believe Bobby agreed to come tonight," Wanda said.

"I think your revelation to him the other day really changed his point of view," Addie replied.

"Mommy?" Bryar peeped from the backseat.

"What, sugar?"

"What does rev . . . revlashun mean?"

"Revelation?" Wanda swiveled her head around to look at Bryar. "It means to tell a story that nobody has heard before."

"Oh," Bryar replied. He leaned his whole body forward in his booster seat. "What story did you tell?"

"It was kind of a grown-up story," Wanda said. "Remember that Mommy talks to other grown-ups about grown-up things sometimes?"

"Yes." Bryar sighed through clenched teeth. "I don't like those stories."

"Speaking of grown-up things," Addie began. "Do you think you might be able to find a sitter for the B-Man in two weeks?"

"I'm sure that I can."

"Great," Addie replied. "I'm going to be twenty-eight that Saturday."

"How come you didn't tell me? We need to have a party!"

"That's why I'm telling you now," Addie said. "I haven't celebrated my birthday in a couple of years. I figure now is as good a time as any to start back up again."

There were cars everywhere when they arrived at the farm. Everyone was dressed in red, white, and blue. Wanda and Bryar were wearing matching star-spangled T-shirts and cowboy boots. In fact, Addie was wearing her very first pair of cowboy boots—they were hot pink. The color thrilled Addie. She hadn't even known that a person could get cowboy boots that color.

People carried baskets with delicious contents and jugs of sweet tea under their arms. Children whizzed past them unattended with sparklers clutched in their fists, glints of fire flickering to the ground below. The air was thick with sweat and excitement.

Bryar skipped ahead of them, occasionally looking back to

make sure his mother and Addie were following. "Mom! Mom! Mom!" he chanted. "Look! Sno-cones!"

"That will flat-out ruin your shirt," Wanda replied.

"I'll be careful. Promise."

"Those sno-cones look pretty good. It is sweltering out here," Addie said. "Let him have one, Mom."

"I could just kick whoever invented the sno-cone. They obviously never had to do laundry."

"My mom never let me have them as a kid," Addie said. "She thought they were too messy. You two would probably get along."

"Fine!" Wanda threw up her hands in defeat. "You two go on and get a sno-cone. But sit down with them!"

Bryar gleefully took Addie's hand and pulled her toward the line. He looked up at her and said, "What flavor are you gonna get?"

"I don't know," Addie replied. "Maybe purple?"

"Purple isn't a flavor." Jasper was standing there, arms crossed over his chest. He wasn't smiling. In fact, he was scowling.

"I'm going to have red," Bryar said.

"Still not a flavor," Jasper countered.

"He's four," Addie said.

"And how old are you?"

"I'll be twenty-eight in two weeks."

"We'd like one red and one purple, please," Jasper said to the man wielding the sno-cone machine.

The man nodded and set himself to work. "See?" Addie nudged Jasper. "He knew what you meant."

Jasper handed Addie and Bryar their sno-cones, tipping his hat to them as he walked away. He didn't say anything else to Addie. She wondered what he was so stressed about.

"Hey! Wait up!" Addie handed an already stained and soggy

Bryar off to Wanda and then jogged after Jasper. "Listen, if you've got other stuff you need to be doing, I understand."

"I don't have anything else to do," Jasper replied. His tone was gruff, agitated. "You just walk too slowly."

"I didn't realize I was supposed to be running a race."

Jasper slowed down. "No. I'm sorry. I forgot you're only about as tall as a nine-year-old."

"I look at least twelve."

"You always have a response for everything?"

"It's part of my charm."

"Actually, if you don't mind, I have a few things I need to check on." Jasper's gaze shifted from Addie to the expansive pumpkin patch. "Do you want to come with me?"

"Sure," Addie replied.

Jasper motioned for Addie to follow him. He led her to a vehicle that looked like a cross between a four-wheeler and a miniature truck. The word POLARIS was written on the side. "Hop in."

"Don't I need a helmet to ride on this thing?"

"No." Jasper started the engine. "There are no helmet laws in the state of Arkansas. Besides, this isn't a motorcycle. It's an off-road vehicle."

"I forgot I was hanging out with a lawyer."

Jasper grinned as they rattled along, his mood lifting with every bump. Addie sulked next to him. It annoyed her that he seemed to enjoy her the most when she was uncomfortable. It was almost as if he did things on purpose just to watch her squirm.

"Where are we going?" Addie called out over the roar of the engine. "It looks like we're leaving the pumpkin patch."

"We are. I've got to go check on a couple of things on the actual farm. We still have to keep it running, you know."

"Oh." Actually, Addie hadn't known. The closest that she'd come to farm life was the time she'd visited a petting zoo in St. Louis. She had a feeling that didn't count.

They slowed down when they approached a field with several machines. "Those machines are harvesting cotton," Jasper said. "Cotton-picking machines use rotating spindles to pick or twist the seed cotton from the burr. Then doffers remove the seed cotton from the spindles and drop the seed cotton into the conveying system."

"Wow," Addie replied. "Is it complicated?"

"It's not so much." Jasper shrugged. "The hardest thing is just keeping the damn boll weevils out."

"The what?"

"The boll weevil. It's the insect enemy of cotton. It can complete an entire life cycle in three weeks, lay two hundred eggs per female—each in a separate cotton square, ensuring the destruction of each—and spread rapidly, covering forty to a hundred sixty miles per year."

"Sounds intense."

"It is." Jasper's voice was serious. "It can destroy an entire crop, which will in turn destroy your bank account. I've got to go over to that machine just to the right of us," Jasper said, pointing to a green machine standing stagnant in the field. "It broke down this morning, and I've got a guy out there working on it."

Addie stood up and followed Jasper. As they approached the machine, she could see a man hunched over to one side, his face hidden. He straightened up as they approached him.

"Mr. Floyd," the man said. "I think I've 'bout got 'er fixed up."

"Good," Jasper replied. "What do you think caused it?"

Addie studied the man in front of her. He looked young. He was smaller than Jasper, with thick dark hair and windburned skin. He looked like a farmer in a way that Jasper did not. Addie stuck out her hand to him and said, "I'm Addie. It's nice to meet you."

"I'm Loren." His gaze was set squarely on her chest. He wasn't even trying to hide it. "So, you and the boss man an item?"

Addie choked back a laugh. "I, uh, well, we're . . ." She didn't know what to say. How had she not thought of this before? What *were* they? She certainly hadn't expected some cowhand in the middle of a cotton field to ask for a status update.

Jasper stiffened. He stepped closer to Addie. "We better get going. I need you to get this thing running before lunchtime."

"Yes, sir," Loren said, a broad smile plastered across his face. "You let me know if you ever figure out that answer, Miss Addie."

This kid was brazen.

Jasper turned and strode back to the vehicle, dragging Addie along with him. "So all this land," Addie said, hoping to break the tension, "belongs to you?"

"It belongs to my father," Jasper corrected her.

"That's what I meant."

"My father and I are two very different people."

"I'm aware of that."

"Then you're one step ahead of most people." Jasper stopped the vehicle. He gazed out into the field surrounding them. "You're new here, so I don't expect you to understand the ins and outs of a place like Eunice."

"I'm trying to understand," Addie replied. "But the people here sure don't make it easy."

"Twelve hundred acres of this land has been in my family for almost two hundred years," Jasper continued. "The Floyd men have always been farmers."

"But you became a lawyer instead."

"The land on the other side of this fence," Jasper continued, "is all my land. It's just about twenty acres, but it all belongs to me."

"Twenty acres sounds like a lot to me," Addie said.

Jasper smiled. "You would think that."

"So what do you plan to do with the old barn and what's left of the house?"

"Demolish it," Jasper said matter-of-factly. "There's no saving it. It's too far gone to be of any use."

"Then what?"

"I'm going to build a house."

"A house? For you?"

"Who else would I build a house for?"

For some reason that response cut her. Of course he was building a house for himself. Just for himself. "What will you do with all that's there now?"

"Throw it away, I guess."

Addie hopped off the Polaris. "Care if I go over there and take a look? I'm dying to see what's inside that barn."

"Snakes and rusty nails are what's inside," Jasper replied, following after her. "I swear, I've never met a person so interested in trash."

"It's not trash just because it's old," Addie said.

"I know, I know."

She waded through the hip-high grass to the entrance of the barn. It was leaning far to its left side, as if one strong gust of wind could topple it for good. "How long has it been since anybody lived here?"

"Decades," Jasper said. "They'd abandoned the place long before it went into foreclosure. We were just teenagers when they moved off. Left all their livestock, dogs, even half their belongings in the house."

"Why?"

Jasper shrugged. "Nobody knows, exactly. Old Man Jones died when Redd and the rest of us were in junior high. I guess his mama couldn't handle it all by herself. She tried for a while, having eight boys and a farm to take care of."

"Eight?" Addie was aghast.

"Not much to do around here but farm and have babies."

"Well, you'd think with all those boys she would've had some help."

"You'd think." Jasper thumped his foot on a stray board. "But that's only because you don't know the Jones boys."

"I ran into him the other day while I was walking Felix," Addie said. "He was sitting in front of some run-down house."

"Did you talk to him?"

"I didn't have much of a choice."

"He give you a hard time?"

Addie shrugged. "He called me a Yankee, which I gather is an insult."

"People around here call everybody who isn't from here a Yankee," Jasper replied. "What were you doing downtown?"

"I told you. I was walking Felix."

"You shouldn't be down there by yourself."

"I'm not a child," Addie said. She rolled her eyes. "I can handle myself."

"It's not safe down there."

"Why not?"

"It just isn't."

"That's not a good enough reason."

It was Jasper's turn to roll his eyes. "There are plenty of places you can walk Felix that don't include getting that close to the Mississippi River."

"Why do I feel like there's something you're not telling me?"

"Just be careful down there," Jasper replied. "Redd Jones hangs out down there for a reason."

"Maybe he knows what happened to Felix."

"I wouldn't go around asking people what they know."

"Well, somebody knows something," Addie said. "Somebody had to have seen or heard something."

"I'm going to give you some advice that you probably won't take too kindly to," he said. "People around here don't want you burrowing into their business. They want to be left alone. A few lonely old women sitting on the front porch gossiping is one thing, but an outsider coming in and asking lots of questions where she isn't wanted is another. It puts people off, Addie. It makes them angry."

"I'm not burrowing into anybody's business."

"Good." Jasper nodded. "Keep it that way."

"But a decent person doesn't just shoot a dog and leave it to die," Addie finished.

"No, he doesn't," Jasper agreed. "And it isn't the kind of person you want to accidentally rub the wrong way."

She decided against telling him that she'd also been *inside* Redd's house with Bobby. Besides, she wasn't sure what to make of what she'd found, and she didn't need Jasper in her head telling her it was nothing. "I'm trying not to do any burrowing or rubbing," Addie said.

A devilish smile appeared on Jasper's face. "Good to know," he replied. "Good to know."

Addie stepped inside the barn. Grass had grown up in between the wooden slats, dirt and debris everywhere. There were rusty tools hanging from the rotting beams, swaying menacingly in the breeze. There was an old couch in the corner, its metal coils sticking out like curls on a child's head. With every step Addie took, something creaked or cracked or was crushed beneath her feet.

"We shouldn't stay in here too long," Jasper warned her. "It's not safe."

"Can I take a few of these loose boards with me?" Addie asked. "Some of them are still in pretty good shape."

Jasper was standing in the doorway, his hands shoved down inside the pockets of his jeans. "What for?"

"I have an idea." Addie bent down and picked up a stray board. That's when she saw it. Coiled inside the couch cushion next to the metal springs. A snake. "Jasper," she rasped. *"Jasper!"*

"What?" Jasper vaulted forward, following her voice. "What's wrong?"

Addie clutched the boards to her chest, afraid to move. It saw her. It was watching her. "Snake . . . snake . . . snake . . ." She repeated the word over and over.

Jasper took several swift steps toward her. "Cover your ears, Adelaide."

Addie wasn't listening. The snake was moving. It was swaying back and forth. If it had haunches, it would have been on them. It was going to bite her. She knew it. She fell back when it lunged, the bullet from Jasper's gun whizzing by her ear. The snake's head popped like a cherry tomato, the bloody body writhing around the coils of the couch.

Addie sat there for a minute, stunned. Her ears were ringing.

She could see Jasper in front of her, but she couldn't hear what he was saying.

"Addie? Addie? Are you okay?" He was shaking her.

She blinked. "I'm okay."

"I told you there were snakes in here."

"Did you shoot it?" She let him pull her to her feet. "With a gun?"

"What else would I have shot it with?" Jasper asked. "I told you to cover your ears."

"Does everybody have a gun in this damn town?"

"You're from Chicago. People have guns in Chicago."

"The criminals have guns in Chicago," Addie replied. "Cops have guns."

"Well, down here we don't wait for the law to show up. We take care of our own business."

Addie grinned at him. "You're such an enigma, Jasper Floyd. A gun-toting farmer with a law degree."

"C'mon," Jasper said. "We better get back to the festivities."

Addie realized that he was still holding on to her hand. She allowed him to lead her back to the Polaris, and only then did he let her go. "Oh, wait!" Addie jumped off the vehicle as Jasper started it up. "I forgot my boards!"

A CROWD HAD gathered near the front porch of the Floyd mansion. There were several Floyd Farms employees standing off to one side as Artemis and Jack had a heated exchange behind them.

"What's going on over there?" Addie asked.

"I don't know." Jasper jumped out of the driver's seat. He made a beeline for his parents.

Addie followed him, stopping next to Bobby and Wanda, who were looking on at the entire spectacle. "Hey."

"Hey," Bobby replied. "You missed half the show."

"What do you mean?"

Bobby tore his eyes away from Artemis, Jack, and now Jasper. "Someone came over the loudspeaker and told everybody to gather out in the front yard for the fireworks display. About that time Jack Floyd come out of the house. They announce his name, everybody turns to look, and he starts yellin' at everybody."

"Why?"

"Hell if I know."

Jasper's arms were crossed, and he was staring down at his father, his mouth set in a hard line. After a few minutes, Jasper threw up his hands and stormed off toward the Polaris. As Addie hurried after Jasper she heard Artemis say, "Okay, everybody! Are you ready for some fireworks? Old Mr. Clyde here is going to start the show!"

Jasper heaved himself down on the seat, his hands gripping the steering wheel so tightly that his knuckles were white.

"Is everything okay?" Addie asked.

"It's fine," Jasper replied through clenched teeth.

"It didn't look fine."

"I don't give a shit how it looks."

Evening was setting in, and mosquitoes droned around Addie's face. She swatted at them with her hands, smacking her bare shoulders and neck. "I've never seen mosquitoes this big. I'm starting to think if I'm not careful they'll carry me off."

"Welcome to the Delta."

"They don't seem to be bothering you."

Jasper reached into his pocket. "Here," he said. "It's a dryer sheet."

"What do you want me to do with a dryer sheet?"

"Put it in your pocket or your shirt or something," Jasper instructed. "It'll keep the mosquitoes away."

Addie arched an eyebrow but wasted no time shoving the dryer sheet into the pocket of her cutoffs. "There are lots of secrets to surviving down here, aren't there?"

"There are secrets to surviving anywhere," Jasper replied.

"This is the first place I've ever lived where I had to put a dryer sheet in my pants to avoid contracting malaria."

Behind them the first of the fireworks burst forth into the sky followed by crackles and pops and oohs and aahs. "I better go make sure Clyde is all right," Jasper said. He stood up and wiped his hands on his pants. "A few years ago he 'bout set himself on fire. My dad had to tackle him to the ground in front of everybody."

"That explains why both your dad and Clyde seemed less than thrilled about the fireworks this year."

"My dad loves fireworks," Jasper replied. "It's about the only thing he likes. This was always his night. His show."

"Then I don't understand—"

"What's not to understand?" Jasper cut her off. "The man didn't want to be pushed out in his wheelchair for everybody to see. He didn't want an announcement that he's a goddamn cripple. That he's not a man anymore."

"Being in a wheelchair doesn't make him less of a man."

Jasper pivoted. "You want to know a secret about living here? About *surviving* here? People either have or they have not. There is no in between. Not here. Generation after generation. You might see us playing nice at the grocery store or at the fair or even here tonight. But everybody knows exactly what the person next to them has. And what they don't. My father could walk into a room and command respect. People feared him. He had power. All of that was taken away from him in fifteen seconds. Now his employees pity him. He thinks I pity him. How can anyone respect a man who needs help getting onto the toilet in the morning?"

"Is that really how you feel?" Addie asked. "About your dad? About everything?"

"Of course not," Jasper said. "Why do you think I left?"

"You could change it. Be different."

Jasper crossed his arms over his chest. "It doesn't work that way, Adelaide. You can't change an entire culture."

"So I guess the best solution is to not even try?"

"You don't get it," Jasper said. "People don't want to change. Not here. Not anywhere. But people like you always want someone *else* to step up to the mic and tell everybody that they're doing it wrong. That you know better. That your way beats our way. That's why people like you never last very long down here. We're all just waiting for you to give up and go home. We never really wanted you here to begin with."

Jasper mashed a boot into the ground, a line drawn into the waning Delta twilight, a line that had not existed until that very second—until his eyes blazed right through her and focused on another muddy Mississippi River secret that Adelaide could not yet see.

CHAPTER 20

ADDIE LAY AWAKE IN HER BED, EYES OPEN, STARING AT THE wall. The man in the white coat plagued her dreams. Jonah plagued her dreams. Jasper's angry face plagued her dreams.

In the darkness, Addie tried to focus on the familiar aspects of the room. The heavy oak dresser and nightstand had belonged to Aunt Tilda, as had the thick blanket under which Addie and Felix were huddled. She thought that maybe if she just concentrated hard enough she could still smell her aunt on the fabric.

She wished more than anything she had more than just a musty, old blanket to comfort her. She wished her aunt was there, stroking her hair and telling her that it would all be okay. She wished she could wander into the kitchen dazed from her bad dream and sit down at the table to a plate of cheese and crackers, her aunt's remedy for any ailment. Most of all, Addie wished that the last vision of her aunt's face wasn't fifteen years old. Addie sat up, choking back the guilt and sobs that threatened to be her undoing. She wasn't going to cry. Not tonight.

In the closet in the spare room, Addie had begun a collection of sorts. Her aunt had used the shelving for quilts. On top of the quilts, Addie placed odds and ends—things that she didn't know what to do with but didn't want to throw away. So far, she'd amassed three light fixtures, four balls of twine, six hand mirrors, and various other knickknacks, including a handful of old doorknobs and dresser knobs—what Addie had come for.

Wandering into the living room, she sat down on the couch and looked at the boards she'd brought home from the farm. Some of them still had the flaking red barn paint on them. Some of the pieces were jagged, and some of them looked like they could be fit right back into the barn's walls as if they'd never been gone.

Jonah hadn't liked to make anything new out of anything old. He was traditional; he wanted only to save what had been lost. There had never been room inside their store for the repurposed creations. Everything had one purpose, Jonah's purpose.

But where Jonah saw barn wood, Addie saw shutters; she saw shelving. Where he saw doorknobs, Addie saw a coatrack. *But doorknobs don't always have to go on doors,* Addie thought. *Paint doesn't always have to be removed.*

Jasper said she didn't understand the Delta, and maybe she didn't. Maybe it was like Jasper said—one person couldn't change a culture. Maybe it was like the wood in front of her; stripping away the paint would make it pretty, make it shiny, but then it wouldn't be the same thing.

Change was something Addie desperately needed. It was the reason she'd moved here, a place most of her friends and family back in Chicago didn't even know existed. She missed Chicago.

She missed the familiarity of it. She missed the restaurants, the weather, and the people. She missed the clients she and Jonah worked with. Many of them had become like family, and just before she left for Eunice, one of them offered her a job. He was the owner of a large auction house in Chicago.

"It wouldn't be much to start," he'd said to her one afternoon over coffee. "You'd be the assistant to my top picker, but he'll be retiring in the next year."

"That sounds wonderful," Addie had gushed. "I'm leaving for Eunice, Arkansas, in a few days, but just for a few months."

"Where?"

Addie laughed. It felt good to laugh. "It's just a little town. Nobody ever knows where it is."

"Well, anyway," he'd continued, "think about it, and when you get home give me a call."

It was, at least, something for her to hold on to—a reason to go back to Chicago when the time came. She'd be starting all over . . . again. Addie took the most jagged paint-covered piece of board and sat it in front of her. Then she took four of the doorknobs and sat them face up on the wood. It looked like something she'd seen in a magazine once, hanging up in a shabby chic bedroom. What she'd hang on the knobs, she had no idea. Tomorrow she'd buy the tools to attach the knobs, and she'd hang it up in this house, her house, at least for now.

CHAPTER 21

"You know," Addie said, peeping at Wanda over a rack of clothes from inside Lily's Resale Boutique, "when I invited you to go to Memphis with me this weekend, I didn't mean that you had to plan everything down to the last detail."

"It's your birthday!" Wanda exclaimed. "You shouldn't have to plan your own celebration."

"It's not a celebration," Addie pointed out. "We're just going into the city for a low-key weekend."

"Right, right." Wanda bobbed her head up and down. "I know."

"Something tells me that you don't know."

"So what are you going to wear on our big night out? Do you think Lily's will have what you're looking for?"

"Somehow I doubt it," Addie replied.

"What are you talking about? Everybody knows that Lily's Resale Boutique is the premiere clothing shop in Eunice!" Wanda rolled the word *premiere* around in her mouth so that it sounded like *pray-meere.*

Both women were consumed by a fit of giggles. Lily's was nothing more than a thrift store with a fancy name and puffed-up prices, but every once in a while there was a real bargain to be had. Addie had found this out the hard way when she'd tried to donate some of her old winter clothing and had been flatly rejected by the priggish woman behind the counter.

"Seriously," Wanda said as soon as they had calmed down. "What are you going to wear?"

"I don't know," Addie replied with a shrug, searching through a rack of pleated dress pants. "Does it matter?"

Wanda rolled her eyes and grabbed Addie by the arm. "Come on. Let's see if we can find something cute in this godforsaken store."

Addie followed Wanda to the back of the store and through an open doorway. "This is where they keep all the nicer stuff," Wanda said. "You know, the stuff donated by people with money . . . the ones in Jasper's tax bracket."

"Apparently that tax bracket is important," Addie mumbled.

"It is for some people." Wanda shrugged. "My granny used to say that none of us had a pot to piss in. Don't suppose I ever will."

"What?"

"It means I don't have anything worth much."

"You have Bryar."

Wanda grinned and said, "And ain't he worth a million?"

Addie was just about to give up when a dress caught her eye. Addie pulled it off the rack and held it up. It was blue chiffon with a floral print. The dress was short and strapless.

"Oh, Addie, you look great!" Wanda gushed when Addie emerged from the dressing room. "Really, I love it."

"Me too," Addie replied. "I have a pair of blue leather pumps that will match perfect." She winked at her friend. "I know how you feel about heels."

"I do love a good heel."

Addie twirled in front of the mirror. She loved it. She knew what her mother would say if she was there. *I like that, Adelaide. You don't have anything that looks like that.*

"It's a little snug on top," she fretted. "But I don't think it looks too obscene, do you?"

"Of course not." Wanda stared down into Addie's cleavage. "Then again . . . a little obscenity never hurt anybody."

Addie glanced around the room. There were paintings with price tags hanging on the walls. There were baby bows made by locals at a booth at the front. There were several refinished dressers with clothes popping out of them, and they all seemed to have price tags as well. She turned to Wanda and said, "Hey, do you think people sell things on consignment here?"

Wanda wrinkled her brow. "You mean, like, clothes?"

"No." Addie pointed to the paintings behind her friend. "Those paintings are for sale. So are half the pieces of furniture sitting in this store."

"Hey," Wanda hollered up to the woman at the front of the store. "Hey, honey, can you come back here a sec?"

"Well, Wanda Carter," the woman said. "I didn't even see you come in."

"Well, you was hittin' that Burger King wrapper pretty hard, Delores." Wanda smiled. It was a smile Addie hadn't seen. "We have a question for ya."

"Shoot."

"Are them pictures up there on the walls for sale?"

"They are. Why? You looking to redecorate?"

"Maybe."

Delores tapped a pointed red fingernail on one of her hips. "These pictures are pretty expensive, seein' as how they were painted by local artists and all. But the Goodwill is just down the street."

"I was actually wondering if you were taking on any consignments," Addie cut in before Wanda could respond.

Delores eyed Addie. "What's your name, sugar?"

"Adelaide Andrews."

"Oh." Her eyes lit up. "I know who you are. Sure, bring a sample of what you've got by. We're always looking for new talent." She turned and walked back up to the front of the store without another word.

"That woman," Wanda fumed. "She thinks her shit don't stink just 'cuz her daddy bought her this store. He bought her that nose, too, you know."

"I didn't know," Addie replied, trying not to smile. "Forget about her."

"She's hated me since high school," Wanda continued. "I've never been able to figure out why."

"Let's just get out of here." Addie hurried back into the dressing room.

"What on earth do you have to consign, anyway?"

"Nothing yet."

"You thinkin' you might get back into the furniture business?"

Addie shrugged from inside the dressing room. "I don't know. Maybe."

"You thinkin' you might stay here a while?"

"At least until I sell the house."

Wanda followed Addie to the register. "Seems like a waste of time gettin' it all fixed up just to sell."

"I'm not ruling anything out," Addie said. She handed Delores the dress. "But the plan was always to sell."

"My mama's a Realtor." Delores handed Addie a strip of paper. "That's her card. She'd be happy to help you sell that house of yours."

"Thanks."

"Any friend of Jasper's is a friend of ours."

Addie turned and raised an eyebrow at Wanda. This must be more of that small-town nuance that she was still becoming accustomed to. Everyone seemed to think there was something going on between her and Jasper.

"It was nice seeing you, Delores." Wanda smiled that smile again. "Tell that little Joey of yours hello from Bryar. They're such good buddies at school."

Delores went rigid. "Joey isn't mine," she whispered.

"Oh, that's right." Wanda slapped the countertop with her palm. "He belongs to McKenzie, don't he? I'm sorry; I keep forgettin' which one of you Troy married and which one of you gave birth to his illegitimate son. Anyway, you have a nice night."

Addie took the bag from Delores's outstretched hand and said, "Thanks for the card. I'll be sure to give your mom a call."

"I guess I know why Delores doesn't like me much," Wanda said once they were outside. "But damn, sometimes that girl needs to be reminded that it ain't just her nose that's fake."

CHAPTER 22

ADDIE STOOD IN HER KITCHEN STARING DOWN AT FELIX. "I promise I'm only going to be gone one night," she said to him.

"He's going to be fine," Geneva, the dog sitter, replied. "Remember, I come very highly recommended by Dr. Dixon *and* Wanda."

"I know, I know." Addie squatted down to give Felix's head a pat. "It's just that we've never spent a night apart since I got him. I don't want him to think I've abandoned him."

Geneva's eyes crinkled. "Honey, I'm going to keep him so busy that he won't even notice you're gone."

"I appreciate you not thinking I'm a crazy person."

"I have twelve cats and four dogs," Geneva replied. "Between the two of us, I can guarantee that you're not the crazy one."

"And remember, don't give him strawberries. They make him puke. And he likes to have a walk at 7:15 P.M. sharp. And whatever you do, do *not* put the TV on Animal Planet. That channel freaks him out."

"I think you hit all the highlights in the three pages of notes you left," the elderly woman replied. "Now, go on. Scoot."

Addie allowed herself to be pushed out the door. She stood on the porch for a second listening for signs that Felix might be unhappy. Hearing nothing, she walked down the steps and out to her car.

Augustus Smoot was sitting on his porch watching her. She waved at him and said, "How are you today?" Augustus didn't answer. He stood up and walked back inside the house, ignoring her. Addie shrugged and got into her car.

When Addie arrived at Wanda's her friend didn't seem nearly as worried about her son as Addie was about Felix. Wanda gave Bryar a kiss on the cheek and skipped out to Addie's car. Bryar and his nana waved from the window.

"Hey," Wanda said. She slid into the front seat. "Let's get this show on the road!"

"I'm so excited about visiting the city for a couple of days," Addie said. "My aunt used to take me there to the movies sometimes when I came to visit. Sometimes we even went down to the riverfront to the little farmers' market."

"You ought to be able to see the riverfront from where we're staying."

"Where are we staying?"

"In a loft downtown," Wanda said. "It's about eight hundred times nicer than any hotel. And it's free!"

"How is it free?"

"That's a surprise."

"Wanda . . . why is the loft free?"

"Promise you won't be mad?"

"No."

"It belongs to Jasper."

A sick feeling slid all the way down Addie's throat. It sat like a rock in her stomach. Jasper had a loft in Memphis? She assumed his life existed entirely in Eunice.

"Addie? Are you mad?"

"No." Addie shook her head. "I just figured when he moved to Eunice that he . . . you know, actually moved."

"I think he's planning to sell it," Wanda replied. "But the last time I talked to his mom, she said he was still traveling to Memphis quite a lot to manage the firm."

"Will he be there?"

"Nope." Wanda fished around in her purse. "Look, he even gave me a key!"

"Oh, okay."

"It's really beautiful," Wanda said. "I've been there once. Back when I was fighting for custody of Bryar. I mentioned to Jasper that you wanted to go to Memphis for your birthday. I thought he might be able to give me some advice about what to do and where to stay. That's when he offered his place."

"Don't you think it's weird that he just gave you a key and free rein over his home?" Addie asked. "I mean, that's pretty trusting."

Wanda shrugged. "He said he owed you."

"I'm going to pull over at the next gas station," Addie said. Her head was swimming. "You can drive after that."

"Okay," Wanda chirped. "I'm so glad you're not mad."

"Don't be silly." Addie forced a smile. "What could possibly go wrong this weekend?" It was then that she did something she hadn't done in a long time. Without even thinking, she brought her left thumb up to her ring finger to twist her engagement ring—the ring Jonah had given her—the ring she no longer had. It had been an old habit, something she'd done when she was nervous or thinking too hard. Addie felt a lump forming in her throat. There was no ring on her finger. She'd given it back, after all, hadn't she, to Jonah's horrible parents at the funeral.

At the funeral, Addie hadn't been allowed to sit with the family. She sat with her mom and Jerry in the back of the crowded church. When it was her turn to walk to the front to face Jonah's closed casket and his stoic parents, she'd given his mother the last thing he'd ever given her, the thing she held most precious—her engagement ring. Addie hoped it would somehow validate her in their eyes. She'd wanted them to embrace her, to cry with her, to remind her of how much their son had loved her. He'd loved her so much he'd given her a ring. He'd loved her so much he'd died trying to make her happy.

Neither of them even said thank you.

What she felt after the funeral went deeper than death, and she didn't know how to explain it to anyone. Her friends soon tired of calling and begging to see her. After a year, they stopped calling altogether. Her mother began suggesting she go out, get out of her childhood bedroom and meet new people, meet new men. She always refused.

Wouldn't her old friends like to see her now? Wouldn't her mother be thrilled to know that she was headed to Memphis with her friend, *her new friend,* to have a lovely birthday? Tonight there would be no more thoughts of Jonah. There would be no more imaginary ring twisting. There would be no more worrying. *I'm going to have a lovely birthday,* she thought. *I'm going to.*

Jasper's loft was located in the downtown cross section of the

South Bluffs neighborhood and the South Main Arts District. It was a hip and artistic area that Addie was drawn to, and she was excited about being in a city once again.

"So, what do you think?" Wanda asked as the two made their way from the parking garage to the lofts.

"It feels like a city," Addie replied. She took a gulp of air.

Wanda's phone began to ring. "It's Jasper."

"He must be telepathic."

Wanda walked ahead of Addie so that Addie couldn't hear the conversation. When she finally hung up, they were standing in the lobby of the building. "Well, Jasper's here."

"What do you mean he's here?" Addie closed her eyes. She wasn't going to worry. It was fine. It was *fine*.

"I mean he's here. In the building," Wanda replied. "Apparently he's been in Memphis since Thursday finalizing the sale of his law firm. He said he's getting ready to leave, so we'll have the place all to ourselves tonight. But he didn't want us to get to the loft and be surprised when we saw him."

"We'll just be surprised in the lobby instead."

"Well, he didn't know we were already in the lobby."

"How far up?"

"All the way," Wanda replied. "Well, not all the way, but almost. He lives on the ninth floor. The tenth floor is like a rooftop garden with a pool."

"Wow."

"So should we let ourselves in or knock?" Wanda clacked the key into her manicured nails.

"Knock?"

"Oh, all right." Wanda returned the key to her purse. "But I was excited about pretending I lived here."

They exited onto the ninth floor. Something about the sterile white walls of the hallway made her feel like she needed to be quiet. Wanda stopped at the door of 901N and knocked. After a few seconds they heard footsteps and then the rustling of the lock.

Jasper stood in the doorway, one arm propped against the frame. "Hey, y'all."

Addie struggled to keep her jaw from hitting the expensive ceramic tile floor in the hallway. The man standing in front of her sounded like Jasper Floyd, but he sure didn't look like him.

The man standing in front of Addie looked like . . . well, he looked like a lawyer.

In the time that Addie had known Jasper, she had never seen him in anything more formal than muddy boots and jeans. She'd never seen his face without three or four days of stubble. But today was different. Today he was dressed in a blue pinstripe button-down shirt with a white collar and white cuffs. He was wearing a paisley tie that was a darker shade of blue and red suspenders with gray slacks and Italian leather shoes. Addie could see a red sock peeking out underneath one of his pant legs. Everything Jasper was wearing fit as if it had been tailored specifically for his expansive six-foot-four frame.

"I've been in meetings all morning," Jasper said, opening the door so both women could step through. "I really had planned on being out of here by now."

"It's your place. You don't have to apologize to us," Wanda replied.

The loft was every bit as posh as Addie had expected it to be after seeing the way Jasper was dressed. It was exquisitely furnished and very clean—much like the carriage house back in Eunice. Every appliance in the stainless steel kitchen was new, along with the white furniture and carpets in the living room. Modern art hung on the walls, as did one of the largest televisions that Addie had ever seen. The bedrooms were the same, and there were three of them. Jasper led each of them to a bedroom.

Addie sat her overnight bag down on the deep purple bedspread and stood there, taking in her surroundings. She hung up her dress and made her way back into the main part of the loft. Jasper was sitting on a bar stool in the kitchen, a glass of water and a sandwich in front of him. Wanda was beside him, busily screwing the cork out of a bottle of wine.

"Wine?" Addie raised an eyebrow. "It's one o'clock in the afternoon."

"Think we should try something stronger?" Wanda asked. "C'mon, loosen up. It's your birthday."

"Technically, it's not my birthday until tomorrow," Addie reminded her. "But whatever. Pour me a glass."

"Glasses are on the top shelf on the right," Jasper said.

Addie could feel his eyes on her as she turned to open the cabinet door. Standing on her tiptoes, she grabbed at the glasses, her fingers just brushing them.

"Let me help you with that." Jasper was behind her, reaching up. He was pressed so close to her that she could smell the starch on his shirt.

"Thanks."

He grinned at her, and it was all at once infuriating and endearing. "Anytime."

"So are you done for the day?" Wanda asked. She poured the glass to the brim.

"I've got to get to my last meeting." Jasper polished off the last bite of his sandwich. "I'll be out of your way in just a few minutes."

"You're not in our way." Wanda snorted into her wine. "Hey, before you go—can you recommend a nice restaurant for supper? I want to take Addie somewhere fancy."

"Well, I actually have supper reservations just a couple of blocks away from here. At a restaurant called Fish," Jasper replied. "I'm sure we could squeeze you two in at our table . . . that is, if you don't mind having supper with a bunch of lawyers."

"Is it a fancy restaurant?" Wanda asked. "I can't tell with a name like Fish. Who names their restaurant Fish?"

"The specialty is fried catfish, but with a special twist. The chef apparently studied in France."

"Then what does he know about frying catfish?"

"I guess you'll have to find out," Jasper replied.

"Sure," Wanda said. "We'd love to go to your weird restaurant."

Jasper stood up and smoothed the nonexistent wrinkles in his pants. "I'll text you directions. See you around eight?"

"We'll be there."

CHAPTER 23

"How do I look?" Wanda asked. "Be honest."

"I think you've had enough wine for both of us."

"I can hold my liquor."

Wanda could hold her liquor better than just about anyone Addie had ever met. And Wanda really did look great in her lacy green minidress, high-heeled boots, and black leather jacket. "You've got such long legs. I envy you."

Wanda's face broke into a wide grin. "Thanks, sugar. My granny used to say, 'That girl's so tall if she fell down she'd be halfway home.'"

"She's not wrong."

Addie was supple and feminine in her floral dress and pink cardigan. Instead of wearing her hair stick-straight as usual, she had ringlets that cascaded over her shoulders.

"Lose that cardigan," Wanda said as they headed out the door and made their way toward the elevator. "You're not going to church."

"No." Addie clutched the top button. "My boobs are about to come out of this dress."

"That's the point. Besides, even at night Memphis is going to be hotter than a billy goat's ass in a pepper patch."

"Another one from your granny?"

"Of course."

"She was so eloquent."

"Let's get a move on. We're going to be late."

All around them, people were buzzing about their Saturday night activities in the balmy Memphis air—couples with strollers full of children licking ice cream cones, teenagers on dates walking hand in hand, dogs on leashes yapping at passersby.

Memphis was different from Chicago in a way that Addie hadn't expected. There was calm to the rush—as if even the busiest person had time to stop and discuss the weather with a friendly stranger. It was both foreign and beautiful, and Addie drank in the city's southern hospitality.

The restaurant was packed by the time they got there—people were waiting at tables outside, sipping on mixed drinks and talking amongst themselves. "Should we just go in and find them?" Wanda asked. "This place is a madhouse."

Addie walked up to the man standing at the podium who was busily checking names off his list. "Excuse me? Can you tell me if my party is already inside?"

"There's a two-hour wait." The man didn't look up. "Give me your name and I'll put you on the list."

"The name is Jasper Floyd."

"You're with Mr. Floyd?"

"Yes."

"He's been expecting you."

They waded through the sea of people to the back of the restaurant where their group sat in a plush half-moon booth.

There were four men and two women at the booth. Jasper sat on one end and slid out to greet Wanda and Addie as they approached. "I was beginning to think you'd stood me up."

"We lost track of time," Wanda said. "You have an excellent wine selection."

"My wine selection pales in comparison to the wine selection here."

Wanda sat down first, followed by Addie and then Jasper. The booth was a tight fit for all of them. Addie's skin tingled when Jasper brushed against her.

"Addie, Wanda, I'd like you to meet a few of my colleagues," Jasper said. "Well, as of today I suppose I should say former colleagues."

"That's right," a balding man on the other end of the booth replied. "Just remember you have to share with the rest of the partners."

"That's all you've ever cared about, Warren." Jasper grinned. "This is Warren Benson and his partner Neil Alexander."

"I'm not a lawyer," the man beside Warren broke in. "When Jasper says 'partner,' he means 'life partner' and not 'business partner.'"

"Neil also owns this restaurant," Jasper finished.

"It looks like you're doing very well," Addie said. "This place is packed."

"So far, so good."

"And next to Neil is Natalie Rains," Jasper continued.

A slight woman with a blond pixie cut smiled over at Addie and Wanda. "It's nice to meet y'all."

"And next to Natalie is her husband, Dan, and then you all might remember Harper Blake."

"Hello again." Harper's voice was low and gravelly.

Addie squinted at her in the dim light. She was just as gorgeous as she'd looked the first night Addie'd met her. She was wearing a tight, pink tube dress. It sizzled against her copper skin. Harper kept her eyes on Jasper as a nervous waiter buzzed about the booth dispensing drinks.

"Everything is on me tonight, ladies," Neil said to Addie and Wanda. "Drink up!"

"Neil, I have a feeling you and me are going to get along just fine." Wanda's head was buried in the wine menu.

Addie opened her mouth to order her usual, but decided against it. She wanted something sweet. Something colorful. "I'll have a Midori sour, please. Extra cherries."

"Oh, that sounds good," Wanda said. "I'll have that, too."

The waiter nodded and rushed off. Jasper had introduced his friends as couples—Warren and Neil, Natalie and Dan, Harper and Jasper? Addie's heart sank. Every time she convinced herself that it didn't matter—that Jasper didn't matter, he did something that proved her wrong.

"Jasper tells us it's your birthday," Natalie said.

"It is," Addie replied. She was thankful for a break from her thoughts. "Well, technically it's tomorrow."

"And you're from Chicago?"

"Yes. I moved to Eunice a couple of months ago."

"If you don't mind me asking," Warren said, "how in good gravy did you get from Chicago to the Delta?"

"To make a long story short, I inherited a house."

"And what was it that you did in Chicago?" Harper asked.

"I owned an antique wood shop."

Neil leaned forward, his elbows on the table. "That sounds interesting. What kind of wood shop?"

"Furniture, mostly," Addie replied. "We bought from estate sales and auctions. Then we'd refinish and sell them."

"We?"

Addie cleared her throat. "My fiancé and I."

"You have a fiancé back in Chicago?" Harper asked.

"No," Addie said. "Not anymore."

"Let's order some food," Jasper spoke up. "Let Addie catch her breath."

Addie let out a sigh of relief and stared down into the menu. Jasper's hand brushed across her bare thigh. In an instant his touch was gone, but it left Addie struggling to read the words in front of her. She looked up through her eyelashes at Jasper. He wasn't looking at her.

"This is the best thing I've ever tasted," Wanda said, marveling at the Midori sour. "I never even knew this drink existed."

"Wanda's right," Addie said to Neil. "Your bartender knows what he's doing."

"Thanks," Neil replied. "I hope you'll say the same thing about the chef!"

Addie sat back and sipped her drink. Wanda was talking to Natalie about their mutual love for leather pants. Warren and Neil were talking to Jasper and Harper about the law firm. Addie marveled at Jasper's animated expressions. He was relaxed and happy—not at all the person he was at the pumpkin patch weeks earlier. There was no brooding, no talk of his father.

Jasper was comfortable, and Addie was jealous. She wanted to relax. She wanted to sit back and enjoy the atmosphere. Enjoy her birthday dinner. And she wanted to know *this* version of Jasper.

Her thigh still burned from his touch.

The food came, and the group ate in silence, reveling in the thick sauces, tender meat, and generous portions all elegantly served by the staff as Neil watched hawkishly from the booth.

"The food in the South has got to be better than anywhere else in the country," Addie marveled, scraping every last bite from her plate. "I could barely squeeze myself into this dress tonight, and now I feel like I might just burst out of it."

"That's how we like our women down in these parts," Warren said.

"And what would you know about that?" Neil replied. "You got secrets I don't know about?"

Jasper's hand was back on her thigh. And this time there was no mistake. His thumb and forefinger made miniature circles over her skin and Addie was on fire with want.

"Well, I hope you saved room, honey," Neil said, forcing Addie to concentrate, "because we haven't even had dessert yet."

Behind Neil, waiters were wheeling in a three-tiered cake with yellow frosting. The words HAPPY BIRTHDAY were painted across it in pink icing.

"Wow!" Addie exclaimed. "Neil, thank you so much. You didn't have to do this!"

"Don't thank me," Neil replied. "All I did was place the order. It was Jasper's idea."

Addie looked up at Jasper, her face flushed with excitement. "Thank you, Jasper . . . it's . . . it's beautiful."

"Happy birthday." Jasper's hand grasped hers underneath the table.

"I think it's time to sing!" Neil raised his glass. He stood up and lit each one of the candles until all Addie could see were twenty-eight little flames blazing in front of her.

It was almost midnight by the time they spilled out onto the streets of Memphis, full of cake and liquor. Natalie and Dan said their good-byes while Warren and Neil debated the agenda for the rest of the night.

"I'm getting old," Jasper declared, stretching his arms to the sky. "I'm ready to go home."

"Hush up, Jasper Floyd," Neil said. "I'm much older than you are. Why don't we all just go back to your apartment? You've got plenty to drink and a great view."

Jasper hesitated. "Okay, but when I say it's time to go, it's time to go. Got it?" He wagged his finger in front of Neil's face.

"Got it," Neil replied. "Homeward ho!"

"I think I'm going to go home, too." Harper spoke up. "Jasper, could we talk for a second?"

"Why don't you all start back to my place?" Jasper said, turning away from Harper. "Wanda has a key. I'll catch up."

As they trekked back to the loft, Addie tried not to think about what Harper and Jasper were talking about. She hadn't seemed at all pleased with the birthday cake.

"Are you having a good time so far?" Wanda asked. "Because I think I might be having enough fun for the both of us!"

"Of course I'm having a good time," Addie said. "This is the best birthday I've had in a long time. Although I have to admit—

going back and falling into bed does sound pretty damn good right about now."

"No talk of bed!" Warren called out from behind them. "Memphis never sleeps!"

Once inside, Addie took off her shoes and heaved herself down onto the white sofa. It looked more comfortable than it actually was.

Wanda handed her a glass of wine. "This room looks like a doctor's office."

"I wonder who decorated this place."

"Maybe it was Harper."

"You think?"

"I doubt it," Wanda replied.

The front door opened and Jasper entered, followed by Harper. "Where are Warren and Neil?" he asked.

"I think they're out on the balcony." Wanda jerked her thumb toward the far end of the living room.

"Let's get a drink before we join them," Harper said.

"Go on ahead. I've got to get this tie off from around my neck. It's strangling me." Jasper tugged at the knot in his tie.

"Don't do that!" Harper slapped at Jasper's hands. "You're going to ruin it doing that." She reached up and expertly pulled the tie away from Jasper's collar. "You're the only man I know who can tie a tie but can't seem to get one off."

Jasper laughed, and for a moment his head was hunkered so close to Harper's that Addie couldn't hear what they were saying. Addie wasn't sure how she could compete with someone whose legs were as long as her whole body. How could Jasper ever be interested in her next to a woman like that?

"Maybe he's a boob man," Wanda whispered to her. "What's Harper doing here, anyway? I thought she was going home?"

"You just read my mind."

Wanda patted her arm. "Sugar, you gotta be pretty on the inside *and* out. Something tells me Harper looks like she was born downwind from an outhouse on the inside."

Addie giggled. "I have no idea what that means, but it sure does make me feel better."

"What are you two laughing about over there?" Jasper asked. He looked up from his conversation with Harper.

"Nothing," Wanda replied. "Just girl talk." She set down her glass of wine on the coffee table. "If y'all will excuse me, I've got to use the powder room." She wobbled off down the hall in search of the bedroom, leaving Addie alone with Jasper and Harper.

The two sat down on the couch. Harper was still holding Jasper's tie in her hands. "So, Addie," she began, "how do you like the Delta?"

"I like it just fine."

"Must be quite a switch from Chicago."

"It is," Addie replied. "But I visited my aunt down here nearly every summer until I was twelve."

"Jas and I always talked about moving the practice somewhere else, someplace exotic." Harper scooted closer to Jasper. "But the Delta is home, I suppose."

Addie cringed. She hated the way Harper said "Jas" like there was some kind of intimate connection between the two of them—a two-person club that Addie wasn't allowed to join. She glanced around the room for an escape.

"Do you want another glass of wine, Addie?" Jasper stood up. "Addie?"

"Oh, yeah, sure." Addie handed him her empty glass. His fingers clasped around hers, and her heart leapt into her throat. She wondered if he felt it, too. Surely he did—hadn't he been the one to kiss her first? Hadn't it been his hands on her hands . . . on her leg? She shook those thoughts from her head. She hadn't come to Arkansas to meet a farmer. She was leaving, she reminded herself. *Leaving.* None of this was going to last.

"Let's go outside with Warren and Neil," Wanda hollered from the hallway. "I want to see that view!"

"Sounds great," Addie said. She was relieved to have something to look at other than Harper's legs.

"Wow," Wanda said once they were outside.

"Jasper has one of the best views in Memphis," Warren agreed.

"Kinda makes ya feel all kinds of Podunk, huh?" Wanda whispered. "Well, not y'all. Y'all are from a city."

"Not everybody living in a city has a view like this," Addie reminded her. "I'll be right back. I don't think I've been to the bathroom since before we left for dinner." Addie slid the glass door open and stepped back inside the loft. She didn't see Jasper following her until it was too late to turn back around.

"Hey," he said. "Have you had a good birthday?"

"Yes. Thank you so much for everything."

"I'm sorry you ended up spending your night with a bunch of people you didn't know."

"Don't be sorry," Addie replied. "I've had more fun tonight than I've had in a long time."

"Good. I'm glad you liked the cake."

Addie held her breath as she slid past him. Jasper stared down at her for a second and continued on his way toward the kitchen. Just before he disappeared out of view she said, “Hey, Jasper?”

“Yes?”

“Is something going on between you and Harper?”

Jasper turned around. His face was sullen. His shoulders tightened. With one question he’d turned back into the old Jasper. “The only thing that’s ever been between me and Harper is paperwork.”

“You couldn’t even fit paperwork between the two of you on that couch,” Addie replied. She instantly regretted what she’d just said. “Forget it. It’s none of my business.”

“You’re right; it *is* none of your business.” Jasper caught her by the shoulder as she turned away from him. “But for the record, I’m telling you the truth.”

“Why are you so angry?”

Jasper pressed himself farther into her until her back was flat against the wall. His fingers traced along the outline of her face, her neck, and her breasts, before planting his hands firmly on her waist. “This dress is a felony.”

The glass patio door opened and muffled voices began to fill the loft. “Jasper!” Warren called out. “I hope you don’t mind. I called a few friends to come over.”

“I’ve got to go,” Jasper said hoarsely, burying his head into the side of her neck. “Jesus Christ . . .”

Addie traced the stubble on his chin with her fingers, resting her thumb on his bottom lip. With a groan, Jasper pulled himself away from her. Taking her hand, he led her from the dimly lit hallway into the living room where their friends were eagerly waiting.

THE NEXT MORNING Addie awoke to a buzzing in her head like she'd had too many cups of coffee. Wanda was snoring next to her, one hand draped across Addie's midsection. Gingerly, she picked up Wanda's arm and slid out from underneath it.

The tile floor was cool beneath her feet and she shivered as she padded into the main part of the loft. She expected to see a disaster in the living room and kitchen—Warren's friends had made quite a mess. Everything looked exactly the same as it had yesterday when they'd arrived. There were no dirty dishes or empty beer bottles. Even the trash had been taken out of the trash can.

On the island in the kitchen there were two cloth bags with the logo from the market Addie remembered seeing down the street. There was also a carafe of orange juice.

Addie plopped herself down onto one of the bar stools and began to riffle through one of the bags. It looked as if Jasper had bought every breakfast food in the entire store. There was fruit, muffins, bagels, cream cheese, and a plethora of other foods. She pulled out a muffin and poured herself some orange juice.

Jasper was sitting out on the balcony reading the newspaper. He didn't look up when Addie slid open the door and stepped outside. "Good morning," he said.

"The view is just as pretty in the daylight," Addie said. She sat down in the chair beside him. "Memphis seems to be your element."

"I love it here."

"Is that why you've never sold your loft?"

"It may be one of the reasons."

"I thought you were building a house in Eunice," Addie said.

"I'm smart enough to know that I'll likely be there for a while, and I want to have a place to come back to that doesn't belong to my father. You aren't the only one who doesn't want to live in Eunice forever."

"I don't hate it there," Addie replied. "I just never thought about making it my home."

"Memphis is my home," Jasper said. "Eunice . . . the farm . . . that's where I was born. That's likely where I'll die. But it isn't my home."

Addie stared out into the abyss of city traffic. "I wish I felt that way about someplace."

"You didn't feel that way about Chicago?"

"I used to. I always thought that Chicago was the best city in the world," Addie said. "But after Jonah died no place felt like home. I couldn't go any of the places we used to go. I couldn't see any of our friends. It was too painful."

Jasper looked back down at the newspaper and didn't say anything else. For once, Addie was grateful for his silence.

CHAPTER 24

Augustus Smoot was sitting on Addie's porch swing, his bathrobe flapping in the early morning breeze, his bony feet tap, tap, tapping against the newly replaced floorboards. She stared at him through the curtains for ten minutes before she opened the front door and stepped outside. The old man didn't speak, didn't look at her, even after the screen door slammed shut.

"Mr. Smoot?" Addie sat down next to him. "You're at the wrong house."

No response.

"Your house is across the street."

No response.

"Do you have someone I can call for you?"

No response.

"Maybe that lady with the nurse's shoes?"

Augustus's feet stopped tapping. "Your dog barks."

"Most dogs do."

"It keeps me awake."

Addie shifted in the swing. "I'm sorry. He is scared a lot, so he barks."

"What's he got to be scared of?"

"I don't know," Addie replied, shrugging. "When I found him down by the levee, he'd been shot."

Augustus turned to look at her for the first time. He raked a finger through his shock of white hair and said, "You went down to the levee?"

"I know, I know, it's not a good place."

"It's my favorite place."

A laugh escaped through Addie's lips. "Well, everybody else says it's a bad place, but my aunt used to take me there as a kid."

"We had picnics there."

"Who did?"

Augustus looked away from her. "Eleonora and I."

"Was that your wife?" Addie didn't want to pry. Then again, the man was half naked and on her porch.

"You shouldn't go down to the levee."

"But I thought you said it was your favorite place."

"It's not safe there now," Augustus replied.

"Do you know what happened to make it that way?"

When he looked at her again, his expression was grim. "The factories left. The river wasn't a means of transportation anymore. Families left their houses in the middle of the night." Augustus pulled at the ties on his robe. "We lost half the town in a matter of a couple of years. The people left had to find another way to survive."

"So they shoot dogs, stuff them in trash bags, and leave them at the riverbank?" Addie asked. "That doesn't make any sense."

"Sometimes what you see on the surface is just a scratch," Augustus said. "What happened to your dog wasn't the cause." He stood up on his spindly legs. "It was the result."

She watched him walk away. He didn't look back, and he didn't say another word to her. He didn't even wait until he was inside to disrobe, and he strolled up his steps in nothing but his underwear. Addie wasn't sure whether her neighbor was a genius or crazy, but somewhere deep down inside of her, she was dying to find out.

A week later Addie sat in the waiting room at the vet clinic, Felix sitting patiently beside her. She couldn't wait to show Dr. Dixon how far he'd come since his last checkup.

"Addie!" Wanda came out from behind the reception desk to give Felix a pat. "What are you doing here?"

"I have an appointment," Addie said. "I've had this appointment for two weeks."

"I don't have you written down."

"I got the other lady when I called," Addie replied. "I think her name was Mavis . . . or something like that?"

"Mable. She was terrible." Wanda rolled her eyes. "She lasted about three weeks, because she never wrote anything down."

"I thought you were the receptionist."

"I'm the vet tech," Wanda said. "And I would really like to get back to my job of being the vet tech. But we've had trouble finding decent help for the front ever since Mrs. Dixon retired. So I've been stuck answering phones since the beginning of August."

"So does that mean I don't really have an appointment today since Mavis didn't write it down?"

"Mable."

"Whatever."

Wanda jogged back around behind the desk and glanced down at the appointment book. "What it means is that we're overbooked. It's you and Mr. LaFoy at nine thirty. Would you mind to wait until ten?"

"We don't mind." Addie scratched Felix underneath his chin.

"Thanks. Mr. LaFoy does not like to be kept waiting."

Dr. Dixon emerged from behind the double doors. "Wanda, I need you back here for a few minutes. We've got a cat with a toenail grown into its pad. I need your magical cat whispering skills."

"Doc, the phone's been ringing off the hook this morning," Wanda replied. "People get mad when they have to leave a message."

"I could answer the phones for a bit," Addie offered. "Felix and I are just going to be sitting here, anyway."

"Great." Wanda rushed to join Dr. Dixon. "Just come find me if you have any questions."

"Can Felix come back here with me?"

"Whatever you want!" Wanda called over her shoulder.

Addie sat down behind the desk and released Felix from his leash. Felix plopped himself on the floor next to her. Addie began an attempt to make sense of the mess. Six hours later, Addie was still there. "You know," she said to Wanda and Dr. Dixon, "you could make all of this a lot easier if you'd keep track of your records on the computer. There are lots of easy programs that are cost-effective."

"Sounds like you've done this before." Wanda peered over Addie's shoulder.

"I kept track of most of our contacts for the business," Addie replied. "I didn't handle any of the financing, but I did a lot of the PR work, which required me to keep accurate records. People don't like it when they commission you to refinish their eighteenth-century china hutch and you forget they gave it to you."

"We are in bad need of a part-time receptionist," Dr. Dixon said. "Are you interested in coming in a few days a week?"

"I'd love to," Addie began. "But I don't know how long I'm going to be here . . . I mean, I could just help until the end of the summer."

"You turn into a pumpkin at the end of August?" Wanda asked.

"That's when I've planned to head back to Chicago."

"Surely we'll be able to find someone full-time before then." Dr. Dixon shifted his attention to Addie's dog, who was panting eagerly beneath them. "Felix is looking wonderful."

"His mange is clearing up," Addie said, beaming. "And he's still scared of some things, like thunder and that blond guy from *Kitchen Nightmares.* But those are totally normal things to be scared of."

Wanda stifled a giggle. "You mean Gordon Ramsay? Girl, he's terrifying!"

"I think the mange has cleared completely," Dr. Dixon replied. "We'll have to do a scraping to be sure, but we don't have to do that today."

"Yeah, you can bring Felix to work with you," Wanda said.

"Really?"

"Really," Dr. Dixon continued. "And if you don't mind, I'd like to put off any lab work for another day. I'm beat."

"No problem."

"Come on." Wanda motioned for Addie to follow her. "Let's get out of here and go back to my place. I'll feed both you and Felix."

Addie didn't protest. She shut down the computer, grabbed Felix's leash, and followed Wanda out of the clinic.

CHAPTER 25

"So you're tellin' me that Augustus Smoot was just sittin' on your porch swing at six A.M.?" Wanda stood in the doorway of Addie's shed, watching her struggle with an oversized box.

"That's what I'm telling you." Addie huffed. "Can you come over here and help me with this box?"

"Sure thing, sugar."

"Why do you think my aunt had so many horseshoes?" Addie asked. "I mean, what on earth would she need with horseshoes?"

Wanda shrugged. "I don't recollect that she ever owned a horse."

"Judging by half of the things I've found in here, I think she may have been just as crazy as Mr. Smoot."

Wanda hung a horseshoe around her index finger and said, "I thought you said he wasn't crazy."

"I don't know." Addie wiped the sweat from her brow, smearing rust all over her forehead. "He seemed sort of normal, except for, you know, him being on my porch in a bathrobe and underwear."

"At least he had the sense to wear a bathrobe."

The two women giggled.

"So have you talked to Jasper lately?" Wanda asked Addie as she counted horseshoes. "You haven't mentioned him at all."

"Nope, not since Memphis."

"One minute he's all hot and heavy and can't keep his eyes off of you, and another minute he's pretending like you don't exist," Wanda replied.

"I don't understand him at all."

"He's a Floyd."

"What does that mean?"

"It means if he had a ham under both arms he'd cry 'cause he didn't have no bread."

"Did your granny just make this stuff up?"

"That one was my uncle Lawrence."

Addie turned around to check on Bryar and Felix. Bryar had his arm around Felix and was stroking Felix's half ear as he watched the news. "Hey, Bryar! What do you think? Are we really going to have tornadoes on Sunday?"

"It is possible," Bryar replied. "On average, twenty-six tornadoes occur every year in the state of Arkansas. But in 1999, a hundred and seven tornadoes were recorded, which is still the most in state history."

Addie shot a look at Wanda who shrugged and said, "He makes me read to him out of the *Encyclopedia of Arkansas* at bedtime. I bet he's memorized every word of the weather section."

"He's four."

"I'm convinced he's really an eighty-year-old man," Wanda said. "You know, like Benjamin Button."

"Or my crazy sprinkler-dancing, porch-swing-sitting neighbor?"

"Or your neighbor," Wanda said. "Have you talked to him again since the porch-swing incident?"

"I tried," Addie replied. "But he pretends like he doesn't know me. I guess he and Jasper have a lot in common."

"Well, he's not known for being cordial."

"If it turns out that Bryar is secretly Brad Pitt, I can't guarantee you that I won't make a pass at him."

"You've got enough man trouble," Wanda reminded her. "Now, let's get something to eat before Bryar predicts the snowstorm of the century."

"I found a recipe in my aunt's recipe box that I've been wanting to try ever since we got back from Memphis," Addie said. "But I'm not exactly sure I can do it."

"What is it?"

"Hush puppies."

"Girl, those are easy."

"Maybe if you've been cooking your whole life," Addie scoffed. She fiddled with the papers inside the box. She felt silly and incompetent. Everybody down here could cook, it seemed. A pang of envy ran through her body for Wanda's knowledge. What if the way to a man's heart really was through his stomach, as her aunt Tilda always said? What would happen if she gave Jasper Floyd food poisoning? Whatever it was, she figured, it wouldn't be good.

"You want me to show you how to fix them hush puppies?" Wanda interrupted Addie's thoughts. "I promise they're real easy, but if you're ever going to make them for anybody"—she stopped and stared at Addie as if she were reading her mind—"you'll need a main course. Hush puppies are meant to be a side. You know that, right?"

"Of course," Addie replied, although she really hadn't known. "Everybody knows that."

Addie woke up on Sunday to rain. The dull gray of the morning made her want to crawl back under the covers and go back to sleep. She curled herself up around Felix and closed her eyes, relishing the warmth of her bed.

The sound of the phone jarred her out of her cocoon. She sat up and shivered. The phone rang again, and Felix started to bark.

"Calm down, ferocious beast," Addie whispered. Felix ignored her and jumped down from the bed, barking and wagging his tail simultaneously. The phone continued to ring.

She felt around on the nightstand, her eyes still adjusting to the odd light of the room. "Hello?"

"Addie? Is that you? I've been calling you for an hour. I thought you were dead."

"Hi, Mom."

"Why didn't you answer your phone?"

"I guess I didn't hear it."

"Jerry said he heard on the news that Arkansas is getting slammed by tornadoes."

"That's the rumor."

"What's it doing now?"

"Raining."

"You need to go to the store and get some provisions."

"Provisions?" Addie asked. "It's a potential tornado. That's all."

"You're not in Chicago anymore," her mother warned. "You can't just walk to the store down there. It's a rural community. Besides, didn't a tornado take out your kitchen window?"

Addie flopped back down on her bed and rubbed her forehead. "I could get 'provisions' if I needed them, Mom. Civilization doesn't end outside of Chicago. It's not like *Little House on the Prairie* down here."

"You could just walk to the store if you needed to? You wouldn't have to get in that tiny car of yours and drive? Is that what you're telling me?"

"That's what I'm telling you," she said, although Addie knew that wasn't entirely accurate. The nearest store was more like two miles instead of two blocks. "And guess what? We also have indoor plumbing!"

"You've really become quite sarcastic. I'm just trying to help."

"I'm not trying to give you a hard time. I'm just tired, I guess."

"Please go to the store and get a few things," her mother urged. "Just in case you lose power."

"Fine," Addie grumbled. "I'll get up and get dressed and go. Okay?"

"You're still in bed? It's almost noon!"

"Bye, Mom," Addie said. She slid off the bed and wandered over to the window, pulling back the curtains.

Augustus Smoot was outside. Addie worried that he'd be stuck in his house during the storm without anything to eat or drink. Or worse—without any underwear.

Maybe she should just go over and check on him.

He was sitting on the porch when Addie and Felix started across the lawn. He didn't look up from the newspaper he was reading, but as Addie neared the steps he said, "Don't bring that dog up here."

"He isn't going to hurt you. He's a good boy."

"Dogs that look like that are dangerous."

"This dog's not dangerous."

"Leave him just the same."

Addie sighed and said, "Sit, Felix. Stay."

The man folded his newspaper and stared down at Addie. "He listens well."

"He's a good boy."

"He barks a lot."

"You told me so already."

"You sound like a Yankee."

"I'm from Chicago."

"I'm Augustus Smoot."

"I know," Addie replied. "Remember, we had a talk on my porch swing?"

"No."

Addie sighed. So he was crazy after all. "Have you heard that we're supposed to get some bad weather tonight?"

"I have indeed."

All she really wanted to know was if he was going to keep himself inside or if she was going to come home from the store to find him blown into her yard like a half-naked lawn ornament. "I'm going to the grocery store. Is there anything I can bring you just in case the weather turns ugly?"

"Magdalene will be along shortly," he said. "She'll bring provisions."

There was that word again, *provisions.* "Okay, then." Addie wondered if Magdalene was the woman who'd shown up at his house the morning of the storm to coax him inside—the lady with the nurse's shoes. She'd seen the same yellow Neon parked outside of the house before. Maybe she was his girlfriend.

Augustus didn't seem to notice or care when Addie turned around and walked back across the street to her house with Felix on her heels. She glanced around the kitchen, making a mental grocery list. Felix probably needed more food. And she supposed she ought to buy some staples like milk and bread, just in case. Her new wine rack, made from the last of the barn wood and the horseshoes, was almost empty. Now, that was a staple she couldn't do without.

CHAPTER 26

By the time Addie got to the grocery store, the parking lot was packed. People streamed in and out of the building, baskets laden with food and supplies. She'd never seen people make such a fuss. Addie was pleased to find that the most important *provisions* she came for were still in stock—dog food and wine. Smiling to herself, she began to load her cart.

"Hey, Miss Addie." Bobby Carter greeted her from one end of the dog food aisle. "How you doin' today?"

"Hey, Bobby," Addie replied. "I'm great. Just trying to prepare for the storm. Last time I got a tree through my window. I'm a little nervous."

"Well, maybe some of that work we did will hold up."

"I'm sure it will. Thanks so much for your help."

Bobby pushed his cart closer to Addie. "Could I ask you a favor?"

"Sure."

"Can I use you as a reference? For a job?"

"Of course you can," Addie said. "What job?"

"There's a trucking company in Mississippi. I could drive one of their trucks till I get up the money to fix my truck. Get me outta town for a while, too."

"Okay. Let me give you my number."

"I already got it from Wanda. I hope that's all right. Maybe you could just tell 'em that I'm reliable?"

"You already bored with all that Eunice has to offer?"

"Nah." Bobby gave her his throaty chuckle. "But I ain't used to spendin' so much time here. A week on and a week off. That's what life I been livin'."

"I thought you were working for Redd Jones."

"Not much work to be had."

"You could be his maid," Addie said with a grin. "Lots of work to be done inside that house of his."

"I ain't got the gumption for that."

"What does he do, anyway?" Addie asked. "I mean, for money?"

"Just takes care of things around the neighborhood."

"What does he take care of?"

"People around here ain't got a lot, but Redd makes sure they got enough to survive."

"When you put it like that, it sounds nice," Addie replied. "But something tells me that Redd's not nice."

Bobby scratched behind his neck. "I've known Redd since we was kids, but we just ain't got the same kind of mind for things, that's all."

"I think that might be a good thing."

"He ain't all bad," Bobby said. "People don't want to come down to those parts anymore. Don't want to look at the ugly part of town. They ain't got no one else to rely on."

"Maybe that's how Redd likes it."

"You may be right about that, Miss Addie." Bobby grinned broadly at her, displaying a row of crooked teeth. "I best be gettin' home. It was nice talkin' at ya."

Addie watched him turn the corner. Bobby was so decent, so caring. How could he get mixed up with a man like Redd Jones? She knew Wanda wasn't at all happy about Bobby living with Redd, and there must be a reason other than the fact that he lived on the wrong side of town. Addie was lost in a deluge of her own thoughts until another familiar voice broke through them.

"It looks like you're planning for a wild evening."

She knew who it was even before she turned around. "It figures that I'd run into half the people I know in this town at the grocery store."

Jasper Floyd grinned at her. "What on earth are you going to do with a month's supply of dog kibble and alcohol?"

"I'm preparing for the zombie apocalypse," Addie replied. "Isn't it obvious?"

"And to think the rest of the town is stocking up on candles and jugs of water."

"I don't have time to educate everybody."

"Is that really all you're going to buy? What if you lose power?"

"I'll drink."

"What if another tree slams through your window?"

"I'll drink some more."

"Eunice is tornado alley. You really ought to take this seriously."

Addie leaned up against her cart and crossed her arms over her chest. "Are you and my mother conspiring with each other?"

"Maybe being without power for an hour or two is no big deal," Jasper said. "But around here people aren't so quick to respond. If you lose power, you'll be lucky to have it back in a day or two. Real lucky."

Addie bit the bottom of her lip.

"You're not in the city anymore, Toto. Come on. I'll help you get what you need."

"Fine," Addie relented. "But I'm keeping my cart full of dog food and wine."

"Whatever you want," Jasper said. He grasped the handle of her cart. His hand brushed up against hers, and Addie's stomach did a flip-flop. "You look like a crazy person."

"I wouldn't be the only one on my block."

"True."

"And how do you think it makes you look to be seen with the crazy person?"

"There's nothing that can be said about me that hasn't already been said."

"I bet I could think of a few things."

Jasper stepped in front of her, and Addie slammed into his knees with the cart. "Listen, I'm sorry about Memphis."

"You don't have anything to be sorry about."

"Yes, I do," Jasper continued. "It was supposed to be your weekend. And it turned into an entire evening spent with me and my friends. I wasn't even supposed to be there."

"I'm glad you were there."

"You don't wish anything about that weekend had been different?"

"Well, I do wish that the cake had been chocolate instead of vanilla," Addie replied. "But other than that"—she met his gaze—"I don't regret anything."

Jasper seemed to accept this response, and soldiered on. It became increasingly clear that he knew everyone at the grocery store—probably in the whole town. Addie counted fifteen times that they had to stop and chat with someone, and each time she was met with a questioning look and a sweet southern smile. Jasper pretended not to notice, and people were too polite to ask. By the time they emerged from the grocery store, the rain was coming down in sheets. Groaning, Addie fished around in her pocket for her keys.

"There is no way you're going to make it home in that skateboard with a motor," Jasper said.

"I'll be fine," Addie replied. "It's just a little bit of rain."

"You told me in the store that your windshield wipers didn't even work."

"I hate to drive in this stuff. In Chicago, I walked or took the El whenever the weather turned ugly."

Jasper threw Addie the keys to the Bronco. "Run on to the car and get in. I'll load up the groceries."

Addie did as she was told. The rain was coming down slanted, and she was reminded of a conversation she'd had with Bryar. So far, his weather predictions had not been wrong, and he'd told her that slanted rain meant tornadoes.

"I don't know how it can be raining like this and still be sweltering outside," Addie said when Jasper jumped into the driver's seat minutes later.

"That's part of the Delta's charm," Jasper replied.

"You look like you've been swimming," Addie said. She reached out and brushed his sopping hair out of his eyes before she could stop herself.

"It's your fault."

Addie's eyes locked with his and her pulse quickened. She wanted to look away, but she couldn't. Every time he was close to her she couldn't think of anything other than touching him. She hated it. It wasn't until Jasper started the car that he looked away from her.

The drive home was quiet. All along the road cars were pulled over, waiting out the storm. When they got to her house, Addie found Felix and let him out into the backyard while Jasper unloaded the Bronco. Felix ran around licking at the rain and sliding in the mud. He looked happier than he'd ever been.

"That's the last of it," Jasper said, heaving two fistfuls of plastic bags onto Addie's kitchen table. "You know, you should really use recyclable bags."

"This coming from the man who drives a tractor to community events. What's that thing get? Five miles to the gallon?" Addie smirked at him.

"Your senseless dog is in the backyard rolling around in the water."

"I guess I'm going to have to go outside and get him." Addie sighed, pulling on her rain boots. "Unless, of course, you wanted to drive your tractor out there?"

Felix was on the opposite side of the yard, ignoring her pleas for him to come to her. "Don't make me come get you," Addie warned. As she spoke, one of her feet slipped out from under her and she fell backward onto the soggy grass.

Behind her, Jasper guffawed. Addie heard him sloshing over to where she lay staring up at the gray sky, droplets of slanted rain stinging her cheeks. "Need a hand?"

Felix bounded over to the two of them. "Some friend you are," Addie grumbled to Felix, allowing Jasper to pull her up. She trudged inside and headed toward her bedroom to change out of her wet clothes. "Why don't you stay for a while?" she called out over her shoulder. For a moment, she cringed, realizing how hopeful she probably sounded. *Screw that,* she thought. *I am hopeful.* Besides, he was the one who'd offered to drive her home, anyway.

"I'm pretty sure the low-water bridge close to the house is washed out, anyway." Jasper was standing in front of her refrigerator, staring intently inside. "There sure is a lot of food in here for one person." He turned around to stare at Addie, who was rushing toward him, one arm still outside of her T-shirt.

"What do you need in there?" Addie asked, red-faced. She put herself between him and the fridge.

"Did I see two bowls full of mashed potatoes?" Jasper asked, looking over her head. "And collard greens? And hush puppies?"

"Maybe."

"Lord, Adelaide. What else have you got in there?"

"I think you've about got it covered."

"Did you have a dinner party or something?"

"No," Addie said. She slunk away from the refrigerator, tugging at her shirt. "I was practicing."

"For what? The invasion of Paula Deen?"

Addie avoided his stare. *For you,* she wanted to say. It sounded so ridiculous inside of her head. It was the twenty-first century. Women didn't do that anymore, did they? She eyed her aunt's recipe box, perched precariously on the edge of the counter by the stove. Maybe some women did. "Feminism is about choices," she mumbled.

"What?" Jasper was giving her his full attention now, the refrigerator and its contents forgotten. "What are you talking about?"

Addie sighed. There was no avoiding it now. "My aunt left me her recipe box. I've been practicing my cooking." She sat down at the table. "I'm not very good at it."

"Oh, I don't know about that," Jasper replied. His eyes were dancing. "Those pies you made were pretty tasty."

"That's a lie," Addie said, not looking at him. "I tasted them myself."

"Well, they weren't awful," Jasper relented. "What did you make to go with the mashed potatoes and the collard greens?"

"Nothing."

"Nothing?"

Addie wished she could disappear. "I haven't worked up to main courses yet."

This time Jasper couldn't keep from laughing, and it was contagious. Addie began laughing, too, and pretty soon they were both laughing so hard that tears were rolling down their cheeks.

Twenty minutes later, Jasper stood hunched over her stove, stirring something that was beginning to smell delicious. "This would be working out a lot better if you had a cast-iron skillet."

"You're lucky I own any skillet at all," Addie replied. "But I think I have one of my aunt's in a box in the closet. I thought it was junk because it was so gross-looking. What are you cooking?"

"I'm attempting to fry chicken, and we can use some of that gravy you said you made this morning."

"Really?" Addie was impressed. She made a mental note to dig out the cast-iron skillet as soon as Jasper left.

"You sound surprised," Jasper replied. "I'm not always the brooding jackass groping women in my hallway, you know."

"Ah, so you do remember that." Addie sat down at the table and took a sip of wine. "I was starting to wonder."

"Of course I remember."

"You can see how I might be confused."

"I felt guilty about it. I guess I still do."

"Why?"

"Considering what happened in Chicago. The whole reason you're here."

"I don't remember saying that's the reason I'm here."

"I didn't want you to think I was trying to take advantage of you," Jasper said. "Of your vulnerability."

"I definitely do not remember saying I was vulnerable."

"It goes with the territory."

"Of what? Of being the damaged ex-fiancée of a dead furniture dealer?"

"Something like that."

"Jasper, what happened was horrible. It was worse than horrible. I swear there were days when I thought I was going to die, too. But I didn't come here to be reminded of what happened."

"Why did you come here?" Jasper asked. "Lord knows it wasn't to stay."

"You're one to talk about staying," Addie shot back. "You're only here because you feel obligated. You're tied to this place, just like me."

"At least I know why I'm here," Jasper pressed. "Do you know why you're here?"

Addie shrugged. She didn't know the answer to that question. She knew she could have sold the house and everything that came with it without actually *moving* to Eunice. "I needed a change. I needed something that wasn't Chicago, and something that isn't stained with the memory of Jonah. I know he'd want me to move on, but I can't do that in a town that has his name written all over it."

"Well, I can tell you one thing about this house," Jasper said. "It could use a little work."

"Couldn't we all?" Addie muttered. "Couldn't we all?"

CHAPTER 27

"THAT WAS WONDERFUL." ADDIE LEANED BACK IN HER CHAIR. "Where did you learn to cook like that?"

"It's something I've always been able to do," Jasper said. "Much to my father's dismay, I spent a lot of time in the kitchen with my mother as a child. Fried chicken was one of the first things she taught me. It's a staple in any proper southern household."

"You're an only child?"

"Yes. My parents were both in their thirties before they had me. They never thought they'd have any children, I guess."

"So you were spoiled rotten."

"Hardly." Jasper stood up and took Addie's plate. "Rotten, yes. Spoiled, no."

"Here, let me do that." Addie jumped up and took the plates out of Jasper's hands. "Sit down." She walked over to the sink, scraping the remainder of Jasper's plate into Felix's bowl. "So, you and your dad . . . you don't get along very well?"

"That's an understatement," Jasper muttered. "But we don't really speak much, so I guess an argument could be made that we get along just fine as long as nobody talks."

"I always wondered what it would be like to have a father growing up. My mom was great, but she worked all the time trying to support us."

"Us?"

"Herself and me. She didn't meet my stepfather, Jerry, until I was in college. They've just been married a few months."

"It must be difficult being away from your mom. I mean, since it was just the two of you for so long."

Addie shifted her weight from one foot to the other, trying to decide how to respond. "It is. But at the same time, I think it's been good for my mother. After what happened . . . after—after I lost Jonah, I think she was afraid to be happy because she thought it would upset me. With me all the way down here, she's finally able to have a life without worrying that she's throwing it in my face."

"Is that why you left?"

"Maybe."

Jasper stood up. "I guess I should probably get on home. It looks like it's letting up, and I don't think you need to worry too much about losing power."

"Okay." Addie dried her hands with a dish towel. "Thanks for the ride, and thanks for dinner."

"Anytime," Jasper said, opening the door. "You want me to go ahead and take you back to your car now?"

Before Addie could respond, a gust of wind shot through the kitchen, and Addie shuddered. "Oh, wait, you forgot your hat." She ran into the living room.

"Is that coatrack some of that old barn wood?" Jasper asked.

Addie pulled his hat off one of the old doorknobs. "Yes, so is the wine rack with the horseshoes in the kitchen."

"That's amazing," Jasper marveled. "You made these?"

"I did." Addie nodded. "And I don't know if you noticed, but the kitchen table and chairs are the same ones you thought were trash the first time you were here."

"I hadn't noticed," Jasper admitted. "But I'm noticing now." He walked back into the kitchen, placing his hands on the back of one of the chairs. "I've never met anyone who could make something most people would throw away so beautiful."

"Thank you." Addie was beaming. It had been a long time since anyone had praised her for her work. It had been a long time since she'd created anything for anyone to praise. "It's my catharsis, you know?"

"It's raw talent, that's what it is." Jasper reached for his hat, accidentally catching part of her shirt, his hand brushing against her naked stomach. Goose bumps pricked up on her skin. Instead of pulling away from her, he let his hand wander around her stomach to the small of her back.

It was too much.

Jasper lifted her up onto the table, pushing her legs apart with his torso. His hands slid up her shirt, pulling her closer to him until she couldn't breathe without feeling his chest against hers. "Tell me you want me," he growled. "Tell me you want me to stay."

Addie couldn't think. Her entire body was on fire. Finally, she found the word she'd been searching for.

"Stay."

As Addie slid off the table, Jasper hooked his thumbs down

into the waistband of her pants and pulled them down to find she wasn't wearing any underwear. "Christ," he mumbled into her ear. "I can't control myself around you." He placed one hand on her bare hip, and his other hand grazed her buttocks and found its way to the inside of her thigh. "I can't think," he rasped.

Addie unhooked his belt as he fumbled with his shirt. She reached out and wrapped her fingers around the length of his excitement.

Jasper moaned at her touch and launched himself forward, until she was lying flat on the table. Lifting up her camisole, he placed his mouth around one of her nipples. He bit down, and she writhed beneath him.

"Please," she begged him. "Please. I can't stand it."

He placed his mouth over hers and then without any warning, thrust himself into her. She wrapped her legs tightly around him, raising her hips to meet his rhythm. His eyes were open, watching her as he moved inside her body. She writhed beneath him, but he whispered to her, "Be patient, just be patient."

Addie could hear her own heartbeat. She could hear Jasper's heartbeat. His hands were gripping the table so tightly that she feared he would get splinters as he found his release. And then for a moment, everything was quiet.

THE RAIN CONTINUED as a slow drizzle. Addie could hear it coming down outside, and she shifted in bed, prompting Jasper awake beside her. She still couldn't believe he was here with her. Felix had been slighted to find him in his place, but had warmed quickly when Jasper invited him up, allowing the dog to curl up at his feet.

"Are you still awake?" Jasper asked. "How long have I been out?"

Addie grinned at him in the darkness as his fingers traced along her spine. "Not long. I'm sorry I woke you."

"No, don't be sorry. I'm glad I'm awake. I love to listen to the rain."

"You do?"

"It's better on a tin roof," he replied. "But I guess this will do."

"Rain makes me nervous," Addie said. She scooted closer to Jasper.

"How come?"

"I don't know," Addie admitted. "Just seems like bad things always happen when it rains."

"The tree limb through the window was a freak accident." Jasper stroked her hair.

"It's not just that."

"What do you mean?"

Addie was regretting this line of conversation. She didn't want to talk about the rain or the bad things that happened in it. She wanted to lie here next to Jasper Floyd, in all his naked glory, and pretend like they were the only two people in the world. Damn rain.

"Addie?" Jasper pried himself away from her. "Why don't you like the rain? Does it have anything to do with"—he paused—"Jonah?"

Addie cringed. She didn't like hearing Jonah's name coming out of Jasper's mouth. It felt wrong. "It's nothing," she said. "Forget about it."

"I don't want to forget about it."

She couldn't see him in the dark, but she knew he was staring at her. She knew she was going to have to tell him. She took a deep breath and said, "Jonah died in the rain. I mean, he died in a car accident, but it was raining."

"I'm so sorry."

"We had a fight," she went on. "I was running late, and we fought. I told him to go without me and he did."

"Where was he going?"

"We were supposed to be getting married in two months. It was our last meeting with the caterer. The food was so important; I guess that's maybe a bit of my aunt Tilda in me, to be so obsessed with food." Addie squeezed her eyes shut. "Jonah didn't understand, but he was so kind about it, even when I picked a caterer an hour away. God, I was so stupid."

When Jasper didn't say anything, she continued, "The roads were slick. It was cold," Addie replied. She fought the tears threatening to flood the space between them. "He was angry. He was driving twenty above the speed limit. He died on impact, and it was my fault."

"Adelaide, it wasn't your fault."

"It was." She couldn't hold back the tears any longer. "It was my fault, and it was for nothing. He died for no reason at all, and I'll never forgive myself."

"Don't say that," Jasper whispered, pulling her close to him. "There's nothing you could have done. Nothing you could have said. Blaming yourself won't bring him back."

Addie didn't say anything. She couldn't say what she wanted to say. She couldn't say out loud that if Jonah hadn't died she wouldn't be here with Jasper, and that the only place she wanted to be was here beside him. The guilt of it all kept her mouth stitched shut. The guilt of it all kept the space between them real and fluid, an ocean of feelings she couldn't explain.

Addie awoke the next morning to sunlight streaming through the windows of her bedroom. She opened her eyes and saw that Jasper was still asleep next to her. She thought about reaching out and touching him, but was afraid that she would wake him and prompt an awkward morning-after-sex conversation that she wasn't sure she was ready to have.

She instead rolled over and glanced at her alarm clock. It was 7:40 A.M.

"Oh, shit!" Addie shrieked, shooting up in the bed like a rocket. "Shit, shit, shit!"

Beside her Jasper stirred. "What?"

"Shit!" Addie said again, this time jumping out of bed. "I forgot to set my alarm!"

"What?"

"I have to work today. It's my first day at the clinic. I can't believe I'm going to be late on my first day!"

"I'm sorry; I'm not really awake yet." Jasper rubbed his eyes. "You have to what?"

Addie rummaged through her dresser for a pair of panties. She found a pair and plopped herself back down on the bed, jamming her legs into them.

"Calm down. You just live five minutes away from there." He glanced down at her underwear and said, "I like those, by the way."

Addie stood up and hurried over to her closet. "But my car is in a parking lot clear on the other side of town, remember?"

"Oh, yeah."

"Do you think you could just take me to the clinic? I can have Wanda take me to get my car later."

Jasper turned away from her, pulling on his pants. He walked past Addie and to the foot of the bed where his shirt lay. He didn't respond.

"Well?"

"What?"

"Can you take me to the clinic?"

"Do you think you could give Wanda a call? You aren't the only one running late."

"Jasper, I've got fifteen minutes to get there, and I haven't even brushed my teeth yet. Why can't you just take me to work?"

"I just have so much to do at the farm. I was gone all night and didn't tell anyone."

Addie narrowed her eyes at him. He wasn't looking at her. And he was standing in the doorway like he was ready to bolt. Why didn't he want to take her to the clinic?

"It's not like I'm asking for a kidney," Addie said. "What's your problem?"

"I know, I know." Jasper shoved his hands down into his pockets. "It's just Doc is good friends with my parents. If he sees me dropping you off, he might get the wrong idea. And I really need to be getting back."

"The wrong idea?" Addie could feel the color rising in her cheeks. She was furious. "Oh, you mean he might think that we spent the night together?"

"That's not what I meant."

"I know exactly what you meant," Addie hissed. "Just leave. I'll call Wanda to come and get me."

"Addie, you're overreacting." Jasper stepped toward her.

"You didn't seem to mind yesterday, pushing my shopping cart all over the place like it was your goddamn civic duty."

Addie recoiled from his grasp. "But I guess everything's different now, huh?"

"Please. Please don't do this."

"I'm sure you'd have no problem giving Harper a ride." Addie glared at him from across the room. "I should have known better than to believe there was nothing going on between the two of you."

"I don't know what you're talking about, Addie." Jasper reached out for her. "I wasn't lying to you. This has nothing to do with Harper."

"I can't believe I told you everything," Addie said, more to herself than to Jasper. "Get out of my house."

"I don't understand why you're making such a big deal out of nothing."

"That's what this is. Nothing."

"Addie, stop it."

"Get out."

Addie followed behind him to the front door. She watched as the Bronco sped away from the curb. She tore her eyes away from the empty street and found that Augustus Smoot was watching her from his porch. He stood shirtless, peeping through the crack in the door like a child. One hand was pressed into the screen. The flimsy aluminum had begun to bow beneath the weight until his hand burst through. Augustus pulled his hand out of the screen and turned to walk back inside his house. And with that, Addie's rage melted into a puddle at her feet, leaving behind nothing but an all-too-familiar numbness.

CHAPTER 28

THE SUMMER STORMS DID NOTHING FOR THE DELTA HEAT except make everything sticky. There was a film over skin, cars, door handles. People seemed to be leaving pieces of themselves behind with every touch.

Those sticky days melted into one another, and Addie found herself dividing her time between her job at the clinic and fixing up the house. She liked the routine of seeing people all day at the clinic and coming home to Felix on the days that she didn't take him with her. In Chicago, there had always been someone at the apartment she shared with Jonah. There were always clients calling for updates about the pieces they'd left to be refinished or clients calling about pieces they wanted to buy. People talk, there always seemed to be people talking. She didn't mind Felix needing her. His language was one she understood even better than her own. For the first time in her life, Addie was content to keep to herself. Besides, the shed out back kept her busy enough for three people.

One evening she ventured out to the backyard, pockets full of dryer sheets, to take a look in the shed. There was a dresser in the back that she'd been eyeing, but it was so heavy that she wasn't confident that she could carry it into the house without help. The dresser was old, even by Addie's standards. It was, as Jonah would have described it, provincial. French, probably, she mused, because of the cabriole legs and scalloped carvings on the drawers. *See, Jonah, I remember things,* Addie thought. *I listened to you.* Years of paint and dust mingled together to make the dresser the color of chalk. She took her finger and grazed the top. She laid her palm flat against it. Even in the twilight, Addie could tell that it would be a lot of work to restore this one. It wouldn't be fun like her repurposed treasures; she'd need to go back to the hardware store for more supplies, and she'd need to bribe Wanda to come help her haul it inside the house. *But maybe,* she thought, *maybe it's still alive under there. Maybe I can find its heartbeat.*

At the clinic, Addie had managed to organize all the clinic's clients and vet records into two electronic files that were easy to locate and use. And for that, Addie had earned the everlasting gratitude of Dr. Dixon. She even found herself at the clinic on her days off, teaching the rest of the staff how to use the system she'd put into place.

Life was altogether slow.

"What do you reckon it'd take for the editor of the *Eunice Daily* to publish an article that isn't about the heat?" Wanda asked. She crinkled the newspaper between her fists. "Does he think we don't *know* that it's hot outside? Like we need someone to be telling us?"

"Doc is going to get you if you rumple that newspaper."

"He can afford to buy another one." Wanda rolled her eyes. "Besides, this isn't 1980. What kind of business doesn't have Internet? This place is a dead zone!"

"People like you are the reason newspapers are going out of business." Addie yawned and stretched back in her chair, accidentally kicking Felix. "Why don't you at least read something interesting like the arrest record or the personal ads?"

"The personals depress me," Wanda replied. "And so does the arrest record. I know too many of the people."

"There's got to be something more interesting than another editorial about the damn heat."

"Let's look at the for sale section. I need a new refrigerator." Wanda skimmed through the page. "Slim pickin's today. Somebody sellin' a tractor motor, somebody sellin' some hogs, somebody wantin' to trade puppies for guns, somebody lookin' to buy a mattress . . ."

"Wait, go back," Addie said.

"To which one?"

"The one about guns and puppies."

"It says, 'For sale or trade: American pit bull terrier pups. Twelve weeks. No papers. Several good prospects, all show gameness. Black and white. Good markings. Will come with one month of supplements. Trade for guns or a few nice springpoles. Will sell for $300 cash.'"

"What's a springpole?" Addie asked. She'd heard the other words before. They'd been in the papers inside Redd Jones's nightstand. She'd meant to look them up, but she'd gotten so distracted by Jasper. She'd forgotten about everything but him for a while.

"Beats me."

"Doesn't that seem a little crude?" Addie asked. "To trade dogs for guns?"

"You can trade anything for anything."

"Is there a number to call?"

Wanda looked up at Addie from behind the newspaper. "Are you going to call it?"

"It sounds like they look like Felix."

"Who looks like Felix?" Dr. Dixon asked, walking into the reception area. He smiled over at them. "Wanda, don't wrinkle my newspaper. You do it every darn day."

"There's an ad in the newspaper. Somebody's got a bunch of pit bull puppies," Wanda replied.

"They want to trade them for guns," Addie said. She wrinkled her nose. "Or a . . . what's it called?"

"A springpole," Wanda finished.

"Yeah, a springpole. What is that?"

"It's a pole that has a spring hanging down that's tied to a rope. It allows the dogs to jump for long periods of time," Dr. Dixon said.

"Why would you want to do that?" Addie asked.

"It strengthens the jaw muscles and back legs. Let me see that ad."

Wanda handed the newspaper over to Dr. Dixon. By the time he finished reading, his facial muscles were tense. He wasn't smiling. "I don't think you're going to want to buy one of these puppies."

"Why not?"

"Just promise me you won't call any numbers for now." He folded the newspaper under his arm.

"Hey," Wanda said. "I wasn't done reading that."

"You're done for today," Dr. Dixon replied. "Now, both of you—promise me."

"Fine, fine." Wanda threw up her hands in defeat. "I promise."

"Addie?"

Addie stared down at her feet. At Felix. She didn't want to promise anything. She had a hunch who those puppies belonged to, and she had a hunch Dr. Dixon knew it, too. There was a reason nobody wanted her on that side of town, and that reason was Redd Jones. "I promise not to call any numbers."

"Now you two girls get back to work."

"What in tarnation do you think that was all about?" Wanda asked as soon as Dr. Dixon was out of earshot. "Sometimes I wonder who that man thinks he is ordering me around like that."

"He's our boss right now," Addie replied. "But he's not our boss when we leave this clinic."

"We both promised him we wouldn't pry," Wanda said.

"No, I promised him I wouldn't be calling any numbers," Addie reminded her friend. "I didn't say I promised not to pry."

It seemed to Addie that the best way to make sure that she never ran into Jasper was to never go out in public. However, as the days counted down to the end of the summer, she began to wonder if he'd picked up and moved back to Memphis. No trip to the store or walks with Felix or even a lunch with Wanda down at Jennie's Joint produced the slightest hint of Jasper Floyd. Addie's anger was beginning to fade into a kind of curiosity that she couldn't shake.

"Just twenty-two more days until fall," her mother chirped into the phone. "Have you started pulling out your sweaters yet?"

"Mom, it's hardly September," Addie said, twirling a strand of blond hair through her fingers. "We're just lucky nobody has died of heatstroke this week."

"We?" her mother asked. "Sounds like you're feeling pretty familiar down there. Didn't you say you'd be home by the end of August?"

"The house isn't ready yet."

"Is that the only reason?"

"Yes, Mom."

Addie's mother sighed into the receiver. "I just thought cooler weather put you in a better mood."

"I'm in a fine mood."

"Obviously," her mother replied sarcastically. "Do you want to talk about it?"

"No."

"Does it have anything to do with that farmer you told me about?"

"It didn't work out, Mom."

"Oh, honey. I'm sorry."

"It's okay. I just don't want to talk about it."

"Adelaide, why don't you come home for a few weeks? We'd love to see you. Jerry and I miss you."

"I miss you, too," Addie said. "But I need to stay here, at least for a little while."

Addie sat down on the couch and absently rubbed Felix's head, thinking about her mother's excitement that Addie might have met someone, even if that meant staying in the Delta longer than either of them had anticipated. It reminded her of the last summer she spent with her aunt. It was the longest she'd ever been away from Chicago—a whole month. She had been twelve that visit and hadn't been particularly interested in leaving the buzz of the city for the pastures of Eunice. That visit her aunt had seemed older—less excited about things and more willing to let Addie be on her own during the heat of the day.

One morning Aunt Tilda woke Addie early, before it was even light outside. "Adelaide, my love," her aunt had cooed. "Get up, angel. I need your help."

Addie sat up in bed. "What? Why are you waking me up so early?"

"You know Ms. Rubina down the street, don't you?" Aunt Tilda said, pulling back the covers of Addie's bed. "Well, her brother is in town for a week. And Ms. Rubina is very old—much older than me." Her aunt paused to chuckle at her own remark. "I'm going to cook enough dinners for them to have for the whole time her brother is here. And I need your help."

"But I don't know how to cook," Addie protested.

"You won't have to do anything but be my assistant for the day," Aunt Tilda promised her. "Now get up. There is no time to dawdle."

Addie spent the rest of the day doing her aunt's bidding as her aunt slaved away over the kitchen stove. Addie remembered the entire kitchen table full of casseroles and, of course, her aunt Tilda's famous fried pies. By the time they finished, the last minutes of daylight were fading from the sky as Addie and her aunt loaded up Addie's red Radio Flyer wagon with a week's worth of food.

Addie remembered the way her aunt had smoothed out the nonexistent wrinkles in her dress before she rang the doorbell at Ms. Rubina's house. "You just smile and be sweet," her aunt whispered to her. "We won't be here long."

A man answered the door instead of Ms. Rubina. He was

well-dressed and older than her aunt. When he spoke, his voice was thick as molasses and drowning in a southern accent. "Why, Tilda Andrews!" he exclaimed. When he said her name, it came out more like *Tilduh*. "I haven't seen you in *forevuh*."

"Hello, Zeke." There was a chill in her aunt's voice. "Rubina told me you were visiting. She's too old for you to be imposing on her like this."

"And I'm too old for you to be scolding," Zeke replied. His voice was firm, but he was smiling. "Now who do we have *he-uh*?"

"This is my great-niece, Adelaide," Aunt Tilda said. "She's visiting from up North."

"Your people in Chicago?" he asked Addie.

"Yes."

"I have known your aunt since she wasn't much older than you. You sure do carry after her."

"How come I've never met you before?" Addie asked.

Before Zeke could answer, Addie's aunt stepped in front of her and said, "Out front there's a wagon loaded with food for the week. No reason for your sister to have to be on her feet cookin' for you."

"I thought maybe I'd call on you one day this week."

"I don't reckon that will be necessary. Don't forget about the food. I'll come back for my wagon."

Aunt Tilda held Addie's hand more tightly on the way home. When they walked through the front door, her aunt said she was tired and went to her room. She didn't come out even at suppertime, even after Addie knocked. She could have sworn she heard her aunt crying in her bedroom that night, but Addie had been too young then to understand. She had been too young to know that her aunt Tilda's tears would be the start of something building up inside of her own soul that night, a pride passed down from generation to generation among Andrews women. And Addie would be left the lone survivor, the gatekeeper to this house, this pride, this ache, the night that her aunt was finally set free in death.

CHAPTER 29

Addie groaned when she saw the beat-up red truck pull into the parking lot at the clinic just as she was about to turn the sign to closed. She stepped away from the door and moved back behind the counter.

"I know it's about closin' time."

"It's all right. What can we do for you?"

The man pointed out to his truck. "One of my dogs is sick. Real sick. He won't even get up to eat."

"How long's he been that way?" Addie asked.

"A couple of days."

"Did something happen to him?"

"Dunno."

"Can you carry him in? I'll go tell Doc. Just bring him on through those double doors behind me."

The man nodded and scurried outside.

Dr. Dixon hovered over the dog in the examination room. "His breathing is shallow," he said. "I'm concerned he might have a blockage."

"What kind of blockage?" the man asked.

"Oh, it could be anything. Food, trash, a dog toy."

"Can you fix it?"

"We'll need to do X-rays first," Doc said. "Then if there is a blockage he'll need surgery."

"I need him better tonight."

The veterinarian peered over at the man from above his glasses. "That simply isn't going to happen."

Even lying listless on the table, the dog was menacing. Addie guessed he was some kind of mastiff mix. He had a slick red coat, wrinkled face, and weighed at least as much as she did. His face was deeply scarred in several places, including one large scar dragging across his eye.

"Redd Jones said to come to you," the man said. "Said you could fix him right up."

"I appreciate the endorsement," Doc replied. "But there's nothing I can do to fix him tonight except to do an X-ray."

"I ain't got time for that."

"He's not well, and he needs medical attention."

"He'll be fine."

"Suit yourself."

Addie glanced from Dr. Dixon to the man in front of her. "What, you're just going to let him go? Couldn't this dog *die*?"

"He could," Dr. Dixon said. He wasn't looking at anyone. He was studying the cracks in the tile floor.

"And you don't care? Neither of you care?"

"I can't force anyone to allow X-rays."

The man was already lumbering out the exam room door, his

arms bulging beneath the weight, the dog's massive head lolling from side to side with each step.

Addie chased after him. "What in the hell is wrong with you? Don't you know that your dog could die?"

The man ignored her. He sat the dog into the bed of his truck and slammed the tailgate shut.

"I'm going to call the police!"

He stopped. He turned around and walked back to the doorway of the clinic where Addie was standing. "You call anybody and it won't be this dog that'll need help."

Addie gripped the doorframe and dug her fingernails into the splintering wood. "I'm not afraid of you," she said.

The man curled his lips into a smile. Then he reached out to her with one hand and began to twirl a loose strand of Addie's hair. "You should be."

Addie recoiled from his grasp and slammed the door in his face, locking it. Outside he laughed for a few seconds before turning around to walk back to his truck. He waved at her as he drove out of the parking lot.

"Just what were you thinking talking to a customer that way?"

Addie turned to glare at Doc. Her blood was boiling. "He was hardly a customer."

"You should have just let him go."

"You should have done your job."

"I don't know who you think you are," Doc began.

"I'll tell you who I am," Addie cut him off. "I'm the only person here who acted like they gave a shit about the dog dying on your exam table!"

"You've probably just signed that dog's death warrant. He might have brought him back tomorrow. But now he'll never come back here."

"So this is my fault?"

"It's not your fault what happened to that dog," Doc said. "But what happened here is your fault."

"I've got to get going." Addie grabbed her purse from behind the counter. "Everything is clean and ready for the weekend except that last examination room."

"I'm just as frustrated as you are."

"How do you know Redd Jones?"

"I'm the only veterinarian within thirty miles. I know everybody."

"That's not what I mean, and you know it."

"You can't just move into a town like Eunice and demand answers to questions that don't have answers," Doc replied. "Forget about what you think you know about that man, forget about what you think you know about Redd Jones, and forget what you think you know about me. You don't know the half of it."

Addie stood outside the clinic for a few minutes trying to collect herself. The evening fell just short of blistering, and the hot tears streaming down her cheeks didn't help. The smell of barbecue wafted through the air and filled her lungs. Fire ants crawled over her feet looking for a toe to bite. Music blared in the distance. She wondered what a place so calm, so small, so quiet could be hiding.

As she drove downtown, she noticed that most of the streetlights were burned out on the cobblestone street, leaving Addie a cover of darkness that she had not anticipated. She was glad that she'd chosen to leave Felix at home. She pulled into the driveway of an abandoned house next to Redd's and cut the engine and lights. People streamed in and out of Redd's house. The dilapidated fence separating the two houses kept Addie hidden as she crept toward the backyard. She stumbled amid the overgrown grass, her only light the full moon shining directly above her. Addie knew she couldn't just walk through the front door, but she had to get close enough to the house to see what was going on.

Behind the house there was a large outbuilding—it had been what she'd tried to get a glimpse of the day she'd been there with Bobby. The lights were on inside and there was someone standing at the door—someone large with his arms crossed over his chest. Nobody went in or out before speaking with the man in front of the building. After a few minutes, the man was beckoned to the main house, leaving the backyard unguarded. Addie pushed at the rotting wood. The fence was already missing several boards. She shoved against it with her shoulder and managed to push enough that she could crawl through.

She crouched on top of one of the empty doghouses and peered through the window. The building was packed full of men. There was a layer of smoke so thick that the view was hazy even though the lights inside were blazing. The men were standing in a circle, many of them shouting and raising their fists toward something below them that Addie couldn't see.

There was one last final outburst, and the crowd dispersed. Redd Jones was left standing in the middle of the room, surrounded by a plywood ring smeared in blood. He was holding a huge pit bull by the collar. The dog was thrashing about, foaming at the mouth. There was another man in the corner, bent over another dog. He was kicking at it, and with each kick the dog lifted its head for a few seconds before it fell back down into the blood-spattered dust.

"Finish him," the man said, stepping away from the dog. "Fucking finish him." He slapped several bloody hundred-dollar bills into Redd's hand and pulled Redd's dog by the collar out of the building, cursing under his breath.

Redd was alone in the room with the other man's dog. He shoved the wad of money into his pocket and wiped the blood from his hands onto one of the plywood boards. The dog struggled to lift its head as Redd neared, tried to drag itself away from his impending shadow. Redd reached behind his back and pulled out a gun—it was the gun Addie had seen in his bedroom—the one with the beautiful design.

He aimed it at the dog's head and pulled the trigger.

Again.

And again.

Addie fell back on top of the doghouse. She tasted vomit. She closed her eyes to keep everything from running together. Just then the door to the building swung open, and people began streaming out. Addie slid down the roof of the doghouse and into the dirt behind it. She hoped that no one had heard the thud of her body hitting the ground. She pulled her knees up to her chest and locked her arms around them.

When the voices drifted back inside the main house, Addie dared to raise her head. That was when she noticed a mass in front of her. Whatever it was, it was breathing—rather, wheezing—in front of her. She squinted into the moonlight. Her eyes followed a thick chain posted into the ground all the way up to the neck of yet another dog. Addie froze with visions of the dogs inside running rampant in her mind. Was it going to attack her?

The animal let out a whimper in Addie's direction, but there was no gnashing of teeth. Instead, the dog crawled toward her. Instinctively, Addie stuck out her hand. The dog sniffed it and slid closer to her. It was then that Addie realized the dog was heavily pregnant. She ran her hand down the length of the dog, and despite the bulging belly, Addie could feel every single rib. At each stroke, the dog's tail hit the dirt with a soft *thump, thump, thump*.

"I have to go," Addie whispered to her. "I've got to get out of here."

The dog licked her hands, and Addie felt her heart sink. The chain around the dog's neck was held with a padlock. The chain led to a stake driven into the ground. She crawled over to the stake and tugged at it. When it didn't come out, she dug into the dirt with her hands until she could pry the stake free. She clenched the stake with both hands, giving the chain a gentle tug. "Come on. Let's go."

The dog stood on four shaky legs. She walked a few paces forward, following Addie. They were almost to freedom when a light shined on Addie's back.

"Hey! Just what in the hell do you think you're doing?"

Addie started to run, pulling the dog behind her.

"Addie? What in tarnation are you doing here?"

She crouched down near the hole in the fence, looping her fingers through the chain. She knew that voice. "Bobby?"

"What are you doing with Delilah?"

"I thought you were going to shoot me."

"Now why would I do that?" Bobby asked. "Where'd you come from?"

"Next door."

"Ain't nobody live next door."

"I parked there," Addie said.

"Why?"

"I wanted to know what was going on in this house." Addie took a deep breath. "And now I wish I didn't know."

"This ain't no place for you."

"You brought me here yourself."

"In the daylight."

Addie stood up. She felt the blood rushing back through her body. "Do you know what's going on here? Do you know?"

"Hush, now." Bobby flicked off his flashlight and caught her by the arm. "If someone else hears you we'll both be in trouble."

"Answer me." She wanted to scream and beat her fists against his broad chest. But neither she nor the white dog dared move.

"I just stand at the door."

"You just ignore what you hear?"

"You gotta get your tail outta here."

"I'm taking her with me."

"That's Redd's dog."

"I'm taking her."

"You ain't."

"Does Wanda know what's going on over here?"

"This ain't her business."

"I'm going to tell her if you don't help me."

"What'll I tell Redd when Delilah comes up missing? She's 'bout to have pups."

"I don't give a shit what you tell him," Addie replied. "But it's the least you can do for her. It's the least you can do for the dog lying in the dirt inside that shed over there."

"You saw that?"

"I saw it all." Addie didn't know why she felt so emboldened. She'd never stolen anything in her whole life, not even a pack of gum, and yet here she was in the yard of one of the most terrifying men in Eunice, with what she could only assume to be thousands of dollars laced through her fingers. But she had to save this dog. She just *had* to.

Bobby reached up with the flashlight and scratched his head. He mumbled something that sounded like *shee-it* under his breath. "Go on, then. I'll figure somethin' out to tell the boss."

"Thank you." A wave of relief washed over her.

"I'm not a bad man, Addie."

"I know you're not," Addie said. And then she couldn't help but add, "But you're keeping secrets for a bad man."

"I got to make a livin' somehow."

"This is no way to live."

"Don't tell Wanda." Bobby was so close to Addie's face that she could smell the cigarettes on his breath. "I got me a job down in Mississippi. I just got to make it through the next couple weeks. I ain't gonna live like this forever, Addie. I swear it."

Addie crouched back down and crawled through the fence, beckoning Delilah to follow. Addie didn't know what would happen once Redd discovered that his dog was gone, but that was for Bobby to figure out. It was, as she'd told him, the least he could do. With that one final thought, she lit out of the driveway and drove as fast as she could to the Floyd farm.

CHAPTER 30

"What in the hell were you thinking, Adelaide?" Jasper paced back and forth across his living room. "You stole a dog. You broke into a man's home and stole a dog. Have you lost your mind?"

"Dr. Dixon isn't answering," Addie replied.

"I have half a mind to make you take her back. I cannot believe you stole a dog."

"Technically, I had permission."

Jasper sighed and sat down on the couch, rubbing his temples. "I don't even have the energy to explain to you how that justification is legally illogical."

"So have me arrested. Call the police and have me arrested. Call Redd and tell him a crazy lady stole his dog."

"You know I'm not going to do that."

"What was I supposed to do, Jasper?" Addie said. "Look at her. Look at her and tell me what I should have done."

Jasper busied himself untangling the massive chain around the dog's neck. He'd already cut the padlock. The chain had been so tight and so thick that it had all but grown into her skin. She was in pitiful shape, and Jasper winced more than once as he worked. "Why were you at that house? On that street? You could have gotten yourself killed."

"I'm not a child. Stop scolding me."

"You didn't answer my question."

"It's not the first time I've been to that house."

"What?" Jasper stopped to gape at her.

"I was there once before, with Bobby. Redd wasn't there."

"Bobby Carter doesn't have the sense God gave him to come in out of the rain."

"That may be true," Addie replied. "But I went there with him just the same. I knew then something wasn't right; I just didn't know how bad it was."

"You shouldn't have gone back there."

"A man came into the clinic today. He had a dog with him. A big dog. Full of scars. He said his dog wouldn't eat, wouldn't walk. Doc suggested an X-ray, but he said he didn't have time. Said the dog had to be better by tonight. Then he said Redd Jones told him to see Doc."

"So?"

"He wouldn't even get the dog treated, Jasper. I knew something was going on at that house. *I knew it,* especially after that ad in the paper. After what I found in Redd's nightstand."

"You were in his room?"

"I found all these papers with these words on them, the same words that were in an advertisement in the paper for some puppies. And I found a gun, Jasper."

"Everybody in Eunice has a gun, Adelaide. We've been through this."

Addie gripped the side of the couch to steady herself. "When was the last time you shot a dog in the head with a .38 special?"

"My God." Jasper couldn't look at her. He stood up swiftly and threw the chain outside. His hands were covered with rust and blood. "This isn't your battle to fight."

"And whose battle is it?" Addie narrowed her eyes at him. "Felix's? That dog over there?"

"We're not getting anywhere," Jasper said as his phone began to ring. "It's Doc."

Delilah, if that was her name, was shaking violently, looking from Addie to Jasper. Addie very slowly sat down in front of her and allowed the dog to sniff her. She knew from taking care of Felix just how slowly she had to start. "I'm sorry," she whispered to her.

An hour later, Dr. Dixon peered over the top of his glasses at Addie, who hadn't moved from Delilah's side. "This dog is covered in fleas. She's terribly anemic. She wouldn't have lasted much longer."

Addie gave a sideways glance at Jasper and said, "But she's going to live?"

"If she survives the birth."

"I stole her from Redd Jones," Addie blurted.

"You did *what*?"

"I stole her. I went to his house. I saw . . . I saw two dogs try to kill each other while men cheered them on." Addie didn't even try to fight the tears forming behind her eyes.

"Thanks for coming," Jasper broke in, giving the veterinarian's hand a shake. "And thank you for being discreet."

Dr. Dixon gave a curt nod. "I'll come back out in a couple of days to check on her. The best things you can give her right now are rest and food."

"We'll make sure she gets plenty of both," Addie promised.

"Addie, I don't condone what you did," Dr. Dixon said. "I know we exchanged some harsh words earlier. But this dog, at least, is lucky you found her."

"Nobody found anybody," Jasper grumbled. "She's just lucky Addie committed grand larceny."

Dr. Dixon cleared his throat. "Jasper, could we go outside and talk?"

"Fine."

Addie strained to hear their conversation but could hear only muffled voices through the thick door. When Jasper walked back into the house, Dr. Dixon wasn't with him. The scowl on Jasper's face, however, remained.

"If you're worried about Redd going to the police once he finds out—"

"That's not what I'm worried about," Jasper cut her off. "Promise me that you won't go back to that house again."

"I promise," Addie replied without hesitation. "I never want to see what I saw again, but Jasper, it was so awful."

"Let me worry about that," Jasper said. "Don't go back out there."

"I can't just stop worrying about it, Jasper. Didn't you hear me when I said that two dogs were attacking and killing each other while people watched? It's called dogfighting. It's illegal. Even in Arkansas."

"I know what dogfighting is."

"Then you know that Felix must have been one of those dogs that Redd was fighting."

"How do you know that?"

"It doesn't take a genius to figure it out."

"You can't prove that, Adelaide."

"Well, excuse me, Counselor. I wasn't aware we were in a court of law."

"I'm not defending Redd Jones," Jasper said. "But I am telling you that there is nothing that you can do about it."

"Like hell there's nothing I can do about it," Addie said. "I can prove it. I know I can prove it. There's got to be enough evidence there for the police to do something."

"I meant it when I told you to stay out of it," Jasper warned her. "Stay. Out. Of. It."

"I'm not asking you for your help."

"Oh, you're not?" Jasper spat. "I was involved the second you brought that dog to my house. You stole a damn dog."

"I know."

"Then please, just leave it alone."

"I don't understand why this doesn't bother you."

"Of course it bothers me," Jasper said. "But I also know the laws in the state of Arkansas regarding animal abuse and dog-fighting."

"Does it always have to be about the laws?"

"It does when you're talking to me about having someone arrested," Jasper said. "Proving animal abuse is difficult, and proving that someone is fighting dogs is even more difficult."

"I saw it!" Addie exclaimed. "I saw it! Look at Delilah! Look at Felix. I'm sure that Redd hasn't had the decency to clean up the bloody body of the dog he shot tonight."

"First of all, you can't prove that Felix ever belonged to Redd or anybody associated with Redd, and you can't prove that Felix was ever involved in dogfighting because you don't have any evidence," Jasper said. "And do not bring up that damn house again."

"*That house!*"

"Look, I'm just giving you the facts," Jasper said. "And the facts are that while dogfighting is a felony in the state of Arkansas, it's just a misdemeanor to be a spectator. That's a thousand-dollar fine at worst. And we can't prove that Redd was anything other than a spectator. Maybe we could get him for a class D felony, which is aggravated cruelty for the way he's treated this dog and the other two dogs you saw out there, but that's a very tenuous maybe. It's more likely that he'd be charged with a misdemeanor."

"Whose side are you on?"

"I'm on your side, Addie." Jasper's voice softened. "I'm always on your side. I wish you could see that. Redd Jones is a pariah. He deserves to go to prison. But we've got to be patient. We've got to use our heads about this. Acting with our emotions won't do us any good."

"I am tired of controlling my emotions."

"You're just going to have to trust me."

Addie glanced from Jasper to the dog. "What are we going to do with her?"

"I'll keep her here for now."

"I'll come over tomorrow and check on her." Addie sighed, defeated. She didn't want to argue any more tonight.

Jasper stepped in front of her, cutting off her path. "Don't say anything to anyone about tonight. Not even to Wanda."

"Okay."

"I'm serious," Jasper continued. "Redd's going to be looking for answers, and I don't know if Bobby will be able to keep this a secret."

Addie reached up and touched his face, and she had to force herself to move her hand away. "I'll be careful."

"Good." Jasper stepped away from her.

She didn't want to leave and something inside told her that Jasper didn't want her to leave, either. Addie walked over to where Delilah was curled up on the floor. She scratched behind her ears and underneath her chin. "This cranky old man is going to take care of you. He's going to feed you. Don't be scared."

"I'll make sure she's comfortable," Jasper said.

"I know," Addie replied. "I know you're mad at me. But I'm not sorry for what I did."

For the first time that night Jasper smiled. "I know you're not," he said. "I know you're not."

Addie turned to leave but stopped at the door. She watched him for a moment until he looked up at her. Their eyes met, and it took all her strength not to turn around and walk away. Instead she said to him, "Are you embarrassed of me?"

"What?"

"Embarrassed." Addie shifted from one foot to the other. "Are you embarrassed of me? To be seen with me?"

"What are you talking about?"

"Come on, Jasper," she replied. "You act like you hardly know me when Doc is around. When anybody is around. You touch me in hallways, in bathrooms. You don't want to be seen leaving my house."

"That's not true."

"You wouldn't even take me to work."

"Are you still mad about that?"

"Forget it," Addie said. "Just forget it."

Jasper followed her outside and into the sticky summer night.

"Wait." He grabbed her arm. "Just wait for a second, will you?"

"Let go of me." Addie tried to shrug him off her.

"No." Jasper's grip tightened. "Listen to me."

"I've been waiting for weeks to listen to you."

"Listen to me now."

"What? What do you have to say?"

Jasper hesitated. He let go of her arm, looking away from her.

Addie pushed him out of her way. "That's what I thought."

This time, when Jasper grabbed her, he didn't let go. Before she could say another word, he slammed his mouth against hers, hard. The force surprised her, and Addie lost her footing. She tumbled to the ground, pulling Jasper along with her.

"Are you okay?" Jasper asked in between feverish kisses.

Addie nodded. She couldn't think. All of her energy was wrapped up in Jasper on top of her. His mouth and his hands searching in the dark.

He pushed her skirt up toward her breasts, lingering for a second on her blue lace panties. He cupped his hands around her buttocks and pulled her panties down in one swift motion. They shriveled at her ankles. Addie lifted herself up to him, begging him with her body, but he pushed her back down into the ground, his mouth leaving her lips to kiss his way down into her nakedness.

Addie cried out and grabbed at Jasper, her hands grazing the top of his sweat-soaked head. She dug her fingers deep into his hair. When his mouth finally returned to hers, she wrapped herself around him until their bodies were synchronized.

THEY LAY THERE together, bodies entwined, staring up into the Arkansas sky. Addie had never beheld such a clear night, never lost count of the stars above her. There was nothing she wanted more than this night, this man, and for the first time in her life she could see, really and truly see, what was in front of her.

Felix was snoring in his bed when Addie got home. He didn't even look up as she came inside. "Some guard dog you are," she mumbled. She didn't understand how someone could have abused him. He was so sweet and gentle, even after everything he'd been through. Even after—she knew, despite what Jasper said—even after Felix survived Redd. Redd had shot that dog as if it were nothing, as if he—she shuddered—had taken a life before. Addie wondered if Redd had shot Felix himself. She wondered how many times Felix had been chewed up and spit out before Redd and his friends had decided he was no longer of use. She wondered how many other dogs had suffered the same fate as Felix—dogs that nobody had saved.

Addie stood up to walk to the bathroom, feeling sick to her stomach. Felix heard her and stirred out of his sleep. He looked up at her expectantly. She crouched down next to him, putting her forehead up to his, just like she'd done with Delilah. Felix licked her face.

"I'm sorry," she whispered to him. "I'm just so sorry."

CHAPTER 31

"Where have you been the last few days?" Wanda asked Addie as they sat in Addie's kitchen. "I called you a million times before you answered."

"I'm sorry," Addie replied, placing a hot dog in a bun. "I just needed a few days to myself, that's all."

"Well, you could have told me that," Wanda mumbled. "Bobby'll be leaving pretty soon. Headed to Mississippi with that new company. Thanks again for being a reference. I'm throwing him a big party later today. The man ain't never lived anywhere else 'cept with Doreen for what amounted to about two weeks."

"I thought he was a long-haul trucker for years."

"He was. But he always comes back here to sleep."

"Oh, well, I think a party is a great idea."

"I want you to come," Wanda replied. "I don't like most of his friends. They take advantage. I love Bobby. He's my only brother.

But he's so dumb he couldn't pour piss out of a boot with the instructions written on the heel."

"Let me guess," Addie said. "Something your granny used to say?"

"You got it. And she used to say it about Bobby."

"Well, I'd love to come. But I don't want to impose."

Wanda stuck a fork into her macaroni and cheese. "It's only imposin' if I don't invite ya."

"Well, I don't know any of Bobby's friends," Addie said. She hadn't seen Bobby since that night at Redd's, and she wasn't itching to see him again anytime soon.

"Please?"

"I just don't want to be in the way."

"You didn't have any other plans, did you?"

"Nope."

"I thought maybe the reason you hadn't been callin' is because you were shacked up with Jasper Floyd."

"You know better than that."

"Do I?"

Addie wanted to tell her the truth. She wanted to tell her about Delilah, and Bobby, and everything she saw at the house on the cobblestone street. She wanted to tell her about Jasper, about *everything* with Jasper. But she couldn't. Even if Jasper hadn't made her promise—she couldn't. "Yes, you do," Addie said finally.

"Speaking of men," Wanda said, a mischievous smile appearing on her face, "Loren Bartwell told me he thinks you're pretty cute."

"Who?"

"He said he met you at Jasper's farm. He's a farmhand there."

"Oh!" Addie replied. "Yeah, I met him once. He's young, Wanda. He can't be any more than twenty."

"He's twenty-five. And he's good-looking."

"Not interested."

"Why not?"

"I'm just not," Addie replied. "Besides, he looks like trouble to me."

"He looks like fun."

"Then why don't you date him?"

"I'm too old for him."

"You're not that old."

"Old enough to know better."

"And you were trying to pawn him off on me!" Addie exclaimed. "Some friend you are."

"I wasn't trying to get you to marry him. I just thought he could help you take your mind off . . . things."

"I'm fine."

"Are you sure?"

"Yes."

Wanda rolled her eyes down at Bryar who shrugged his shoulders as if he knew what the two women were talking about.

"This bun is soggy," he said. "Miss Addie, you are *not* all right."

Addie gave Bryar the best smile she could muster. She was fine, she guessed. She was fine for a woman who was keeping secrets from her only friend for at least two thousand miles. She was fine for a woman who couldn't stop thinking about a man she couldn't have, and she was fine for a woman who had landed herself smack-dab in the middle of an illegal dogfighting ring that she couldn't do a damn thing about.

Yep. Adelaide Andrews was just fine.

"Here," she said to Bryar, handing him a plate. "Try my Ooey Gooey Butter Cake. You'll have to tell me what you think."

Wanda eyed Addie suspiciously. "You're still baking?"

Addie shrugged. "I'm just trying a few things."

Bryar was still focused on his hot dog in the soggy bun and didn't even notice when Wanda took the plate from his hands. She took a bite. "Addie, this is good." She took another bite. "No, this is amazing. It tastes just like your aunt's!"

"Just like it?"

"Hmmm . . ." Wanda chewed thoughtfully. "Not exactly like it. There's another flavor there, but I can't put my finger on it."

Addie grinned, this time with no effort at all. "It's my special ingredient. I added something that wasn't in the recipe."

"Well, slap my ass and call me Sally!" Wanda exclaimed. She motioned for Addie to bring the entire pan of cake over to the table. "You may just belong right here in Dixie."

By the time Addie said good-bye to Wanda and Bryar, changed her clothes, and managed to get out to Jasper's house, all the lights were off. She knocked on the front door. When he didn't answer, she knocked again and said, "Jasper? Are you there? It's Addie . . . I . . . I just came to check on Delilah."

Addie heard Delilah bark, and after a few seconds there was a thumping around inside the house. She stepped back when the porch light flickered on and the door opened.

Jasper stood in front of her rubbing his eyes. "I'm sorry. I must've fallen asleep."

Addie felt a wave of relief wash over her. It was irrational, she knew, but for a few terrible seconds, she'd thought maybe Jasper wasn't alone. Felix rushed out from behind her and into the house, needing no invitation. Delilah waddled happily after him. "She looks even bigger than she did last week," Addie managed to say.

"I think she's going to be having the puppies soon." Jasper stepped aside for Addie to enter. "Every time I came to check on her today she was nesting."

"Nesting?"

"Yeah, it's what dogs . . . what all pregnant animals do, really . . . to prepare for birth. She's been tearing newspaper, ripping up the old blankets I gave her, and gathering toys over in that corner to create a nest."

Delilah and Felix were curled up together, and Delilah was licking the insides of Felix's ears. "Are you ready to be a mommy?" Addie asked her. "You look like you're ready to pop!"

"I'm glad she's focusing her attention on Felix," Jasper said. "She's been grooming herself like crazy and pacing around the house."

"It amazes me that she even likes dogs. She can't have had too many good experiences with dogs or people living where she did."

"Dogs are resilient."

"Well, they shouldn't have to be." Addie knelt down and stroked Delilah's head. "I brought her some more blankets and food."

"You look nice." Jasper looked Addie up and down. "Are you headed somewhere after this?"

"Thanks." Addie crossed her arms over her chest, suddenly feeling self-conscious. "Wanda is having a going-away party for Bobby."

"I heard Bobby got a job."

"Yeah, somewhere down in Mississippi?"

"That's what my mom said. They're headed down that direction for a week or two. My dad made some joke about hoping they didn't meet him on the road."

"So you're here alone?"

"Yep."

"Then I'll stay with you," Addie said.

"Go on to the party. Wanda will never forgive you if you don't go," Jasper said. "I've known Wanda a long time. You don't want her sore at you."

"I don't want to leave you all alone."

Jasper rolled his eyes. "I hate to break it to you, but I've been alone before."

"I was just trying to be nice."

"I know you were."

Addie stood there awkwardly. She wasn't sure what else to say, but she knew she had to say something. The tension between the two of them was driving her crazy. "Jasper, do you want to talk about things?"

"What things?"

"You know, things between us."

"I don't know if that's a conversation I'm ready to have," Jasper replied.

"Look," Addie began, "I don't want to be the girl who needs some sort of definition, but I'm tired of secrets. I'm tired of not knowing the answers to so many things. To everything. I don't need for everything to make sense, but I'd like it if I had just a few more pieces of the puzzle."

Jasper took a step toward her, but he wouldn't meet her gaze. "That's just not something I can give you right now."

Addie bit the bottom of her lip. "I've got to go." She thought maybe he'd say something, anything to keep her from leaving like he had the night she brought Delilah. That seemed to be what they were best at—feverish refusals to leave. But Jasper said nothing, and Addie realized that she was going to have to make good on her threat. Without another word, she opened the door to his house and walked back through it.

CHAPTER 32

Cars were lined up on either side of the street when Addie arrived at Wanda's house. She didn't recognize any of them, and the way she was feeling, she wished she'd just gone home and made up an excuse. Surely Wanda would forgive her for being sick or possessed or caught up in the zombie apocalypse.

"Addie!" Wanda flung open the door. "Come in! Come in!"

"Sorry I'm late." Addie put on her best smile.

"Where have you been?"

"I couldn't figure out what to wear."

"You couldn't answer the phone to tell me that?"

"I guess I didn't hear the phone." She avoided looking directly at her friend. Wanda had a way of being able to tell when someone was lying, and this was especially true when it came to Addie. Looking directly at Wanda was a little like looking directly at the sun. Blink once at the glare and she'd call your bluff.

"Well, you look great," Wanda said. "Let's get you something to drink."

"I haven't worn this in forever." Addie glanced down at her denim skirt and black silk tank top. "It's nothing fancy, but this is my favorite skirt."

"Nothin' fancy is my motto for life." Wanda handed Addie a red plastic cup filled with an amber-colored liquid. "Drink up, sugar."

Addie took a sip and winced. "This is awful!"

"I know."

"Why did you give it to me?"

"Because you look like you needed it."

"I do, but I don't want to throw it back up. Don't you have beer or anything?"

"Loren would love to get you a beer." Wanda nodded toward the couch in the living room. "He was starting to think you stood him up."

"What are you talking about?"

"Just go over there and talk to him."

"I don't want to."

"Don't be rude."

"I'm not being rude."

"Yes you are. He's watching us."

"What did you tell him?"

"I didn't tell him anything other than that you'd be here," Wanda whispered. "I also might have told him that you are not, in fact, dating Jasper Floyd."

"That's true," Addie muttered. She wished the words didn't sound so resolute, but there they were, out there for everyone to hear. She was *not* dating Jasper Floyd. He'd made that very clear. She cringed as she thought about how she'd asked him if he *wanted to talk.*

"Just go talk to him," Wanda said, shoving Addie forward. "Stop looking around like one of these people ran over Felix and try to have a good time. It's not going to kill you to talk to him."

Addie tugged at the hem of her skirt. Squeezing past a group of people having a heated conversation about Chinese food, she made her way over to the couch. With his thick hair and dark features, Loren was good-looking; of course it wasn't going to kill her to talk to him.

"Hi there, Adelaide," he said. His drawl was thicker than Wanda's, slower. "Have a seat. Can I get you something to drink?"

"A beer would be great," Addie replied.

"Be right back."

Addie sighed and leaned back onto the couch. She avoided Wanda by looking down at her hands. She couldn't stop thinking about what Jasper had said to her. If that wasn't a conversation he was *ready to have,* then she wasn't prepared to sit around and wait for him.

"Here ya go, sweetheart." Loren sat down next to her. "Coors Light okay?"

"Not really, but I'll live." She didn't like him calling her sweetheart, even though she knew it was more a southern thing than it was Loren being patronizing. Still, she didn't like it.

"Too good for cheap beer?" Loren's dimples deepened.

"I'm not too good for cheap beer. But I am too good for crappy beer." Addie took a swig from the bottle.

Loren let out a hearty laugh and ran a tanned hand through his thick, dark hair. "That's all that's left, so I apologize if I've offended your delicate palate."

"You don't sound much like a farmhand."

"Is there a certain way a farmhand is supposed to sound?"

"I just mean that you don't sound like most farmhands I've met."

"And how many farmhands have you met?"

"You don't sound like Clyde."

"Sweetheart, I'm in trouble if you're comparing me to Clyde."

"I guess you're right," Addie said. "It's not really fair to compare you to Clyde. He's such a gentleman."

"You're a clever girl, Miss Addie."

"Thanks." Addie sank back into the couch. Maybe being called sweetheart wasn't so bad.

"Wanda tells me you're from Chicago."

"I am," Addie replied. "What about you? You're not from Eunice, are you?"

"I'm originally from Jackson."

"Mississippi?"

"Is there another one?"

"How'd you get all the way up here?"

"I followed a girl," Loren replied. "It didn't work out, but I thought I'd stay for a while."

"What was a girl from Eunice doing in Jackson?"

"College or something." Loren's response was slow and thick. "Hey, is there a reason Redd Jones is glaring at you?"

Addie's heart leapt up into her throat. Redd was standing in the kitchen, his meaty hands clasped around a six-pack. She turned back around to Loren and said, "I don't know. I hardly know him."

"He sure seems to know you."

Addie squeezed her eyes shut and pretended that Redd wasn't

walking over to where she and Loren sat. He didn't see her; he didn't care about her. She had no reason to be worried.

"Hello, Adelaide," Redd said.

"How are you, Redd?" Addie opened one of her eyes. He was towering over her. *He knows,* she thought. *He has to know.*

"I coulda sworn the rumor was that you and Jasper Floyd was seein' most of each other." He sneered down at Loren and Addie. "You plan to get around to every man workin' on that farm?"

Loren stood up. His forehead came up to the middle of Redd's neck. There was something large about him, however, something about the way he carried himself. "You've got a fresh mouth there, boy."

"Who you callin' *boy*?"

Addie could already see where this was headed. And it wasn't anywhere pretty. "It's okay, Loren," she said. She stood up. Then, looking up at Redd, she said, "I'm not seeing any part of anyone on the Floyd farm."

"That's not the way I hear it."

"I can't help what you hear."

"You reckon I heard wrong?"

"I don't reckon anything," Addie replied. She wanted to run. She wanted to be anywhere but where she was, perched precariously between Loren and Redd. But she knew she couldn't run. Guilty people ran. Besides, he probably knew where she lived. She couldn't let him know she was afraid of him. "The way I hear it, part of the Floyd farm used to belong to you. But I think that was before that part ended up being auctioned off on the courthouse steps."

Redd broke off one of the beers in the six-pack, slinging the remaining five down onto the couch. "That what them Floyds tell you?"

"That's what everybody tells me."

"You think you know people in this town?" Redd asked, but it was more of a statement. He wasn't going to give her any time to respond. "*I* know the people in this town. *I* know what they want, and *I* give it to 'em."

"Good for you" was all Addie could manage to say. He was standing so close to her now that she could feel his hot breath beating down onto her face.

"You don't fuckin' know me." Redd pointed to himself with force, his right thumb pressing hard into one of the buttons on his shirt. "And if you don't know me, you don't know this fuckin' town."

"I think it's time you be movin' on," Loren said through his teeth. His jaw was clamped shut so tightly that the muscles in his face were working overtime.

"I ain't goin' nowhere."

"Redd!" Bobby appeared very suddenly, stepping in between Redd and Addie. "What are you doing here?"

"I heard there was a party."

"Just a little get-together."

"Sure looks like a party to me."

"It ain't much."

The two men faced each other, neither one breaking eye contact. There was a conversation going on, but nobody's lips were moving. Finally, after what felt like years, Redd spoke. "So that's how it's gonna be, huh?"

"I 'spose."

"After everything I done for you?"

"What have you ever done for me 'cept get me into trouble and addicted to nicotine?" Bobby reached into his pocket and pulled out a pack of cigarettes. "You think I owe you somethin'? Here, take these."

Addie stared at the pack of Marlboro Reds that Bobby thrust into his friend's chest. There must have been at least fifteen cartons of that brand inside the trash bag on the day she found Felix. She'd peeled pieces of the blood-soaked cardboard off his body, tiny pieces sticking to his wounds. There had been ashes in his eyes and cigarette butts in his stomach. Doc told her he must've been so hungry he'd eaten the discarded butts of the person—the man Addie knew was standing in front of her—who abused him. Fury filled her all the way from the bottom of her feet to the top of her head. She wedged herself in between the two feuding men until she was so close to Redd that she could smell the dirt underneath his fingernails. "I think it's pretty obvious that nobody wants you here."

Redd wrapped his bear paw of a hand around one of Addie's arms. "Shut up."

"I know who you are. I know exactly who you are, and you're nothing like this town." Addie looked him dead in the eyes. "You're nothing but a coward."

Redd gave Addie's arm another bone-crushing squeeze before he let go, sauntering out of the living room with Bobby on his heels. He was as calm as ever, a kind of furious apathy that was one of the most unsettling things Addie had ever seen, and she was afraid.

"Well, what in the hell was that?" Wanda asked. She had been watching the scene unfold from the kitchen. "I was ready to come over there and jump on that man's back if he didn't let you go."

"I'm fine," Addie said. She looked down at her right arm. She could still feel the burn of his skin up against hers.

"Redd and Bobby had a fallin' out, but Bobby won't tell me why. You know somethin' about that?"

"No."

"Yes you do."

Addie's phone began to ring. She stood up and walked away from Wanda toward the back of the house. "Hello?"

"Addie?"

"Jasper?"

"Sorry," Jasper said. "I'm a little distracted. Delilah is in labor. I thought you'd want to know."

"She's in labor? Did you call Doc?"

"I did. But he's out of town. He can't be back much before the morning."

"I'll be there as soon as I can." Addie hung up the phone and returned to Wanda. "I have to go. I'm sorry. I promise you that I'll tell you everything soon."

"Where are you going?"

"I'll call you tomorrow."

"You can't even tell me where you're going?"

"I'll tell you," Addie promised. "Just not tonight."

"You need to be careful going wherever you're going," Wanda replied. "Redd's as mad as an old, wet hen."

Addie was pulling away from the curb when Loren stepped out in front of her car. He waved and gave her a sheepish grin. "Are you leavin' so soon?"

"Yeah, I've had all the excitement I can stand for one night."

Loren leaned in through the window and said, "Well, I was hopin' I might take you out one night."

"Thanks," Addie replied. "But I don't think so."

"Why not?"

"I just can't right now, that's all."

"It's just dinner," Loren said. "I promise no shitty beer."

Addie laughed for the first time that night. She tried to remember what she'd told herself about not waiting for Jasper, about not waiting for anyone. "I guess I've got time for dinner."

JASPER WAS PACING the floor when Addie arrived. He looked like he'd been up all night, even though it was scarcely one A.M. His hair stood on end and he was barefoot. He was wearing sweats and a ratty old T-shirt. It was, in fact, the shirt Addie borrowed the night Felix had raided the chicken coop.

"How is she doing?" Addie asked. "Where is she?"

"She's in the closet," Jasper replied. He led Addie to the closet in his bedroom. "I made a whelping box so that she wouldn't try to hide."

"You made her a what?"

"A whelping box. It's just a place where she can give birth comfortably. Sometimes dogs try to hide when they're in labor. *Whelp* means give birth. Her temperature is ninety-nine degrees. I think she'll be having these pups pretty quick."

Addie hurried into Jasper's bedroom and peered into the closet. "Eeeew."

"Hush," Jasper said. "That's not a comforting sound. She needs to be comforted."

"I'm sorry," Addie whispered, sitting down next to Jasper. "How can you tell it's time?"

"Well, the discharge that you squealed about for one," Jasper said. "But also because her belly is hard as a rock. Here, feel."

Jasper grabbed Addie's hand and placed it on Delilah's stomach. "See?"

"Wow."

"Hopefully we won't have to help her much," Jasper continued. "But we need to stay close just in case."

"Okay. You know a lot about this kind of thing."

"I grew up on a farm," Jasper replied. "I've assisted in many live births."

Addie giggled. "You've assisted in many live births?"

"Yes," Jasper said, humorless. "Grab those old towels behind you. We may need them."

By the time Addie turned back around, Delilah was licking the first of the puppies. Addie watched in awe as puppy after puppy was born. She counted six before there was a lull in the labor.

"Is it over?" Addie asked. "Is she done?"

"There's another one," Jasper said. "But I think it's lodged."

"What does that mean?"

"It means I'm going to have to help." Jasper leaned over Delilah and gently began pulling the pup, twisting slightly. After a few seconds, the puppy slid out next to its mother.

The puppy didn't move.

"Jasper, is it breathing?"

"No."

"Is it dead?"

Jasper picked up the puppy. "Fold one of those towels over."

"Okay."

"Now, fold the top of the towel over him and rub gently," Jasper replied. "Very gently. Don't stop."

"He's still not breathing."

"Keep going," Jasper urged. "Just keep going."

Addie rubbed the little puppy inside the towel, whispering to him words of encouragement. At Jasper's instruction, she placed the puppy back into the box next to his brothers and sisters. After what felt like forever, the puppy gave a short, shuddering sigh.

"He's breathing!" Addie rejoiced. "He's breathing! We did it!"

"We'll have to keep an eye on him until morning," Jasper said.

"I can't believe she had seven puppies. Do you think she's doing okay?"

"She seems to be okay for now." Jasper wiped his hands on one of the unused towels. "I need to move her food and water bowls over. And Doc will be here later this morning to check on her."

Addie yawned. "What time is it?"

"It's five A.M. Why don't you go lay down? You look exhausted."

"What about you?" Addie yawned again.

"I'm going to stay up and keep an eye on things."

"I'll stay up with you."

"You can hardly keep your eyes open."

"I'm fine."

"Just go lay down." Jasper pointed toward the bed. "I'll wake you up if something happens."

"Okay," Addie said. "I feel like I've been run over."

"About earlier tonight," Jasper began. He sat down at the foot of the bed. "I didn't mean for what I said to sound uncaring."

"It's okay."

"It's not," Jasper continued. "I want to talk about it, about us, but I just can't right now."

Addie wanted to ask him why, why he couldn't talk about it.

Why couldn't he talk about the way he looked at her, the way he touched her? Did it have something to do with Harper? But she was just so tired. She didn't want to ruin what she'd just experienced, what she'd just seen, because as far as summer nights went, there wasn't another one in her twenty-eight years that compared to this.

CHAPTER 33

ADDIE AWOKE TO VOICES COMING FROM JASPER'S LIVING ROOM. Groggy, she sat up. She tiptoed over to the closet to check on the puppies. "It's just me, Delilah," Addie whispered.

She gave the dog a scratch on the head before making her way into the living room. When Doc and Jasper saw her they stopped talking. "I thought you were going to wake me up when Doc got here," she said.

Jasper crossed his arms over his chest. "I tried. You told me to go away. More than once."

"It's true," Doc said. He looked up at her from his cup of coffee. "You didn't even open your eyes, but you were quite threatening."

"I'm sorry," Addie replied. "I can get pretty hateful in my sleep. So how are the puppies? How is Delilah? Are they all healthy?"

"They all seem to be doing fine. I can give the puppies the care they need from here, but I think we'll need to bring . . . Delilah, is it? I think we'll need to bring her into the clinic for some tests—

things we couldn't check while she was pregnant. Not now, mind you, but relatively soon after the pups are weaned."

"Is that . . . is that going to be okay?" Addie asked. "I mean, what if someone recognizes her?"

"We can do it after-hours," Doc replied. "But really, Adelaide, I don't know who would recognize her and put two and two together. From the looks of her, she's had little to no veterinary care her entire life. I doubt she's ever even been off of the property until now."

"So you've never seen her before?"

"Never."

Addie's brow furrowed. "But I thought Redd came to you with his dogs. Isn't that what the guy at the clinic said yesterday?"

"I've seen some of his males, never any of the females," Doc replied. "I don't see how anyone would recognize her."

"There are people over at that house all the time. And Redd acted like he knew something last night at Wanda's."

"Redd was at Wanda's party?" Jasper asked. "Why didn't you tell me?"

"I guess I forgot."

"Why would Wanda even invite him?"

"She didn't," Addie said. "And he and Bobby had some kind of argument, so I know it wasn't Bobby. I was sitting there talking to Loren, and then Redd came over and was, as Wanda put it, 'as mad as an old wet hen.'"

"Loren was there?"

"Yes."

Jasper looked as if he was about to say something else but, looking from Doc to Addie, thought better of it. After what seemed like forever, he said, "Did Redd threaten you?"

"Not exactly," Addie said. "But I might've . . . I might've said something to make it worse."

"What did you say?"

"Well, it started with him accusing me of sleeping with just about everyone in all of Eunice," Addie began.

Doc cleared his throat. "That's quite an accusation."

"I called him a coward."

"I wish you'd told me this earlier." Jasper's hands were clenched tightly at his sides. "This isn't Chicago. You can't go around saying things like that to people. Not people like Redd. Didn't I ask you to let me take care of it?"

"Why? What were you going to do?" Addie asked. "Go find him and beat him up?"

"It's crossed my mind a few times."

"Well, you weren't there."

"That's not going to fix anything," Doc said. He pursed his lips together. "The best thing any of us can do right now is keep a low profile. Just don't talk to anyone."

"It's going to be hard to hide those puppies in a few weeks," Jasper said. "The farmhands know about Delilah, but I told them she was a stray."

"Strays have puppies all the time," Doc concluded. "Just keep on like normal."

"Why is everyone so scared of Redd?" Addie asked, the anger she felt earlier flooding back. "I mean, Jasper, you're a lawyer. What's a guy like Redd have over this town that he thinks he owns all the people in it?"

Doc walked over to where Addie stood and planted his hands squarely on her shoulders. "This is much bigger than you could ever imagine."

"What do you mean?" Addie asked. He was staring so deeply into her eyes that it caught her off guard. It was like he was trying to tell her something without saying any words. She didn't understand.

"He just means that Redd Jones had been terrorizing this town for years before you came around pushing his buttons," Jasper said.

Doc took a step back from Addie. "I've left some vitamin supplements for the pups in the bedroom. And you might want to think about getting some puppy chow for Delilah. That will help her keep her energy and weight up while she's nursing. The extra protein will be good for her."

"I'll get some today," Addie promised.

Jasper led Doc outside and shut the door behind them. Addie crept to the window and pulled back the curtain. The two men were standing close to each other. Doc had his glasses off and was using them to rap Jasper on the chest as he spoke. Jasper's nostrils flared with each *tap, tap, tap* of the glasses.

"I don't think you understand," Jasper was saying.

"No, *you* don't understand," Doc cut him off. "This is getting out of control. *She* is getting out of control."

Jasper looked up and saw Addie at the window. She backed away and let the curtain fall, leaving the two men to their conversation outside in the muggy Delta morning.

CHAPTER 34

ADDIE WAS EXHAUSTED BY THE TIME SHE PULLED INTO HER driveway. She'd avoided six phone calls from her mother and spent twenty minutes on the phone convincing Wanda that she would explain everything once she'd had more than two hours of sleep. All she wanted to do was crawl into bed. But as soon as she walked through the front door, the half-sanded dresser called to her from the spare bedroom.

Felix watched her work, curiously tilting his head from side to side each time the sandpaper made a sound against the wooden dresser. He wouldn't get near her while she wore her mask, staying at a safe distance in the living room. Loud voices scared him. Hats scared him. Cigarettes scared him. And Addie's mask scared him. She tried talking to him in a quiet voice, but it didn't do any good while she wore the mask.

She couldn't get what happened at Redd's house out of her mind. It didn't matter if her eyes were opened or closed. It didn't matter if she was awake or asleep—it was always there, lingering, in the back of her mind. Jasper had tried to take her mind off it, and he had for a while, making love to her in the grass at the farm. His touch left her head fuzzy for a few days, but Addie could still see the gleam of Redd's gun whenever something shiny caught her eye, whenever the sun was out. How could Jasper and Dr. Dixon be so nonchalant about it? How could they tell her to calm down? They hadn't seen what she had.

An hour later, she was jolted out of sleep by the ringing of the doorbell and the howling of Felix. "Be quiet and maybe they'll go away," Addie whispered.

Instead of going away, the ringing continued. Felix, in an excited frenzy, jumped off the bed and ran to the front door.

Addie pulled herself out of bed. Cursing, she made her way to the front door where Felix sat pawing and whining. "Traitor," she said to him.

She swung open the door to see her mother and Jerry standing in front of her. "Mom?" She blinked. "Jerry? What are you doing here?"

"Well, that's some greeting," her mother replied. "Aren't you going to invite us inside?"

"Of course!" Addie said as she unlocked the screen door and held it open for them. "I'm sorry! I'm just surprised!"

"You just sounded so depressed when we talked a couple of weeks ago, I couldn't stand it," her mother replied. "So we booked a flight to Memphis, rented a car, and here we are!" She flung her arms out wide to embrace her daughter. "I tried calling you all morning, but you never answered. I thought I was going to have to call the police!"

"I'm so happy to see you," Addie murmured into her mother's shoulder. From the corner of her eye, she could see Felix sitting on top of Jerry on the couch, both paws resting on Jerry's shoulders as Jerry sat there with a mix of horror and amusement on his face. "Felix!" Addie yelped. "Get off of Jerry!"

With one swift lick to the side of Jerry's face, Felix leapt down and trotted to his bed, where he plopped himself down with a snort.

"I couldn't tell if he was going to eat me or lick me to death," Jerry said finally, taking out a handkerchief from his pocket to wipe off his glasses. "You hear all these terrible things about pit bulls. I wasn't sure what to expect when your mother told me you had one."

"He's about as vicious as a gnat," Addie replied.

"He seems very sweet," Jerry agreed. "If not a little excitable."

"I'm so sorry," Addie said. "He forgets his manners sometimes."

"That's okay." Jerry grinned. "So do I."

"When was the last time you greeted someone like that?" Addie asked.

"Last night when your mother told me we were boarding a plane to the Delta of Arkansas." Jerry laughed.

Addie leaned down to give Jerry a quick peck on the cheek. "I'm so glad you came. Thank you."

"Of course."

"I haven't been here in so long," Addie's mother lamented. She walked into the kitchen. "But I swear it even smells the same."

"Some of the furniture and decorations are the same," Addie said. "The kitchen table was Aunt Tilda's and so were most of the pictures on the walls. The bed in the spare room was hers. Some of her belongings were donated when she died, mostly clothes and linens—but she left a few things with the house. Most of it was out in the old shed. I don't think anybody ever thought to look there."

"Did you refinish the table?" her mother asked. "It looks lovely."

"I did," Addie replied. She felt a surge of pride. "I'm working on an old dresser, too."

"Jonah would be so proud of you."

"I don't know about that." Addie looked away from her mother. "I haven't exactly been doing things the way he taught me."

"No matter about that." Her mother took Addie's hands in hers. "I always thought you spent too much time trying to please him, anyway. Now, tell us, what are your plans for the day?"

"I don't have any plans."

"I wanted to take Jerry down to see the river. And maybe we could get some lunch?"

"Sounds good." Addie shrugged. "There is a cute restaurant over by the clinic."

"It's been so long since I've been to a little southern town," Addie's mother said. "I'm so glad to be here."

Addie grinned and wrapped her arms around her mother's neck. "Me too, Mom."

Three Sisters was a diner located on the sole strip of highway that ran through Eunice. It was run by three women—sisters who had never been anywhere their whole lives except to the next town over, and any one of them would tell you that they didn't like it much. They lived in the same house they were born in, in 1938, 1939, and 1941. The house was right behind the diner, the last remaining house left on the business side of the town.

Patty Mae, Fannie Lou, and Opal Ruth were, in Addie's

mind, responsible for some of the best food she'd ever eaten in her entire life. The first time Wanda took her there she'd eaten until she was sick.

"Addie!" Fannie Lou exclaimed when Addie, her mother, and Jerry walked through the door. "So good to see you."

"Hi, Fannie Lou," Addie said, a broad smile crossing her face. "How are you?"

"Oh, the usual." She squeezed one of Addie's hands. "And who do we have here?"

"This is my mother, Miranda, and my stepfather, Jerry."

"Howdy," Jerry said. He stuck out his hand to greet Fannie Lou.

Fannie Lou raised an eyebrow at Addie. "Howdy."

"You've got a lovely place."

"Why don't I show y'all to your table?" Fannie Lou beckoned them to follow her. "Where's he from—that stepfather of yours?" she whispered to Addie.

"Chicago," Addie replied. "Where are Patty Mae and Opal Ruth? I've never seen you up front by yourself before."

"Patty Mae's at home today. She's under the weather," Fannie Lou replied. "And Opal Ruth is in the back fixin' up the usual for Mr. Smoot."

"Augustus Smoot?"

"You know him?"

"He's my neighbor," Addie said.

"Lord, child."

"He's not as crazy as people think."

"He's a might younger than me," Fannie Lou replied, "but I've known him all my life. He don't speak to nobody now. Magdalene always answers the door. It's the same thing every week—chocolate gravy and biscuits."

"What is chocolate gravy?" Jerry asked.

Fannie Lou stopped dead in her tracks. "You ain't never had chocolate gravy?"

"I can't say that I have."

"Well, bless your heart!"

"Why do I feel like she's insulting me?" Jerry asked Addie as they were led toward the dining area.

"Because she is."

"But she was so nice about it."

Addie was about to respond when she saw Artemis Floyd waving at her. Artemis wasn't alone. Both Jasper and his father were seated at the table as well.

"Would you all like a booth or a table?" Fannie Lou asked.

"Either is fine," Addie's mother piped up.

Artemis stood up from her table and started to walk over to the booth where Addie, her mother, and Jerry were about to sit down. "Hello, Addie," Artemis said. "How are you, my dear?"

"I'm good, Mrs. Floyd. How are you?"

"Call me Artemis. I know I've told you that before. Is this your mother and father?"

"I'm Miranda," Addie's mother said. "And this is her stepfather, Jerry."

"It's so nice to meet you both," Artemis replied. "I'm Artemis Floyd. Your daughter and my son, Jasper, are good friends, I believe."

"I think I've heard Addie mention a friend named Jasper a time or two."

Addie wanted to crawl under the nearest table and stay there. "Mom, we should probably sit down and look at the menu. The lunch specials will be over soon."

"Why don't you all come over and sit with us? We'd love to have the company."

"We were actually thinking about taking our food to go."

"No we weren't," Addie's mother said. "We'd love to join you, Artemis. What a nice offer."

Fannie Lou busied herself making the table ready for six people while Addie tried to ignore Jasper's eyes on her. She knew how awful she looked after hardly any sleep, and she knew how awful it was going to be having to sit through an awkward lunch with four nosy parents.

"Sit!" Artemis commanded.

Addie said nothing as her mother and Jerry made small talk. After a few seconds Jasper cleared his throat. "Hello, Addie."

"I thought you said your parents were out of town," she whispered.

"They were out of town. They came home unexpectedly last night."

"Oh."

"Why are you acting weird?"

"I'm not."

"Yes. You are."

"I didn't even know your dad went out in public."

Jasper put the menu in front of his face. "He's paralyzed, not dead. Besides, where did you think 'out of town' was? The barn next door?"

"So, Jasper," Addie's mother said, drawing their attention back to the group. "I don't know if I've ever heard how the two of you met."

"I was there the night she brought that disaster of a dog into the clinic," Jasper replied.

"You don't work there, too?"

"No, no," Jasper said. "I was there talking to Doc about something or other when Addie came rushing in."

"I see."

"She saved that dog's life," Jasper continued. "He would have died without her."

"That's what we heard," Jerry said.

"He's quite a dog, especially considering all he's been through."

"He sure gave me a hero's welcome." Jerry chuckled. "I told Miranda I was worried about Addie having a pit bull . . . you know, because of all the terrible things you hear about them."

"I've seen animals endure less and come out meaner than a bag of snakes," Jasper replied. "He's got some kind of spirit."

"Some of us see more than our fair share of cruelty in life," Addie spoke up. "The only difference between people and animals is that people are cruel on purpose."

"Well," Jasper began. "Felix is lucky to have you, then. I don't believe there's a cruel bone in your body."

Jasper's gaze was on Addie, searing into her. It was the same look he'd had in the hallway of his loft in Memphis, and the same look he'd had that night in the kitchen at her house.

"How long will you folks be in town?" Artemis asked, breaking the awkward silence between Addie and Jasper.

"Just until tomorrow," Addie's mother replied. "I'm a nurse, and I've got to be back at work for the weekend shift."

"Oh, that's too bad. The Delta Blues Festival downtown starts this weekend."

"That sounds like fun," Jerry said.

"It is," Artemis said. "Isn't it, Jack?"

"Huh?" Jack grunted. "Oh, yeah. A blast."

"Sometimes Jasper even plays in a bluegrass band," Artemis continued. "Jasper, honey, have you decided if you'll play this year?"

Addie choked on her water. "Jasper plays in a bluegrass band?"

"He plays the harmonica. It's a family tradition."

"Really?"

"Oh, yes," Artemis said. She grinned at Jasper. "We always have a get-together at the farm with some of the musicians after the first night of the festival. Addie, honey, you ought to come. I'm sure Jasper would love that."

The scraping of forks against plates was the only response as Jasper stared down at his food. Everyone was silent, waiting for a response. "Yes. I would like that," he said finally.

Addie concentrated on the menu in front of her. What had taken him so damn long to respond? She was so busy being irritated that she didn't even hear Artemis talking to her until the entire table was staring at her.

"Addie, honey?"

"Hmm? Oh, I'm sorry. What was it? I didn't hear you."

"I was just asking you about your job. Jasper tells me you're working at the clinic with Dr. Dixon?" Artemis asked.

Addie nodded. "Yes. I've been there a few weeks. I really like it."

"Doc said you've brought the whole place up to date electronically."

"It's nothing fancy," Addie said. "But they were working with a few older programs, and it was causing some trouble."

"You have some kind of degree in computers?" Jack Floyd spoke up, looking at Addie for the first time.

"No. I have a degree in fine arts. But I know a thing or two about computers."

"That what those two paid for while you were at college?" Jack pointed at Addie's mother and Jerry with his fork. "You want to work there for the rest of your life?"

"I have no idea what I'm going to do with the rest of my life, Mr. Floyd," Addie replied. "No idea."

"Nobody's ever been able to tell Adelaide that she has to do anything," her mother said. "She gets that from me."

"Well, then it sounds like your kid and my kid are two peas in a pod."

"Oh?"

"If I told Jasper the sky was blue he'd spend all night tellin' me that it was green."

"Well"—Addie's mother shrugged—"you know what they say—you can't put an old head on a young body."

Jack Floyd smiled and gave a hearty laugh that turned into a cough so loud that Artemis had to clap him on the back. Addie had never seen Jack smile. She'd never seen him laugh, and judging from Jasper's reaction, he rarely saw it, either. He was giving her one of his very own lopsided grins, and it occurred to Addie how much Jasper looked like his father. For a second, everything was perfect. Addie resisted the urge to reach underneath the table and take Jasper's hand in hers.

"Actually," Jasper began, "Addie knows a lot about furniture, too."

"Moving it?" Jack grunted.

"No, Dad." Jasper rolled his eyes. "She took some of the old barn wood from the Jones place and"—Jasper paused—"what is it that you call it, Addie?"

"Repurposed," Addie finished.

"I saw some of that kind of thing on HGTV," Artemis said.

"It was really quite interesting. Have you been doing this a long time?"

"About six years."

"What got you started?" Artemis asked. "I just love learning new things."

And there it was. The question. Talk of furniture always led back to Jonah. When was it going to be easy to say his name? "I had a fiancé back in Chicago. He taught me. We owned a furniture store together."

"Oh?"

"I sold it before I moved here. I managed to save a little from the sale, but not much," she continued. "That's one reason I've started to work on projects while I'm here. I'm hoping to get back into the business."

"What made you decide to leave Chicago?" Artemis wanted to know.

"Well," Addie began tepidly, "my aunt died."

"Yes, honey, and we're all so sorry."

"That's okay." She knew what Artemis was really asking. She was asking, "So, you were practically married and had a business. Why would you pick up and move and leave all that?" Addie couldn't stand it. She knew what was coming next, and she waited.

"And your fiancé, he was okay with you moving all the way down here alone?"

Addie could feel her mother shifting uncomfortably next to her. Jerry was looking at her sympathetically. Part of her wished that Jasper had told them so that she wouldn't have to, so that they wouldn't be having this conversation. But she knew he never would have violated her trust like that. She was going to have to explain it. All of it. "He's dead," she blurted.

The table fell silent.

"My fiancé died," Addie repeated. "We owned a store together, but I sold it alone because he died in a car accident."

"Oh, honey. I'm so sorry."

They were all staring at her. She knew what they were thinking, even her mom and Jerry, and it made her sick. They felt sorry for her. They felt sorry for asking questions. They would go home and talk about it with each other. They'd ask her how she was doing the next time they saw her. "I'm not feeling very well." Addie stood up, the chair scraping against the concrete floor. "I think I'm going to go outside and get some air."

"Are you okay?" Addie's mother asked. "Do we need to go home?"

"I'm fine."

"You look green."

"I just need some air." Without waiting for her mother's response, Addie hurried out of Three Sisters.

CHAPTER 35

"How are you feeling, honey?" Addie's mother put the back of her hand up to Addie's forehead. "You don't have a fever."

"I'm better."

"Do you want to talk about it?"

"That's the last thing I want to do," Addie replied. "I'm fine, but I'm sorry I ruined our afternoon."

"You didn't ruin anything," her mother said. "We came here to see you."

Addie flipped absently through her aunt's recipe box. She was looking for something, a recipe she'd seen earlier with chocolate and coconut. "I would have cooked something if I'd known you were coming."

"You would have *what*?" her mother asked, in shock.

"I would have cooked for you."

After a few stunned seconds, her mother burst out laughing. "When you moved down here, you couldn't boil water."

"You're the one who suggested I bake when I needed to apologize to Jasper," Addie replied indignantly.

"So I was."

Addie turned her attention back to the recipe box. It didn't matter that she couldn't find what she was looking for. She doubted she had the ingredients for it, anyway. She made a mental note to get to the Piggly Wiggly ASAP. Maybe she could find something quick, with just a couple of ingredients. As she leafed through the yellowed index cards, her nails scraped against a piece of paper that was larger than the cards. It wasn't yellowed like the rest. It had been carefully folded over several times. In her aunt's handwriting was a recipe for something called boiled tea.

Boiled Tea (You'll need this for when you have company, Adelaide.)

In large glass pitcher add 1–2 cups of sugar. Place metal knife in pitcher.

On stove boil 2–3 cups of water. Add 2 family tea bags. Cover and let steep.

(Remember, Adelaide, the longer you steep, the stronger the tea.)

Remove the tea bags and pour hot tea slowly into pitcher.

(Remember, Adelaide, the metal knife will absorb heat so glass won't break.)

Now add cold water until tea is the color you desire.

Stir well!

(Don't forget what I said about the tea. People down in

these parts like strong tea. But if you steep for too long, you'll become bitter. There's a fine line between strong and bitter, my angel. Don't become bitter.)

Adelaide fought the tears she could feel forming in the corners of her eyes. Her aunt had known she'd come here. She'd known Addie wouldn't throw away her beloved recipe box, and more importantly, she'd known Addie would open it.

"Do you think Aunt Tilda would be proud of me?" Addie asked her mother after a few minutes.

"Oh, honey, she *is* proud of you," her mother replied. "I can feel her all around this house."

Addie smiled. "I think I'm going to sit out on the porch for a while. Want to come?"

"I'm going to stay in here with Felix. You go on."

Jerry was sitting in the porch swing. Long curls of smoke siphoned out through his nose and mouth. He gave his stepdaughter a sheepish grin. "Don't tell your mother. She thinks I quit."

"She's going to smell it on you."

"Have a seat," Jerry said. "That is if you can abide my secondhand smoke."

"I think I'll be okay."

"So," Jerry began after a few minutes of silence. "Do you really like it down here?"

Addie shrugged. "I guess so."

"You guess?"

"Yes," Addie paused. "I mean, yes."

"You don't sound very confident."

"I like it," Addie said. "I guess I just thought things would be different."

"Different?"

"Uncomplicated."

Jerry ground his cigarette onto the rim of a soda can. "You've had a rough go of it for the last little while. I don't think anybody could have handled it any better than you have."

"Not counting my little outburst today."

"Counting it," Jerry said.

"Thanks."

"I know I'm not your father. I know you were an adult when your mom and I met." He furrowed his brow, and a cascade of wrinkles tumbled down his forehead. "But would it be okay for me to give you some fatherly advice?"

"I think it's about time someone started giving me some fatherly advice."

"No matter where you move, life is going to get complicated. It's going to get messy."

"I'm tired of messy. I'm ready for normal."

"Good luck with that. I felt the same way about my life when I met your mother. I'd just gotten out of a divorce, just moved to a new city, just started out on my own for the first time in a long time. The last thing I wanted was to meet someone new."

"So then why did you start dating my mom?"

"As if I had any choice in the matter. Do you know your mother?" Jerry laughed. "She's quite persuasive. But it was more than that, Addie. I fought it for a while, but then I realized that it was silly to continue fighting what was right in front of me for some idealized version of life I'd built up in my head. That kind of normal just doesn't exist."

"You're right," Addie replied. "I know you're right. It's just that my whole life, all my plans, all my dreams, everything was destroyed with one accident. Now I'm starting all over, and I don't want to be sad again. I don't want to cry. I don't want to hurt. I don't want to answer any more questions."

"I know."

"Do you?"

"Well, no," Jerry admitted. "I don't know. Not really." He reached into his pocket and pulled out an envelope. "I've been waiting to give this to you all day."

"What is it?"

"Just open it."

Addie looked inside the envelope. It was a check. "Jerry, no. I told Mom I don't want your money."

"She told me. But you and your mother aren't the only ones who can be stubborn, you know. She tells me you may be staying longer than you anticipated, and I thought you might need the extra help."

"Just an extra month or two," Addie said. "I'll pay you back."

"Just let me be your father this one time." He put his arm around Addie and pulled her close. "Now, you like this Jasper fellow? The one we had lunch with today?"

"Yes."

"Well, he seemed nice enough," Jerry said. "Kind of stuffy, but nice. His father, he's a real asshole, isn't he?"

Addie covered her mouth to stifle a giggle. The giggle turned into a laugh, and before they knew it, both she and Jerry were roaring.

"What on earth is going on out here?" Addie's mother demanded, sticking her head through the doorway. "Jerry, what's that smell? Have you been smoking? *Have you been smoking?*"

"Of course not!" Jerry protested, trying to catch his breath.

"Addie and I were just solving the world's problems, weren't we?"

"Absolutely. Come out and sit with us, Mom," Addie replied. "You won't believe the things your husband has been saying about you."

THE NEXT MORNING, as Addie's mother and Jerry packed their bags, she found herself wishing that they could stay longer. Part of her longed for the solitude of her empty house, yes, but she thought she could forgo that solitude for a few more days.

"Are you sure you all have to leave today?" Addie asked. "You never miss work, Mom. Don't you have some time?"

"You know how busy this time of year is, Addie," her mother replied. "The end of summer brings out the stupid in people. I can't tell you how many drunks we stitch up on a daily basis."

"Don't forget about the guy who accidentally glued himself into a gorilla suit," Jerry said with a wry grin. "That one's my favorite."

"How do you accidentally glue yourself into anything, let alone a gorilla suit?"

"We never got the whole story." Addie's mother laughed. "But I'm willing to bet my nursing license it had something to do with several shots of whiskey."

"People are ridiculous," Addie agreed. "But I still wish you could stay."

"I know, sweetheart," her mother replied. "We've had such a good time. Maybe we can visit again soon."

"I hope so," Addie said. "This house is too quiet sometimes."

"Your aunt used to say that. That's what she would always say when she called to ask if you could come and visit."

"I remember." Addie thought about the recipe she'd found the night before. She was filled with a longing for her aunt. She wanted to rush back into the kitchen and take out the recipe from the box and pore over it. She wanted to see her name written in her aunt's scrawling cursive.

Addie's mother leaned over and gave her a kiss on the forehead. "We should probably head on outta here. We've got to have that car back before noon if we only want to pay for half a day."

"Will you call me when you get home?"

"Of course we will," Jerry said. "Now, get over here and give me a hug."

Addie bounded over to Jerry and wrapped her arms around his neck. "It was good to see you, Jerry."

"You too, kiddo," Jerry replied. "Don't forget about our talk."

"I won't," Addie promised.

"Let's move it, Jer," Addie's mother said, pulling her rolling suitcase toward the door. "I'm not paying for a full day!"

CHAPTER 36

ADDIE COULD SEE LOREN SITTING ALONE INSIDE JENNIE'S. HE was concentrating on the menu, one hand stuck inside the peanut bowl. She thought about leaving, making up some kind of excuse so that she didn't have to go in. She couldn't remember why she'd agreed to the date in the first place. She felt the same pang of guilt she'd been feeling since she left her house—what about Jasper? Would he be angry if he knew she was going to dinner with another man, another man who was technically one of his employees?

It's only dinner, she thought. Besides, she hadn't even spoken to Jasper since her mother and Jerry's visit. He hadn't called. He hadn't texted. He hadn't made a single attempt to have any kind of contact with her, and *it's only dinner*, she repeated inside her head.

Loren looked up and waved. His hand knocked over the bottle

of beer in front of him as she stepped inside, and it spewed out onto the table.

"Well, you look right pretty this evening." Loren stood up to greet her.

"Thanks," Addie replied.

"Thought maybe you'd changed your mind."

"What makes you say that?"

"I saw you standing outside." Loren pointed to the window. "Looked like you were tryin' to make up your mind."

"I was just checking my reflection," Addie said.

"Well, ain't no reason for that."

"Hey, y'all." Jennie appeared in front of them. "What can I get ya?"

"I haven't had time to look at the menu," Addie said. "Do you have a suggestion?"

"Everything's good, darlin'."

"I'll just have the usual." Loren pulled the menu away from Addie's face. "I'd recommend the burger. With everything."

"I'll have that, but with no tomatoes."

"Good choice." Jennie winked at her.

"How long have you been here, in Eunice?" Addie asked Loren once Jennie meandered off.

"A few months."

"And you already have a usual?"

Loren grinned. "I come here just about every day for lunch. Jennie's brother Jerome is a great cook."

"I've just been here one time," Addie admitted. Her cheeks flushed as she thought about that night.

"So what have you been doing since you moved here?" Loren asked. "Well, other than making the locals angry at parties."

"That's why I don't go out. I always end up making people angry."

"Something tells me Redd Jones is always angry."

"Something tells me you're right."

"Do you know why Redd has it out for you?"

"I don't know that he has it out for me." Addie shifted in the booth. The bends of her knees were sweaty. "We just got off on the wrong foot is all."

"You think it has anything to do with that dog staying with Jasper?" Loren took a swig of his beer.

"So you've seen her."

"Everybody on the farm has seen her," Loren replied. "It's kinda hard to hide a big white pit bull."

"She's not that big."

"Not since she's had them pups."

"So you've seen them, too."

"They're cute, but rumor has it that they're not Jasper's."

"Oh, yeah?" Addie bit the sides of her cheeks. "Where did you hear that?"

"Just around." Loren shrugged. "You know anything about it?"

"No."

"You sure?"

"Why do you care what I know?" Addie reached down to scratch her sweaty legs. "I thought this was dinner, not an interrogation."

"Why are you being so defensive?"

"You know," Addie said, twisting herself out of the booth, "I think I'm just going to leave."

"Aw, come on, don't be like that." Loren followed Addie outside. "I was just curious, that's all."

"What's it matter to you, anyway?"

"It doesn't." Loren jammed his hands down into his pockets. "I'm just nervous, that's all. You came in looking so pretty. I didn't know what to say."

Addie sighed. "It's all right."

"Come on back inside."

"I can't," Addie said. "Look, you're really nice. And you seem like a good guy, but this was a mistake."

"Gee, thanks."

"It's not like that." Addie struggled to come up with the right words. "I just can't do this right now. I'm sorry."

"Are you seeing somebody?"

"I don't know," she replied. "I don't even know how much longer I'll be living here. I hadn't planned to be here this long."

Loren gave her a half smile. "You don't know much, do you?"

"I don't know anything right now."

"Come on." Loren reached out and clapped her on the back. "I'll walk you to your car."

JASPER WAS SITTING on the front porch when Addie got home. She wondered what it was about her front porch that made people think they could just walk on up and sit down. He didn't say anything when he saw her.

"What's wrong?" she asked. "Is everything okay with the puppies?"

"They're fine." Jasper stood up. "How was your date with Loren?"

Oh, shit. Addie scratched the back of her head. Her ponytail suddenly felt very tight. "It was dinner."

"I heard you two looked pretty cozy up in that booth."

"We were on opposite sides. And I left after about ten minutes. Whoever calls that cozy needs to consult a dictionary."

"What were you doing there with him, Addie?"

"I was having dinner."

"That's it?"

"That's it!" Addie threw her hands up in the air. "That's it. And I didn't even get to eat because I left."

"Why?"

"How much do you know about him?" Addie asked. "I mean, did you run a background check or something before you hired him?"

Jasper narrowed his eyes at her. "What do you mean?"

"He was asking a lot of questions about Delilah. Wanted to know if she had anything to do with Redd."

"What did you tell him?"

"Nothing!" Addie exclaimed. "And it's a good thing since everybody seems to have a Dixie cup attached to a piece of string in this damn town."

"You can trust Loren," Jasper said.

"I tell you what," Addie began. "Why don't you make me a list of the people I can talk to and the people I can't talk to. Go ahead and make me a list of the people I can go to dinner with while you're at it."

"Don't think I haven't thought about it."

"I can go to dinner with whoever I want!" Addie slammed her key into the lock. "I can talk to whoever I want! Last time I checked, you didn't *want* to have that conversation with me."

"That's not what I meant," Jasper said. "I want to have that conversation, but not right now."

"Well, I want to have it right now."

"I can't."

"Then what are you doing here, Jasper?"

"I don't know."

Addie opened her door and stepped inside. She turned around to face him one last time and said, "Maybe it's about time you figured it out."

CHAPTER 37

THE CHECK FROM JERRY SAT ON THE KITCHEN TABLE, AND ADDIE sat staring at it. She tipped back in her chair, thinking. It was more than enough to get her through for the next few months—enough for her to fix the house and enough for her to survive until she could start selling some of the pieces on which she was working. It was enough for her to start a life in the Delta, a life that wasn't temporary.

Addie couldn't bring herself to do anything with it other than stare. She stared and stared. As she stared, she heard a sharp crack beneath her. Before she could react, Addie was on the floor in a heap of wood.

It wasn't the first time she'd broken a chair. Once before, several years ago, she and Jonah had been perusing a flea market just outside of the city. Addie found a vintage wingback chair and fell in love. Jonah had argued with her, said that the structure was weak. But all she'd seen was an opportunity to reupholster the chair in a funky fabric for one of their clients.

"Can't you just see Carmelle in this chair?" Addie had asked. "It's exactly what she's been looking for."

"No way," Jonah had replied. "That chair is good for one thing and one thing only—kindling."

That was when Addie had plopped herself down into the chair. She teetered for a moment on the cushion before falling completely through it to the asphalt below. It seemed like everyone at the flea market stopped to stare as Jonah and the chair's owner struggled to pull her out from its clutches.

She remembered laughing about it during the ride home, but Jonah hadn't thought it was quite so funny, especially after paying the two hundred fifty dollars to the owner. They argued for hours about it, a running theme in their relationship those final months.

She lay on the floor of her kitchen. She'd never told anyone about that day; there were so many days she never mentioned. It didn't make sense to her how those memories could feel so far away and also as if they happened yesterday. How could she feel both free and tangled up? How could she, after those years with Jonah, move on? But Jonah would want that, wouldn't he? From her? He'd wanted that from people and furniture. He'd reveled in the reaction of his clients when he showed them what he'd done with their once dirty and decrepit pieces of furniture. That revival of life had been Jonah's greatest joy.

It was time for her to find *her* greatest joy.

Addie knew Jasper would be angry if he knew she was even thinking about telling Wanda about Delilah and the puppies, but Addie couldn't come up with an excuse that would pacify Wanda for bolting from her party and ignoring her phone calls, and she was too tired to try. She knew she was going to have to tell the truth.

"So, what you're saying is that you've been lying to me for weeks." Wanda leaned back in her chair at the kitchen table. "Addie, I thought we were friends."

Addie pulled two tea bags out of a fresh pitcher of tea. "We are friends, Wanda."

"Then why didn't you tell me about all of this?"

"Jasper made me swear I wouldn't tell."

"Since when did you start listening to Jasper?"

"Since I broke the law and dragged him into my giant mess."

"Well, that explains why Redd came to the party. He knew you'd be there." Wanda put her fingers to her temples. "Lord have mercy, I thought he was having a stroke."

"That's another reason I didn't tell you," Addie replied. "I promised Bobby, too."

"I oughta kick Bobby's ass," Wanda said. "He shoulda gone straight to the cops."

"I think he wanted to." Addie placed her hand on Wanda's reassuringly. "It seems like Redd Jones has some kind of hold over this town. Over Bobby. Over Jasper. Even over Doc."

"I know my brother. He can tolerate a little roughness, but there's no way he would let Redd get away with that kind of shit."

"Maybe that's why he left."

"What does Jasper say?"

"Jasper says to be patient," Addie said. "He says he'll take care of it. But I don't know. Everybody is keeping secrets."

"If Jasper says he'll take care of it, he will," Wanda said.

"I'm tired of waiting on Jasper." Addie was tired of waiting on Jasper for more than one reason. She wanted to tell Wanda more about that, too, but she knew that Wanda would ask even more questions that she didn't have the answers to. She bit her lip.

"He'll take care of it, Addie."

"Redd knows I took Delilah," Addie continued. "Doc told me not to worry, but I saw it in his eyes at your party. He knows. And if he knows, that means someone else knows."

"Redd's meaner than a junkyard dog, but he ain't stupid. And comin' to my house the other night, well, that was stupid. Somethin's got him off his game."

"I hate to admit it, but he scares me," Addie said.

"You've just got to lay low for a while," Wanda replied. "Keep a low profile. Give Redd some time to forget about it."

"Let's talk about something else." Addie shook her shoulders in an attempt to rid the chill she felt. "I heard there was some kind of music festival in Eunice next weekend?"

"Every year."

"Why didn't you tell me?"

"Honey, it ain't like we've been talking much here lately," Wanda said.

"I know," Addie replied. "I'm sorry."

"I figured you already knew about it. It's front-page news."

"Artemis Floyd told me that Jasper plays harmonica." Addie let out a giggle. "I swear I about fell out of my chair."

"The man can flat-out play!"

"Seriously?"

"We'll have to go down and watch him."

"Artemis said the same thing," Addie replied. "And then she invited me to some kind of party afterward."

"You got invited to the Floyds' Delta Blues party?" Wanda squealed. "Everybody who's anybody will be at that party."

"Yes, and Jasper didn't look happy about it, either."

"How did he look?"

"Uncomfortable, mostly."

"Relax." Wanda placed her hand over Addie's. "That's just Jasper's regular look."

"I just can't figure out why he wouldn't want me there."

"So are you going to go?"

"You said so yourself—I need to lay low for a while."

"What we need is to go to that party," Wanda replied. "I've never been invited, and I'm dying to know what actually goes on there."

"We're not going."

"We are."

"I haven't talked to Jasper since the day I went to lunch with Loren," Addie said. "He isn't going to want me there. I promise."

"Well, he didn't invite you, did he?"

"I'm not going."

Wanda stood up and walked into the living room. "That party is going to be amazing. What do you think I should wear?"

"Are you even hearing me?"

"No. I'm watching your half-naked neighbor," Wanda said. "Doesn't it drive you crazy to live near him?"

Addie shrugged. "Not really."

"Well, I guess I better get going. I've got to go pick up Bryar. I'll call you and we can make plans!"

Addie waited until Wanda's car had disappeared down the street before she walked over to Augustus's house. He was still standing in the yard as she approached him. "Why do you act this way?" she demanded. "You know you freak people out, right?"

He wasn't looking at her. His gaze was fixed on Felix, who was at the window. "Those dogs can be mean," Augustus said. "I prosecuted a couple cases as a D.A. Those were the days before they passed laws banning people from owning them."

"Felix isn't mean," Addie replied. "We've had this conversation, remember?"

"He seems like a good dog."

"I think it's people who are mean," Addie said. "I found him inside a trash bag. He'd been shot and left to die. I don't know any dog that could do that."

"You may be right." Augustus finally turned his attention to Addie. "Would you like to come inside?"

Addie had never seen anybody over at his house except for the woman she assumed was Magdalene. Not a single visitor. Her curiosity was killing her. "Sure."

"Lovely," Augustus replied. "I'll put on some tea."

Addie had envisioned a potential episode of *Hoarders,* but the house was clean. Except there were books everywhere. There were books on the dining room table. There were books on the chairs and on the kitchen counters. Addie had to put her hands into the pockets of her jeans to keep from peeking beneath their covers. "Have you read all of these books?" she asked.

"Yes," Augustus replied. He pulled a robe around his pale, bony body. "I'm a collector of sorts."

"I've never seen so many books."

Augustus smirked at her. "You've never been to a library?"

"That's not what I meant."

"Of course it wasn't."

"May I look at them?"

"Make sure your hands are clean," Augustus said.

Addie looked down at her hands. They seemed fine to her. She picked up the book nearest her and opened it. The inside showed that it was a first edition of *Lolita.* There was a name scrawled on the inside, but she couldn't make out what it said.

"Have you ever read that book?" Augustus asked. "It was one of my wife's favorites."

"I read it once in college." Addie leafed through the pages. "Is that your wife's name written on the inside?"

"I'm sure that it is," Augustus said. "Eleonora."

"Like the short story?"

"Yes. Just like the short story by Edgar Allan Poe."

"That's a beautiful name."

"I've always thought so." Augustus handed Addie a glass filled with an amber-colored liquid. "So Tilda Andrews was your aunt, eh?"

"She was." Addie sniffed at the glass. "I thought we were having tea."

"Rye whiskey beats tea," he replied. "I always liked her, your aunt."

"Did you know her well?" Addie put the glass to her lips and winced. The smell burned her nostrils and all the way down her throat.

"They got on well," Augustus replied.

"Who got on well?"

"Your aunt and my wife were good friends with another one of our neighbors, Rubina." Augustus seemed exasperated at Addie's question. "Although I believe they moved her to a nursing home this past March."

"I met Ms. Rubina once. But I never met your wife."

"They had a falling out many years ago," Augustus said. He

poured himself another glass of whiskey with a shaky hand. "It was all over Zeke."

"I met Zeke once, too."

"Nobody liked him much. Not even Tilda liked him. But she sure did love him."

"If he was so awful, why did she love him?"

"Your aunt was stubborn as a mule."

Addie smiled. Her mother had always said that her aunt was the most stubborn woman alive. She didn't doubt that the reputation had followed her into death as well. She remembered the words scrawled across the recipe: *Don't become bitter.* Had her aunt become bitter? "Did your wife and my aunt make up before your wife died?"

"No," Augustus said. "They never did make up, and I don't think your aunt ever forgave herself. My wife has been dead for over a decade. Tilda would come and see me sometimes, and I think it was just because she missed being inside this house."

"May I ask you another question?"

"I don't see what I could do to stop you."

"Why do you let everybody think that you're crazy?"

Augustus swirled the whiskey around in the glass. He took several long sips until it was once again empty. "It's easier."

"Easier than what?"

"Than everything else."

"You're lucky they don't lock you up," Addie said. "Or put you in a nursing home like Ms. Rubina."

"Magdalene would never let that happen."

"Who is Magdalene?"

"She's my caretaker."

"Does she know that this is all a big scam?"

Augustus smiled, his lips curling up into his gums. "I think she has her suspicions. But unlike some people"—he nodded toward Addie—"she respects my privacy."

"You invited me into your house."

"Only after you charged over onto my property."

"Because you scare my friends."

"I don't believe anybody scares Jasper Floyd."

"I wasn't talking about him," Addie said. She glanced down at the book still in her hands. "But I'm pretty sure that I scare him plenty."

"Jasper has always been very willful, very stern—especially when his daddy is around. Jack Floyd expected too much of that boy, I always thought."

"He's a lawyer now," Addie said. "Well, he doesn't practice anymore, but I think he was probably a good one."

"I'm sure he was," Augustus said. "Of course, once a lawyer, always a lawyer. That's not a job from which a man can simply walk away."

"You did."

"But I'm crazy, remember?"

"That's the rumor."

"I like you Adelaide Andrews." Augustus poured Addie another drink. "I like you just fine."

CHAPTER 38

Downtown Eunice was buzzing with the arrival of the Delta Blues Festival. Men with clipboards and earpieces yelled at other men backing up trucks full of musical equipment down the barricaded streets. Stages had been built on all corners, and banners hung all over town touting names like Andy Coats, Gregg Allman, and the Backbone Blues Band. There wasn't a stage or an ear or a crack in one of the sidewalks not filled with music. Even the mighty Mississippi River seemed to be crashing to shore to the beat of a bass guitar.

Addie was in awe. She couldn't think of a single thing in all her twenty-eight years to compare it to.

"So, are you glad you decided to come?" Wanda gave her friend a sideways glance. "It gets bigger and better every year."

"It's impressive," Addie agreed. "How long does it last?"

"Three days." Wanda turned around to face Bryar, who was

licking an ice cream cone inside his red wagon. "But the first day is always the best, huh?"

"It is, Mama," Bryar replied. "Can I get a caramel apple next?"

Addie grinned down at him. "It's so funny that ice cream and caramel apples can be eaten during the same season around here. Further up north, where I'm from, kids eat ice cream in the summer and caramel apples in the fall."

"It can be ninety degrees in the fall," Bryar replied. "Lasting cold doesn't arrive until November."

Addie glanced from Bryar to Wanda, who just rolled her eyes. "How old are you, anyway?" Addie asked him. "Some days I think you're four, and some days I think you're forty-four."

"Meemaw says I'm an old soul."

"I believe it."

"Well, let's go find Meemaw and Pawpaw." Wanda pulled at the wagon with a grunt. "You eat too much more and I won't be able to pull that old soul of yours!"

Wanda's parents were sitting in lawn chairs in front of one of the main stages. People were littered in the grass all around them. There was no missing Leon Carter, and there was no mistaking where Wanda and Bryar got their red hair and smattering of freckles. He looked like one of Peter Pan's Lost Boys all grown up—all elbows and ears. He broke into a broad, toothy smile when he saw them.

"I wondered when you three was gonna find us." Leon lifted Bryar by the back of his overalls out of the wagon. "Boy, you look bigger than the last time I seen ya."

"You saw me yesterday!" Bryar said, bursting into a fit of giggles.

"Don't get him all riled up, Lee," Wanda's mother said. She wagged a long, red fingernail in his direction.

"Calm down, Priscilla. We ain't hurtin' nobody."

Priscilla pursed her lips and turned away from her husband to Addie and Wanda. She was every bit the antithesis of her husband. Priscilla Carter was almost sixty, but Addie ventured to guess nobody *ever* mentioned that fact in front of her. "What are you girls up to today?"

"Just here for the music." Wanda shrugged. She bent over to spread the blanket along the grass. "How many bands have we missed?"

"Lord, child," Priscilla said. "Are you trying to make Daisy Duke jealous with those shorts?"

"Mama, it's almost eighty degrees outside."

"That don't mean you gotta let all that God gave you hang out."

"Mama, I'm not sixteen."

"Precisely my point."

Wanda sat herself down onto the blanket with a harrumph. "Better sit down, Addie," she said. "Before my mother finds something wrong with you."

"How are you, Adelaide? You're here just in time!"

"In time for what?"

"I reckon Jasper and Jack Floyd is gettin' ready to play," Leon said. "At least, that's the rumor."

"Neither one of them have been to the festival since . . ." Priscilla trailed off. "Well, since what happened."

"You oughta hear Jack sing," Leon continued. "Got a voice sweet and thick as honey."

"I don't get it," Addie whispered to Wanda.

"You don't get what?"

"Jack Floyd wouldn't even be seen at the Fourth of July celebration. And that was at his own house."

"He ain't got his legs, Addie. But he sure as heck's got his voice. Nobody will notice that chair once he opens up his mouth." Wanda shrugged. "This festival . . . it just does things to people."

"This heat does things to people."

There was a hushed excitement as Jack Floyd wheeled himself out onto the stage and in front of the crowd. He was alone. "I'm a man of few words. But before we begin, I want to tell y'all that I appreciate all the encouragement to come back to the stage after this last year." Three men and two women walked out onto the stage to join Jack. One of them was Jasper. He had a look on his face that Addie hadn't seen since Memphis. He stepped up beside his father and said, "We're gonna start out with a classic by Charley Patton. It's called 'Mississippi Bo Weevil Blues.'"

Addie had never heard the song before, although just about everyone else, including Wanda, knew the song by heart. Despite the heat, people began dancing, and a few of the men took their shirts off.

The crowd roared when the song was over. Jasper stepped over to the middle of the stage and next to his father. "Now, as most of you know, my dad believes that any blues song written after 1950 isn't a real blues song," he said. He glanced down at his father and gave him a quick grin. "But I like more contemporary music."

"Every year them two get up there on stage and mend fences," Priscilla said. She shook her head.

"But they haven't played together for a while, right?" Addie asked.

"Musta been rough around that farm."

"One of my favorite contemporary blues artists is Jonny Lang," Jasper continued. "My dad has agreed to play one of Jonny's songs if I'll agree to sing."

The crowd erupted.

"Now, this is a surprise," Wanda hollered at Addie over the throng.

"Jasper doesn't usually sing?"

"Not since he was a young'un," Leon replied.

The music began once again, and Jasper said, "This one is called 'To Love Again.'"

I'd been sleepin' way too long.
Searched for the answers but couldn't find one
Thought I had it under control,
Yeah, I was dying and didn't even know.

Jasper's voice was like Jack's and, as Leon had said, thick as honey. But where Jack's voice was smooth, Jasper's was rough. Where Jack let notes run out, Jasper cut them short. Each word sounded like shoes scraping through gravel.

I needed something.
You showed me how to love again.
How to love again
When I had nothing
You showed me how to love again
How to love again.

"He's singing to you," Wanda said.

"He doesn't even know I'm here."

"He had to know you'd show up."

"Like I'm some kind of a stalker?"

"Hush."

Addie did as she was told when she saw Harper Blake walking out onto the stage. She was smiling and waving to the crowd. She stepped up in between Jasper and Jack. She slipped her arms around Jasper's middle when Jack began to talk.

"I'd like to introduce one of my son's good friends," Jack said. "She's joining us from Memphis, but she's originally a New Mexico girl. I've known her for the better part of a decade, and she's like family to me. Please welcome Miss Harper Blake."

"Thanks for inviting me, y'all."

The men without shirts began to whistle and cheer.

"She's struttin' her stuff like she's the damned queen of the Delta." Wanda crossed her arms across her chest. "She ain't even from here."

"Neither am I."

"Yeah, but you know better than to say a word that don't belong in your mouth in the first place."

"I think I'm ready to go home," Addie said. "I'd literally rather be anywhere but here."

"Sure thing, honey," Wanda replied. "But we're still going to the party tonight, right?"

"Jasper doesn't want me at that party."

"Sure he does."

"Harper is going to be there."

"Who cares whether she's there or not?"

"Please, let's just get out of here."

"Fine." Wanda sighed. "Just let me give Bryar a kiss. I had to beg my parents to keep him tonight, by the way. They had reservations at some fancy steak house at one of the casinos in Tunica."

Addie wasn't listening. She was instead replaying Harper putting her arms around Jasper over and over again. She'd been so nonchalant about it. Like it was something she did all the time.

All the time.

Wanda took hold of Addie's hand. "Try not to think about it, sugar."

"I'm fine. I just want to go home."

"Well, let's get you home. I'll fix ya a good stiff drink."

"No," Addie said. "I want to go *home.* To Chicago."

Wanda stopped short, jerking Addie back with her. "What?" She let go of her hand. "Why? Because some stupid lawyer who doesn't know her 'y'all' from her ass had her hands all over Jasper Floyd?"

"It's not just that."

"Then what is it?"

"I just don't fit here, Wanda." Addie bit the bottom of her lip. "I don't belong here any more than Harper does. It's time for me to sell my aunt's house and get back to a place I understand."

"Well, that's about the dumbest damn thing I've ever heard."

"I never planned on staying here forever," Addie reminded her. "This was always temporary."

Wanda opened up the car door with a harrumph. "Well, excuse me if I thought maybe I mattered to you."

"I can't stay here for you, Wanda."

"So you're just gonna leave us all behind?" Wanda asked. "That it, Addie? Just gonna walk away from everything and everybody down here 'cause your life ain't so easy?"

"Wanda—"

"No," Wanda cut her off. "Don't say nothin' else. I just thought more of you is all."

Addie leaned up against the car. The metal bumper of the old car singed the back of her legs. The music continued from the stage, and all around her people were eating, drinking, and laughing. It was the most alive she'd ever seen the sleepy little town. As much as she hated to admit it, it was the most alive she'd been in a long time.

Two figures broke away from the crowd and galloped toward her, a mass of arms and legs glinting in the sunlight. "Addie!" they shouted in unison.

"What are you two doing here?" Addie pushed herself off the car. Her legs throbbed.

"We came down with Harper this morning," Warren replied. "We've been here since nine A.M."

"Since nine A.M.," Neil repeated. "I drank an entire chai latte before we got here. But there are only"—he leaned in to whisper to her—"porta-potties here."

"We've been searching all over God's green earth for a toilet that flushes," Warren continued.

"Jasper really should have warned us," Neil finished.

Wanda got out of the car. She didn't look at Addie. "Is this your first time at the festival?"

"Artemis invited us. She told us about it a while back when she came up to help Jas clean out his office."

"Did she invite Harper, too?"

"She was standing right there when Artemis was telling us about it."

"You're both welcome to come back to my house," Addie said, fully aware where Wanda was headed with her line of questioning. "I do have indoor plumbing. But I don't think I'm going to the party."

"Why not?" Neil asked.

"I'm exhausted."

"Nonsense." Warren dismissed her. "You can rest when you're dead."

"I've really got a lot to do at home."

"Yeah, like pack," Wanda mumbled.

"Are you going on some kind of trip?" Warren asked.

"Not exactly."

"She's leavin'," Wanda spat. "Movin' on from our hick town."

"That's not what I said," Addie protested.

"If you're planning to leave, what better reason could there be than to go to a party?" Neil threw his hands up in the air.

Addie couldn't think of a worse reason, but she didn't say that. She knew Neil and Warren wouldn't stop pestering her and that Wanda wouldn't stop scowling until she agreed to go. It wasn't like she had to stay once she got there. It wasn't like anyone would notice, anyway.

CHAPTER 39

Addie had never seen a more spectacular sight than the Floyds' house all lit up for the party—even the scene of the blues festival downtown couldn't compare. The outside of the house was decorated in blue and gold lights, and there seemed to be a constant stream of cars pulling into the long, winding driveway.

"Where am I going to park my car? That field over there on the right?" Addie asked Warren.

"I don't know. Follow Wanda and Neil."

"I can't see them. It's raining too hard."

"You've got an umbrella in here, right?"

"No."

Warren turned to her, his horrified expression evident even in the darkness of the car. "What kind of a person doesn't keep an umbrella in her car?"

His face was so preposterous that Addie had to laugh. In that moment, she was glad she'd been pestered into coming to the party. She could leave her packing for tomorrow.

By the time Addie and Warren made it to the front porch, they were soaked to the bone. Wanda and Neil were waiting for them.

"Y'all look awful," Wanda said. She looped her fingers through her curly hair.

"Addie didn't have an umbrella," Warren mumbled. "She's a degenerate."

The four of them made their way to the bar, which was right in front of several tables and chairs that no one was using.

"Everybody here is old," Wanda whispered, taking a look around.

"I'm sure not everybody is old," Addie replied. "Maybe just everybody in this particular room is old. It's still early yet."

"I'll have a gin and tonic," Wanda said to the bartender. "Addie, what do you want?"

"Do you have Midori?" Addie asked. She wondered if this meant Wanda was speaking to her again. She'd been ignoring her since their argument at the festival.

"Sure do," the bartender replied. "Midori sour?"

"Yes, please. Could I have three cherries?"

"You got it."

Wanda was right. There were a lot of old people there, and Addie didn't know any of them. She assumed, of course, that they were all friends of Artemis and Jack. They stood in clumps, drinking wine and laughing. It wasn't much like the rowdy party Addie had expected after a blues festival. Of course, nothing about the Floyds' house was rowdy. It was genteel and elegant, a lot like, Addie thought, Harper Blake, who was standing alone with Jasper at one end of the room.

They saw Addie at the same time that Addie saw them, and there was nothing she could do to escape the embarrassment she felt as they both stared at her. She knew she couldn't run away, but that was the only thing she could think about when she locked eyes with Jasper.

"C'mon," Wanda said. She scowled over at Jasper and Harper. "Let's go find another room full of old people to hang out in."

"No, it's fine. It's not a big deal."

"Since when?"

"They're coming over here," Addie whispered. "Oh, God. I want to die."

"Shut up. Smile. And stop bein' so dramatic," Wanda shot back. "For the life of me, I can't figure out what's goin' on with you today, Adelaide."

Addie wished she knew.

"Hello, ladies," Jasper said. "I'm glad to see you two found Warren and Neil after they abandoned Harper."

"You didn't tell us that it was going to take an act of Congress to find a working restroom," Neil replied. "Adelaide was kind enough to allow us the benefit of toilet paper."

"Don't seem like Harper was abandoned," Wanda said. "Seems like she managed to get here just fine."

"Jas gave me a ride," Harper replied. She linked her arm through his. "Looks like you all got drenched."

"How bad do I look?" Warren asked. "On a scale of one to ten . . . how bad is it?"

"Seven," Harper replied without blinking.

"I've got to go find a mirror."

"It's too bad you all dumped me," Harper continued, ignoring Warren. "I got to come in through the private garage." She raised an eyebrow. "There is an elevator."

"I think I'm going to follow Warren to the bathroom," Addie said. She hurried off without waiting for a reply from anyone. She thought about Jasper and Harper alone inside the elevator together. She felt so angry and stupid. This was not how she wanted to feel. This was not what she signed up for when she packed up her life in Chicago and moved into her aunt Tilda's ramshackle house. It was supposed to be peaceful, serene. The Delta was supposed to heal her wounds, not rip them open and pack them with Mississippi River mud.

Instead of going to the bathroom, she wandered into another room just off to the side of the main part of the house. She doubted this was meant to be used as one of the party rooms. There was a white leather chaise at one end. She went over and sat down. Out the window she could see streams of cars rolling in despite the rain.

The stupid rain.

She didn't really want to look in the mirror. She knew what she'd find—limp strands of hair stuck to her neck and face, mascara where it shouldn't be, and a pink bra that was showing through her sopping white silk tank top. She lay back on the chaise.

"What are you doing in here all alone?" Harper stuck her head in the room. "Everybody is looking for you."

"Just trying to dry out."

"Well, your friend Wanda is on her third drink."

"She can handle herself."

"I'm sure she can," Harper replied drily. "She looks like she comes from sturdy stock. She says you're ready to go home to Chicago?"

"I might be." Addie stood up.

"Well, that's probably for the best." Harper walked over and put her arm on Addie's shoulder.

"What do you mean?"

"What would you do here, anyway?" Harper asked. "Your little antique business is cute, but it's not a living."

"Who told you that I have an antique business?"

"Jasper."

"Well, I don't have a business," Addie said, "not anymore."

"All the more reason for you to go back to where you came from."

Addie tilted her head back. "What do you mean, back to where I came from? What do you care where I live or what I do with my time?"

"I don't care," Harper replied. "As long as you don't live or spend your time here."

Addie took a step away from Harper. "You need to back off."

"I've worked too long and hard to land Jasper Floyd." Harper wagged a sinewy finger in Addie's face. "And no blond piece of trash from Chicago is going to come in here and take that away from me."

Addie looked around the room to see if anyone else was hearing the same conversation that she was. "If you were going to *land* Jasper, you would have done it by now," she whispered in the calmest voice she could muster. "Now if you would please get out of my way, I need to refill my drink."

Harper took a step back and allowed Addie to brush past her and out of the room. Addie's blood was boiling. She could feel the heat steaming up from her body and penetrating through her shirt. It made it even worse. She felt like she was trapped in a sauna. She trudged back to the heart of the party.

"I'm telling you, Neil"—Warren slammed his glass down onto the table—"if you go up to that deejay and ask him to play Journey, I'm leaving right this second."

"It doesn't have to be Journey," Neil protested. "I just want a *decent* song. And I'd prefer for it to be an eighties song."

"This is not a junior high dance," Warren replied. "And there is no possible way that *decent* and *eighties song* can be used in the same sentence."

Neil leaned back into the chair dramatically. As he rolled his eyes, he caught a glimpse of Addie. "Addie! I didn't even see you sitting there! Where's Jasper? I thought he went off to find you."

"I haven't seen Jasper." Addie looked over to the opposite side of the room where Wanda was sitting at her own table with at least three drinks. Wanda and Addie locked eyes, but Wanda looked away before Addie could motion for her to come over. "I'm going to go over and check on Wanda."

"I'm sure we'll still be debating the necessity of Journey when you return."

Wanda was slumped in her chair staring down at her hands when Addie sat down next to her. "What are you doing all the way over here by yourself?"

Wanda didn't look up.

"Aren't you having any fun?"

"I guess so," Wanda said. "You know, in all the years I've known Jasper and his family, this is the first time I've ever been inside his house."

"Really?"

"I thought it would be nicer."

"Yeah, it's kind of a dump, huh?"

Wanda took a sip of her drink and then grinned over at Addie. She burst into a fit of giggles. "I mean, did you *see* that kitchen? It's bigger than my whole house!"

"I got lost the first time I was here," Addie confessed.

"You know what my granny used to say about rich people?"

"No, but I have a feeling you're about to tell me."

"She used to say that half the stuff rich people own are about as useful as tits on a bull."

"Which means?"

Wanda put her hand on Addie's. "Honey, I ain't got time to explain to you why tits on a bull is useless. But it means that rich people buy junk they don't need just because they can. And after bein' in this house, I can tell ya she was right."

"I'm sorry about earlier," Addie said. "I didn't mean to upset you. I don't hate it here. I just don't know what I'm doing anymore. And that's not your fault or Jasper's fault or the fault of this town."

"Bein' lost is the only way you can find yourself. You wouldn't believe how many different versions of me I've found."

Addie grinned. "Maybe you can help me find my way."

"Come on." Wanda stood up. "Let's go back over and sit with Warren and Neil."

"I can't."

"Why not?"

Warren and Neil had been joined by Harper and Jasper. The argument had been replaced by the silent act of lips pressing to crystal full of mixed drinks. Harper wasn't smiling.

"Harper practically attacked me earlier," Addie explained.

"She told me to move back to Chicago, stay away from Jasper, and called me trash."

Wanda made a gurgling sound into her drink. "She said *what*?"

"She was pissed."

"She ain't seen pissed." Wanda stood up.

"Sit down!" Addie grabbed Wanda's arm.

"I ought to go over there and show her just exactly what trash means."

"Believe me, that's something I'd like to see," Addie replied. She watched Harper from a distance. Harper's mouth was set in a hard line. Her shoulders seemed to slump. Her hair didn't seem so glossy, and her eyes didn't seem so bright. "But she's not worth it."

CHAPTER 40

ADDIE WAS RELIEVED THAT JASPER WAS SITTING AT THE TABLE. She knew that neither Wanda nor Harper would say a word with him there.

"Jasper says he's going to have to leave the party early," Warren said. "I don't think he fully grasps the notion of being a host."

"I'm *not* the host," Jasper reminded him. "My parents are the hosts."

"So what are we supposed to do while you're gone?"

"I'll be back." Jasper stood up.

"Does this have anything to do with that phone call you got earlier?" Warren asked.

"What phone call?"

"The one you got just before you headed off to look for Addie."

"No," Jasper replied. "It doesn't."

"Why don't I go with you?" Harper was already standing up.

"It is raining like crazy outside," Jasper replied. "And it is awful muddy. You sure don't want to walk all the way down to the barn to check on a calf."

"That's what the phone call was about?" Warren asked.

"No."

"Will you at least find your parents for me before you leave?" Harper asked. "I wanted to see your mother for a bit."

It was clear she didn't want to be anywhere near Addie. At least not without Jasper in her sights.

"They're around here somewhere," Jasper replied. "The last time I saw them they were upstairs. Why don't I take you and Addie up there before I go?"

"Why do I need to go?" There was something about Jasper's disposition that didn't seem right. He wasn't looking at her when he spoke. He wasn't looking at any of them.

"My mom's been asking about you." Jasper shrugged. "I just thought I'd kill two birds with one stone."

"Fine," Addie said. She followed behind Harper, who also wasn't looking at her.

"I remember two years ago we must've played bridge with your parents all night," Harper said. "Do you remember that night? Upstairs in one of the extra bedrooms. I think it was New Year's Eve."

"I do seem to remember that," Jasper replied. "Wasn't that the year my dad got mad that we won and threw his cards all over the table?"

"Yes!" Harper giggled. "He was so angry he stormed off and your mom made him come back in and apologize to us."

"That's right! My father never apologizes."

"He must really like me."

"I'm fairly certain that if he ever needed a lawyer, he'd hire you. And I'm willing to bet that they're playing bridge up here right now."

Harper squeezed his arm and said, "I really miss those days, Jas."

Jasper cleared his throat and pushed open one of the doors on the right-hand side of the hallway, and a roar of conversation came tumbling out. He entered the room where Artemis and Jack Floyd sat with two other couples. "I'm going to have to go down and check on one of our calves," he said. "I'll be back in about an hour or so."

"How long have you ladies been here?" Artemis didn't look up from the cards in her hands. "I've been so involved in this darn game I've forgotten to be a decent host."

"Not too long," Addie replied. "Just long enough for Jasper to leave."

"He's not a very good host, is he?" Artemis asked with a wink.

"I'm not the host!" Jasper threw his hands in the air. "You are the host!"

"You're right, son." Artemis stood up. "I've got to get. I'm sure there are a million things I've forgotten to do tonight."

"You can't leave me here, Art!" Jack yelled at his wife. "We're not done here, woman!"

Artemis waved at him from the doorway. "You're an educated man! Figure it out."

Jack grumbled and wheeled his chair around to face Jasper, Harper, and Addie. "She acts like I can just slide down the banister and dance around all night."

"Can't you?" Jasper replied.

"Sure. Just give me your legs."

"Oh, Jack," Harper said, leaning down to give him a hug. "Who needs legs when you've got such a charming personality?"

"You're a liar, but a pretty one, so I'll let it pass."

"Thank you."

"Hey, I don't suppose you'd do an old man a favor and be his bridge partner, would you?" Jack asked. "I can't beat these two knuckleheads all by myself."

"Oh, I don't know a thing about bridge."

"I can teach you."

Addie glanced around the room. Jasper was gone. "You know, I should probably go back. Wanda is downstairs alone with Warren and Neil. There's no telling how much she's had to drink already."

"That girl could drink most sailors under the table," Jack replied. "Don't tell her I said this, but I respect that in a woman."

"Your secret is safe with me."

"Well, I guess I could play a few hands with you until Artemis gets back," Harper interrupted. She sat down in Artemis's chair.

"I'll teach you everything I know," Jack said. He shifted his attention to Addie. "Go on, get out of here. We don't need any distractions."

"Yes, sir." As she turned around to shut the door behind her, she caught Jack's eye. He gave her a little wave, and just before the door clicked shut she could have sworn she saw him wink.

From the top of the stairs, Addie saw Jasper at the front door. He didn't see her, and she knew he wasn't going to check on any calf. She knew there had to be a reason he left so quietly. It had to have something to do with that phone call he hadn't wanted to discuss.

"Addie!" Wanda stood at the bottom of the stairs. "Come on

down here, honey. Let's get another drink. The party's really starting to pick up."

"I'm coming. Give me just a few minutes. I've got to go to the bathroom."

"Didn't you go once already?"

"I never actually made it there."

"Well, hurry up," Wanda called over her shoulder. "I'm tired of listening to Warren and Neil arguing over eighties hair bands."

Addie considered following Wanda back into the party. Instead she opened the front door and walked out onto the porch. There were two men standing on the steps, smoking cigars. "Did either of you see where Jasper Floyd went?"

One of the men clenched the cigar between his teeth and said, "Saw him head out in his Bronco a few minutes ago. Looked like he was headed to town."

"Thanks."

She parked at the bottom of the driveway and tried to call Jasper. There was no answer. The rain was coming down so fast and so hard she struggled to see. She wasn't even sure where she was going. She fumbled through her purse when her phone began to ring, but before she could answer, the phone slipped through her hands and landed on the floorboard of the passenger's seat. She grabbed at it and looked back up to the road.

Addie saw the deer standing in the middle of the road, but it was too late. She didn't have time to honk. She didn't have time to swerve. She clipped the animal with the front driver's side and her car spun around in the muddy gravel.

Addie tasted blood, and within seconds it was over. When she came to, she was sitting halfway in between the driver's and passenger's seats. She was covered in glass and blood, and she touched her nose and winced. Her phone was still ringing and was still in her hand.

"Hello?"

"Addie?" Jasper's voice sounded far away. "Addie, are you there?"

"I hit a deer."

"You what?"

Addie winced again. Every time she spoke it was as if a thousand needles were poking at her brain. "I'm fine."

"Where are you?" Jasper's voice was becoming more and more panicked.

Addie hung up the phone and slid herself over into the driver's seat. Pushing the door open with her foot, she slid out into the rain. One of the headlights remained intact and was shining out onto the road. The deer was nowhere to be found. Addie wasn't sure what she was supposed to do—try to drive the car back to the farm or call the police. Did the police even come out this far for an accident? This wasn't a problem she'd ever encountered in Chicago, as rogue deer very rarely plagued the busy, pedestrian-lined streets of the city.

She wondered if Jonah felt any pain before he died. It was something she'd wondered over and over throughout the years, even though practically everyone told her that his death was immediate. There hadn't been time for him to feel anything. It had been the only thing that brought her comfort in those first weeks. Her mind wandered back to Jasper before she could stop it. Had she called him? Had he answered? She couldn't remember. Where had she been going, anyway?

Addie got back inside the car, her only shelter from the downpour, got the car to start after a few tries, and drove back toward the farm. The cigar-smoking men were nowhere to be found when she stumbled up the steps of the house. She wandered into the main room where she'd left her friends. It was then that she realized just how she must look. There were hundreds of eyes staring at her. She clutched the entryway for support.

A woman she didn't know rushed up to her and said, "Lord, child, what happened to you?"

"I hit a deer." Every word was painful.

The woman helped Addie over to a chair and eased her into the seat. She handed her a cocktail napkin to blot her nose. Addie tried to take the napkin from her, but the woman was dangling three of them in front of her, and she couldn't get a firm grasp on any of them.

Jasper's hands were on her shoulders and he was talking to her. "Addie? Addie? Are you okay? What happened?"

"I hit a deer. I want to sit down."

"You are sitting down." He turned to the woman in gray and said, "Clementine, go get Dr. Iverson."

"I'm fine."

"You're covered in blood."

"My head hurts."

"Come on." Jasper took her by the hand and helped her up. He led her back into the room with the white chaise. "Sit down and lay your head back. Try not to talk."

All around her there were voices. Try as she might, she couldn't make herself open her eyes. "I feel so stupid," Addie said. "I didn't even see the deer until it was too late."

Jasper put his hand gently behind Addie's head and replied, "Believe it or not, people hit deer all the time around here."

"Do you think I killed it? I looked for it, but I didn't see it anywhere."

"Probably not," Jasper said.

"Good."

Jasper stood up when Artemis came into the room followed by a man carrying a 1950s-style doctor's bag. He kneeled down in front of Addie. "What happened here?"

"I hit a deer," Addie mumbled. "I'm fine."

"My name is Dr. Iverson. Can you open your eyes for me?"

Addie's eyes fluttered open, and the doctor shone a light into each one. He blotted at the blood on her face and nose, listened to her heart, and asked her questions about the wreck.

"I don't think she needs to go to the hospital," he said. "I'm not worried about broken bones or any internal bleeding, but she may have a slight concussion. Her nose isn't broken. She may have a couple of black eyes in the morning, though. She has some cuts, and she will be banged up."

"I think she should stay here tonight, Mom." Jasper turned to his mother. "I don't want her spending the night alone."

"I think that's a good idea, Artemis," the doctor broke in. "She probably doesn't need to be by herself."

"Of course," Artemis agreed. "Of course."

"I can't leave Felix for a whole night."

"I bet Wanda will go check on him." Jasper nodded toward Wanda, who was standing in the doorway. "Won't you, Wanda?"

"Sure thing," Wanda said.

Jasper ushered everyone out of the room, stopping for a moment to shake the doctor's hand. They were alone in the room. "What in the hell were you thinking? Following me? Don't you think if

I wanted you to go with me that I would have asked? You could have gotten yourself killed."

"Who says I was following you?"

"C'mon, Addie. I'm not stupid. Besides, Bill and Ed said you asked where I was headed."

"Just like I'm not stupid enough to believe you were going to check on a bull."

"It was a calf."

"Same thing."

"Not really."

"The last thing I need is a lecture from you about honesty." Addie tried to stand up, but the room began to spin. She fell back onto the chaise in a heap.

Jasper sat down next to her. He took a handkerchief from his pocket and wiped her face. "I've never seen a person so wet and bloody."

"I've never seen a person younger than ninety years old carry a handkerchief."

"Just let me take care of you."

"I'm mad at you."

"Oh, really?"

Addie stood again, holding herself up with the back of the chaise. "Yes. Don't think you can come in here and take advantage of me because I've got brain damage."

A smile threatened the corners of Jasper's mouth. "I don't think you have any brain damage, Addie."

"You know what I mean." She pointed a wobbly finger at him. "You can't boss me around. You think just because you're gorgeous with those long eyelashes and those perfect teeth and all that you've got . . . underneath your shirt . . . you aren't foolin' me, mister." She didn't know why she was saying these things. It wasn't what she wanted to say at all. But she didn't seem to have any control over her mouth anymore.

"Do you think you can walk back to my place?" Jasper asked. He tried not to flash his perfect teeth at her as he laughed. "You need to rest where someone can keep an eye on that concussion you've obviously got."

"I'm not leaving Felix."

"He'll be fine for one night."

"Will you take me home first thing in the morning?"

"First thing."

"Fine."

Jasper tucked a loose piece of blood-covered hair behind her ear. "Come on, I'll help you."

Addie took his hand and shuffled toward the door. There were still several people waiting in the hallway. One of them was Harper. She stood with her arms crossed over her chest, eyeing the two of them as they came out of the room.

"I don't like her." Addie pointed to Harper.

"She doesn't know what she's saying," Jasper said. He pushed Addie's hand back down to her side. "She has a concussion."

"Well, I don't have a concussion, and I don't like her none, either," Wanda said, just loud enough for everyone to hear. She took Addie's free hand. "Let me help y'all."

Jasper stopped at the porch of the carriage house and said, "I can take it from here."

"Are you sure?"

"Yeah, no problem."

"I want to take a nap," Addie said once they were inside.

"Nope," Jasper replied. "No way."

"Just a quick one."

"No." Jasper led her into the bathroom. "You are covered in blood and dirt. We need to clean you up." He sat her down on the edge of the tub.

"Are you going to give me a bath?"

Jasper's cheeks reddened. "No, I'll just wet a washcloth."

Addie kicked off her sandals. "I want to take a bath."

"I'm not leaving you alone."

"Fine!" She squirmed until her dress was up to her thighs and yanked it off. It hurt to lift her arms above her head. There was no way that dress was going back on tonight. "Turn on the water."

Jasper did as he was told. "I'll just turn around, how about that?"

"You've seen me naked before. I look the same."

"This is different."

Addie tried to roll her eyes, but the pressure in her head was too intense. She sank back and let the water rush over her. Everything was fuzzy. She looked down at her bare legs as the water cascaded down over fresh bruises. Did her face look like that, too?

They sat in silence for a while, listening to the whirring of the water hitting the porcelain tub. Addie stared at Jasper's back, watched the slow, rhythmic motion of his breathing. She wondered what he was thinking about.

"Jasper?"

"Yeah?"

"Are you in love with Harper?"

"What? Why would you ask me that?"

"Are you?"

"No."

"Turn around so I can see your face."

"Addie, listen to me." Jasper turned around. "I am not in love with Harper. I have never been in love with Harper. I am never going to be in love with Harper."

"Then why won't you talk to me? Why are you keeping secrets from me?" Addie demanded.

Jasper turned back around. "I don't want to hurt you," he said. "I don't want to be another reason for you to blame yourself."

"Blame myself for what?"

"For anything," Jasper replied.

Addie traced one of the bruises on her leg with her finger and said, "I need some soap or something."

"It's behind you."

"No it's not."

Jasper grabbed the bottle of bodywash. "See? It's right here."

Addie knew she ought to be embarrassed about him seeing her in such a state. Each steam-filled breath cleared her head just a little bit more. But Jasper wasn't turning back around and she didn't want him to.

She handed him the washcloth and said, "Could you help me?"

Jasper didn't say anything as he wet her skin with the washcloth from her neck down into the small of her back. He moved around to her stomach and worked his way up to the space between her breasts. Addie couldn't help but allow a pleased sigh escape her lips when the washcloth grazed her nipples. Jasper was on his knees beside the bathtub, and abandoning the buffer, used his bare hands to explore her body.

Finally, Jasper slipped his hand into hers and helped her stand. She allowed him to admire her, relished in the delight of his eyes on her. She wasn't afraid of her steamy nakedness, of the slick feel of her skin. Addie pulled him into her, cringing only once when his belt buckle pierced a bruise.

"I'll be gentle," he murmured into her ear. His voice was thick and hoarse with desire.

Jasper cupped one hand behind her head, resting his forearm on the tiled wall of the shower. He used the other to curl one of her legs around his waist and thrust slowly inside of her. He was deliberate, controlled. Addie could see it in his eyes that he was holding back, afraid that he would hurt her.

She didn't care if it hurt. She wanted him.

Addie buried her face into his chest and bit down. Jasper's pace quickened. Arching her back, she allowed him to pick her up by her ass, settling her other leg around his waist. He ground himself into her until they were both collapsed in a heap at the bottom of the bathtub.

CHAPTER 41

Addie woke up to little wet sponges touching her skin. She opened her eyes to find seven puppy tongues licking her bare arms. At the foot of the bed, Delilah was looking on.

"You guys are getting so big!" Addie exclaimed, pulling herself to a sitting position. Pain shot through her entire body. Every muscle hurt.

"I thought I heard you awake in here," Jasper said. He appeared in the bedroom doorway.

"It's hard to stay asleep when you've got puppies all over you," Addie said with a grin. "But I'm not complaining."

"Delilah was spending all her time running back and forth checking on you and checking her pups," Jasper explained. "So I put the puppies up on the bed, and she's been fine ever since."

"Their eyes aren't even open yet," Addie marveled. "Are you sure it's okay for them to be out of their box?"

"Sure. It won't hurt them any." Jasper moseyed over to the bed and sat down, plucking puppies out of his way. "Your nose doesn't look as swollen as it did last night."

Addie reached up to touch her nose. "It hurts."

"It's going to hurt for a little while," Jasper said. "You've got bumps and bruises everywhere."

"Are my eyes black?"

"Yep."

"I must look ridiculous."

"You do," Jasper agreed. "But that's mainly because you have drool dried on your chin."

Addie's hands flew up to her mouth. "Don't look at me!"

"I'm just glad you got some sleep." Jasper dodged the pillow she threw at him.

"What time is it? I need to get home. Felix will be going nuts."

"How about some breakfast first?"

"I thought I smelled bacon," Addie replied.

"Let me move the puppies back, and then I'll help you up."

Addie grimaced as she swung her legs over the side of the bed. She watched Jasper carry the puppies back to the box in twos, whispering and nuzzling each one of them before he put them back. Delilah followed him for each trip, wagging her tail.

"I had your car towed this morning," Jasper said after the last of the puppies was moved from the bed. "I just had it towed back to your house."

"Couldn't I have driven it home?"

"I really don't think you're going to be in any shape to drive for a couple of days." Jasper held out his hand to help Addie off the bed. "Careful, now."

"I hardly remember anything from last night," Addie said with her mouth full of toast.

"You don't remember anything?"

"I remember *that.*" Her cheeks turned pink. "I just don't remember a whole lot from before we got back here."

"It's probably a good thing you don't remember much," Jasper said with a wry smile.

"I ruined the whole night." Addie looked over at Jasper. "I'm sorry. I shouldn't have followed you. I really don't know what I was thinking."

"I've learned many things about you, Adelaide," Jasper began. "And one of them is that you really can't help yourself. Besides, you didn't ruin the night. In fact, it gave me a great excuse to keep you in my bed all night."

"I didn't mind that part," Addie said.

Jasper looked down at Addie's empty plate. He was suddenly very serious. "You've been through so much already. The last thing I wanted was to get you involved in this mess."

"What mess?"

"I can't explain it all right now," Jasper replied. "But I promise that I will. Whatever this is that's going on between us—I like it, Addie. I want to keep it."

"I like it, too."

"Can you trust me just a little while longer?"

"I think so."

"I'll go out and get the Bronco started." Jasper stood up. "Stay here until I come back in and get you. I don't want you falling down and hurting yourself."

"You're bossy."

"I mean it."

Addie rolled her eyes as the front door slammed. She stood up after a few unsuccessful attempts. Everything hurt, but she wanted to go and see Delilah and the pups before she left. She stopped when she heard Jasper outside talking to Clyde.

"How is that mama takin' to them puppies?" Clyde asked. "I ain't seen her out much since they was born."

"She goes out enough," Jasper replied. "I don't like for her to stray too far from me."

"Afraid someone might steal her?"

"Not exactly."

"She's a pretty dog."

Jasper crossed his arms over his chest. "She'd be a lot prettier if someone had taken better care of her."

"You reckon?"

"I reckon."

"Well, I guess I don't know about all that, Mr. Floyd. I ain't much of a dog person."

"What are you doing up here today, Clyde?" Jasper asked him. "I thought this was your day off."

Clyde took off his green Floyd Farms hat and scratched his greasy head. "Oh, I just forgot some of my tools in the barn is all." He looked up to the porch and saw Addie watching them. "Hello there, Miss Addie."

"Hello, Clyde."

"No offense, darlin', but you look like you've been rode hard and put back wet."

"If that means that I hit a deer with my car, then you're right."

"Are you ready to go?" Jasper turned his attention to Addie. "Hurry up, we're wasting time."

"I thought you wanted me to stay inside until you came to get me."

Jasper walked up the steps two at a time. "I don't remember asking you to eavesdrop at the door."

"I didn't mean to," Addie said. "Is everything okay?"

"Clyde's just an idiot, that's all."

"Are you mad at him about something?"

"Left his tools at the barn," Jasper scoffed. "Clyde hasn't done any work on this farm in twenty years. I'd fire him, but he's practically an institution around here."

"There's something not right about him."

"He's an odd duck, all right."

"I guess the meaning of southern charm was lost on him."

Jasper grabbed Addie's hand and guided her down the stairs. "Lots of things were lost on ol' Clyde," he said. "Now, come on. Let's get you home."

The ride to Addie's house was silent. Jasper's mood was dark since his conversation with Clyde, and he spent most of the time scowling at the road ahead of them. It wasn't until they pulled into the driveway that he spoke. "You should probably put some ice on your nose and take it easy today."

"I will," Addie promised. "In fact, I have some ice packs in the freezer. One of the benefits of having a nurse for a mother."

"Do you miss your mom?"

"What?" Addie was taken aback by the question. "Yeah, I guess I do. Especially when I'm having trouble making a decision. She's always prying into my life, but I secretly like it that way."

"My mother is the same way."

"I suppose all mothers are."

"All the good ones," Jasper said. "Warren and Neil told me

last night that you were thinking of going back to Chicago. For good."

"That was the plan at the beginning."

"Is that the plan now?"

"I don't know." Addie leaned back in the seat. "I don't know much of anything anymore."

Jasper squinted through the windshield at her house. "Is your door off its hinges?"

"It wasn't when I left yesterday. Maybe it was the storm?"

"There was rain, but not much wind." Jasper slid out of the driver's seat.

"Slow down." Addie followed him. She really did feel as if she'd been hit by a bus. Jasper went rigid. "Addie, don't come any closer . . . stay where you are."

"What's wrong?"

"I said stop!" Jasper leapt off the porch and into Addie's path. "Go back to the Bronco."

Addie tried to see around him. "Move out of the way."

"Please." Jasper grabbed her hand. "Just don't go up there. Go back to the Bronco and I'll tell you."

"No. It's my house. I'm going inside." Addie scrambled past him and up the steps. What she saw made her wish that she'd listened. Just beyond the broken door, on the floor of the porch was a dog lying in a pool of blood. The dog wasn't moving. Or breathing. She crept closer to the animal, but with every step it became more and more evident that the dog was dead. She turned and stumbled back into the yard, falling to the grass in a heap. "I think I'm going to be sick."

"I told you not to go in there." Jasper hovered over her. "I told you."

"I've seen that dog before. I've seen him."

"What do you mean you've seen him?"

"The man who came into the clinic and then refused to let us treat his dog. That's the dog. That's *his* dog."

"Jesus Christ." Jasper paced in front of her. "Jesus fucking Christ."

"This is my fault." Tears dribbled down Addie's cheeks.

"It's not your fault."

"Felix." Addie picked herself up off the ground. "Felix. I've got to go check on Felix." She didn't wait for Jasper to respond, pausing only a moment at the porch before bursting into the house.

"Felix! Where are you?" Addie's heart leapt into her throat. He wasn't in his bed. *"Felix!"* She heard the clicking of paws on the hardwood floors. She found Felix in her bedroom, unharmed. He stretched and yawned, looking curiously up at her.

"Is he okay?" Jasper panted. "Is he okay?"

"He's okay. He doesn't even know what's going on."

"I was afraid . . ."

"This is Redd. I know he did this. Why would he do this?"

"I don't know." Jasper sat down on the bed and put his head in his hands.

"We've got to call the police."

"We're not calling the police."

"Why not?"

"You're going to have to trust me on this."

"I do trust you."

"You've obviously made Redd very angry. And he's dangerous."

"That's why we need to call the police."

"I'll clean it up," Jasper said. "But we cannot call the police."

"What aren't you telling me?"

"Addie, please just listen to me." Jasper grabbed her around the waist and pulled her close to him. "Please. Just trust me. I promise this will be over soon."

"I don't even know what you're talking about."

"I know."

"I'm not stupid. I know you're hiding something from me."

"Addie, listen to me—"

"No, *you* listen," Addie cut him off. She dissolved into tears, tears she was frustrated she couldn't hold back.

"It's okay," Jasper whispered. "It's going to be okay."

Addie lay on the bed petting Felix. He was snoring next to her. She wished more than anything she could sleep, but all she could think about was Jasper out on the porch. There wouldn't be enough bleach in the entire Delta to get rid of what she'd seen that day.

She slipped off the bed and padded into the living room. Taking a deep breath, she opened the door to the porch. The dog was gone. The screen door was leaning idly against the house. Jasper sat with his back to her on the porch steps.

"Can I help with anything?" she asked.

Jasper shook his head. "I thought you were in your room with Felix."

"I was. Felix is asleep. I thought maybe you could use some help. You shouldn't . . . you shouldn't have to take care of this by yourself."

Jasper stood up and turned around to face her. "It's okay."

"What did you do with him?"

"I wrapped him in a couple old blankets and put him in the Bronco," Jasper replied, looking down at the hammer in his hands. "I thought I'd go ahead and fix this door."

"I want to bury him," Addie replied.

"I'll bury him at the farm tonight."

"No," Addie said. "I want to bury him in the backyard."

"Why?"

"I owe him that."

"Can you come over here and steady this door for me?"

Addie walked down the steps and held the door open. She was silent for a few minutes as they worked and then she said, "Could you tell how he died?"

"I think he was shot."

"Do you think it was quick?"

"I think it was quick enough."

"I hope he didn't suffer." Addie felt a sudden throbbing in her head. How many times was she going to have to ask about suffering? How many lives were going to evaporate in front of her? Her eyes darted around the room. Who was next?

"Let's go inside for a few minutes." Jasper waved her away from the door. "I'm not going to get this fixed today. You need a new hinge."

Jasper sat down at the kitchen table while Addie searched the cupboard for clean glasses. "Do you want some sweet tea?"

"You need to know that none of this is your fault."

"You know, people keep saying that to me; you keep saying that to me. And yet here I am, right in the middle of it."

"Maybe you're being too hard on yourself."

"Maybe you don't know me as well as you think."

Jasper sighed. "I don't think it's safe for you here."

"What do you mean?"

"I think scaring you was just a pleasant side effect of the real meaning behind all of this."

"Which is?"

"He's telling you to leave."

"He wants me to leave my house?"

"I think he wants you to leave Eunice."

Addie exhaled, crumpling in her seat. "And you think this is his way of making that happen? To kill a dog and leave the body on my porch for me to find?"

"I do."

"Well, I'm not leaving," she replied. "I live here, and if I decide to go, it'll be *my* choice."

"I'm not suggesting you leave town. But I do think it would be a good idea if you come and stay with me. Just until things"—he paused—"blow over."

"How could staying there help anything?"

"Redd will be arrested if he sets foot onto my farm," Jasper replied. "Any part of it, whether it used to be his or not."

"He hates you just as much as he does me."

"I'm sure he does. And that's another reason I think you ought to come stay with me. He knows that we're connected. I don't want him coming after you in retaliation."

"How do you know he didn't do this in retaliation?"

"I guess I don't," Jasper replied. "But either way, you'll be safer where I can keep an eye on things."

"I'd be safer if we went to the police."

"Addie."

"What?"

"Don't start this again."

"Redd Jones can't scare me out of my own house."

"Don't be stupid."

"Tell me why we can't go to the police, and I'll go with you."

"I can't."

"Then I'm staying here."

Jasper slammed his fist down onto the table so hard that his glass of tea toppled over and onto the floor. The glass shattered at his feet. Within seconds, Felix bounded into the room, barking frantically.

"Shit," Jasper mumbled, pushing back his chair. "I'm sorry."

"Felix, go to bed!" Addie pointed at his bed in the living room. *"Go!"*

Felix whimpered and sulked back into the living room, heaving himself down. He eyed the kitchen warily.

Addie knelt down to pick up shards of broken glass off the floor. "We've both had a long morning. I'm tired. You're tired. I'm sore as hell. After we"—she swallowed—"after we bury the dog . . . why don't you just go home?"

"Please just reconsider."

"I'm not leaving."

"You don't even have a car."

"I'll call you if I start to worry," Addie reassured him. "Right now, all I want to do is take a long, hot bath and go to bed."

"I'd stay here if I could," Jasper said. "But I've got the farm to take care of. And Delilah and the puppies."

"I know."

"I'll come back by tomorrow and finish up with that door."

Addie watched him walk down the steps and out toward the Bronco, her hands full of glass. So far, the first two days of the Delta Blues Festival had turned out to be disasters of epic proportions. Despite her best efforts to shake the feeling, there was something inside of her warning her that this was merely the beginning.

CHAPTER 42

"Je-sus." Wanda looked from Addie to the door propped up against the side of the house. "Girl, if it wasn't for bad luck, you wouldn't have none at all."

"I know."

"And your poor face."

"I know."

"You think Redd did this?"

Addie nodded. "I do, but Jasper doesn't want me going to the police. Did you see anything last night when you checked on Felix?"

"Half the cops are probably related to him, anyhow," Wanda replied. "But it does seem fishy that Jasper won't let you say nothin'. When I stopped by, everything was right as rain."

"He's supposed to come back later to fix the door, but I want to go ahead and get it fixed, especially if I'm going to be alone here. Would you mind to take me to the hardware store?"

"How are you going to fix your door, sugar?" Wanda asked. "You need help putting on a shirt."

"That's what I've got you here for." Addie tried to grin, but her face was so sore that it came out as more of a grimace.

"Oh, great. We better get some vodka while we're out," Wanda replied. "And don't go tryin' to charm nobody with that face of yours. You'll scare 'em away."

As they drove to the hardware store, the town was ghostly quiet. Not a soul walked along the streets. There were no cars at the gas stations, and even the parking lot at Linstrom's was surprisingly empty. Addie guessed the men who usually frequented the place, like everyone else in town, were at the festival.

"Stay here in the car with Felix, and I'll be right back," Addie said, unbuckling her seat belt.

"Are you sure?" Wanda asked. "I can run in for ya. You're walking around like Frankenstein."

"I've been lying in bed all afternoon. I need to walk around a little bit."

The inside of the store was just as empty as the parking lot. The store was almost always full of people milling around, looking for caulk, or whatever it was that people went to the hardware store for. Most of the time, Addie was in the minority. Most of the time there were men wearing boots and heavy belt buckles shooting the shit with each other in every aisle. She found the nearest salesperson and said, "I need a hinge just like this." She held it up. "Do you carry this?"

The man squinted at the hinge. "If we do, it'll be over in aisle 6."

"Thanks." Addie hadn't told Wanda, but she was relieved to have something on which she could concentrate, even if it was something as menial as a door hinge. There were too many other things going on in her head that she didn't want to think about. And she was scared, another thing she hadn't told Wanda *or* Jasper. She'd been scared since that night of the party at Wanda's. Jasper was right—she couldn't really help herself, but now she was in so deep that she wasn't sure how she was going to dig herself out, and she didn't even know what kind of a hole she was in.

She scanned the aisle for the hinge that was in her hand but didn't see a single one that matched. Addie walked to the end of the aisle, looking for the guy who'd helped her minutes earlier. That was when she saw someone familiar walking in through the sliding doors of the hardware store. The closer the person got to her, the more convinced she was that she knew it was him. She wouldn't be forgetting his glue-like skin anytime soon.

It was the man from the fair; the man from Jasper's yard. Frank, was it? She followed him to the back of the store. He pulled a list from his dingy pocket and began to read silently, his lips moving with each word.

"Hey," Addie said, hurrying toward him. "Don't I know you?"

The man looked at Addie like the deer in front of her car had the night before. He wanted to run away but was caught. So he just stared at her, not saying anything.

"Frank, right?"

"I, uh, yeah."

"I thought so." Addie mustered a smile, but remembered Wanda's warning and allowed her face to fall. "You're friends with Redd Jones."

Now his skin really was the color of glue. He looked back down at his list. Then at Addie. Then back down at his list. "I work for him."

"Oh, yeah? What is it that you do?"

"Odds and ends."

"Do you know much about door hinges?"

"Not especially."

Addie took a step closer and held up the piece of metal in her hand. "I don't either, but I have to buy a new one. You think you could help me?"

Frank swallowed, clearly debating his odds of making a clean getaway.

"It won't take but a second."

"I 'spose I can help ya," he relented. His smile wasn't much better than hers.

Addie led him back over to aisle 6 and handed him the hinge. Frank looked up and down the shelves, but after a few minutes handed it back to her. "I don't see nothin' that matches it."

"I didn't, either." She closed her fist around it. "I think it might be an antique. Most everything in my house is."

"Sorry I couldn't help ya." He tipped his hat to her and started to walk away.

"Oh, wait!" Addie started after him. "I've got another question if you don't mind."

"Go ahead."

"You killed any dogs lately?"

"Huh?"

"Did you and Redd Jones leave a dead dog on my porch?" Addie clenched the hinge tighter. "You know, after you broke my door?"

"I need to be goin' now."

"Yeah, I bet you do," Addie called after him.

Frank didn't look back at her. He hurried out of the store without buying anything just as fast as his skinny legs would carry him.

CHAPTER 43

ADDIE HARDLY RECOGNIZED HERSELF IN THE MIRROR. HER FACE wasn't nearly as swollen as it had been the day before, but there were bluish rings around both of her eyes. Her top lip was bruised and puffy. She looked like she'd been on the losing end of a fist-fight with a deer rather than a car accident. As she sat on the back steps and watched Felix trot through the dew-filled grass, steam from her coffee soothing her face, she thought maybe all things looked better in the morning.

Maybe sleep really was all that she needed, but she couldn't sleep. Not when she was afraid of who might be sneaking onto her porch while her eyes were closed. She knew Felix would bark at the slightest disturbance, but it wasn't the disturbance she worried about—it was what always came afterward. Addie heard some-one stomping up the steps, and her heart leapt into her throat. She peeked through the curtains to see Augustus standing on her porch.

"What have you been telling people about me?" Augustus hollered at her through the window.

"What?"

"People! What have you been telling them?"

Addie opened the door. "I haven't told anybody anything."

"That's a lie." Augustus strode past Addie and into her house. "Those women from the restaurant told Magdalene that I'd been talking to you."

"You mean Fannie Lou?" Addie asked. "That was before I knew . . . I mean, that was when I didn't know it was a secret."

Felix began barking furiously, jumping up and down in place.

"Tell that dog to hush up."

"I won't." Addie crossed her arms over her chest. "This is his house. And you weren't invited inside. I'm tired of keeping secrets for everyone. I can't remember from one day to the next what's a secret and what's not. So you'll have to forgive me if I didn't realize that you were pretending to be crazy so that you don't have to deal with the fact that your wife is dead."

The scowl on Augustus's face turned to one of pain. It was a look Addie hadn't seen him wear before. He began to wring his hands. "Forgive me. I've been acting crazy for so long that I sometimes forget my manners."

"Here, sit down." She took his arm and led him over to her couch.

"I used to be a good man." Augustus stared down at his hands. "I used to be an honest man."

"I'm sorry. I shouldn't have said that about your wife."

"It's just too hard to be without her."

"I understand."

"No you don't."

"I do," Addie said. "I lost someone. Someone I loved. That's why I moved here."

"I doubt you loved him like I loved Eleonora."

"You're probably right." Addie looked down at her lap. More and more she was starting to realize that perhaps the guilt she felt wasn't entirely about the way Jonah died. Maybe it was about something more, something deeper that she hadn't quite fleshed out yet. "I did love him," she continued. "And losing him was hard. It was so hard. For a long time I wanted to lock myself up and throw away the key."

"You're too young to have suffered in that way."

"But I didn't do that," Addie continued. "And neither can you."

"I can do whatever I want."

"Neither one of us can escape life. It keeps on happening whether we want it to or not." Addie shook her head and continued, "And if there's anything that living down here has taught me, it's that I cannot stop things from happening."

Augustus took a deep breath in through his nose and out through his mouth. He did this several times. "I don't want to be here without her."

"Is this how she'd want you to behave? Like this? Shutting everyone out?"

"You can't go around telling people that we're friends."

"I never told anybody we were friends," Addie said. "Wait, are we friends?"

Augustus stood up. "Get some rest, young'un. You look like hell." He turned on his heel and marched out the front door and down the steps, cursing as he crossed the street. Addie could still hear him even once he was inside.

There's a fine line between strong and bitter, Addie thought. *A fine line between sane and crazy, too.* Felix jumped up and trotted over to her, his body wagging back and forth. He settled himself on her lap, resting his head underneath her chin.

"Come on, buddy," she said. "Let's go get you a treat." Addie took out the last hot dog from the package and set it onto a plate. She then cut up the hot dog into several pieces and set it on the floor for Felix to eat. "There you go. I'm going to go and take a bath."

Addie padded back to the bathroom and turned on the faucet in the tub. The only thing that sounded good to her was a hot bath with a warm washcloth over her face. She settled into the tub and tried to relax. When she'd moved to Eunice, she held out hope that something good would come of the nightmare she had endured in Chicago. At that moment, it was hard to tell if the nightmare had ever ended.

There were, of course, good things about Eunice. Jasper and Felix were two of them. Wanda and Bryar were two others. Addie was grateful that they had welcomed her so readily. If she'd never found Felix lying desperately down at the levee, chances were that she never would have met any of them.

Addie remembered Jerry's words to her: *No matter where you move, life is going to get complicated. It's going to get messy.*

The people she loved were full of suggestions.

She just hadn't anticipated it would get *this* messy. She thought about what she'd just said to Augustus. Had she really not loved Jonah as much as she thought she had? For so long she'd felt guilty having the slightest negative thought about him, but when it came down to it, she hadn't loved him like Augustus loved his wife.

And that was okay.

She was okay.

Felix was once again barking furiously. "Felix! Hush!"

He ignored her. Addie wrapped a towel around her body and hurried into the living room. Felix was standing on top of the couch with his nose pressed up against the windowpane. Addie leaned over him and strained to see what Felix saw. "Felix, you scared me half to death. There's nothing out there."

His barking became more intense. Before she could reprimand him, Addie's phone rang. She ran back to her bedroom to grab it while Felix continued to snarl.

"Hello?"

"Hey, Addie. It's me."

"Oh. Hey, Wanda."

"What's wrong?"

"Nothing," Addie replied. "My dog thinks that there is something out in the yard, and he won't shut up about it."

"Oh," Wanda said. "Maybe it's just a squirrel."

"That would be my guess."

Wanda paused, breathing into the receiver. Finally she said, "I was just calling to check on you. I know you don't want to talk about it, but I just want to make sure you're okay."

"Thanks," Addie replied. "I really do want to talk about it. I just don't want to talk about it right now." She closed her eyes. She sounded just like Jasper.

"I know. But I'm here when you do."

Addie heard a dull pounding coming from outside, followed by more howling from Felix. "Hang on a second," Addie said to Wanda. "I think I heard something outside."

Felix was now standing in front of the door, his bark lulled to a low, guttural growl. Addie walked over to the window and strained to see outside in the impending darkness. There were no cars parked outside that she could see. No animals scurrying through the bushes.

"What's wrong?" Wanda asked.

Addie crept closer to the window. Her eyes scanned every inch of the yard. Just as she was about to turn away, she saw a shadow move in the driveway. It was a human shadow, and it was headed toward her house.

"Wanda, hang up the phone and call Jasper. Tell him there's someone outside my house," Addie whispered into the receiver.

"Addie, what's going on?"

"Just do it," Addie breathed. "Please. Do it now."

Addie hung up the phone and grabbed Felix by the collar. Her hands were trembling. "Come on," she pleaded. "Let's go."

Felix hesitated, more interested in what was happening outside. Eventually he relented and followed her back to the bedroom. She opened her closet door and coaxed Felix inside. She cradled the phone in her chest and listened for noises inside the house.

Addie could hear someone at the front door as if they were trying to get inside. She heard the door crash into the wall as it flung open. She scrounged around the floor for something to wear, anything but a bath towel. She froze when she heard voices in her bedroom.

"I know she's here. I saw her looking at me through the window."

Addie clapped her hand over her mouth. Felix began to bark. In a matter of seconds the closet door swung open and revealed them both.

"I found her."

Addie looked up into Frank's pitted face. "Get out of my

house," Addie said. She tried to keep her voice steady. "Get out or my dog will attack you."

"Now, I don't think he'll be doin' that." Redd Jones's voice pierced the bedroom. In one hand was his .38-caliber handgun. "Now, come on out of there."

"No."

"Get up."

"I won't."

"Get up or I'll shoot you and that fucking dog," Redd growled, pointing the gun at Felix.

Addie stood and held up one hand; the other hand was wound around Felix's collar. The T-shirt she had flung over her head barely covered her. She'd never felt more exposed or frightened in her life. At any moment, she thought, her heart was going to beat right out of her chest.

Redd kept the gun on the dog and said, "Just you. He stays in the closet."

"Stay," Addie said to Felix, but Felix was no longer listening to her. He lunged forward and snapped at Redd. He caught the end of Redd's pant leg and tore it before Addie managed to get the door shut.

Redd stepped back, cursing under his breath. "That damn dog."

"Please don't hurt him."

"I'm going to shoot him if you don't shut up."

Addie backed up until her back was against the closet. She could feel Felix sniffing and scratching at it inside. There had to be a way out of this. If she could just get her brain to think.

"I'd thought you'd be long gone out of here," Redd continued, scratching his forehead with the barrel of his gun.

Addie turned her head slightly, trying to muster the courage to look Redd in the eyes. “Felix would rip your face off if I gave him the chance.”

“Naw,” Redd said. “That dog doesn’t have it in him. He never was prospect material.”

“How would you know?”

“I know.”

“Was he your dog?”

“He was never nobody’s dog.”

“He’s my dog now.”

Redd grabbed Addie by the arm and pulled her over to the bed, forcing her to sit down. He leered at her bare legs for a moment before he said, “My colleagues and I think it is about time you were movin’ on.”

“Where do you expect me to go?”

“I don’t reckon I give a shit.”

“I live here,” Addie said. “I own this house.”

“Maybe it’s time to sell.”

Addie looked away from Redd. She couldn’t figure out why she was arguing with him. Why couldn’t she just say okay and beg for him to leave? She could pack a bag right now and take Felix and run. She could disappear. “And what if my answer to that is no?”

“You’ve got a lot of nerve, girl,” Frank said suddenly. Addie couldn’t tell if the look on his face was one of awe or contempt. “Most days Redd don’t give people an option.”

“I can handle this, Frank,” Redd replied. “I ain’t asking you to get out. I’m tellin’ you.”

“Was it your idea to kill a dog?” Addie asked. She looked away from Redd over to Frank. “Or did your boss over here order you to do it?” She couldn’t leave it alone. Scared as she was, she wanted answers. Maybe if she couldn't get them out of Redd, she could get Frank to talk.

"Come on, now." A grinchly smile crossed Redd's face. "I can't be held accountable for that."

The fear in Addie was spiraling into fury. The nerve of this man to think he could just come into her house and order her around. The nerve of him to pretend like he didn't know anything about anything. "Just like we both know that you're not accountable for leaving Felix to die in a trash bag. Just like you're not accountable for the dogs that die on your property. Just like we both know you're mad as hell that you won't make any money off of that pregnant dog that mysteriously disappeared," she said all in one breath. Addie knew Redd could kill her before help came. She knew that, but it didn't matter. Felix mattered. Delilah mattered. Those puppies mattered. She wasn't going to let another living being die because of her.

Redd's free hand clenched into a ball. He brought the gun up under Addie's chin. "Tell me, darlin'. What else do you know?"

"Isn't that enough?" Addie could feel the cold steel of the barrel against her flesh. She couldn't breathe. He was going to kill her. This was it.

"Don't play stupid with me. Who are you working for?"

The question caught her off guard. "What are you talking about?"

"Are you working with that idiot DEA agent?"

"What DEA agent?"

"I don't think even the Floyds know they've got an undercover cop working for them." Redd puffed out his chest. "But I know."

"I don't know who you're talking about."

"Clyde said you'd play dumb." Frank threw himself back into the conversation.

"Clyde the farmhand?" Addie felt control of the conversation slipping away from her. She was lost.

"How do you think I found out about the undercover cop? How do you think I found out about you?"

"I'm not working for anyone."

"You must think I'm stupid."

"I don't think you're stupid," Addie replied. "Honestly, I don't." She didn't think Redd was stupid. She thought he was mean. She thought he was terrifying, but she didn't think he was stupid.

"What were you looking for when you went snooping around my house?"

"Which time?" Addie replied without thinking. Shit, this was getting her nowhere. So far, she'd managed to accomplish nothing but make Redd even angrier.

"Yeah, Bobby told me he'd brought you 'round. I shoulda decked him for that shit." The armpits of Redd's T-shirt were sopping with sweat. His face was melting into a puddle on Addie's floor. "You didn't find nothin', though, did ya?"

"I found that gun you're pointing at my face," she replied. "You shot another man's dog with it when your dog beat his in a fight. You shot Felix with it. I bet you shot the dog buried in my backyard with it." *Shut up,* she screamed inside of her head. *Just quit talking!* Why couldn't she quit talking?

"You're pretty slick, ain't ya?"

"It's an awful pretty gun to be doing such ugly things with."

"Redd?" Frank interrupted. He peered through the curtains of the bedroom window. "Redd, I think there's someone here."

"Take care of it."

Frank slunk out of the room muttering under his breath. Addie had underestimated him. The first time she talked to him, that day on Redd's lawn, he'd seemed slow and uneven, but friendly. He'd been downright scared of her at the hardware store. But he wasn't afraid right now. He didn't seem to have a problem breaking into her house and watching Redd Jones threaten her with a loaded weapon.

"Why don't you just put the gun down and we can talk," Addie said. "Maybe we can get this all figured out." The closet door threatened to burst open every time Felix jumped up against it, and Addie was afraid Redd might notice how close Felix was to escaping.

"Shut up. Maybe I should just shoot you for taking up so much of my goddamn time." He aimed the gun.

"I don't think you want to do this." Addie held up her hands. "Can't you hear the sirens? They'll be here before you can escape."

"But not before I can kill you."

"What do you want from me?"

Redd cocked the gun. "I want you to beg."

"What?"

"Get on your knees and beg."

Addie dropped her hands to her sides. She stepped away from the door where Felix was trapped. She knew he was going to kill her. It didn't matter if she got down on her knees. It didn't matter if she begged. He was going to aim that beautiful gun at her head and kill her. She took a breath, the air sticking inside of her throat so that she hiccuped slightly. With one hand behind her she pulled open the door to the closet. "I'm not going to do that."

The shot went off a second before Felix was on top of Redd, his teeth sinking into the soft tissue of the man's neck. Redd let out a yelp, dropping the gun.

Addie was watching the scene underneath water—as if someone heavy had cannonballed right into her. The bullet shattered her left shoulder and knocked her backward onto the bed. She lay there and listened to the commotion on the floor beneath her. She tried to jump up and help Felix, but she couldn't get her legs to cooperate. She pulled herself along the side of the wall and out into the hallway. Nothing was working right. It was then that she realized the warm sensation down her left side was blood.

Her blood.

Then there were people hovering over her, talking to her, touching her. Jasper was there. He was saying something but she couldn't make out the words. *Maybe this is all a dream,* she thought. Like those dreams about Jonah and the man in the white coat. Maybe the last few years had been a dream. Maybe she'd wake up back at the store or their apartment, surrounded by furniture and sandpaper. Maybe it was her birthday and Jonah was letting her sleep late because he'd stayed up all night building her a bench for her breakfast nook.

No, Addie tried to say out loud. *No, I don't want that. I want what's here. I want this life.*

But nobody was listening. Nobody was paying attention at all. They were too busy. And her eyes were so heavy. *If it's okay,* Addie thought, *I'm going to close my eyes now. I'm just going to rest my eyes for a while.*

CHAPTER 44

THE NEXT TIME ADDIE OPENED HER EYES SHE WAS IN AN UNFAMILIAR room. There were white walls surrounding her, machines beeping next to her, and everything smelled sterile.

"Where am I?" Addie's throat was raw. "Can anyone hear me?"

"Adelaide! You're awake!" Addie heard her mother's voice. She grabbed Addie's hands and face. "We were all so worried!"

"Mom. Quit. You're hurting me."

"Oh, I'm sorry!" Her mother gasped. "I forgot. Your shoulder."

"What's wrong with my shoulder?"

"Don't you remember?"

"No."

"Honey, you were shot."

"I got shot?"

"Yes, you were shot. Two days ago."

"At my house," Addie said.

"Yes, at your house."

"In my bedroom?"

"Yes."

Addie blinked. It was so foggy inside of her head. "I think I remember," she said. "I was at home. I was taking a bath. Felix started barking."

"Wanda said you were on the phone with her."

"I was." Addie's shoulder was throbbing. "Someone was outside the house." The memory of the entire incident came flooding back to her. "I remember! It was Redd! He was outside my house. And Frank. They were both there. Redd shot me, didn't he?"

"Yes." Her mother's voice was shaking. "Oh, baby. I'm so sorry."

Addie remembered everything. Redd. Frank. The closet. Felix. "Mom, where's Felix? Where is he? Is he okay?"

Her mother clasped Addie's hand from the side of the bed and said, "He's fine. He's just fine. He's staying with Jasper at the farm."

"I think he saved my life, Mom."

"Jasper told us that he was still on top of Redd when the police got there."

"But Felix is okay?"

"He's just fine."

Addie heard a voice in the doorway. Jerry was standing there. He was staring at her as if he were seeing her for the first time. "How are you, kiddo?" He clutched his hospital coffee tightly in both hands.

"I guess I'm going to live," Addie replied, trying to smile. "My shoulder really hurts, though. Everything really hurts."

"Why don't I go and see if I can find the nurse," Addie's mother said. "See if we can't get you something for that."

Jerry bent down and kissed Addie gruffly on the forehead. "I'm glad to see you back with the waking world."

"I feel like crap."

"I bet you do," Jerry replied. "Jasper told us that you hit a deer a couple nights before . . . all of this happened. The doctors said that's probably the reason for your black eyes and the bruising on your ribs."

"Where is Jasper?"

"He's had quite a few things to take care of."

Addie didn't know what that meant, and she was afraid to ask. She reached up and touched her face. It didn't hurt as much as she remembered. "Are my eyes still black?"

"Just barely." Jerry smiled at her. "You looked so awful when we got here"—he swallowed at a lump in his throat—"your mom and I were so worried."

"I'm okay." Addie reached out and took Jerry's hand. "I love you, Dad." It was the first time she'd ever called him that.

Jerry looked up at her, his eyes rimmed with water. "I love you, too."

There was a knock at the door, and Wanda stuck her head in. "Is it okay if we come inside?"

"Sure thing." Jerry stood up. "Come on in. I'm going to go and check on your mother, Adelaide."

Bryar skipped over to the bed and looked up at Addie, his eyes as wide as quarters. "Mommy said you got hurt," he said.

"I did get hurt," Addie replied. "But I'm going to be okay."

"And the bad man is gone."

"Yes," Addie replied. "The bad man is gone."

"Bryar, honey, be careful over there. Don't hang on Addie."

"Can I tell her our surprise, Mommy? Can I?" Bryar's eyes danced around the room. "Please?"

"You better go outside and check to make sure that it's time," Wanda said with a grin.

Once Bryar was out of the room, Addie turned her attention to her friend and whispered, "The bad man *is* gone, right?"

Wanda stroked Addie's hair. "Girl, we've got to get you to a shower."

"Wanda, tell me Redd is gone."

"He's gonna be, sugar," Wanda said. She was using the reassuring voice she usually reserved for Bryar. "But right now he's just down the hall."

"What are you talking about?"

"Well, it took them sixteen stitches to close him up after Felix got hold of him," Wanda replied. "And then Jasper shot him, Addie. Shot him right in the belly."

Addie struggled to sit up, but the searing pain shooting through her body prevented her from being successful. "He shot him?"

"He had to."

"I'm going to need you to be more specific."

Wanda scooted closer to Addie and said, "According to Alice Baker—her mama answers phones down at the police department—she heard that the wet-behind-the-ears police officer put the cuffs on Redd all wrong and didn't even pick up his gun afterward. Well, everybody thought this kid was watchin' Redd in the other room, but he wasn't, and Redd got outta them cuffs, picked up his gun, and was comin' back for ya, Addie, so Jasper had to shoot him. He just had to."

Addie closed her eyes. The skin of her lids burned. "But Redd's not dead?"

"Nah, but he's a lot worse off."

"And he's down the hall from me?"

"Ain't but one hospital in this town."

"Great."

"They've got guards at his door all the time," Wanda said. "Redd's cuffed to the bed and cuffed right. They won't let nobody in or out of that room. He's part of a federal investigation now. That's why Jasper ain't been here to check on ya. He can't be near Redd till everything's all sorted out."

"Because Redd shot me?"

Wanda shook her head. "No, 'cause of somethin' else, but nobody will say nothin' about it."

Before Addie could formulate a response, her mother and Jerry came back into the room with Bryar.

"Look, Addie! Look! It's Felix!"

Felix dragged Bryar over to the bed, slobbering and whining the whole way. Before Bryar could stop him, Felix jumped up onto the bed and was licking Addie's face.

"I missed you, too." Addie laughed in between licks. "Watch my shoulder, buddy."

"He sat at the door every night waiting for you," Wanda said. "I told him you were coming home, but I don't think he believed me."

"I'll be home soon," Addie whispered to Felix. "I promise."

Felix wagged his tail so hard that his entire body started to shake.

"Hey, quit it!" Bryar squealed, swatting at Felix's swishing tail. "You're hitting me in the face!"

"When will I get to go home?" Addie asked. "Have the doctors said anything?"

"Someone is coming in to talk with us," her mother replied. "I think I overheard someone say it could be as early as tomorrow."

Felix settled down on top of Addie, his paws resting on her chest. His weight was killing her, but she couldn't bear to make him move. "What about something for my shoulder?"

"The nurse should be on her way."

"We need to get Felix down off your bed," Wanda said. "It was like pullin' teeth to get him in here, and that nurse will blow a gasket if she sees him sittin' on your bed." She took his leash from Bryar and gave it a tug.

Felix didn't budge.

"Go on," Addie said to him, giving him a nudge.

Felix yawned.

"Looks like we're going to have to get a new gasket for the nurse," Jerry said with a chuckle. "He's not going anywhere."

"That's okay. I owe him my life." Addie buried her head into his fur and caressed his half ear. "Thank you for returning the favor."

CHAPTER 45

JUST AS ADDIE'S MOTHER HAD PREDICTED, THE DOCTORS allowed her to leave the very next day. There were strict orders to abide, and many follow-up visits prescribed, but Addie felt relieved to be leaving the beeping monitors and the looming presence of Redd Jones just feet away from where she slept.

Although she understood that Jasper couldn't come to the hospital because of Redd, it didn't make any sense to her that he wouldn't at least call. Nobody, not even the DEA agents who'd come to speak with her the day before, would tell her about the investigation. All they could do was assure her that Jasper wasn't in any trouble and that Redd wouldn't be going *anywhere* without handcuffs for a long, long time.

"Are you about ready to get out of here?" Jerry asked.

A nurse in bright pink scrubs pushed a wheelchair into the room.

"Oh, I don't need that," Addie said.

"Doctor's orders."

Addie swung her legs over the bed. Getting dressed had been more difficult than she'd anticipated, and her mother had to go buy her several oversized button-up shirts that she could put on by herself. The tank top she was wearing had taken her fifteen minutes to put on, and that had been with the help of her mother *and* an orderly. Secretly, Addie wondered if she'd ever be able to button another pair of pants. Her mother, true to form, made sure that everyone in the hospital knew that she was a nurse with thirty years in the field. By the time Addie was ready to leave, everyone, including the doctors, was calling her mother Nurse Miranda.

"Sit down, sweetheart," her mother said. "Let's get this show on the road."

The nurse backed her out of the room, making beeping noises as she did so. When Addie turned around to look at her, the nurse grinned and said, "Hey, I've got to get my kicks where I can."

Addie was so relieved to be going home that she felt a sense of unexpected euphoria. Despite the pain, despite everything that had happened, she wanted nothing more than to be sitting with Felix in the living room of her little house.

"Do y'all want me to turn around and go the other way?" the nurse asked. She looked behind her to Addie's parents. "We can go through the doors at the end of the hall and walk around to discharge."

To Addie's left, there were two men standing at the door of one of the rooms. They were big men, and they were both bald. She could see the black wires hanging out of their ears. In fact, everything they had on was black, all the way down to their shoes, which were so shiny that she could see the reflection of the floors in each one of them.

They were the agents Wanda had told her about, which meant that Redd Jones must be inside that room. "Just a minute," Addie said. She stood up.

"You've got to ride out in the wheelchair," the nurse reminded her. "Sit down."

"I'll sit down in a minute." Addie was already walking toward the men. They looked down at her. They weren't smiling. "Is Redd Jones in there?"

"Sorry, ma'am. No admittance."

"You see this cast? This sling?" Addie pointed with her good arm. "That man in there shot me, but I suppose you know that by now."

"Yes, ma'am," one of the men said.

"I want to see him."

"We can't let you in," the other one said.

"I won't say anything."

"We're sorry."

"Just open the door and let me look inside," Addie pleaded.

The men exchanged glances with each other.

"Please."

"Just for a second," one of them said.

They both took a step sideways, allowing Addie to push the door open. Redd was lying back on the bed, and he was indeed handcuffed to the metal sides. He was staring blankly at the television screen. He looked insignificant compared to the last time she'd seen him, when he was looming over her with a gun pointed at her forehead.

She opened the door an inch more to get a better look, and that's when he saw her. Their eyes locked, and Addie had to fight the urge to look away—to run, to turn around and not look back.

Redd was the first one to look away. He pushed the button on the side of his bed, struggling to reach it through the cuffs. The volume on the television shot up, and he fixed himself once more staring at the movement on the screen. He didn't look at her again.

She closed the door and took a step back between the two men. "Thank you," she said to them. "Thank you."

Addie hadn't anticipated the circus awaiting her when she arrived home. Jerry could hardly get down the street for all the cars and people milling about.

"Did the blues festival move to my house?"

"We wanted it to be a surprise," her mother replied. "Some of the locals wanted to welcome you home."

"Some?" Addie was incredulous. "It looks like the whole town is here!"

"If you're too tired, we can tell them to go home."

"No, that's fine." Addie waited for her mother to unbuckle her seat belt. "I'm just surprised, that's all."

The first thing that Addie noticed was that her screen door had been fixed. It was back on its hinges perfectly, and even the tricky handle had been replaced. Wanda was standing in the doorway when they approached, and Felix was on her heels.

"Addie!"

"Are you behind all of this?"

"I don't know what you're talkin' about," Wanda said. She winked at her friend. "I really didn't know there would be so many people. I'm sorry about that."

"It's okay," Addie replied. "Did you fix my door, too?"

"What?" Wanda turned around to look at the porch. "No, that was Jasper. Had to go two towns over to find the damn hinge."

"Looks good," said Jerry. "Looks real good."

"Come on in, y'all." Wanda ushered them inside. "There's food!"

And indeed, there was food. The Three Sisters had cooked up quite a spread. It was all set out and gleaming on Addie's kitchen table. Patty Mae, Fannie Lou, and Opal Ruth stood beside it proudly.

"You did all of this for me?" Addie asked.

"Sure did, sweetheart," Patty Mae replied.

"I'm going to have food for weeks!"

"That's the plan," Opal Ruth said.

"There's even some chocolate gravy for string bean over there." Fannie Lou pointed to Jerry. "Eat up, sugar!"

Addie didn't know what to say. She hardly knew these women, and yet here they were in her kitchen, with enough food to feed a small army and then some. She felt warm from her head to her toes. They'd cooked for her, for her family, and that food was love. Addie knew this because it was what Aunt Tilda would have done if she were alive. It was what she'd done for Addie, and it was, Addie now realized, what her aunt had done for Zeke that summer. The love her aunt poured into that food was the love she couldn't have expressed for him. It filled up the wagon and spilled over into Zeke's hands that sticky day in July. It was years and years of being strong that had somehow turned to bitterness. It was her aunt's only way of saying what needed to be said. She hoped Zeke understood. Addie clutched the recipe box to her chest. She wouldn't let her aunt down. She wouldn't be bitter.

As her mother and Jerry busied themselves filling their plates, Addie counted the chairs at her table. There were four. "Wanda?" Addie called out. "Did somebody fix my broken chair?"

"I'll give ya six guesses as to who it was," she hollered back. "And the first five don't count!"

"Jasper," Addie mumbled. Where was he?

"How are you feeling, Adelaide?" Doc was in front of her, a half-eaten piece of pie on his plate.

"I'm okay. A little overwhelmed, but okay."

Doc nodded. "I tried to tell Wanda that this would be too much." He gestured around the room. "But she insisted. You know how she can be."

"Oh, I know." Addie laughed. "I just can't believe so many people even wanted to come."

"We care about you," Doc said. "Despite our disagreements, I am quite fond of you."

"About that," Addie began. "I need to apologize to you . . ."

"Don't," Doc cut her off. "Talk to Jasper first, and then you can decide whether you want to apologize."

"Where is Jasper?"

"I don't know. But I'm sure he's around here somewhere."

Doc wandered off, and Addie was left alone in her kitchen. People were buzzing all around her, eating food, laughing, and waving in her direction. She knew most of them. They were clients from the clinic, friends of Wanda's and Jasper's, and people from around the neighborhood. Sitting on one corner of her couch, alone in a tweed blazer, was Augustus Smoot. Addie could hardly believe her eyes.

"Mr. Smoot, what are you doing here?"

Augustus looked up at her. In his hand was a glass of whiskey, his own; Addie recognized it from the day she'd been there. "I was invited."

"I'm glad you're here." Addie sat down beside him. "I'm just surprised, that's all."

"Eleonora and I had a talk," he said. "She told me I was being crotchety and that I should be nicer to the pretty neighbor."

Addie grinned. "I think I like her."

Augustus took a sip from his cup and said, "I know you would have."

"Addie." Her mother was calling to her from the other side of the room. "Come over here."

Addie stood up and took Augustus's hand in hers. "Maybe we could have tea one day this week?"

"I'll have Magdalene clear my schedule."

Addie made her way over to her mother and a woman who looked vaguely familiar. She couldn't place her, but she knew she'd seen her face somewhere before.

"Addic, this is Dclorcs. She says you've met."

"I think so," Addie replied. "But I just can't remember where."

"Lily's Boutique," Delores said. "I own it."

"Oh!" Addie's eyes lit up. Now she remembered. "How are you?"

"Well," her mother cut in, "Delores was just telling me how she asked you to bring some of your creations to the store and you never did."

"I guess I forgot."

"Well, now you have my official request." Delores gave Addie a broad smile. "Any friend of Jasper's is a friend of mine."

"Have you seen Jasper?"

"I think I saw him out back a few minutes ago," Delores replied.

"You two will have to excuse me for just a minute," Addie said. She walked away from them despite protests from her mother.

She opened the back door and Felix followed her. At the other end of the yard, she finally found Jasper. He was standing on a ladder in front of the shed, holding on to a brand-new door. The fresh wood stood in stark contrast to the wood around it, and Jasper was cursing and coaxing it into position.

Felix barked and bounded down the steps, and Addie followed him. "Jasper, what are you doing out here?"

"What does it look like I'm doing?" he huffed. "I'm trying to fix this door. There are just too many things to fix in this house. Too many."

"Come down from there," Addie demanded. "You're going to give yourself heatstroke."

"I wanted to have everything fixed by the time you got home."

"Please, come down."

Jasper sighed and stepped down off the ladder. He squinted into the sunlight at her. "You look better than the last time I saw you."

"I'd hope so," Addie said with a laugh. "I was covered in blood and lying on my bedroom floor."

"I remember."

"Why aren't you inside with everyone else?"

"I've been trying to make everything perfect for you."

"Why?"

"Are you in a lot of pain?"

"Yes. But it's only when I move. Or talk. Or breathe."

"Addie, I'm so sorry. I should have told you everything. I never should have left you alone here."

"You came back."

"I got there too late," he muttered.

"You shot him!" Addie exclaimed. "You shot him, Wanda told me."

"I figured you'd find out before I could tell you."

"You saved my life, Jasper."

"It's because of me that your life was ever in danger," Jasper said.

"I don't understand."

Jasper twisted the hammer in his hands. "This whole time you thought you'd brought this trouble into *my life* when it was the other way around."

"Jasper, you're talking in circles," Addie said. She took a step closer to him. "What are you trying to say?"

"What do you remember about that night? About what Redd said to you?"

"I don't remember a whole lot of the conversation." Addie shrugged. "But I told the police that he kept asking me who I was working for, which I thought was strange."

"What else?"

Addie thought about it. That night was a cloud resting in her brain somewhere, and bits and pieces were still breaking through. "He said something about a DEA agent? On your farm. Said you didn't know anything about it."

"That's what I should have told you about all along."

"Tell me now."

Jasper took a deep breath. "The Jones family has been suspected for decades of manufacturing and selling drugs all over Eunice and the state of Arkansas. But nobody could ever really prove anything. When Redd's daddy died, he took the family business to a whole new level."

"What kind of drugs?"

"Meth, primarily," Jasper replied. "Redd took the operation across state lines into Mississippi, Louisiana, and Tennessee. When the Jones farm was foreclosed on and I bought the property, the DEA came to me to ask for help. I agreed to work undercover. So did Doc."

"Doc was in on this, too?"

"This had been going on for a year before you moved here, Addie," Jasper continued. "We were deep in the middle of things. And then you found Felix. And started asking questions. We were all afraid you were going to find out and word would leak out to Redd . . . or worse, that you'd end up getting hurt."

"So this was bigger than Felix," Addie said. She was talking more to herself than to Jasper. Pieces of the puzzle were starting to come together.

"Dogfights were just one way to distribute and make contacts."

"That's disgusting."

"I agree."

"Did you know about it?" Addie asked. "I mean, before I jumped in the big middle of it."

"We had a hunch. We couldn't confirm it, but that's one reason that Doc had to work with Redd and his guys. We figured if he helped with the dogs, that he might be able to garner information."

"But those dogs," Addie replied. "They were fighting them and nobody was doing anything about it."

"Addie, we just couldn't prove it. We couldn't take a chance that those charges wouldn't stick. We had to wait until we could get him for something that would keep him behind bars."

"I wouldn't have told anyone."

"If someone had found out that you knew anything, you would have been at risk." Jasper swallowed. "I thought I could keep you safe if I didn't tell you. Clearly I was wrong."

"We were both wrong about a lot of things."

"The DEA agent that Redd told you about," Jasper continued, "is Loren."

"Loren?" Addie repeated. "But he's so young!"

"He's actually thirty." Jasper laughed for the first time. "This was his first undercover case. Admittedly, he made some mistakes. That's how Clyde found out, and somehow he got it in his head that you and Loren were working together. I guess because you both showed up here within a couple months of each other."

"This is insane," Addie murmured.

"And you're never going to believe this," Jasper said. "Augustus Smoot called the police. He called in even before Wanda called me."

"What?"

"He said he saw some suspicious activity over at your house. He was even wearing pants when the police showed up. Nobody quite knows what to make of it."

"I can't believe it."

"I know it's a lot to take in," Jasper said.

"How many people were involved? I mean, in Redd's operation?"

"Redd, Frank, Clyde, and five others have been arrested. They'll be charged with drug trafficking across state lines," Jasper replied. "The list of charges is about a mile long. But Redd Jones will go away for the rest of his natural-born life if I have anything to say about it. Right now he's being held on your attempted murder."

The words *attempted murder* bounced off Addie's ears and pinged around the yard. *Attempted murder. Someone had tried to murder her.* She closed her eyes.

"I would have killed him, Addie," Jasper continued. "I wanted to kill him."

Addie took the hammer from Jasper's hands. "I'm glad you didn't."

"I never wanted to lie to you. Please believe me. I never wanted any of this."

"From now on, just tell me the truth."

"From now on?" Jasper looked from his hands up at her. "Aren't you going to go back to Chicago with your parents?"

"Why would I do that?"

"You said so yourself that you never planned to stay here. And after everything, I figured this would be the last place you'd want to be."

"You figured wrong, Jasper Floyd."

"You want to know the truth?"

"Yes," Addie said. "I want to know the truth."

"The truth is that all I've ever wanted, from the first time I saw you, is just to be next to you."

Despite her shattered shoulder, despite the pain, despite everything that had happened, Addie felt something she never thought she'd feel again—she felt safe. It was a feeling she hadn't felt in a long time, a feeling she hadn't felt in years. She allowed Jasper to pull her close. There was nothing in that moment that she wanted more. "And that," she said, burying her head into his chest, "is why I'll stay."

Acknowledgments

It is with sincere affection and admiration that I'd like to thank the following:

Priya Dorwaswamy—for taking a chance on me and this novel, for being my biggest cheerleader, and for being patient when it was obvious that I had no idea what I was doing.

Lucia Macro—for being the best editor that anyone could ask for, for being hilarious, and for being a fellow Idiot Girl.

Nicole Fischer—for answering every. single. stupid. question.

My husband—for putting up with the light of the computer, the iPhone, and the iPad at 3 a.m.

My son—who gives me strength I never even knew I had.

My mom and dad—for always encouraging my ridiculous dreams, for always giving me a place to live, and for setting an example that only fictional characters could ever dare to top.

For Mimi—for being a writer.

Nicole Hunter Mostafa—for her unflinching loyalty and nearly two decades of friendship. I could not have done this without you. I love you, Lucy!

Brittany Carter Framer—for reading (and writing!) fan fiction with me fifteen years ago and for the hours spent quoting Blink-182, *NSYNC, and Richard Marx.

Lindsey Davis—for reading my drafts with an eagle eye. You are, without a doubt, one of the most talented people I know.

Louis, Ruthie, Lillie, Winnie, and every other rescue dog out there—for teaching humans what it truly means to love and be loved. This book is for you.

About the author

About the book

Insights,
Interviews
& More . . .

Meet Annie England Noblin

Annie England Noblin lives with her son, husband, and four rescued bulldogs in the Missouri Ozarks. She graduated with an M.A. in creative writing from Missouri State University and currently teaches English full-time for Arkansas State University in Mountain Home, Arkansas. Her first novel, *Sit! Stay! Speak!*, was inspired by the year she spent teaching developmental English in the Delta of Arkansas, a place she says still has her heart. Her poetry has been featured in publications such as the *Red Booth Review* and the *Moon City Review.* ~

Recipes

Fannie Lou's Chocolate Gravy

4 Tbsp. cocoa
1½ cups sugar
1 stick butter (*not* margarine)
3 cups milk (whole milk)

Mix dry ingredients together. Put in skillet or pan, add milk slowly so there will be no lumps. Cook on medium heat so it doesn't burn. Best made in black cast-iron skillet. Serve over hot buttermilk biscuits.

Ms. Rubina's Cornbread

1 cup yellow cornmeal
½ tsp. salt
¼ tsp. soda
1 tsp. baking powder
1 tsp. sugar
1 egg
1 cup buttermilk

Combine in mixing bowl. Set aside.

Heat oven to 425°F, put 2 Tbsp. of grease in black skillet. Put skillet in oven to heat it up. In mixing bowl, make a well in the center of meal mixture. Drop in 1 unbeaten egg. Add 1 cup buttermilk. Mix well. Take skillet out of oven. Pour hot grease into mixture. Stir well. Immediately pour mixture back into skillet. Bake 25–30 minutes till done. Serve with molasses butter.

Aunt Tilda's Hush Puppies

2 cups yellow cornmeal
1 Tbsp. flour ▸

1 tsp. soda
1 tsp. baking powder
1 tsp. salt
6 Tbsp. chopped onions
1 whole egg
1 cup buttermilk

Mix together all ingredients. Drop by spoonfuls into hot grease in black skillet. Turn in grease 2–3 times till golden. Serve with fried catfish. In a pinch, perch will do!

Aunt Tilda's Buttermilk Biscuits

1¾ cups unsifted flour
4 tsp. baking powder
½ tsp. salt
½ tsp. cream of tartar
¼ tsp. soda
⅓ cup shortening or lard
¾ cup buttermilk

Mix together dry ingredients and then cut in shortening in pea-sized portions. Add buttermilk. Knead on floured surface till soft.

Pat out dough. Dip small glass in flour and cut out biscuits. Place in pan. Cook in hot oven at 450°F for 12 minutes.

Artemis Floyd's Cheese Grits

4 cups boiling water
1 tsp. salt
1 cup grits
1 stick oleo
1 egg, beaten
½ roll garlic cheese

Boil water, salt, and grits for about 5 minutes. Add oleo and cheese. Beat together. Add beaten egg. Pour into greased casserole dish and bake 25–30 minutes at 350°F.

Southern Spoon Bread

3 cups milk
3 eggs, beaten
1 cup yellow cornmeal
3 level tsp. baking powder
1 tsp. salt
Melted butter—about the size of a walnut

Stir meal into 2 cups milk. Let come to a boil, making a mush. Add remainder of milk, well-beaten eggs, salt, baking powder, and melted butter.

Bake in moderate oven for 30 minutes or until brown at 350°F. Spread and serve in baking dish.

Aunt Tilda's Sugar Cookies

1 cup butter
1 cup white sugar
1 cup oil
1 cup powdered sugar
2 eggs
4½ cups sifted flour or 5 cups unsifted flour
1 tsp. soda
1 tsp. cream of tarter
1 tsp. salt
1 tsp. vanilla

Mix dry ingredients together. Add to creamed mixture. ▸

Preheat oven to 350°F.

Drop by spoonfuls on greased cookie pan. Press flat with glass dipped in sugar. Bake 8 minutes.

Jasper Floyd's Fried Chicken

Cut large fryer into individual pieces. Wash well in cool water. Set aside.

Flour Mixture:
Add 3 cups all-purpose flour to large bowl. Add salt, pepper, and garlic salt. Mix together.

On high heat add 2–3 inches of oil to frying pan. Heat oil. Drop a little flour in oil to see if hot enough. When flour sizzles, that means the oil is hot enough.

Coat chicken well and add coated pieces to hot oil. Brown and turn chicken. Reduce heat to medium/ medium-high. Continue to turn chicken till brown, golden, and crispy. Cook around 30 minutes till done.

Jasper Floyd's White Gravy

In heavy black skillet, heat 3 Tbsp. of grease.

In large jar, add about 3 cups of milk. Add 3½ Tbsp. flour to milk. Stir flour into milk.

Pour all at once into hot oil. Whisk till smooth. Add salt and pepper to taste. May add more milk to thin gravy. Cook till bubbly and thickened. Serve with biscuits. May add sausage to gravy as desired.

Aunt Tilda's Fried Pies

4 cups all purpose flour
2 tsp. salt
1 cup shortening
1 cup milk

In a large bowl, mix together flour and salt. Cut in shortening until mixture is crumbly. Mix in milk and stir until dough forms a ball. Roll out dough and cut into eighteen 6-inch circles.

Set aside.

Filling:
14 oz. dried fruit (peaches, apples, cherries)
¾ cup white sugar
Water to cover fruit

In large saucepan combine fruit and sugar. Add enough water to cover fruit. Cover pan and cook over low heat until fruit is falling apart. Remove lid and cook till water is evaporated.

Place 2 cups of oil in black skillet over medium heat.

Place spoonful of fruit into center of each circle. Fold in half. Seal pastry with fork dipped in cold water.

Fry a few pies at a time in hot oil, browning on both sides. Drain pies on paper towels. Sprinkle with sugar.

Aunt Tilda's Ooey Gooey Butter Cake

Cake:
1 18¼-oz. package yellow cake mix ►

1 egg
8 Tbsp. butter, melted

Filling:
1 8-oz. package cream cheese, softened
2 eggs
1 tsp. vanilla
8 Tbsp. butter, melted
1 16-oz. box powdered sugar

Heat oven to 350°F.

Combine the cake mix, eggs, and butter and mix well with an electric mixer. Pat the mixture into the bottom of a lightly greased 13-by-9-inch baking pan.

In a large bowl, beat the cream cheese until smooth. Add the eggs, vanilla, and butter and beat together.

Next, add the powdered sugar and mix well. Spread over cake batter and bake for 40–50 minutes. Don't overbake—the center should be a little gooey.

Addie's Boiled Tea

In large glass pitcher, add 1–2 cups of sugar. Place metal knife in pitcher.

On stove, boil 2–3 cups of water. Add 2 family-size tea bags. Cover and let steep. The longer you steep, the stronger the tea.

Remove tea bags and pour hot tea slowly into pitcher (the metal knife will absorb heat so glass won't break). Now add cold water until tea is the color you desire. Stir well!

Reading Group Discussion Questions

1. This novel deals with issues of home, family, and remembrance. At one point Addie thinks that if Jonah, her late fiancé, were with her he would have "picked through each piece of furniture" in her late aunt's home. "He would have asked for stories about each one, stories Addie had long forgotten." Are there any mementos or heirlooms in your life that tell a story?

2. Addie saves Felix from certain death, but Felix is not just a cuddly dog; he's a pit bull, a breed that often has a bad reputation. What do you think about the author's choice in making Felix a pit bull? Does this make Felix's gentle disposition more of a surprise to you?

3. Many people attribute human characteristics to their pets, especially to dogs. In fact, Addie thinks that Felix "looks a lot on the outside like she felt on the inside. She had a feeling that Felix wasn't the only dog to have been dumped bleeding and struggling for his life." Do you think that dogs and pets can feel things the way humans do?

4. Addie resists telling Jasper that Jonah is dead, although she does say he is her "ex-fiancé." What do you think holds her back from telling him the entire truth at first? ▸

Reading Group Discussion Questions
(continued)

5. Food means a lot in this novel. At one point Addie finds her aunt Tilda's recipe box and remembers her saying, "A woman's recipes are like her diary. They aren't meant for anyone else's eyes but hers." Do you agree? Disagree? Why?

6. At one point Addie enters Redd's room. Redd is a criminal and yet his room is clean and well-furnished. Does this surprise you? Why do you think Redd has such a well-put-together place in such a disorganized and filthy house?

7. Although the United States is one country, there are regional differences even in today's highly connected world. Jasper accuses Addie of trying to change "an entire culture," saying, "That's why people like you never last very long down here." Do you think that it's true that you can't change an entire culture? Should Addie be trying to change things or not?

8. Jasper tells Addie that "Memphis is my home. Eunice . . . the farm . . . that's where I was born. That's likely where I'll die. But it isn't my home." What is the difference between home and where you live? Can they really be two different concepts?

9. Addie's neighbor Augustus says that "acting crazy is easier than everything else." Is this true?

Why do you think he has chosen to act crazy all these years? Has it made his life easier? Or has it actually cut him off from other aspects of life that could have brought him joy?

10. In the end, we discover that while crimes against animals are very real, the true crime being investigated is meth. Did this surprise you? And do you think that television shows such as *Breaking Bad* have actually glamorized meth production as we root for the criminals there to succeed?